Praise for the novels of James Tucker . . .

"Sly, unpredictable, and cunning. This newcomer is one to watch."

—H. Paul Jeffers, bestselling author of *Who Killed Precious?*

"Jim Tucker has pulled together some unforgettable characters in a wonderful page-turning whodunit. He brings his love of magic and understanding of medicine and mixes them up and presents the reader with a real gift."

—Nancy L. Snyderman, M.D., Medical Correspondent, ABC News

"A real page-turner! I couldn't put it down."

—*Valley News Dispatch*

"A well-written, gripping first novel."

—*Tribune-Review* (Pittsburgh)

TRAGIC WAND

James Tucker

AN ONYX BOOK

ONYX
Published by New American Library, a division of
Penguin Putnam Inc., 375 Hudson Street,
New York, New York 10014, U.S.A.
Penguin Books Ltd, 27 Wrights Lane,
London W8 5TZ, England
Penguin Books Australia Ltd, Ringwood,
Victoria, Australia
Penguin Books Canada Ltd, 10 Alcorn Avenue,
Toronto, Ontario, Canada M4V 3B2
Penguin Books (N.Z.) Ltd, 182–190 Wairau Road,
Auckland 10, New Zealand

Penguin Books Ltd, Registered Offices:
Harmondsworth, Middlesex, England

First published by Onyx, an imprint of New American Library,
a division of Penguin Putnam Inc.

First Printing, November 2000
10 9 8 7 6 5 4 3 2 1

Printed in the United States of America

PUBLISHER'S NOTE
This is a work of fiction. Names, characters, places, and incidents either are
the product of the author's imagination or are used fictitiously, and any
resemblance to actual persons, living or dead, business establishments, events,
or locales is entirely coincidental.

As always, I write for my wonderful family
Peter, Brad, Scott,
and Kim

ACKNOWLEDGMENTS

One of the most enjoyable aspects of writing has been the opportunity to learn more about both medicine and criminology. I am grateful to everyone who was willing to offer advice.

Plastic surgery plays a significant role in *Tragic Wand*. I am fortunate to know two of Pittsburgh's finest plastic surgeons: Jack Demos, the heart and soul of Surgicorps, and Joe Falcon. Both were always available for a curbside consultation.

My friend Bill Cohen was invaluable in helping to shape the chapters involved with hypnosis. Chip Jungreis worked with me on the subtleties of neuroanatomy.

I was fascinated to speak with Wayne Reutzel, Pittsburgh's latent fingerprint examiner. He is knowledgeable enough to make his complicated science simple enough for me to understand and write about.

Without Jennifer Janssen from the toxicology crime lab, Paul Schiff from the department of pharmacy at UPMC, pharmacist John Yakim, and Rob Askew from the crime lab, the book would have lacked verisimilitude.

Frank Dermody, Bill Steiner, Arthur Feldman, Ira Bergman, Jeff Baum, John McCarthy, the guys at the Allegheny River Arsenal, and Bob Deringer offered their expertise.

As always, Jeanne Baseman added her golden touch, and my wonderful parents were there to encourage me.

I am indebted to my editor, Dan Slater, whose thoughtful red pencil made the story better. Once again I thank my superb agent, Jake Elwell, for giving me the opportunity to have the time of my life.

And in the end it is for my family that I do this. Peter, Brad, and Scott inspire me. My wife, Kim, gets the first read. It is a horribly tough job and she does it with grace. It is not a book until she says it's a book.

Thank you all.

Prologue

Miami Beach, Florida

Raymond Phillips was an absolute magician. With a brilliant touch of his scalpel he could tighten loose flesh on the face or perk up a sagging pair of breasts. He was considered to be one of the finest plastic surgeons in southern Florida. At age thirty-eight he was tall and muscular, without the bulky look of a bodybuilder, and his perpetual tan gave him an aura that positively glowed. Nearly all of his clientele were passionately entrenched in the battle against age and gravity and were flush with cash, which was good for business because insurance companies rarely, if ever, paid for the type of surgery for which he was known.

His building, The Phillips Cosmetic Surgery Center, was a single-story octagonal structure that reminded one of a giant layer cake, iced with a coarse, green pastel stucco. Occasionally, maybe three or four times a year, Phillips shut down the surgi-center to his regular patients in the middle of the week. On these special days all but a few of his staff were treated to a day off with pay as Phillips devoted every bit of his attention to one special patient.

Today was one of those days, what Phillips and his staff called a marathon. This particular surgery would take more than nine hours. The patient, a thirty-nine-year-old man, was fat and ugly with little moles dotting his chin like barnacles on a fishing boat. His name was Harold, but he wasn't some Miami Beach local clinging to his youth or a Wall Street tycoon shopping for a new image. Harold was from the streets, the type of man Raymond Phillips never ran into at fancy soireés or weekend pool parties. He was the sort of guy to be known by a nickname, something like Switchblade or Weasel.

Starting at eight a.m. Harold spent four hours wide awake, sitting upright in a special chair while Phillips, decked out in a pair of tailored scrubs that hung from his sleek frame like something from the Armani collection, re-implanted almost a thousand hair follicles from the back of the scalp, where Harold had many, to the front, where he was nearly bald. Harold didn't have much to say during the tedious process. He leered at Phillips's pretty medical assistant, licking his parched lips whenever he caught her eye. When one of his EKG leads came loose and the medical assistant bent over to re-attach it, Harold reached out and grabbed one of her breasts, squeezing hard enough to make her jump. She looked to Phillips for help, but the surgeon remained fixated on his work and did his best not to notice.

When the front of Harold's scalp finally sported enough hair to comb over to one side, the anesthesiologist, a gentle man named Sammy with a huge ethnic nose, doped up Harold. Once he was asleep, the tension in the room abated remarkably, and Phillips quickly started with the eye lift and Silastic cheek implants. Then it was on to the rhytidoplasty—the face-lift—and a nose job.

Then some liposuction. And finally another Silastic chin implant to make him look a little more like Jay Leno.

By the time the anesthesia had worn off enough to allow Harold to grope the medical assistant, his head and neck had been swathed in heavy bandages, leaving only tiny slits for his mouth, nose, and eyes. He looked like a mummy.

"You better call me a taxi," Harold said to Phillips as he was being helped off the table.

Sammy had stationed himself right next to Harold in case he got woozy and had to be caught. "You have to wait in recovery until you can drink some ginger ale," he reminded him.

"Forget it," Harold answered, dismissing Sammy's concern with a quick wave of his hand. Turning to Phillips he said, "Look, Doc, I gotta go. Just have the girl with the jugs call me a taxi." Harold clumsily cupped both his hands in front of his chest as if he were testing a couple of cantaloupes for ripeness. "Where is she?"

"Don't you have anyone to pick you up?" Phillips asked with some genuine concern. As much as he detested Harold he didn't want him to do anything foolish that would compromise nine hours of work.

"Just call me a taxi," Harold ordered as he slowly shuffled his way to the little dressing room. "Oh, yeah, lemme get the money I owe ya."

"I'll . . . uh . . . I'll be in my office." Without any front office personnel, Phillips despised what was to happen next. It wasn't as though he didn't want the money, but he felt that the brief act of collecting it was beneath him.

While Harold disappeared into the fancy dressing room, Phillips mumbled to Sammy, "Forget it. Let him do what he wants." Phillips quickly retreated down the lushly carpeted hallway, past the darkened office where Sammy would do his post-operative paperwork, toward his own beautifully appointed office. In the middle of the room was Phillips's showpiece: a magnificent mahogany desk, the type of massive piece behind which leaders of nations had themselves photographed when they signed important treaties. He plopped himself into a plush chair, sinking a good four inches into the expensive leather, and rubbed his eyes.

"Hey, Doc, whaddaya got, a migraine or sumpin'? You 'bout ready to do this?" Harold was quite a sight. The mummy had dressed himself in a short-sleeve light green shirt, unbuttoned at the collar to show several garish gold chains around his neck, a pair of shiny, gray pants, and leather dress boots that looked as if they'd been spit polished. In his right hand was a battered leather attaché case that he crudely dropped right on the desk's beautifully polished surface.

That was enough to clear Phillips's head. Instantly, the plastic surgeon sat up to survey any damage caused by the attaché while Harold worked the two latches. Without a word, Harold began withdrawing stack after stack of crisp twenty-dollar bills, eleven in all, each bound with straps of paper like they had just come from the bank. He piled them neatly on the desk. Then he snatched a twelfth pack, snapped the paper strap in two, and gave his thumb a practiced quick lick that made Phillips recall that Harold was probably used to dealing in large quantities of cash. Working like a Vegas dealer, Harold smoothly counted out twenty-five bills, creating a perfect fan with the money. Squaring up the pile he declared, "Twenty-two five. Go ahead, Doc, count it."

Phillips made no move to reach for the money. Instead he shook his head. "That's okay, Harold, I trust you."

Harold's eyes opened wide and for a moment he seemed to be smiling through the bandages. "Yeah . . . I guess so. Whaddaya know. I'm a goddamn new man.

No reason in the whole fucking world not to trust me. Huh?" Harold turned and slowly shuffled toward the door. "I wish I could say 'See ya around, Doc' but I'm outta here," he called over his shoulder. Harold gave a little wave, then headed down the hallway to wait for his taxi. As he passed by the operating room where his metamorphosis had taken place, he made a little detour in order to pat the medical assistant on the ass. As she recoiled and moved away from him, Harold held out a couple of twenties as though he was tipping a stripper after a lap dance. "Go ahead," he said as he waved the money about in a tantalizing way, "take it. Buy yourself sumpin' nice."

All this while Raymond Phillips vanished into his private changing room, showered quickly, and slipped into a powder blue, custom-tailored shirt, a beige suit, and a brilliant blue tie that he had purchased specifically to wear with the ensemble. As he walked purposefully down the carpeted hallway, he felt tired, as if he needed a vacation, or at least a couple of stiff drinks by the pool while he cooked a nice steak on the grill. He mumbled a weary goodnight to Sammy as he went by, hopped into his pearl-colored Lexus, popped a Mozart piano concerto into the CD player, and sped away from The Phillips Cosmetic Surgery Center as quickly as traffic would allow.

It wasn't until he was nearly twenty minutes into his drive home that he remembered the little bricks of cash that were piled up on his desk. "Oh my God!" he exclaimed, drawing a horrible mental picture of the cleaning crew arriving and pocketing what would certainly take the lot of them more than six months to earn.

Phillips did a frantic U-turn, then raced all the way back to his twenty-two thousand, five hundred dollars, running a couple of stop signs in the process.

Every light was on in the surgi-center. There were two cars in the lot, Sammy's blue Chrysler and the crappy, rusted-out Chevy the cleaning crew drove.

Phillips pulled the front door open and broke into a trot down the hallway. The cleaning crew was nowhere to be found. "Hey, Sam, good thing you're still here. I left the money out," the surgeon called as he shot by the anesthesiologist's office. He didn't bother a side glance into the office to see why Sammy was hanging around so late. The only thing Raymond Philips could think about was the money.

From the threshold of his darkened office he spied it, eleven neat little packages, each held tight with a paper strap, precisely where Harold had left it. He let out a sigh of relief and immediately stuffed the twenty-five loose bills into his pocket, scooping up the rest of the money into his arms and hurrying over to the corner of the office where he knelt down and dumped his valuable bundle on the carpet. A colorful wicker basket needed to be pushed out of the way before he could see the metal door of the safe that had been installed directly into the floor. Phillips dialed the combination, pulled the inch-and-a-half-thick door open and placed the bricks of money into the dark well one by one. As he closed the door and gave the dial several random turns, he checked his watch. It was too late now to go home and fix himself something decent to eat. His little mishap with the money was going to cost him the evening he deserved after the kind of day he had put in. Unless he changed his plans right on the spot, dinner was going to be whatever he could rummage in his refrigerator. Still kneeling on the floor, he hollered, "Hey, Sammy. Let's get outta here. I'll buy you a steak."

He made his way down the hallway toward Sammy's office. "What do you say, Sam? Where should we eat?"

Phillips asked, breezing into his anesthesiologist's office. Before he could get out another word he realized the entire Mexican cleaning crew—Miguel, his wife, and two sisters-in-law—was packed into the tiny office, staring silently at Sammy, who sat behind his small desk.

One look at Sammy and he knew something was dreadfully wrong. The anesthesiologist had his head down on his desk, like a college kid who hadn't made it through an all-nighter in the library. But Sammy's head wasn't comfortably turned to one side, and he wasn't using his forearm as a pillow. Sammy had his head nose-down on the desk, as if he had slumped straight forward and never recovered.

"What's going on?" Phillips demanded of Miguel.

"Meester Sammy, he no move," Miguel answered in his broken English and stood next to his wife, who looked as if she might cry.

Phillips stood in the doorway, not yet daring to enter the room. "Sammy! You sleeping? Wake up, Sam!"

Sammy did not stir. Phillips noticed some papers were scattered on the floor near the desk. Carefully, afraid of what he might encounter next, Phillips crept his way around the desk. Placing one hand on the anesthesiologist's shoulder, he gave him a firm shake. "Sam?" he said loudly. Phillips had a sick feeling Sammy was no longer in the room.

As soon as Phillips took his hand away, Sammy began to slump to one side. A trail of blood appeared as his face slid across the desk. The three female Mexicans huddled together in one corner of the room, trembling like terrified Siamese triplets. There was nothing to stop Sammy from falling from his chair. Slowly his head reached the edge of the desk, then he tumbled onto the carpet. Phillips and Miguel watched in horror as the front of Sammy's blue scrub shirt came into view. It was wet with blood, and in the center of his chest was a jelly-like curd that clung to the shirt.

"Was anyone else here, Miguel?" Phillips snapped.

"No. Nobody was here. Just Meester Sammy."

"Listen to me, Miguel." Phillips swallowed to moisten his throat. He was frightened and it showed in the way he was raising his voice. "Do *exactly* as I tell you."

"Yes, Meester Phillips," Miguel said and began wringing his hands together.

"You have the women over there check *every* room. I mean every goddamn room in this place, every closet, under every desk. Make sure no one is here. You hear me?"

"*Sí,*" Miguel answered, slipping back into his Spanish, staring at Phillips as if he expected more direction from the surgeon.

"What are you waiting for, Miguel? Now!"

Miguel turned toward the women and spoke very quickly in Spanish, gesticulating wildly with his hands. When they did not move quickly enough, he screamed, "*¡Ahora! ¡Ahora!*" Now! Now! The three women scurried from the room and disappeared into the hallway.

The sight of the blood caused Phillips to suck in a mouthful of air and bring his hand up to his mouth as if he were about to vomit. He felt dizzy. It required an incredible effort of self-control just to squat down and reach out for Sammy's hand in order to feel for the pulse in his wrist.

Immediately, Phillips palpated the rapid tapping of Sammy's pulse with his index finger. "He's alive!" Phillips blurted out.

Miguel responded by clenching his hands together and praying out loud.

Phillips's own heart was pounding madly in his chest. When it struck him as odd that Sammy's pulse could be ticking away just about the same speed as his own was, Phillips realized his diagnostic error.

And in that frightening moment Phillips couldn't quite tell what he was feeling.

The surgeon placed his left index finger on his right wrist to monitor his own pulse while he simultaneously used his right index finger to palpate Sammy's pulse a second time.

The two were in perfect unison, beat for beat. If Sammy's heart was still pumping, his pulse would beat out its own rhythm. What Phillips had felt was the frantic pulse in his *own* fingertip.

Phillips bent over the anesthesiologist, taking care not to let his clothing brush against the blood-stained scrubs, and placed his ear close to Sammy's mouth so he could listen for the wispy sound of breathing. But there was none.

Sammy was dead.

Raymond Phillips needed to get the hell out of there. He felt trapped in the tiny office. Without thinking about the twenty-two thousand dollars he had just dumped into his floor safe, he headed for the hallway and nearly ran into Miguel's wife and her sisters as they were returning from their mission.

"No, señor, no!" Miguel's wife said to Phillips, trying to communicate that the office was otherwise empty.

"Meester Phillips," Miguel said in a heavy Mexican accent. "Are you going to call 911?"

Phillips turned to look at Miguel. The little cleaning man was sweating profusely. "There's been an accident, Miguel. You better get out of here if you know what's good for you."

"You said Meester Sammy is alive."

"You hear me, Miguel?" Phillips was practically screaming. "Get the hell outta here!" Phillips reached into his pocket and grabbed the five hundred dollars. "Here," he said, taking Miguel's hand and slapping the money into it. "Go!" The three women, understanding the fury more than the words, scattered down the hallway.

Still Miguel just stood there, craning his neck so he could stare at Sammy on the floor, confused as to what was happening.

Feeling a tremendous sense of panic, Phillips shook his head and brushed past Miguel. He passed the Siamese triplets by the front door, not wasting any more time to explain the danger they were in, and shot out to his car.

He jammed the Lexus in reverse, did a screeching semi-circle out of his parking space, then squealed the tires as he tore away, spraying crushed red stones at the front door of his surgi-center.

Not for one second did Phillips even think about the twenty-two thousand dollars until he was a hundred miles north of Miami. He stopped once for gas, then kept driving right into Georgia, not stopping again until he was almost to the South Carolina border.

That's when he took a break at a crowded truck stop in order to make a single long-distance phone call to a man he hardly knew, a man who was furious as hell that he'd been awakened in the middle of the night. Finally, just an hour or so before daybreak, Raymond Phillips allowed himself a brief respite from his nightmare and sat down at a booth and ordered himself two cups of coffee.

While the waitress hurried off to fetch his caffeine, Phillips couldn't get Sammy out of his mind. He knew all too well that the anesthesiologist wasn't the one who was supposed to be dead. He gulped down the coffee, threw some money on the table, headed back to his Lexus, and kept driving.

Chapter 1

Six years later. Pittsburgh, Pennsylvania

The last light of day was nearly extinguished when Stanley Stilwell pulled his heavy Buick off Route 28 just before Harmarville. He inched his way down the long road so he wouldn't miss the sign for the plastic surgery clinic. There wasn't much traffic this late in the day, so Stilwell felt pretty relaxed. He was a short man, no more than five foot four, but powerfully built. Stilwell looked rough, not the sort of man anyone would dare to piss off deliberately, and he had a full head of gray hair that he wore long—not fashionably long in a ponytail, but long and greasy. He combed it straight back, and it stayed that way until he ran a comb through it the next morning. There was a huge scar that ran halfway down his right cheek, but when people thought about Stanley Stilwell, there was only one thing they could visualize: his nose. It had been broken at least five times and sliced up pretty badly by a hunting knife. Now it looked more like a snout, broad and flat up near his eyes, with a pair of huge upturned nostrils that were grotesquely out of proportion to the rest of his face. Stanley Stilwell appeared to be the hideous result of human crossbreeding with a pig. He couldn't stand the way he looked, and mirrors were something he carefully avoided.

As soon as he spotted the fancy sign he pulled the Buick onto the crunchy gravel shoulder, turned off the engine, and waited. The cheap sunglasses and baseball cap were probably a bit much now, what with the sun going down, so he took them off and tossed them on the empty seat next to him. He looked around, craning his neck as far as it wanted to go. He took advantage of the Buick's side and rearview mirrors to make absolutely certain he hadn't been followed. Rolling down his window, he worked up a mouthful of spit and shot it toward the white sign. Two times he read it, the second time aloud. "The Cutter Institute for Cosmetic Surgery." He spat again. "You better know what the fuck you're doing, Dr. Cutter, that's all I gotta say." He rolled the window back up and checked the mirrors again.

The white sign was the centerpiece for a little garden, landscaped to perfection. Each of the letters carved into the wood was painted with a shiny gold enamel that spelled a class operation to Stilwell. The oval patch of ground surrounding the sign was groomed with wood chips that were a rusty shade of red. Sprouting up in little clusters were dozens of tulips and daffodils, all standing at attention. Wherever he looked it was pretty.

When he looked beyond the garden he saw robust boxwood hedges running around the periphery of the magnificent piece of property. An acre of green lawn ran up a gentle hillside to the surgi-center. He wondered whether the perfectly manicured grass might really be Astroturf.

If Stanley Stilwell had been a regular sort of guy he might have thought it looked like something at Disney World, but Stanley Stilwell wasn't a regular sort of guy. The closest he ever got to the Magic Kingdom was driving Route 95 on his way to Cocoa Beach with some hooker's head bobbing up and down in his lap.

He gazed up at the surgi-center, an impressive colonial-style building that looked more like a mansion in an expensive new development than a place to go for a face-lift. It had a pitched roof, white clapboard siding, dark green shutters, paneled doors, several trellises with flowering clematis, and a white porch. The only concession to its commercial purpose were the double glass doors where the front door should have been.

All of a sudden Stilwell was aware of a car coming up the road behind him. It's headlights looked like a pair of eyes watching him off in the distance.

Instantly he was filled with the sort of panic that makes brave men do crazy things. His hand shot under the seat and pulled out a small package wrapped in a greasy rag. It was pure instinct, an act he had performed hundreds of times over the years. Quickly discarding the rag, his hand slipped around the stippled grip of a Heckler and Koch USP pistol. The weapon was matte black, enhanced by both a laser sight and a six-inch silencer. It was loaded with ten hollow point .45 caliber bullets.

And, if it hadn't been stolen, it would have set Stanley Stilwell back nearly three grand.

His hands knew what to do without him looking down. He racked the slide and listened for the reassuring sound of the first bullet slipping into the chamber. If push came to shove he was ready. "C'mon," he hissed as he turned the key roughly in the ignition.

The engine roared to life. Stilwell's eyes were locked on the rearview mirror as he gunned the engine. The reflection of the approaching car was growing. Without setting the H&K down, Stilwell rammed the car into drive, one foot on the brake, one giving it the gas. The Buick was a coiled spring waiting to explode.

Closer and closer the car approached, creeping too
slowly for someone on his way home from work after a
long day. Quickly he shifted his eyes from the rearview
to the driver's side mirror. Back and forth his eyes alter-
nated, desperate for a glimpse of whoever was driving
the car.

Stilwell was getting hyper, his heart racing faster than
the engine, icy bullets of sweat popping out all over his
body. The skin on the back of his neck prickled. He
worked the gas pedal. Hearing the engine roar made him
feel powerful, and he played with the gas like a hot-
rodder about to explode at the start of a drag race.

His breathing was hard and noisy, as if he'd been running for some time. Spittle formed at the corner of his
mouth, and his tongue shot out and licked it away.

*Turn the car around. Turn the goddamn car around
and put the sucker on notice.*

A voice was screaming in his head, the words echoing
as if he was in a great empty room. Without thinking,
he pulled his left foot off the brake and the car lurched
forward onto the road. Using both hands he yanked the
steering wheel hard to the left. The Buick did not respond with the crispness of a smaller car, instead jerking
heavily across the macadam toward the white sign and
bright spring flowers.

In less than a second his front tires were three inches
deep in the rusty red bark. Now the Buick was sideways
on the road, as if he were setting up a roadblock.

Immediately Stilwell put the car into reverse without
lifting his foot off the gas. A horrible grating noise
erupted from the engine as if the transmission was about
to fall out of the bottom of the car. Gripped with a fear
that was growing with each passing second, he revved
the engine, spinning the front tires in the soft earth and
sending a flashy rooster tail of red bark flying up from

under the car right in the direction
The Buick headed backward. A single
ing wheel and Stanley Stilwell was facing
head-on. *Roll down the window.* Thirty ya
he slows down . . .

Stilwell held up the H&K, steadying his wris
aim. The Buick's engine whined as Stilwell clench
jaw shut and pulled his lips back to expose two rows
yellow teeth. His foot stomped some gas to the roaring
engine. *How the hell did they follow me?* In less than a
second it happened.

The oncoming car slowly cruised by him.

In that brief moment he stole enough of a look at the
driver to know exactly what had happened. All the panic.
All the flowers that were destroyed. The rusty red bark
that would have to be raked back in place. And the
beautiful white sign that would probably need to be
sprayed down with a powerful hose.

All for nothing.

The driver of the oncoming car—a Buick just like the
one Stilwell drove but newer—was a skinny old woman
with white hair who was doing about twenty-five miles
an hour in a forty-five-mile-per-hour zone. An old lady.
Shit! After all he'd been through. After everything he'd
seen, the people he'd done, the crap he'd taken. Faked
out by an old broad who probably couldn't see two feet
in front of her.

The Heckler and Koch slipped from his fingers and
tumbled to the floor. Stanley Stilwell hated being reduced to this, freaking out over some old hag. He had
to admit it, he was scared, terrified, as a matter of fact,
that he would be found out. What a horrible way to live,
hiding in one cheap motel after another. But in another
week or two it would all be worth it. He could disappear
forever. Leaning over so he could see his reflection in

arview mirror, his fingers touched his horrible nose
y. What was about to happen was the most impor-
thing in the world to him, and he was prepared to
anything to keep his secret safe.

Twenty minutes later he summoned the courage to
urn the car around, this time guiding the Buick away
from the flower beds, embarking on the short trip up the
cobblestone driveway to Marshall Cutter's office.

Jack Merlin had been standing in front of the large
mirror in the wooden frame, engrossed for so long he
didn't hear the front door open. He was at the top of
the stairs of the cozy two-story clapboard house he had
been sharing with Tory Welch for the past several years.
They lived in Aspinwall, a quiet community with beautiful old homes across the Allegheny River from the city
of Pittsburgh.

Although quite handsome in a Waspy sort of way,
Merlin wasn't vain. Whenever he took the time to look
in the mirror, he liked what he saw but was too busy to
dwell on it. He never wasted time fluffing his hair or
smoothing his eyebrows. How he kept his six-foot frame
in shape was a bit of a mystery, what with putting in
ridiculous hours starting up a practice in general surgery
and devoting every other waking minute to Tory. His
face was thin, and he sported medium-length brown hair
that usually looked as though it needed a workout with
a comb.

After six years of residency, including one as chief resident, Jack Merlin had finally gone out on his own. Not
surprisingly, he was immediately busy, seeing patients in
his office at the Pittsburgh University Medical Center
two days a week and operating the other three. Not only
was he a superb clinician and technical surgeon, but he

had an appealing personality, and the au— nicate easily with his patients.

Over and over, for nearly an hour, Merlin practiced a sleight with an old deck of cards, the torn remnants of a selected card between his without once looking at his hands, training his gaze his own reflection in the mirror to observe exactly wha his audience would see. Although quite accustomed to performing before groups of all sizes, he wanted this par— ticular trick to be flawless.

"Hey, Narcissus, since when did you have to *practice* that trick?"

It was Tory, breaking his reverie. She was halfway up the stairs, brushing a wisp of her shiny dark hair away from her face and tucking it behind her ear. Rolling her eyes at Merlin, she grinned. An assistant district attorney in Allegheny County, Tory worked almost as many hours as Merlin.

She was wearing a thin running suit, dark blue in color with a Nike swoop on the jacket. She had a runner's body, long legs and a body-fat percentage that was in the single-digit territory. Her skin was already reacting to what little sun Pittsburgh enjoyed, and it made her smile all the more radiant. Now that they were well into spring and the days were growing longer, Tory had re— sumed her runs home from the courthouse. On a good night she covered the seven miles in just under fifty min— utes, bounding into the house looking so fresh and vital sometimes it was difficult for Merlin to keep his hands to himself.

Merlin returned the smile and immediately headed down the narrow stairs. As he gave Tory a kiss his fingers found the red elastic that held her short ponytail in place and released it.

"I've been practicing ever since I was asked to teach

magic in the management of pain to a group
...tudents," he answered with some bravado.

...o you're a professor now?" Tory mused. She slipped
...hand into Merlin's and led him downstairs to the
...ving room. *The room was small and in need of some
new furniture. What they had was nothing more than an
eclectic gathering of the used junk each had brought to
the relationship. Their one prized possession in an otherwise ordinary room was a watercolor of a creamy tran-
quil Cape Cod marsh the two had purchased at a small
art gallery in Wellfleet last summer.* "How'd this come
about?"

"You remember Tanner Valdemar."

Tory plopped herself onto the sofa. Her fingers immediately fiddled with some loose threads on the upholstery
as a wistful expression spread across her face. "Of course
I remember him," she said ever so softly. As she fixed
a mental image of the psychiatrist in her mind she
couldn't help but smile. "He was wonderful to me. I like
his weird hair and the way he talks with his hands."

Merlin chuckled when he thought about his colleague.
Valdemar did have weird hair, a thatch of wiry steel wool
that covered his head like a cheap toupee. And he did
talk with his hands, moving them about animatedly each
time he had anything to say in a social situation. "Anyway," Merlin continued, "Tanner's doing some sort of
class for the medical students on hypnosis and pain management——"

Tory furrowed her brow. "I thought you were a magician. I didn't know you knew anything about hypnosis."

"Obviously there's a lot you don't know about me."

"Okay, Svengali, do me."

"Many magicians dabble in hypnosis——"

"Do me."

"What do you mean, 'do you'?"

"Hypnotize me. Make me think my belly button's disappeared or that I'm a duck," Tory teased.

Merlin waved her off with one hand. "Forget it."

"Hey, how 'bout turning me into a courtesan, and I'll fill all your erotic fantasies," Tory said with a sly smile. Her eyes squinted with delight.

"You already fill my erotic fantasies."

"C'mon Merlin, strut your stuff." Unable to resist the opportunity to chide him, she lowered her voice in a cheap Vincent Price imitation and said, "Put me under your spell. Look deep into my eyes." Then she held up both hands toward Merlin, and wiggled her fingers around like a hypnotist in an old movie.

"I don't do parlor hypnosis. Your belly button will have to remain exactly where it is."

"I got it," Tory said as a new idea popped into her head. Cupping both hands over her small breasts she bubbled, "Pamela Anderson! Turn me into Pamela Anderson and make me look like I'm shoplifting honeydews." Tory was laughing so hard she had to hold on to Merlin to keep from falling over.

Merlin shook his head. "How do you know I haven't already hypnotized you? You know how gooey you get every time I whisper how much I love you in your ear?" Merlin paused for dramatic effect. "And when I snap my fingers you start to—"

"All right, Merlin. Take a lap. Gee, I shouldn't get you started." She leaned over and kissed him. "Seriously . . . could you hypnotize me if you wanted?"

"Yes." Merlin hopped to his feet and crossed the living room. He grabbed a stuffed chair and carried it to where Tory was sitting. Once he was seated directly in front of her, he began. "You comfortable?"

"Always," Tory answered and straightened up.

Actually Merlin had no formal training in hypnosis,

but he knew enough to render a demonstration when asked. "All right. Why don't you close your eyes and hold both hands out in front of you."

Tory closed her eyes and held both arms out, hands palm down.

"First thing, you have to stop smiling." His voice had become smooth and reassuring and he watched the giddy smile disappear from Tory's lips. "I want you to feel relaxed. I want you to think about your breathing for a little bit and try to slow it down as if you were sleeping." Silently, Merlin watched Tory for almost thirty seconds, waiting for her breathing pattern to get into a relaxed rhythm. "That's good. Breathe innnnnnn, now ouuuuuut . . . goooood . . . innnnnnn . . . ouuuuuut . . . innnnnnn . . . ouuuuuut. Now think back to our trip to the Cape last summer. I want you to put yourself on the beach. Remember taking those rickety wooden stairs down the dune, carrying the towels? Smell the air . . . the salty sea air. Take a deep breath in and smell the ocean." Merlin watched Tory breathe with the relaxed, peaceful cadence of someone on the beach who was just about to drift off to sleep. "Listen to the sound of the waves as the tide comes in. I want you to be there. The bright sun is in your eyes."

Almost imperceptibly Tory's eyelids tightened. Merlin watched for this and studied her breathing for a few more seconds.

"There's a bucket in the sand, Tory. Can you see it?"

Tory's eyes moved beneath her lids. "Yes," she said evenly.

"Tory, tell me the color of the bucket."

"Red."

"A red bucket," Merlin repeated slowly, letting the words hang in the air to reinforce the image. "Does the bucket have a handle?"

Tory nodded. "Yes."

"Innnnnnn. Ouuuuuut. Good. Breathe innnnnnn, breathe ouuuuuut. Smell the salt in the air. I'm going to hang the empty bucket on one of your hands." Merlin was deliberate in not saying which of Tory's hands was going to receive the bucket. Neither of her outstretched arms moved a fraction of an inch. "Good . . . innnnnnn . . . ouuuuuut . . . Feel the sun on your face . . . innnnnnn . . . ouuuuuut. Now Tory, I'm going to take a red plastic shovel and place a scoop of sand in the bucket." Merlin did not move a muscle. Instead he waited almost ten seconds before continuing. "All right, now a second scoop." He allowed another ten seconds to pass. "Here comes a third shovelful of white sand." Ten seconds elapsed. "I'm going to put another shovelful of sand in the bucket. Can you see the sand in the bucket?"

"Yes."

"Good. How about one more shovelful of sand?" Ten seconds. And then something amazing happened. Before Merlin could announce he was putting more sand in the bucket, Tory's right arm drifted downward, almost an inch below her left. "Another shovelful. Now the bucket's more than half full. Innnnnnn. Ouuuuuut. Here come two more shovels of sand."

Tory's right arm was drifting downward under the weight of the sand.

"Now, Tory," Merlin said, his voice like wet velvet, "keep the bucket on your hand but notice a green-headed horsefly is buzzing about." The corner of Tory's mouth flinched. The green-headed horseflies had been out in full force when they were on the Cape, inflicting brief but wickedly painful bites on any unprotected patch of skin. "The green-headed horsefly zips around, looking for a place to land. Bzzzzzzzzzz . . ." Merlin imitated the fly softly, holding the sound on his tongue as long as his breath would last.

Tory's right arm, heavy under the weight of the bucket and hanging beneath her left one, apparently started to get tired because it now was a full six inches lower.

"Notice that the green-headed horsefly is no longer buzzing about. It is nowhere to be seen . . . or heard. The wind is blowing. The waves are crashing. But no buzzing. You look about but cannot find it. Listen to the wind. Hear the waves. The green-headed horsefly is silent for one reason. It has landed."

Tory's breathing quickened. She'd been through the routine too many times before. The moment the horrible green-headed horseflies stopped dive bombing—*Wham!*—you got bit, contorting your entire body in an attempt to shoo the wicked insect away, all the while scratching madly at the bite mark.

"Innnnnnn. Ouuuuuut. That's it, slow your breathing down. Let me put one last shovelful of sand in the bucket . . . there. Tory, I want you to notice something on your neck. Tiny legs tickling your skin, walking about, looking for the right spot. Someplace juicy. Someplace tender. The green-headed horsefly has found it and instantly you feel a lightening bolt of pain shoot—"

Abruptly Tory dropped her right hand in an effort to slide the heavy bucket off her arm. In a single sweeping gesture she slapped hard at the back of her neck. Her hand made a loud smacking noise, then remained for a few seconds scratching wildly at her skin, nursing her wound. Now her breathing was hard and her cheeks flushed crimson.

Merlin's voice brightened considerably. "Tory, I want you to open your eyes."

Tory's lids fluttered lightly then opened. She squinted as if her eyes hurt from the sun. A sheepish smile crept across her face at the thought of what she had just been through. "My God! That was so real." Her fingers went back to her neck and scratched some more.

"You okay?" Merlin asked sympathetically.

"Yeah, but I can't stop scratching," Tory said and let out a little laugh.

"And *that's* why Tanner Valdemar asked me to help teach his class."

"You are incredible. I mean, that was so real I actually feel like there's bug bite on my neck that I can't stop scratching."

Merlin smiled the sweet, confident smile of success. As far as he was concerned, he could watch Tory scratching like a cocker spaniel all night long.

"Merlin, I mean it," Tory said. "I've got some kind of a bite or something. Is this one of your little tricks? Did you slip me some itching powder when you undid my hair?"

"Nooooo," he said, drawing out the word. "The power of suggestion, that's all."

"The power of suggestion, my ass. I know a bump when I feel one. Here, take a look." And with that Tory turned and lifted her hair off her neck.

Merlin leaned in close, close enough to get a whiff of her wonderful scent. "Bend forward." Then he used his hands to position her so that the light from the ceiling fixture illuminated her neck. "Well, you're right about feeling a bump, but it's not a bug bite. It's just a mole. I never noticed it before. No big deal."

"Is that bad? I mean, maybe it's new." A tone of concern crept into her voice.

"No, it's nothing. I guess I haven't been kissing that part of your anatomy enough."

Tory didn't seem to be able to remove her fingers from

her neck. Her lips curled down into a frown and she looked pale. "Damn," she said.

"Hey," Merlin said softly, shifting from the stuffed chair to a spot on the sofa right next to Tory. "No reason to get upset."

"But you don't understand. My grandfather and my uncle died of skin cancer."

"It's only a mole. Nothing serious. It's not cancer."

"Cancer," Tory repeated, sounding fearful. "Oh, God," she said and her eyes got wet. "Maybe I need to have someone check me out."

"If there's one thing I know, it's your body." Merlin reached down and picked up Tory's right foot and smoothly untied her Saucony. He slid off the running shoe and then her sock. "I know how your little toes curl under just a bit." He kissed her foot. Then he undid the zipper on her jogging pants that ran from her ankle to her knee. "I love how gracefully your calves rise from your ankles and how you've got three freckles right here." He traced a triangle on her skin, running his finger from freckle to freckle. "And I'm not even going to remind you about your appendix scar, but I'll tell you something you probably didn't know. You've got two dimples on either side of the small of your back. And when you towel off and the light catches them just right, I practically pass out. I know everything about your face. The way your eyes crinkle up when it's sunny and the dozens of different smiles you have. I've spent so much time kissing and biting your wonderfully long, sexy neck that I can tell you for sure there are no other moles and now that I've seen this one I'm certain it's benign." Merlin smiled confidently.

Tory didn't seemed to relax. "I want it off."

"So, we'll get it taken care of. No big deal," he said reassuringly.

"Good. I'll cancel a few things and come to your office tomorrow—"

"Not so fast. I thought we agreed I'm no longer your doctor."

"I trust you."

"No," he said definitively. "I'll refer you to someone else—"

"Hey, I know. One of the secretaries at work just had her breasts done by someone she absolutely loved. A Dr. Cutter."

"Cutter and restore her," Merlin joked. "You don't need a plastic surgeon for something on the back of your neck. Besides, all he does is face-lifts and breast jobs."

"Is he good?"

Merlin considered the question. "He's terrific," Merlin finally admitted. "An absolute magician. And women adore him so much they keep coming back for more."

"Sounds like I have my man."

Merlin started to unzip the jacket of Tory's warm-up. Underneath she was wearing a white T-shirt that read YALE in blue letters, the Y and the E gracefully following the curve of her breasts. "He can take care of that little mole on your neck." Merlin reached out and gently began to massage her breasts. "But don't let him touch the old bulldogs. Cutter's good, but he's not God."

"Is that Stilwell with one L or two?"

Stanley Stilwell had just entered The Cutter Institute for Cosmetic Surgery and was ignoring the question asked by the beautiful young woman on the other side of the long black reception desk. He was looking back through the glass front doors at a reproduction of the Venus de Milo in a small garden.

Timidly, he had stepped into the world of Marshall Cutter and was overwhelmed by what he saw. An enor-

mous tank filled with silvery bubbles and fish more intensely colored than a box of Crayola crayons. Polished
wood. Furniture swathed in chintz and silky smooth
leather. Crystal and fine china.

And the beautiful receptionist who was patiently attempting to enter Stanley Stilwell's information into the
computer. "Mr. Stilwell," she tried again, sounding
chirpy and sexy at the same time.

Stilwell had sidled up to the reception desk and leaned
against it as if he were in a bar. Wherever he put his
hand a moist print lingered on the shiny enamel. He
looked the pretty receptionist up and down but did not
smile at her, even though she grinned at him in the most
appealing way. Not for a moment was he struck by her
beauty, her lustrous black hair cropped close enough to
reveal a high forehead and stunning face. She wore a
pink sweater combination consisting of a thin pullover
and a cardigan of matching fabric. Only a single button
on the cardigan was fastened, the one over her breasts.
Its intention was to draw eyes to her ample chest, but
the effort was lost on Stilwell.

"Where's the doc?" he wanted to know in the kind of
tone that gets fights started.

"Dr. Cutter's been expecting you. I believe he's in his
office—"

"We'll get him out here," Stilwell growled.

"Absolutely, sir," she said in her perky voice. "Why
don't you fill out the forms in the living room while I let
him know you're here."

"What kind of forms?" He didn't sound pleased with
the prospect of filling out paperwork.

"Just some information about yourself, health questions, that sort of thing. Won't take but a minute." She
held out a clear plastic clipboard with the forms and a
pen. "By the way, how *do* you spell your last name?"

Stilwell didn't like the way things were going. "Who are you, anyway?"

"I'm Gretchen. I'm one of the receptionists." She smiled prettily.

Stilwell let out a sigh of exasperation. "Shit . . . it's Stilwell. S-T-I-L-L-W-E-L-L. No one said anything 'bout forms. Let's get the doc out here," Stilwell demanded as he took one step closer to Gretchen and snatched the clipboard away from her.

"He'll be right with you." Gretchen began to type something into her computer. "S-T-I-L-L-W-E-L-L, is that what you said?"

"Right. No, wait. That's not right." Stilwell was gripped with the sort of terror people feel when they have to introduce someone whose name they've forgotten. He rolled his eyes up in his head and silently recited the spelling of his name. "S-T-I-L-W-E-L-L. One L, *then* two. Ya gotta listen better."

"Okie doke," Gretchen agreed, typing the correction into the computer. "Everyone gets a little nervous when they come to the doctor's office. I know just how it feels. You just have a seat in the living room. Since tonight's only a consultation I can get you some sherry if you'd like."

"Who's that?" Stilwell sounded exasperated. He looked about, expecting to find another person to deal with. Finally, he shook his head as he glanced at the clipboard and checked out Gretchen's breasts for the first time. Then he headed in the direction of the room that Gretchen pointed out, which was not far away. It was a heavily decorated room, thick with draperies and carpet. He had his choice of flowery sofas and over-stuffed easy chairs. Small tables were scattered about the large room covered with ladies' magazines and huge lavish coffee-table books.

Stilwell sat stiffly in one of the easy chairs, looked about the empty room, and reluctantly began to fill out the health form. It took him ten minutes to fill in all the blanks and put checks in the appropriate boxes. When he was finished, he pushed himself out of the deep chair and was just about to move in the direction of the black reception desk when a man approached.

"Mr. Stilwell, I'm Marshall Cutter. Won't you join me in my consultation room?" Marshall Cutter was dressed in a perfectly tailored brown suit, a pale brown shirt, and blue tie knotted tightly at the neck. Even in the dim lighting of the hallway Cutter was an imposing figure, tall and lean, like a swimmer. A lifelong bachelor, he had fostered quite a reputation for squiring a number of different socialites around town, including several his magic scalpel had touched.

The two briefly shook hands, then Cutter led his patient down the darkened hallway, past several small examination rooms toward the only room on the corridor that was lighted.

Before Stilwell entered the room he paused in the doorway and looked about. For a man whose idea of a living room was a grimy sofa and a television set, Cutter's private office was magnificent. Paneled walls. A patterned carpet on the floor. Elaborate crown molding. Two huge windows looking out on a small garden illuminated from above by brilliant floodlights. An antique desk and chair stood on one side of the room, while two leather sofas faced each other on the other side.

"Why don't we sit over here?" Cutter suggested as he strolled across the thick carpet on his way to the sofas.

"You said if I came late no one else would be here," Stilwell declared from the doorway.

"Please," Cutter said grandly. He was standing with

his hand out, the consummate host, in a pose he supposed Stilwell might never have seen before.

Stilwell made a face and padded across the room to take a seat.

"We have a new computer system. Gretchen's been helping with the conversion of data. There's nothing to be alarmed about. I have a lot of patients who want privacy, men and women in politics and television. Having someone arrive after hours is nothing out of the ordinary."

"Yeah, well, I want to keep this as hush-hush as possible, if you know what I mean."

"Of course," Cutter said somewhat magnanimously.

"Which reminds me, the day I get cut, who all's gonna be here?"

"Personnel will, as I assured you, be kept to a minimum. My anesthesiologist, Brian Trilby, and, of course, my medical assistant. But all front office personnel will be given the day off."

"So I won't be seeing what's her name . . . Gretchen . . . again?"

"I don't believe so."

Stilwell leaned forward toward the doctor. He waited for a few seconds to let Cutter know something important was coming. "You listen to me, Doc. I only want to say this one time. What I'm going through here is real fuckin' important to me. I bet you know what I mean."

"I believe I do," Cutter said quietly but with utmost confidence.

"Not so fast. I may seem all sweet and nice sitting here on this fancy furniture with all these pretty pictures on the wall, but my looks are my life. I don't like crowds. I don't like forms. For crissake, I don't want to discuss how to spell my name or where the fuck I live. And I don't give a crap about your computer. I ain't some broad coming in at night for a tit job so her friends at the country club don't know she's getting blown up. Okay? It's the three of you and that's it. Am I making myself clear?''

If Cutter was unnerved by the crude talk he hid it well. He sat very calmly, legs crossed, and when he finally spoke his voice sounded as relaxed as a disk jockey on an easy listening FM station. "Mr. Stilwell, I understand precisely how important your privacy is. That's why I suggested we meet after hours, and why I will give our front office staff a paid holiday."

"And that's why you're so expensive."

"No, I'm expensive because I'm good. Now, with that out of the way, let me tell you what I have in mind for you."

Stilwell brought his finger to his nose and flicked it. "Not a lot of details, Doc. Just the skinny."

Cutter studied Stilwell's coarse features. "You've got some very good features that I want to bring out. You'll be given general anesthesia so you won't feel a thing. I'll do a routine face-lift to tighten everything up. That loose skin under your neck will be gone. Then I'll fix that scar on your cheek." Cutter paused to study Stilwell's nose. If he was having trouble looking at it, he hid his feelings. "Then I'll work on your nose. I'll take a small flap of skin from your forehead and use it to reshape your nose. Your nostrils will be smaller and they'll be in proportion to the rest of your face. The whole thing will take about six hours but it will knock twenty years off. Your own mother won't recognize you."

Stilwell considered Cutter's plan, nodding silently to himself until Gretchen's voice called out, "Goodnight," from another part of the surgi-center. "That's it." He sneered at Cutter. "If I have to hear that bitch's voice one more time, I'm gonna bust this place up but good."

Stilwell had crossed the line. Cutter was now thoroughly disgusted. "Listen to me. I can't work like this. I'm sorry to have to tell you this, Mr. Stilwell, but I don't believe I can operate on you."

"Huh?" Stilwell sounded surprised. "You don't got no choice."

"Listen to yourself. You're threatening me. I'm not going to operate on someone who threatens me. Goodnight, Mr. Stilwell."

Stilwell rose to his feet. He didn't seem put off or disappointed. This wasn't the first time in his life he had to convince someone to do things his way, but he was determined to leave the Heckler and Koch in his car. His hand disappeared inside his corduroy jacket and withdrew a thick roll of cash held in place by a doubled-over rubber band. He held it up for Cutter to see the hundred-dollar bill on the outside. Slipping his index finger under the rubber band he gave it a swift yank and snapped it in two. The tightly coiled money unfurled and Stilwell dropped it on the floor at Cutter's feet. Stilwell smiled. "So what's with the statue in the garden without the arms? Don't that scare the broads away?"

Chapter 2

Most of Marshall Cutter's front office employees were strikingly attractive women, giving hope to the patients that they, too, might someday walk out of the surgi-center with luscious full lips, a nice tight neck, and breasts that promised to stand at attention long after everything else on the body had migrated south.

Privately, Cutter joked with his staff that if some of his regulars scheduled one more face-lift they would be surprised to look in the mirror and see they were sporting a beard. Of course Cutter never breathed a word of this to any of his wealthy clientele. In fact, his reputation was stellar, attracting a huge following from all over western Pennsylvania over the last five years.

After the first face-lift of the day was safely in recovery, Marshall Cutter strolled into the staff lounge for a glass of fresh orange juice. Sitting at the oval butcher block table was beautiful Gretchen, furtively smoking a cigarette.

"This is as good a time as any," Cutter said, pulling out a chair for himself at the table. "I think we should talk."

"I know what you're gonna say, Dr. Cutter. I gotta smoke outside. I'm really, *really* sorry. It won't happen again." Gretchen smiled sincerely and blinked her pretty eyes, knowing from past experience that she could disarm any situation with the right flash of her physical features.

"I'd appreciate it."

Gretchen smiled again.

"Is everything okay?" he asked with an avuncular tone. "Lately you seem—"

"I'm fine," the receptionist quickly said, nodding reflexively. "Why?"

"Well, there've been quite a few scheduling mix-ups. Patients coming in for appointments they don't really have. Others not coming in for appointments on the book. Is anything going on I should know about?"

Gretchen hesitated. Her eyes got wide and for a moment her visage was as pretty and frozen as the reproduction of the Venus de Milo. Cutter expected her to blurt out something like her mother was dying of cancer or that her boyfriend had gotten her pregnant. But Gretchen said nothing of the sort. "I guess with the new computer I'm just stressed out a little."

"Maybe you need some time off. You have any vacation coming?"

Suddenly, Gretchen's face burst into a cover girl smile. "As a matter of fact, I'm going on vacation tomorrow. Acapulco."

"Wow!" Cutter said, more at the thought of Gretchen in a sexy thong than at her good fortune to be off on vacation. "Come back tan and rested."

"Okie doke," Gretchen gushed, the mere mention of her two weeks in Acapulco invigorating her. She hopped up from the table. "No more ciggies in the lounge, no more scheduling mistakes." Then she gave a friendly little salute to Cutter, giggling, and headed back to her front office position.

* * *

"Hey, Tanner, you got any medical students with you today?" Merlin said into the phone without bothering to identify himself. He was wearing street clothes; dark brown pants, a light blue shirt, and a tie adorned with a rabbit poking its head out of a black top hat.

"Who is this?" Valdemar asked.

"It's Merlin." He was sitting in the nursing station of the emergency room at the Pittsburgh University Medical Center, printing the name Tony Schaffer on an eight of spades with a black Sharpie marker before folding it twice and slipping it into his pants pocket. One of the more popular doctors at the Medical Center, Merlin was known as much for his surgical skills as his abilities with a magic wand, sponge ball, or a deck of cards. "I'm just about to go in with an incarcerated hernia in the ER. You told me to page you the next time I had something for your hypnosis class."

"Incarcerated hernia, huh? This I've got to see. Let me gather my students and I'll meet you in, say, ten minutes."

"Make it five. I hear the kid's miserable." Although incarcerated hernias were quite painful—a loop of bowel having popped through a small hole in the abdomen to the point where it had become trapped and swollen—they weren't a surgical emergency if the bowel could be coaxed back inside. Often, though, the patient was so tight with anxiety it took a slug of Valium to relax the muscles in the abdominal wall.

Three and a half minutes later Tanner Valdemar hurried into the ER. In his early sixties, he was thin almost to the point of being frail, and he wore his mop of kinky hair long enough to add almost three inches to his overall height. He had three gold teeth, all molars, and they managed to catch the light whenever he smiled. Merlin had never seen him in anything but a three-piece suit, a dark blue one today with a pocket watch tucked into the side of his vest. A looping gold fob hung in an eye-catching catenary, tracing the dangling course from the pocket to a button on the front of the vest. Of course this was an affectation that might be reviled in another, but Valdemar was deservedly respected for his success with clinical hypnosis. His eccentricities were tolerated by the medical staff, who routinely dumped all of their difficult patients on him. Although the running joke in the medical profession was that psychiatrists went into their chosen field to gain a better understanding of their own neuroses, Valdemar had impressed Merlin from the start, mostly because he had a sense of humor. Whenever there was a general staff meeting and Valdemar's beeper went off, his hands would flutter about his head while he stage-whispered that one of his patients must be on a bridge. But Valdemar took his profession seriously. And Merlin discovered just how superb his clinical skills were when Valdemar counseled Tory after she'd been forced to kill a man in self-defense. She was having wicked nightmares that made her terrified to fall asleep. Tanner Valdemar was the one who made them go away. Merlin would do anything for his friend.

Valdemar led three medical students who had decked themselves out in short white coats with reflex hammers, little flashlights, and expensive stethoscopes hanging from every pocket and button hole, as if their initiation to the medical profession required that they display every piece of equipment they owned. The students clutched little notebooks and followed in tight formation behind the psychiatrist.

"All right, Merlin, let's see your stuff," Valdemar said as he found his colleague in the nursing station, re-viewing the patient's chart.

After handshakes all around, the medical students making sure to enthusiastically pump the hand of anyone who might write them an evaluation later in their clinical experience, the small group made its way into a private observation room. "Okay, who's in charge here?" Merlin said in a Muppet-like voice, then winked at the twelve-year-old boy lying on a stretcher. The child's mother was huddled right next to the head of the stretcher, stroking her son's sweaty forehead. Dad was not far away, holding Junior's hand.

Both parents looked up to greet Merlin and his on-lookers. "You must be Dr. Merlin. I'm Judy Schaffer. The nurses said you were going to be seeing our Tony." Mrs. Schaffer did her best to smile bravely.

"I hear Tony has some pretty bad belly pain."

"Do you think you'll have to operate?" Mr. Schaffer wanted to know.

"Why don't I get to know your son before we decide anything." All eyes turned to the youngster curled up on the stretcher, wearing one of those horribly unflattering, bare-backed hospital gowns. "Ohhhh, so *you're* Teddy," Merlin asked again with a silly voice, seeming befuddled.

Tony almost smiled at Merlin, but a spasm of pain sent a grimace across his young face. "No, I'm Tony," he replied in a weak voice.

"Tony Baloney," Merlin said and laughed.

The gold teeth twinkled in Valdemar's mouth when he saw the young boy crack a brief smile.

"Can I see your hernia?" Merlin asked, getting closer to the stretcher.

"You're not going to hurt me, are you?"

"No way, I already hurt a couple of kids today." Merlin gently helped Tony lie flat on his back and lifted the hospital gown. Carefully, Merlin explored the boy's groin with his fingertips. There was a bulge on the right side no bigger than a grape. "Doesn't look too bad to me."

"Really?" The boy sounded hopeful.

"Really?" his mother echoed.

Merlin looked at, and spoke directly to, his patient. "Oh yeah. No biggie. All we have to do is wait for it to slide back inside and then we're done for today."

"It won't go back in," Tony said, looking down at himself as Merlin covered him up. A tear meandered down his salty cheek. "All they do is keep pushing on it and that makes it hurt."

"Wanna bet?"

"No," the boy said indignantly.

"Tell you what," Merlin reached into one of his pockets and pulled out a pack of playing cards. "Let's try something." Merlin open the deck and fanned it for his young patient, showing it to be a very ordinary-appearing deck. But ordinary was precisely what this deck was not. In magic parlance it was called a rough-smooth deck. What made this deck special was the fact that every second card was an eight of spades. In addition, the face of each eight of spades was chemically 'roughed up' so that they would stick to the back of the next card, making every two cards travel as a couplet when they were shuffled. When the cards were fanned in the face up position, with pressure from the magician's fingers, the couplet stayed together as one. All twenty-six of the eights of spades remained perfectly hidden from view. The deck of cards could even be cut without disrupting any of the couplets. Then, when the deck was turned facedown and fanned again, each of the cards offered to the audience was actually an eight of spades.

It was the simplest way to force a predetermined card.

"I'll just make a couple of quick cuts," Merlin said, squaring up the deck after he turned it facedown and proceeded to make a series of legitimate cuts. "Why don't you choose any card you want?"

Tony's small hand reached out and pointed to a card in the middle of the deck. Merlin cut the deck so that the chosen card was on top. "You sure?" Merlin asked as Tony nodded. "This is the one you want?" Again, Tony nodded. Merlin turned the card over. "Eight of spades. You okay with the eight of spades?"

"I guess so," Tony said. He tried to prop himself up on his elbows but it hurt the boy too much.

"Well let's make sure we remember which card you chose." The magician removed the Sharpie marker from his shirt pocket and neatly printed Tony Schaffer on the card. "Okay, Tony Baloney, would you tear up the card for me?"

The young patient obliged and handed Merlin the little pieces of the card. This is when Merlin's magic truly began.

"Now I want you to listen to me very carefully, Tony," Merlin said, his voice becoming softer and melodic. The magician held the torn pieces of the card between his thumb and forefinger, working them in a slow pill-rolling technique as if he were a Parkinsonian. "I need your help making these pieces go back together, Tony, but you have to put all your energy into it. Watch my fingers, Tony. Think about the little pieces. That's gooood . . . watch the pieces . . . think about the pieces going back together."

Merlin was holding his hand about eighteen inches in front of the boy's face, working his thumb against his forefinger. "Relax all your muscles. Start with your shoulders. Go ahead, think about relaxing your shoulders." Merlin watched as the skinny shoulders sagged. "Good," Merlin murmured, switching the torn eight of spades from his right hand to the left. "Now your arms . . .

that's right . . . let your arms float away from you. Good, Tony, watch my fingers work the little pieces. Keep your eyes right here. The pieces want to go back together. Only you can make it happen." Merlin moved his left hand several inches closer to the boy's face, then switched the pieces back to his right hand and continued rolling them between his fingers. "Now the muscles in your chest. Let them go nice and gooey. Ohhhh, I can feel the pieces finding each other, working their way back into the eight of spades. Try to slow your breathing down."

Although the sounds of a hectic ER continued in the background, it seemed so quiet in the little observation room that Tony forgot where he was. The pieces of the card made little wispy noises as they slid over one another.

Again Merlin switched hands, moving the cards closer and closer to Tony's face. "Watch the cards . . . I can feel them working their way back together . . . watch them, Tony." Merlin switched hands and continued rolling the pieces for another minute, only this time he leaned over and gingerly laid his hand on the boy's groin.

Tony's eyes were at half mast. His shoulders sagged and one of his hands dangled over the side of the stretcher. With each breath, his chest moved up and down, slow and steady as if he had been asleep.

"Good, Tony, we're almost done, I think they're just about back together." As Merlin continued his hypnotic patter and worked the torn pieces, his other hand began to apply gentle pressure to the hernia. Gradually he pressed harder, feeling the hernia beneath his fingertips until *pop*, the pesky loop of bowel suddenly slipped back inside the abdomen.

The boy didn't flinch.

Merlin then brought his hands together. Working delicately, he began to open the card that, up until a minute earlier, had been safely tucked in his side pocket. The switch had been simple, executed perfectly during one of the times Merlin handed the torn pieces from one hand to the other.

The magician didn't rush. This was the payoff and he prolonged the moment of suspense. When the card was fully unfolded Merlin showed Tony the back of the card first. Merlin worked his fingers around the four corners of the card, moving them in a most delicate way as if his digits were in a slow motion ballet.

Not for a moment did Merlin take his eyes off the boy's face. Tony looked absolutely dreamy, totally mesmerized by the wondrous event unfolding right in front of his eyes. Finally, Merlin turned the card over. "Here, Tony," he said softly, "here's your card."

Tony reached out for the restored eight of spades. His movements were the clumsy efforts of someone groggy from sleep.

"We're done. You can go home now," Merlin stated.

"What!" Tony exclaimed, looking down at Merlin's hand. "It doesn't hurt. Mom! It doesn't hurt!"

Mrs. Schaffer, who had remained in the shadows with Tanner Valdemar and the three medical students, couldn't help but jump to the side of the stretcher. "You fixed it, Doctor?"

"Temporarily," Merlin answered. "Once Tony relaxed, it slid right back inside."

"What about the operation?" Tony wanted to know.

Merlin leaned in a bit closer to Tony and gently went eye-to-eye with him. "I still have to fix your belly so it doesn't happy again, but we'll wait a couple of days. Nothing's going to hurt you. And I promise you an even better trick just before we let you fall asleep."

"A new trick?" the boy asked eagerly.

"Yeah. And you won't even have to sleep in the hospital overnight."

Tony smiled and reached out for his mother.

When it was all over and Merlin had had a chance to go over all the details with Mrs. Schaffer, he retreated to the nursing station to find Valdemar and the three students.

"Just a simple magic trick," Merlin bragged with a mock bad-boy smile.

"That wasn't so simple," Valdemar admired. "Thanks, I owe you one."

Tory Welch drove up the long driveway to The Cutter Institute for Cosmetic Surgery. It would have been easier to phone for an appointment from her downtown office, but she'd heard about the impressive building and was curious to experience for herself what so many of her friends buzzed about.

There was a certain aura about Marshall Cutter.

The type of women who wanted their jewelry from Hardy and Hays, their car a Land Rover, their second home in Ligonier, and their husbands to say yes to any request that involved money, wanted to be done by Marshall Cutter. Nose jobs, eye lifts, and breast augmentations were scheduled around Cutter's availability rather than going someplace else. The bruising and swelling that accompanied a newly upturned nose or a fresh set of perky, squeezable breasts was not hidden behind closed doors or on an island where no one would notice. Recovery was done in Pittsburgh, at the Giant Eagle supermarket, by the pool at the club, or at one of the flashy soireés benefiting whatever was the charity of the moment. Bruises became badges of honor, membership cards to an exclusive club that proclaimed the bearer had been touched by the deified hands of Cutter. More than once, a pampered society gal arriving at a summer bash in a backless dress and a face full of bruises could be heard bragging she'd been "Marshalled." Once the word got out, she became the belle of the ball, attracting a throng of envious women who decided right on the spot that they, too, were going to be Marshalled before Labor Day.

Tory pulled into the crowded lot just as three perfect women, all dressed up and permanently on vacation, strolled out the front doors beaming with pride. Their slender necks sparkled with jewelry that attracted the sunlight like brilliant little magnets. The happy trio got into a shiny white Mercedes, slipped on fashionable sunglasses, and smoothly cruised out of the parking lot.

Tory paid less attention to the little threesome than most women would. The surroundings, with the manicured gardens, Venus de Milo reproduction, and white porch seemed more like a resort than a plastic surgery clinic. Pulling open the heavy glass doors, she entered the world of Marshall Cutter. Women were everywhere. The waiting room was full of beautiful Barbie dolls beaming in anticipation of their post-op sessions with the doctor, while Cabbage Patch Kids anxiously awaited their turn to be Marshalled into perfection.

A young woman in her late twenties emerged from the hallway to Tory's right. Jewelry jangled merrily from her delicate wrists, and by the way she was prancing it was obvious she couldn't contain herself. Instead of heading to the reception desk or the front door, she turned and strutted back into the waiting room to see which of her best friends might have arrived while she had been in consultation with the doctor. Immediately she squealed, "Pa - tri - cia," and shot her friend a garden club wave—arm straight out, palm toward her friend, thumb to the side and fingers flapping up and down as if she were working a hand puppet.

As the giggly reunion commenced, complete with smooches on the cheek and conversation loud enough for everyone in the room to enjoy, Tory made her way around the huge fish tank and toward the black reception desk. The small business office was fully stocked with a Neapolitan ice cream assortment of comely receptionists. A silvery blond and a stunning redhead were perched at small desks in the back while a striking brunette sat alone at the reception desk, talking quietly on the phone.

While waiting patiently for the raven-haired beauty to finish her call, Tory read the name on her chest— Gretchen—and couldn't help but catch the tail end of her conversation. "Just give me a few more days," Gretchen was saying. "I need some more time . . . Okay. *Okay*, bye." Once Gretchen hung up the phone she stared off into space, not seeming to notice anyone standing in front of her. Tory had the sense Gretchen was going to burst into tears.

Tory had waited long enough to be polite. In fact she was thirty seconds beyond the outer reaches of polite when she took two steps sideways to position herself directly in Gretchen's line of sight.

Now Gretchen was staring through Tory as if she were in a deep trance.

"Excuse me," Tory said.

Gretchen did not stir.

"Gretchen!" Tory implored, this time quite a bit louder.

Gretchen batted her expertly made-up eyes several times and looked around as if she'd just awoken from a nap. "Oh, can I help you?" she said to Tory.

"I'd like to set up an appointment to see Dr. Cutter." Tory noticed Gretchen looking her over, wondering

which part of her anatomy she wanted enhanced or reduced or smoothed over.

Gretchen shook her pretty head. "For a consultation,
we're looking at . . ." Gretchen was making a clicking
sound with her tongue as she gazed into the computer
monitor to check what appointment times were available.
"I'm afraid his schedule is quite busy in the next few
weeks. Gosh, he's booked all the way through . . . oh
my, wait a sec, you're in luck. How's next Tuesday?"

It was four seconds after five o'clock when Gretchen
bounced out the front door of The Cutter Institute for
Cosmetic Surgery. As she flew past the Venus de Milo
she burbled, "See you in two weeks."

She hopped into her Firebird, cranked up the tunes on
her radio, and felt better than she had in the last ten
days. All that stood between Gretchen and an Acapulco
tan was a couple hours of packing and a good night's
rest.

Gretchen stopped at the drugstore on her way home,
bought sunscreen and two tubes of gel for her diaphragm, then went home to pack. She whipped up a
pitcher of margaritas just to get in the mood and began
throwing things into her suitcase, one sip of the sweet-
ened tequila for every item she packed. By eight-thirty
she was so tanked she didn't even hear the *clunk* of the
Lock Ness Monster.

The man took care to back his car up to the rear door
of Gretchen's little townhouse. He sat alone in his car,
the radio turned off, staring up at the second floor as he
watched the slender figure cross back and forth in front
of the window. Before he stepped onto the cement walk-
way he donned leather gloves and slipped a wool ski
mask over his head. Now he was dressed in black from

head to toe, the only spot of color being a light tan
sheath strapped to his belt that hung over his right hip.
Made of leather, it was quite similar to the type of sheath
hunters wore to secure knives, but it was longer and
quite a bit more narrow. Poking out of the top was a
wooden handle, old and dull, that looked as if it had
been forgotten in the back of a drawer for years.

On the seat next to him was a device that at first
glance resembled a giant metal syringe. It was nothing
of the sort the medical profession would ever sanction.
An aluminum dowel, fifteen inches in length and three-
eighths of an inch in diameter, had a cross-bar attached
at one end and a rugged sheet-metal screw at the other.
The only moveable part was a chunk of lead, the size
and shape of a six-ounce can of tomato paste. It was
wrapped around the metal dowel so that it could be slid
up and down its length.

This was the Lock Ness Monster. It was neither neat
nor pretty, but in the right hands it could open a locked
door in less than seven seconds.

The back of Gretchen's townhouse was quiet. Nevertheless, the man in the black ski mask scanned the area
several times to make absolutely certain no one would
see what he was about to do. Then he approached the
back door.

The lock was a newer model, one that was advertised
as being absolutely pick-proof. First the metal screw was
injected into the narrow keyway by turning the cross bar
until the threads caught and drove the screw more and
more deeply into the lock. When it would turn no more,
the man grabbed the lead weight and carefully slid it all
the way down to meet the doorknob. In one forceful
movement the lead was yanked back until it slammed
into the cross bar. The Lock Ness Monster instantly
ripped the keyway and the cylinder out of the knob, and

the back door of Gretchen's townhouse was ready to be opened.

Gretchen was tossing bikinis and tank tops into her suitcase when she remembered her diaphragm. Grabbing her margarita for the short trek to her bathroom, she scolded herself, "The gel doesn't do much good without the 'phragm." Then she headed across the hallway.

That's when she saw him, not six feet away from her.

Although she had never seen his face, this was not the first time she had been forced to meet with this man. But this time he was inside her house. Being alone with him absolutely terrified her. "I don't want to wait a few more days," he said.

When she heard his voice the glass slipped from her fingers and tumbled to the carpet. Tequila splashed everywhere as she took several frantic steps backward before banging into the wall. Both of her hands shot out in front of her in a feeble attempt to stop the onslaught of the intruder.

He charged her immediately, not stopping for a second, spinning her around and grabbing her roughly around the neck, choking her hard with one hand as his other clamped over her mouth.

"Anyone else here?" he demanded.

Gretchen's eyes were so wide she looked like a ridiculous caricature for cosmetic eyelid surgery. All she could manage was a frightened little shake of her head.

"Now, I'm gonna take my hand away from your mouth. You scream, you die. You understand?" Gretchen nodded quickly, and the grip on her mouth was released. In one swift move he changed his choke hold to a half-nelson. "You got what I want?"

"I told you on the phone. I need more time. It's the

new computer system. I can hardly make appointments. Please . . . please give me a little more time."

The man peered into the bedroom and noticed the opened suitcase on the bed. A stack of clothing waited next to it. "Going someplace?"

When Gretchen didn't answer quickly enough the man tightened his hold around her neck and jerked her off the ground.

"Answer me."

"To my boyfriend's. For the weekend," Gretchen strained to say.

With his right hand, the man grabbed hold of the worn wooden handle at his side and pulled an ice pick from its leather sheath. As poorly maintained as the handle was, the slender pick was polished to dazzling perfection. The tip had been honed on a whetstone until it was needle-sharp.

First he held it up to Gretchen's face, scratching a thin red line across her unblemished skin. "I don't want to use this."

"Please don't. I just need—"

"You tell anyone?"

"No! You said not to. I swear. I wouldn't tell anyone."

"Don't you lie to me. You lie to me and that's it." The ski mask was getting itchy, but he was too angry to pay it much attention.

"No, really, I'm not lying—"

"You goddamn better not be."

"Maybe you could ask someone else. Someone who knows how to access the files—"

"What makes you think anyone else is on the case?" Again he jerked his left hand up and lifted Gretchen up in the air. "I asked you, and that's all you need to know."

"I'll do it. I swear," Gretchen pleaded, saying anything she could think of to temper the situation.

"When are you gonna know enough to get me the info?"

"I don't know. A week maybe."

"You'll have it in one week?" the man demanded, his arm still constricting Gretchen's neck.

Gretchen nodded quickly, willing to agree to anything the man wanted.

"Then why're you booked on USAir outta P-burgh tomorrow, landing in Dallas eleven-thirty-seven on your way to Acapulco? Now, maybe I'm thick or something—I ain't no receptionist at the Marshall Cutter Beauty Academy or nothing—but I gotta ask you, how the hell you gonna get me the names I need by next week?"

The blood drained from Gretchen's face. Her knees gave out and if it wasn't for the man's grip on her neck she would have collapsed to the floor.

"Found your ticket downstairs."

"Please, let me go."

"Wanna dance?" The man in the black mask moved the ice pick from Gretchen's cheek to the back of her neck, right at the point where the skull ends and the tissue becomes soft and fleshy. "You know what I'm talking about. If you don't want to dance, tell me what I need to know 'bout who's been visiting the doctor."

"I'm gonna be sick."

"Time's up." The man put gentle pressure on the ice pick. Effortlessly it pierced through Gretchen's skin. The pain was instantaneous, a sharp, stinging sensation that made Gretchen suck in her breath and hold it. Slowly the intruder advanced the cold steel of the pick, no more than a millimeter at a time, slicing through muscle and fascial planes.

Gretchen made little whimpering noises, sounding like a small animal in the talons of a much larger predator. The room was starting to spin. *Tell him something. Make up a name. Tell him anything.* It was hard to think. She could not tell what the man was doing with the ice pick, but she knew he had stabbed her with it. *Stilwell. Something Stilwell.*

"You listen to me. The tip of this ice pick ain't no more than half an inch from your brain. 'Member what I told you about the wicked dance? Trust me, hold very still, pretty Gretchen. Breathe as gently as you can. I don't want to slip."

"There was a man the other day. Seemed kind of . . . Ow!" The ice pick had crept forward.

"Kind of *what*?" he growled through clenched teeth.

"He was rough."

"What's his name?"

"Stilwell. I don't remember his first name."

"Stanley?"

"Yes, yes. Stanley. That's it. He saw the doctor. I'll get more."

"I need to know now. Stilwell I know. Keep going."

"I . . . can't." Gretchen was crying softly.

"Feel the ice pick? In a few seconds it'll slide up into your brain. Think, Gretchen. Think."

"I'm trying," she said with a desperate tone of failure in her voice.

"Last chance."

Gretchen was sobbing.

"Good-bye, pretty Gretchen," he said and with a quick thrust, advanced the steel point of the ice pick into the base of Gretchen's brain.

In five seconds it was over.

Chapter 3

A crew of men was fussing with the little garden around the white sign at the bottom of the long driveway. Three of them were on their hands and knees re-planting brightly colored flowers. Another was shuttling a wheelbarrow full of rusty red bark, dumping it between the newly planted flowers so that the men on their knees could spread it by hand until it looked perfect.

A fifth man, evidently the crew chief, was dressed in khaki slacks and a dark green pullover. He was working with a large chamois, wiping every nook and cranny of the white sign, even wrapping some of the cloth around one of his fingers so that he could clean each of the gold-colored carved letters individually.

Two trucks, one a rusted-out pickup with a load of wood chips, and the other a brand new Ford, were parked across the street. Just as Tory was about to make the turn into the driveway she spotted a sixth man, dressed in dark slacks and a dark shirt, staring through a pair of binoculars. He was looking in the direction of the surgi-center, scanning the beautiful green hillside. With the sound of the tires crunching on the gravel drawing his attention he lowered the glasses momentarily and peered at Tory's Honda.

The whole scene seemed a bit excessive, five men to tend to one little garden, one man to survey the property with a set of binoculars. But as Tory started up the brick driveway and noticed the tightly trimmed boxwood hedges and magnificent landscaping, she appreciated the statement Marshall Cutter was making.

The day was true Pittsburgh drab, a sky full of gray but the breeze blowing off the rivers was mild and temperate. Guiding her Honda up the gently curving driveway of Cutter's clinic, Tory glanced in her rearview mirror. The five men were still diligently tending to the little garden. The sixth man, standing almost motionless, seemed to be tracking the progress of her car through his binoculars. It was a moment that invited contemplation, one that she would certainly dwell upon in the future. But as she entered the parking lot her thoughts were interrupted by the site of Merlin's red Jeep Cherokee parked among four other cars in an otherwise empty lot.

Tory fleetingly thought it was strange that the large parking lot was so empty for such a busy practice, but her thoughts quickly turned to Merlin's surprise visit to the clinic.

Tory noticed two things as she stepped around the magnificent fish tank in the reception room. The first was Merlin, happily ensconced in an easy chair, his head buried in one of the glossy cocktail table books.

The second was there was no receptionist working the front desk. The Neapolitan girls were gone.

Merlin sensed Tory's presence and pulled his eyes away from the book.

"What are you doing here?" Tory asked through a sly smile.

"Protecting you from flying implants." Then in a whisper, "An opportunity to check out the high-rent competition." Merlin admired the expensive surroundings. "You know, we ought to get this book. It shows the wonderful work they're doing with breast implants." Although too far away, he held the shiny pages up for Tory to see. "Can you see yourself in a pair of forty-four Ds?"

For a moment Tory held both hands out six inches in front of her own modest chest, cupping huge imaginary breasts. "Anyone around?" she asked, turning briefly toward the darkened hallway that led back to the examination and operating rooms.

Merlin shook his head.

Tory wandered over to a sign that instructed her to SIGN IN HERE and waited at the shiny black reception counter for several minutes.

The phone began to ring. Tory fully expected one of the Neapolitans, whichever flavor was supposed to answer the phone, to whip down the hallway with powdered sugar all over her mouth. The phone rang six or seven times. Then it was silent. Tory leaned over the reception desk and checked out the telephone. One of the lines was lit. Evidently, someone had picked it up in back.

Not knowing quite what to do, Tory joined Merlin in the waiting room. He realized how nervous she was. She fidgeted, her hand reaching behind her neck to play with the mole, then she checked her watch and straightened her sleeve.

The sofa she chose was incredibly comfortable, but she could not relax. Several times she crossed and uncrossed her legs, finally grabbing one of the glossy hardcover coffee-table books that depicted before and after shots of men and women who had undergone plastic surgery. Not until she found the section that featured breast augmentations was she able to smile. For several minutes she was mesmerized by the ridiculously buxom middle-aged women who looked like they had huge udders in need of a good milking.

"Uh, excuse me. Can I help you?"

Tory looked up and snapped the glossy book closed as quickly as a teenager caught with a *Penthouse*. An attractive middle-aged woman stood across the room. Apparently she had just emerged from the darkened hallway. She was in pink scrubs and red clogs. Her hair was streaked with blonde that probably hid the first signs of gray, and the skin on her face and neck was tight, almost to the point of being shiny.

"Hi, uh, I'm Tory Welch. I have a ten-thirty appointment with Dr. Cutter."

"A ten-thirty. I didn't think we had—" The woman cut herself off in mid-sentence and strode purposefully around the reception counter and efficiently tapped several keys on the computer console. "Ten-thirty, ten-thirty," she repeated quietly to herself. Finally she murmured, "Gretchen," and made a little clicking noise with her tongue. She looked back at Tory and Merlin and said, "I apologize for keeping you waiting. Dr. Cutter wasn't supposed to be seeing . . . um . . . new patients today. When did you call for your appointment?"

"It must have been sometime last week."

The woman in pink scrubs shook her head in mild disgust. "Did you talk to a woman with a high-pitched voice?" Tory nodded. "Sounded like someone who should be serving drinks in Hooters?" Tory nodded again. "Gretchen. She's on vacation, two weeks on some tropical island or something. An amazing scatterbrain. The closer she got to her vacation, the more mistakes she made."

Tory could take a hint. "Well, it doesn't really matter," she said, looking at her watch. "I've got an appointment in town at noon and with traffic I probably should re-schedule and get going."

"What are you here for?" the woman in pink scrubs finally asked. She was eyeing Tory up and down in her dark-blue suit and red blouse. It was obvious by her expression that she couldn't imagine what Cutter and Restore Her could offer this woman.

"I've got a mole on my neck that just sort of appeared and—"

"Is that all?" The woman in pink scrubs sounded relieved. "Oh, I'm sure Dr. Cutter can take care of that in less than ten minutes. Why don't you come with me." Turning toward Merlin she asked, "Do you want to join us?"

"Oh, no. I'll come in after," Merlin said, not wanting to embarrass Tory with extra people in the room while she undressed. It seemed like an odd thing to do as he saw her naked every day, but he read the situation correctly. Tory seemed relieved he didn't want to be in the room for the exam.

"By the way, I'm Carol, Dr. Cutter's medical assistant. Let me put you in an exam room. You can fill out the paperwork while you wait. I'll make sure you're out of here in twenty minutes."

In a flash Tory was out of her chair, hurrying to catch up with Carol, who was already walking briskly down the hallway. Though artwork decorated the walls, most of the tiny overhead spotlights were darkened and it was nearly impossible to see what was in the frames.

Carol opened the door to a small, windowless examination room and flicked a switch that immediately lit up the room, not in the harsh glow of three-foot fluorescent lights, but with a series of hidden cove lights that bathed the room in a most pleasing soft glow. Hanging from the ceiling on an adjustable metal arm, was a round operating-room lamp the size of a small pizza. On one wall was the requisite stainless steel sink set in a deep azure counter, and in the corner sat a small secretary-type chair, also in blue, with a minuscule backrest held in position by a chrome arm. A small cushioned table waited for Tory in the middle of the room. It had been placed at a forty-five degree angle to the walls so that it sat on a diagonal from one corner of the room to the other. Quite obviously it was too short to allow any adult to stretch out. The footrest was folded down and could be operated by a foot pedal on the floor.

Carol opened one of the drawers beneath the little sink and pulled out a skimpy pink cotton examination gown that tied in the back. "The mole's on your neck? Take everything off above the waist and put this on." Carol placed a clipboard on the blue counter with several sheets of paper.

Tory seemed surprised. "Will Dr. Cutter want me in a gown?"

"I suppose, especially if he decides to remove it today. That way you won't have to change. Would you mind filling those out while you're waiting?" Carol smiled and pulled the door closed behind her.

Behind the door hung several hangers, not noisy wire ones that clanged against each other every time the door moved; these were dark blue wooden ones that must have been special-ordered to match the rest of the decor. Tory slipped the shapeless leather bag she always carried from her shoulder and hung it on one of the hooks. As she removed her jacket and placed it on a hanger it struck her as odd that the color of her jacket nearly matched the rest of the blue in the room. It set her to wondering whether a slick operation like Dr. Cutter's had examination rooms in a variety of hues so his ritzy patients wouldn't clash with the decor.

In several minutes Tory had removed her red silk blouse and bra and slipped into the examination gown. She modestly clutched the thin fabric to her chest as she walked about the small room. She had seated herself on the crinkly exam table paper and had begun to fill in the blanks on the paperwork when she was startled by the door being opened.

It was Carol. "Everything okay?" Tory nodded and before she knew it Carol had disappeared, this time leaving the door slightly ajar, which Tory took as a good sign that Dr. Cutter wouldn't be long.

Tory had worked her way to the bottom of the first page of questions when she heard men's voices filtering through the door. The words were too garbled to understand, but the conversation went on for several minutes. A new voice joined the others, a woman's, possibly Carol's, sounding as if she might be standing directly in front of Tory's examination room door. She was saying, "The restroom is right down the hall, sir."

For the next couple of minutes it was quiet and no voices of any kind could be heard. Tory was nearly done with her paperwork when she looked about the windowless room. Each of the three blue cabinets was closed. The sink was empty as was the counter except for a single book that was also blue. She noticed a faint odor permeating the room that smelled like disinfectant from some previous surgery. Tory breathed it in and tried to imagine how her procedure was going to feel. The cold swab dripping with antiseptic. The sharp sting of the needle on her neck delivering its payload of anesthetic before the real work began . . .

The door to her examination room pushed open. Tory looked up and smiled. She was about to greet Dr. Cutter when a man walked into the room wearing nothing but one of the little pink examination gowns and brown over-the-calf socks. He looked to be about fifty, with greasy gray hair swept straight back in the shape of a gladiator's helmet and a deformed nose that made her want to look away. The way Stanley Stilwell sauntered into the room with his head down made Tory realize he had made an embarrassing mistake. Suddenly he jerked his head up and stood there staring at her, his lower jaw working feebly but no sounds coming out. Finally he demanded, "Who the hell are you?"

Although not showing any skin, Tory's right hand shot up to her chest and pressed the cotton gown tightly to herself. "Uhhh, sir, I think you're in the wrong—"

"Where'd you come from?" Stilwell barked, this time raising his voice and taking an aggressive step toward the examination table.

"Excuse me!" Tory exclaimed loudly. She hopped off the table and took two steps backward, maneuvering herself on the other side of the exam table to put herself as far from the angry man as the small room would allow. "You are in the wrong room, sir. Please get out!"

With one quick kick of his foot, Stanley Stilwell sent the door banging closed. Now the two patients, wearing identical pink cotton examination gowns tied in the back, stood face-to-face. "There ain't s'posed to be anyone here today. This is my day." Before Tory could react, Stilwell took two mores steps toward the small examination table.

Thinking the man was going to lunge at her, she flung the clipboard at him, catching him in the shoulder. Stilwell quickly bent down and picked up the forms and began reading them. "Let's see. Tory Welch, huh?" He was sliding his fat index finger down the page so he wouldn't miss anything. When he reached the bottom he cast the clipboard aside. "Now I ain't goin' round and round wit you. I'm only gonna ask sweet one more time.

What the hell you doin' here?" Stilwell notched the volume up.

Tory was trapped with this hideous man in the small examination room. Her first instinct was to scream, but she was afraid that the man might go berserk and attack her. Then she remembered her pocket-sized .25 caliber Beretta. It had been purchased by Merlin and he insisted she carry it at all times. Unfortunately it was across the room, tucked safely away in the bottom of her leather bag on the back of the door. The man was close enough to block any attempt to grab her bag and rummage through it.

Somehow she had to get to the door.

"You're in the wrong room. I'm a patient, just like you are. Go back into the hallway. Leave me alone."

There was a fire burning in his eyes. He was leaning over the examination table, both hands on it for support. The pink gown he was wearing had shifted forward exposing a pair of filthy boxers that were several sizes too big. Every few seconds he swiped his hand across his mouth and hunched his shoulders forward nervously, which rendered the flimsy gown more and more worthless until it became a bib in front of him.

Suddenly it hit Tory. The man was a mental patient. What other explanation made sense? "Why don't you tell me your name?" Tory asked softly, as if addressing a lost child.

"Don't play with me. The two of us ain't that different." He hissed his words and took the first step around the table.

Paranoid schizophrenic. "Okay, how about if I leave and I promise never to bother you again?" Again Tory spoke slowly, measuring her words. Each time he took a step, she responded in kind with one in the opposite direction, keeping the distance from him constant.

"Cutter said no one would be here. It was bullshit. Bullshit!" Another step.

"It's just a mistake. I shouldn't be here. Ask him yourself."

Suddenly he jumped at her, throwing himself onto the small table as he grabbed for her. Tory jumped back, and his hands came up empty. Instantly Tory turned and darted toward the door.

Stilwell was no fool. He knew where she was going and pulled himself off the exam table and jumped in the direction of the door. "Stop!" he demanded.

Tory had her hand on the knob and was turning it when he reached her. With a clumsy move he threw his entire weight crashing against the door. Then he grabbed a handful of the flimsy pink cloth that was Tory's only protection from this madman and yanked her close enough to give her a whiff of his body odor.

"Get outta my way!" Tory screamed. Her hand reached up and clawed at his face.

Ignoring Tory's attack, Stilwell held one shoulder against the door like an offensive lineman protecting against the blitz. He was powerful and smart enough to know someone would be coming soon. "You know sumpin'? That was pretty stupid of you to think I wouldn't notice you eavesdropping on me. I got too much riding on this. You hear me? Way too much." He released his grip on the pink gown and viciously grabbed Tory by the neck. His fingers wrapped around her like a boa constrictor. It felt as if he could lift her off the ground with one hand.

"Help," she managed to say but the words barely crossed her lips before they disappeared into the noisy scuffle. Locked in the small room with a paranoid schizophrenic, her options were limited. He was going to kill her. As her mind raced, she forced herself to think what he wanted her to say. All of a sudden it dawned on her. In a coarse whisper she uttered, "My ID. Let me show you . . . my ID. I'm just a secretary downtown."

Before Stanley Stilwell had the chance to think about what Tory had said they heard the crisp metallic sound of the doorknob being turned from the outside.

Merlin had heard the ruckus all the way from the waiting room. Springing from where he was sitting, he raced to the examination room just as Marshall Cutter shot out of another room. Cutter looked elegant in his blue scrubs and white clogs, more like an actor who played a doctor on a soap opera than a bona fide surgeon about to operate. Two others quickly followed Cutter, Carol in her pink scrubs and Brian Trilby, Cutter's anesthesiologist, also in scrubs and clogs. The four of them clustered tightly around the door.

While Merlin vigorously worked the doorknob back and forth he said to Marshall Cutter, "Who's in there with her?"

Cutter was red in the face. "Another patient. In for a face-lift."

"Mentally unstable?"

"I don't know," Cutter said defensively.

"Call the police."

Cutter's tongue flicked out of his mouth and licked his lower lip. He stared at the door.

Merlin dropped to all fours and turned his head sideways so he could get one eye as close to the floor as possible, trying to see under the door.

Each breath was a tiny miracle. Tory was no longer waging war on Stilwell's face. Her hands were on his, trying to pry his fingers loose from her neck.

There was a loud banging on the examination room

door that made Stilwell jump. Then a voice shouted, "Open this door. Do it *now!*"

It was Merlin. The sound of his voice lifted Tory's spirits and she tried to scream, "Call the police," but she sounded like someone in need of a Heimlich.

"Mr. Stilwell," a second voice called, this one trying to sound calm and reassuring. Cutter was doing his best to sound the way a psychiatrist would if he were defusing an argument between a couple having marital problems. "This is just a misunderstanding. Why don't you open the door?"

"Yeah, well, I tole you, no one else here or I bust the place up!" Stilwell screamed.

Tory's windpipe was in danger of being crushed. The pain was horrible as her breathing became raspy like a straw trying to suck the last bit of milkshake from a glass. "Let me show you my ID. I'm a nobody," Tory tried to say, but Stilwell didn't hear her.

"Yeah," Stilwell said, turning his attention back to Tory. "I knew someone was following me. I seen you in my mirror. I heard you at the motel. I ain't stupid. You were listening. Why else was the friggin' door open?"

"He's wedged up against the door," Merlin said quietly, getting up from his hands and knees after scanning what he could from the narrow view under the door.

"He's just upset, that's all," Cutter said to Merlin, then immediately turned to the door and raised his voice. "Mr. Stilwell. She's a patient just like you. Why don't you open—"

"Turn the knob and hold it," Merlin quietly instructed Carol. Then, pushing Cutter out of the way, Merlin took several steps back and prepared to ram the door with his shoulder.

Trilby, a silent bystander in the situation, also moved

away until he was flush up against the wall. He was sweating profusely and hyperventilating, looking about as if planning the easiest route of escape.

Cutter was still trying to appeal to Stilwell, optimistically assuming the lunatic had a rational side. "It was a scheduling error, Mr. Stilwell. That's all," he implored. "Please open the door."

"You're a fucking liar, Cutter." Stilwell's anger filled the hallway.

Tory was desperate. Her eyes were no longer able to focus as Stilwell maintained his grasp on her throat. The room was beginning to get darker. *The Beretta.* Why she thought of it at that moment didn't make sense, but she realized it was less than two feet away from where she was being pinned against the door. Blindly, she reached for the leather bag. Stilwell didn't seem to notice what she was doing. He was busy screaming through the door at Cutter, threatening to kill him. Hooking her fingers on the leather strap, Tory tugged until the bag slipped off the hook and dropped to her side.

"How did you find out I was here?" Stilwell was saying right in Tory's face.

All Tory could manage were gurgling sounds coming from someplace deep within her throat.

"Hey!" he snapped when he realized what Tory was doing. His other hand swiped hard and knocked the leather bag to the floor.

Almost immediately the door burst open, knocking both Stilwell and Tory into the middle of the room. But Stilwell maintained the powerful grip on Tory's neck. He craned his head around and watched as Merlin, Cutter, and Carol raced into the room. *"Goddamnit!"* His eyes were crazy with rage as he decided what to do next.

No one noticed that Brian Trilby was nowhere to be seen. When the door was forced open, he used the diversion to discreetly disappear into the bathroom and was vomiting his breakfast into the commode.

"Stay back. I'll snap her neck," Stilwell warned. He maneuvered Tory over to one of the walls, leaning into her, pinning her roughly against it so that her eyes bugged out. Her face was bright red and swollen from the pressure. Stilwell's gown was wide open in the back, showing off two gaping holes in his underwear.

Merlin held his hands up to show Stilwell he wasn't a threat. He positioned himself so that he could see that Stilwell wasn't holding a weapon to Tory's neck. When Stilwell turned to glare at Cutter, Merlin stepped over to the counter to grab a copy of the *Physician's Desk Reference*, a compendium of every prescription drug on the market that doctors kept handy for quick reference of dosages and side effects. The dark blue tome was a monster, three-and-a-half-inches thick and weighing in at over seven pounds. Two quick strides and he could be at Stilwell. One quick swipe with the book and Stilwell's greasy menace and vice-like grip on Tory's neck would be history.

Merlin raised the book above his head.

Seeing what was about to happen, Marshall Cutter inserted himself between Merlin and Stilwell. "No!" he implored, both to Stilwell and Merlin. Then he spoke to his patient. "Stanley," he said, modulating his voice as he approached the out-of-control man. "There's no reason to hurt her, Stanley." He placed a hand on Stilwell's shoulder in an avuncular way and lowered his voice even more. "Why don't you let her go. I swear to you, Stanley, I knew nothing about this. Believe me. She's just another patient who was scheduled on the wrong day."

Then to Tory he said, "You okay?" Tory's eyes widened as she tried to gasp for air. "I'm sorry. Some of my patients don't want people to know they've had plastic surgery—"

"Shut up, Cutter," Stilwell snapped, but his breathing was starting to ease up and he seemed to be calming down. He turned his head to look Tory up and down. Even in his highly agitated state he recognized Tory wasn't in any obvious need of plastic surgery. "Why're you here?" He loosened his grip for the first time.

Merlin remained in position, *PDR* over his head, no more than six feet from smashing Stilwell's skull. As long as Cutter was making progress he would wait.

"A mole. I have a mole, on my neck." Tory gasped out her words as she turned her head so that Stilwell might have a look.

He leaned in close, squinting his eyes. "Yeah, right. That little thing?"

Tory nodded hard, feeling the madman relax his grip even more. She sensed the incident was about to come to an end and remained still.

"That's it, Stanley," Cutter said. "Let her go and we'll go down to my office and talk before it gets too late." Now Cutter was making little circular motions with his hand on Stilwell's shoulder, massaging away whatever pain the man was feeling. "Let's get started so we can finish up quickly. You'll have a chance to lie down before you go home."

"I don't trust any of ya," Stilwell barked. He jerked his hand from Tory's neck and released her.

Immediately, Tory's hand went to her neck and began rubbing away the pain. Bright red welts had already appeared in the shape of Stilwell's fingers. "I'm okay," she said hurriedly, letting Cutter know his priority was getting Stilwell out of the room, not attending to her.

Merlin threw the *PDR* onto the exam table and embraced Tory while Cutter led Stilwell from the room. Just before disappearing into the darkened hallway, the plastic surgeon turned back to Tory and mouthed the words, "I'll be right back." Then he was gone.

"I sat in this room one week ago and you swore up and down everything was gonna go real smooth." Stilwell's wet thighs were sticking to the sofa, his filthy underwear pressed up against the expensive fabric.

Cutter was sitting directly across from him. Looking very solemn, he placed both hands on his chest as he spoke. "Stanley—may I call you Stanley?—I take full responsibility. I . . . swear . . . to . . . you. You listening? I swear that this is all a misunderstanding."

Stillwell glared at him.

"Look, Stanley. You're my patient, and I'm in this with you. You 'n' me. A hundred percent."

"You think so, Cutter? My face is my life right now."

"I know that. But don't you realize that if I'm the one giving you the new face I have to care about your privacy. My God, Stanley, you locked yourself in that room and tried to strangle one of my patients. And what did I do? Did I call the police? No. I kept it under control so no one's asking a lot of nosy questions neither of us wants to answer."

"So what if she starts nosing around?"

Cutter let out a big sigh. "She has no reason to go nosing around. She has a mole on her neck. That's all. You let me take care of things. I know exactly how to handle this."

"Yeah, how?"

"You go in and apologize to her."

"What! ?" Stilwell jumped off the sofa in shock. "No fuckin' way!"

"Just listen to me, Stanley. Go in and say something about being embarrassed about having plastic surgery. Then I'll go in, schmooze her a little, and kick her the hell outta here. Done."

Stilwell was slowly shaking his head back and forth. "I don't know."

"Trust me. Everything's under control."

The pink gown Stanley Stilwell was wearing was horribly askew. Now that he was calming down he noticed how he looked and worked the gown's material back into place. "Just so you know—if this gets out of hand, I'll kill you." He stood for a full minute, scratching himself behind his neck, looking out the open doorway into the dark hallway. Finally, just as Cutter was about to say something, Stilwell shuffled out the doorway with the enthusiasm of a man about to meet his executioner.

The walk to the exam room where he had held Tory hostage was short. Under his breath, Stilwell mumbled to himself, "Sorry. It was a misunderstanding. Sorry." When he got to the door he neglected to knock, instead grabbing the knob and opening it halfway.

Merlin was half-seated on the exam table. Tory was hurriedly buttoning her red silk blouse as the door opened. An involuntary noise, as if a lap dog were yelping, came through her lips as she got an eyeful of Stanley Stilwell. Merlin jumped off the table and started toward Stilwell, his hands raised in fists.

"No, it's not like that," Stillwell went, holding one hand up in an unenthusiastic demonstration of contrition. His eyes were drawn to the welts on Tory's neck that had already begun to turn purple. "Forget it. Sorry 'bout before. That's all. I . . . I didn't 'spect anyone else here and I sorta freaked."

Merlin backed off. Tory didn't say a word. She just

stood there, holding her blouse together, waiting for Stilwell to leave her alone.

"So we can forget about it, huh?"

"Get out!" was all she said before Stilwell slammed the door as he left the room.

Thirty seconds later there was a soft knock at the door.

"Who is it?" Tory said quietly.

"Marshall Cutter. May I come in?"

"Go ahead," Tory said curtly.

The door opened and Cutter entered the room. "Merlin, I'm so sorry," was the first thing he said. Instantly this infuriated Tory, Cutter choosing to acknowledge Merlin before he recognized her presence in the room.

The room became uncomfortably quiet. Merlin looked at Tory, and Cutter realized his mistake. "I'm sorry." His tone was deferential. With one hand out he offered her a seat on the exam table. "Please." By now the paper was no longer in place, but dangling off one side of the table and swaying gently in the soft breeze from the overhead ventilation system.

"I'm okay right here."

Cutter examined Tory's bruises from afar. "How's your neck?"

"She's fine," Merlin snapped. "Where's the police?"

"We don't need the police."

"Are you crazy? That maniac had his hand around her neck. Look at the bruises! For chrissake, what if we hadn't gotten into the room so quickly? You had no idea the situation was under control before we got inside."

"It was a judgment call, Merlin." After an appropriate pause to allow everyone in the room to take a breather, Cutter continued, "Miss Welch, you have my most humble apologies for what happened."

"What did happen?"

"The gentleman who was in here is a new patient. Very eccentric. He has privacy issues. Obviously he's quite sensitive about being here and—for reasons that certainly seem obvious at this point—I preferred not to have him in the surgi-center with other patients."

"Why did he freak out about my being here?"

Cutter held out both hands, palm side up. "Who knows? I had assured him no other patients would be in the office today. It had nothing to do with you. He would have reacted the same way to *anyone* he stumbled upon. I'm sorry it had to happen to you. How's your neck?"

"I'm fine."

"If you never want to see me again, I'll certainly understand. But I'd like to examine your mole if you would allow me."

"Let me ask you a question," Merlin said.

"Of course," Cutter encouraged.

"Who is he?"

"Look, it's over."

Knowing that Cutter was not going to divulge another patient's identity, Merlin held him in his gaze, his face tight with anger. No way was he going to let him off that easy.

Cutter sensed as much. He lowered his eyes to the floor as if he were about to make a bold admission. "As important as the results are that I achieve with my patients, the atmosphere here takes a close second. One part of me didn't want the police here. It would destroy my reputation. It was selfish of me." Now he looked up at Tory. "If my patients—or my potential patients— thought these kind of things happened here . . . my God . . ." Cutter's voice trailed off to an inaudible whisper. He looked as though he were overcome with emotion.

"Let's just forget about it," Tory said, ready to dismiss

the whole incident. She stepped toward the door and slipped her blue jacket from the hanger.

"Shall I have a quick look at that mole of yours?"

Tory made a face. "Why don't I call and set something up."

"No, Jack, let it go," Tory said. They were alone in the examination room, modulating their voices so no one in the hallway could hear them.

"The guy tried to kill you. I want to call the police. I want to know who the hell he is."

"His hand was around *my* neck, not yours. He's some sort of psychopath. What are the police going to do? You want me to tell you? I know about these kinds of people. They'll take him down to the station and sit him down. He's probably on Haldol or something. Even if I wanted to press charges, he's not spending the night in jail. He's going home. But he'll know who gave him trouble. And someday soon he'll come looking for me, wanting to settle whatever score he makes up in his mind. I know what I'm talking about. Until he goes out and kills someone the system favors him. No police, Merlin."

"He's not crazy. He's got a hidden agenda. He paid to be alone in this office. He's hiding something. I want to know what we stumbled into."

"I stumbled into it, Merlin. I've got the bruises, and I don't want him in my life ever again. Forget it."

Merlin was furious. "I can't believe you." He walked toward the door.

"Don't you go through that door until we resolve this. Are you blind to what I just went through? You go through that door and we change forever."

Merlin turned back to confront Tory. "This is going to come back and haunt us."

"Not if we drop it, goddamnit." Tory brushed past

Merlin on her way out of the room. She took one look back at him. Tears streaked her face. "I'm not kidding," was all she said as she disappeared into the darkness of the hallway.

Chapter 4

Nine miles from downtown Pittsburgh, Stanley Stilwell had taken up residence at a sleepy little mom and pop motel consisting of twelve rooms, six out and six back, with parking in between. The place had no official name, just a sign by the road that screamed 22.95 FREE TV in huge yellow letters on a jet black background. It didn't take a Michelin guide to figure out what you got for twenty-two ninety-five. An eight-by-ten room with a double bed smack dab in the middle. One straight-backed chair in case you didn't want to throw your coat on the floor. A three-drawer bureau made of composition board covered with peeling wood-grain contact paper. And for entertainment, a television set, bolted to a plastic stand and chained to the wall lest some sticky-fingered guest get the idea that free TV meant take it with you.

No Gideon Bible. No little soaps wrapped in paper. And no cable.

Two things, though, were evidently important to the elderly proprietors. Theirs was a price that none of the chains could beat. At least once a week young studs with their nervous dates would ask whether the twenty-two ninety-five got them an hour. This would be followed by a donkey bray of self-conscious laughter as if they were the first ever to ask the question.

The second thing was, of course, the choice of colors on the big sign by the road. It was vital for the owners to show off the Steeler colors. It was not a business decision. Customers were not more likely to frequent a motel just because it had a black and gold sign. It was more a loyalty that went to the very fiber of the football fans in Pittsburgh, whose cold weather months were consumed with one topic, and one topic only.

No one really took much notice of the man in room six, the one way at the back out by the trash cans. His was the best room, what they called the presidential suite, but really it was just a regular room with an old refrigerator that ran Stilwell an extra three bucks a day. The motel had no fancy in-room movies that could be ordered up with a push of a button on the remote control. Each room did have a VCR, some off-brand model with a name that was supposed to make you think of Panasonic, but actually had a couple of different letters so that it was easy to get mixed up.

The night before his surgery, Stilwell had wandered out to the front desk and was given a sheet of paper with about fifty titles of videos that could be rented. The titles were handwritten and appeared in different colors of ink as though the proprietors were adding to their video collection in piecemeal fashion.

Stilwell's choice had come from a small group of six titles on the other side of the page: *Naughty and They Know It.* Before he had the money out of his wallet, one of the owners, an offensive woman with long gray hair and an upper denture plate she swirled around her mouth as if it was two sizes too big, gave him a look that said she knew exactly what he was all about.

Now that his face was swathed in bandages and he was

supposed to be taking it easy for a day or two, he had given up on the thought of renting *Naughty and They Know It 2* and was killing time in front of the TV.

Eating and drinking were practically impossible. His face throbbed, swollen as though he'd been in a fight. He'd finally settled on an old stand-by: a tall glass of iced vodka with a raw onion. Not a sweet Vidalia, but a pedestrian white onion, big and juicy with a pungent aroma that could irritate your eyes until you cried.

His mouth was unable to open more than an inch, so he had to resort to using a hunting knife, slicing off bite-sized slivers of the onion the way his grandmother used to cut up apples when he was a baby. When he went for the vodka, it was with a straw, sipping carefully so as not to disturb the stitches around his mouth.

By late afternoon he was wasted, burping up the bitter taste of onion and hitting the can every ten minutes, urinating loudly, which Stilwell thought was good because the last thing Cutter had said to him was to make sure he was drinking enough. What Cutter had in mind was water and fruit juice, not vodka, but as far as Stanley Stilwell was concerned drinking was drinking.

Finally the alcohol caught up with him. A tremendous fatigue set in and he crawled underneath the covers, leaving the late afternoon news on the television. Mostly the local media busied itself with house fires, traffic accidents, and the weather. Occasionally there was some real news, and when Allegheny County District Attorney Frank LaBove took the podium at a news conference to discuss the latest development in whatever case had captured the imagination of Pittsburgh, Stanley Stilwell sat straight up in bed.

Standing behind Frank Labove, just to his right and looking very prosecutorial, was an attractive woman with dark hair and eyes that appeared as if they could look right through a man. He moved to the foot of the bed to get a better look at her neck. Bruises, one on the right, three or four on the left. She was wearing a suit, but it was impossible to tell what color it was on the crappy TV. Maybe it was brown. Maybe it was green. Stanley Stilwell couldn't give a shit.

All he cared about was *who* was in the brown or green suit.

Stanley Stilwell held out his right hand, his third, forth, and fifth fingers curled up. His thumb pointed up in the air and his index finger stretched straight out like the barrel of a small handgun. "Pow!" Stanley Stilwell said as his hand jerked with an imaginary recoil.

It was the end of a long day. Marshall Cutter was between patients. A perfect little Barbie doll had just given him a wet one on the lips to say thank you for making her even more beautiful. Cutter hardly noticed. While Carol was busy ushering in a homely Cabbage Patch with a flabby neck that she discreetly covered up with a silk scarf, Cutter retired to his elegant office, ensconced himself in his ergonomically perfect chair and picked up the phone.

"It's me," Cutter said after waiting too many rings for someone to pick up. "Listen, about that referral. . . . Yes, *that* one. He damned near ruined me yesterday. . . . Listen to me!! He *attacked* another patient, barricaded himself in an exam room and tried to strangle her. . . . I know, I know. Of course I promised him. One of the girls up front made a scheduling mistake. . . . He was going to the bathroom when he walked into the wrong room. We almost had to call the cops. . . . No, no. No one's suing. I handled it, even got him to apologize, but let me warn you: this guy's a loose cannon. He's dangerous. He could go off at the slightest provocation. . . .

You're not listening. I run a class operation here. I've created something that can't be fixed once it's broken. I don't need some lowlife with one of my faces to start picking off children with a high-powered rifle or something. . . . No, all I'm saying is have a little chat with him and convince him to mind his P's and Q's. . . . I'd appreciate it. . . . Of course the surgery went fine." Feeling satisfied with how he had handled the Stanley Stilwell situation, Cutter pushed himself up from his chair and headed toward the consultation room next to his office where the hopeful Cabbage Patch waited for him with an optimistic smile.

By ten-thirty Stanley Stilwell had nipped a car.

Once the Tory Welch problem had presented itself, Stilwell instantly formulated a plan. It started with a slow peel of the endless Coban dressing that covered every speck of skin on his face and neck. Cutter had promised that the use of the tightly bound Coban would keep swelling to a minimum and would delay the purplish discoloration for at least two or three days.

Stilwell remained on the bed, slowly unwinding the Coban, purposefully holding off on that first look in the mirror, keeping one eye on the television just in case they did another piece on the D.A.'s office. Finally, the bandages removed, he did a gentle Braille evaluation of Cutter's handiwork. Whatever swelling there might be, his fingertips enjoyed the tightness of the skin on his neck, the firm prominence that had once been a saggy double chin, and the proud cheekbones that seemed to swell out of his face. It made him wonder if he might now look like a rugged movie star. Stallone, maybe. Then he touched his nose, ignoring the pain while his fingertips marveled at how small his nostrils were.

Heading into the grimy bathroom, he flicked on the

lights and stared at his new face in the cracked mirror. He appeared more youthful, maybe fifteen years younger. His nose was . . . ordinary. Not beautiful. Ordinary. And that's what Stilwell wanted. No longer was it a horrid magnet drawing attention away from the rest of his face. He saw his features for the first time in years. His chin was powerful, jutting out in a way that made him think of Kirk Douglas, hold the dimple. And his cheeks looked so . . . so . . . Stilwell had trouble finding the word.

Strong!

That was it. Stilwell looked *strong*. Happily he extended his neck and inspected where once there had been a gobbler. What a pain in the ass it was to shave. Sometimes he let it go for days rather than pull and stretch the skin so his razor wouldn't carve him up like a Thanksgiving bird.

He put his fingertips to his Adam's apple and tugged gently on the skin, marveling on its firmness.

He examined two suture lines, stitched in blue. Each began where his sideburn ended, running down and around the lobe until they disappeared somewhere behind his ears. With a little hand fluffing of his hair in front of his ears, Stilwell had no trouble hiding the stitches.

Forgetting Tory Welch for a moment, Stanley Stilwell smiled. His rebirth had begun.

Stepping back into the bedroom, he found the brown paper bag from the drugstore and pulled out a box of Nice 'n Easy, color #121; Natural Deep Brown. Reading the directions for the third time, Stilwell began the process that would finish his metamorphosis. But there were complications. The flimsy clear plastic gloves were designed for the petite hand of a woman and tore apart before he'd mixed the two bottle of chemicals together.

Squirting the smelly goo onto his hair, Stilwell gagged until he nearly vomited. When it came time to massage the color into every strand of hair, Stilwell was without the safety of gloves. Thirty minutes later, when it was time to step in the shower and rinse off the dye, the palms of his hands looked as though he'd spent the afternoon replacing an engine block.

By nine-thirty he was done. His luxurious brown hair, still wet from the treatment, was carefully tucked beneath a Yankees baseball cap. He donned running shoes, blue jeans, and a windbreaker. He stuffed a pair of thin leather gloves in one of the pockets.

Then he called for a cab, which seemed to take forever, and ended up waiting in the tiny front office under the gaze of the old woman who clicked her upper plate as she stared at his new face.

Stilwell pulled his baseball cap lower and counted tiles on the floor.

"Why'nt you taking your own car, Mister?" the woman wanted to know, just as a red taxi rumbled up to the building.

For a moment Stilwell debated saying something about not driving under his surgeon's orders, but instead mumbled something about not wanting to drive drunk. Then he was out the door.

As Stilwell slid into the cab and gave the rusty door a good hard pull, the old woman was at the window, looking out at him with both arms crossed under her sagging bosom.

"Where're you going?" the cabby wanted to know. He had an accent and held a pen poised to write Stilwell's destination on a small clipboard.

"Uh, the country club."

The cabby paused. "Which one?"

"You know," Stilwell said, trying to act natural, "the big one."

"Rolling Hills, you mean? Wife works up there, big event tonight."

"Big," Stilwell said and sat back to enjoy the ride.

Merlin watched the candles from where he was sitting in the living room. Two of them, practically down to a nubbin. He passed the time wondering which was going to burn out first.

The table in the kitchen was set, and the dinner had been warming in the oven for so long that Merlin had forgotten about it. The house seemed more quiet than he knew it could be.

Finally the back door opened. Tory came into the kitchen quietly. She paused briefly by the candles. It was almost ten o'clock.

"Please talk with me." Merlin was standing in the doorway between the kitchen and the living room.

"Candles," she said softly. Then she sniffed twice.

Merlin walked over to the oven and opened the door. "You hungry?" He slipped his hand into an oven mitt and removed the dried out casserole and placed it on the stove.

"I ate something already, just a sandwich."

"Then let's talk."

Tory blinked twice, heavy, wet-eye blinks. "After what that monster did to me, I needed your arms around me last night." Wearily she walked toward the living room. Merlin stepped aside, out of her way.

"The bedroom door was closed when I got home."

Tory stared at him for the longest time not quite knowing what to say. "I didn't get much sleep. I'm so tired."

"Me too."

"Where'd you sleep last night?"

"Sofa."

"I didn't hear you get up."

"I left when I heard the clock radio. I figured you didn't want to see me. But I can't stand this."

Tory started up the stairs. "Me neither. Let's talk tomorrow."

"I still don't understand why we didn't go to the police."

Tory wiped a tear. "I can't fight with you about it now. I . . . just can't."

"I've thought nonstop about this. I'm still trying so hard to understand you," Merlin called up from the bottom of the stairs.

"It shouldn't be that hard. I've never been so scared in my life, Merlin. If you went to the police it would only make everything worse." Tory proceeded up the stairs slowly, tears streaming down her cheeks.

"If we don't do something, he'll always be out there."

Tory looked down at Merlin. "You still don't get it. But I'm too tired to go through it again. Maybe we'll talk about it tomorrow."

Merlin stood looking up the stairs until he heard the sound of their bedroom door closing.

Nine minutes later, the cab pulled into the employee parking lot at Rolling Hills. Stilwell paid the cabby and made the long trek toward the showy brick clubhouse. When he got close enough to see all the rich people getting out of their expensive cars, he stopped to study the layout.

The clubhouse was surrounded by towering oak trees and huge leafy bushes that provided more than ample shadows in which Stilwell could move around.

He approached the lot where attendants parked the cars. Hiding behind a bush, he watched for several minutes as the valets locked each car and placed a little white ticket under the wiper blade.

When no one was in sight, Stilwell pinched one of the little white tickets, then snuck back toward the drop-off area and waited for a cluster of cars to arrive simultaneously. He lingered behind a huge rhododendron, biding his time for the perfect opportunity. It soon happened.

Four cars pulled up to the front steps of the club with only three parking attendants to accommodate them. As the third attendant drove off leaving the fourth car behind, Stilwell made his move. He jogged toward a Chrysler Concorde whose owner and his wife were looking around impatiently for someone to give them a little parking ticket so they could go inside and start drinking.

"Sorry you had to wait, sir," Stilwell said breathlessly. "Really busy tonight." He handed the member the white ticket.

"Yeah, yeah," the member mumbled, not giving a crap how busy things were for the hired help. He never even bothered looking at Stilwell as he slipped the ticket into the inside pocket of his peach-colored sports coat and took his wife's arm to lead her inside. The man's back was turned completely when Stilwell slipped on the pair of thin leather driving gloves.

"Have a nice time, sir," Stilwell called in a friendly sort of way as he hopped into the car and put it in drive.

Ten minutes later he was heading back to the 22.95 gold-on-black sign, taking care to park the car in a secluded area on the other side of the trash cans.

Chapter 5

The entire time Tory and Merlin were inside the restaurant, Stanley Stilwell waited across the street, unnoticed by either of them. This was supposed to be a date, a chance for Tory and Merlin to hold hands and get that special feeling they had for one another going again. Merlin was impatient and didn't want to wait for time to heal the wounds. The first thing he had done that morning was to send a single long-stemmed rosebud to Tory with a note asking her out to dinner.

And now Stilwell was watching the steps leading down to the front door of the restaurant in the rearview mirror. All of the windows were down to let out the smoke from his cigarettes. He had been there for over an hour and a half, leaving the only Chrysler when a fat meter maid had made her rounds.

He sipped some Coke. Tonight he needed to stay sober.

On the seat next to him, covered by a greasy rag, was his Heckler and Koch semi-automatic. A couple of times he grabbed hold of the rearview mirror and twisted it around so that he could inspect his nose and his rejuvenated hair hanging down around his ears. He was pleased with the color, a dark shade of brown. Although it looked phony as hell on a man Stilwell's age, he thought it revitalized him and cursed at himself when he realized he should have asked Cutter for some Viagra before he paid up.

How the hell did the D.A. know he was at Cutter's office? That was the biggie. It annoyed him that he couldn't figure it out. *Shit!* She was pretty. No way did she need a plastic surgeon. And no way should he have bought that crap about a mole. For crissake, you couldn't even see it unless she lifted up her hair.

Nothing made sense to Stilwell. Even though he had a new face—Cutter said his own mother wouldn't recognize him—the whole thing bugged the hell out of him. His world was crumbling around him, and Stanley Stilwell wasn't the sort to sit around and let it happen.

Merlin had taken Tory to Pasta Piata, a restaurant located ten steps underground in trendy Shadyside. It was a celebration of a new beginning. The bruises on Tory's neck had not yet begun to fade, but they were changing. The angry purple hue of freshly injured skin was beginning to wander across the color spectrum toward a less harsh shade of yellowish-green.

The meal started with a marvelous house salad sprinkled liberally with gorgonzola. Tory speared a grape-sized chunk of the white cheese but nibbled on it as if she weren't hungry. Just watching the way she was eating, Merlin knew she was thinking about the incident again.

"So, who're you having dinner with?" He followed his comment with a warm smile, then reached across the white tablecloth to hold Tory's hand.

And, in that moment, Tory realized *that* was what she loved most about Merlin. The way he knew her inside and out. The way he reached out and held her without needing to be asked. And the way he knew when she needed a hug, even when she needed to be wrestled to the floor and showered with kisses.

Having spent another night alone in their bed made her want him even more.

Suddenly, the strong smell of the Italian dressing filled her head and she realized she was ravenous. She enjoyed her salad. "I can't get that monster out of my mind," she eventually said. Merlin remained quiet, preferring for the moment just to listen. "But you want to know what scares me most? What if I had gotten my hand on the Beretta? I was so overwhelmed, I mean"— she paused for a couple of cleansing breaths and a sip of red wine— "would I have panicked and killed him?"

"You would have done the right thing. You've proven that before."

"I don't know if I can go through the nightmares again." Tory thought about all the sessions with Tanner Valdemar the last time she had used her Beretta. It had taken months to recover.

Merlin stroked her hand. "I don't believe for a moment you would have shot him if he'd backed off. And if he didn't he would have deserved it."

"Cutter said he was just eccentric."

"He wasn't eccentric. Tanner Valdemar is eccentric. That guy was maniacal. Sure, clearing the surgi-center for his own private use, *that's* eccentric. Attacking a woman in the next exam room is crazy, desperate. What kind of a normal person does that? For some reason he didn't want anyone to know he was there, not even a stranger. I'd say he's probably more in need of a shrink than a plastic surgeon."

As the evening progressed they devoured calamari and spinach over linguine, using the last of the bread to sop up the delicious red sauce. An entire bottle of wine disappeared in the process, Merlin pouring each time their glasses were empty. By the end of the meal Tory had relaxed to the point where she seemed to be having a good time.

Afterward, the two held hands as they ascended the staircase to street level. Whenever the weather got warmer, dessert meant a trip up the Allegheny River to one of the region's last remaining frozen custard stands, a small cone for her, a medium for him.

Traffic was light coming out of Shadyside. Tory and Merlin chatted away, telling each other what had happened at work over the past two days. Neither was the least bit wiser about the shiny new Chrysler Concorde trailing behind. Even when the Concorde missed the light heading onto the Highland Park Bridge and ran the red, Merlin and Tory in the Cherokee were oblivious, singing along with the Beatles on CD.

You can't see me, I'm right here, but you can't see me. Stilwell marveled at how easy it was to follow someone who was not expecting it. There was even a moment, as the two cars sped north on Route 28 toward Cheswick, that he pulled right alongside the Jeep for several seconds just to get a good look at Merlin. "We're gonna get to know each other real good," he said aloud.

Once across the Allegheny, it took less than fifteen minutes to get to Glen's Custard. As always the undersized lot was nearly packed, but Merlin smoothly slipped into the last available space.

The Chrysler Concorde parked across the street. Stanley Stilwell watched and waited. He saw Merlin talking and laughing with the man behind the little window. Then while they waited for their cones, Merlin put his arm around Tory and kissed her.

Stilwell's hands were all sweaty in the leather driving

gloves, but he knew not to take them off. A drop of sweat formed behind his ear where the tiny blue stitches disappeared into his hairline. As it scooted down the back of his neck he scratched at himself as if he'd just been bitten by a mosquito.

Long ago he'd run out of Cokes and probably would have enjoyed one of the creamy custard cones, but this wasn't the time. Mindful of the handgun on the seat next to him, he adjusted the greasy rag, making certain no part of the Heckler and Koch was exposed. "C'mon, hurry up. Ain't got all day." He was talking to himself, anxious to get on with it.

But Stanley Stilwell was smart enough to know the importance of waiting for an opportunity.

Merlin and Tory found a spot at one of the wooden picnic tables behind the small custard stand and lingered over their cones, talking quietly and whispering secrets into each other's ears.

The moon was full in the darkening sky. It was time to go home. Hand in hand, the lovers walked back to their car. Merlin backed the Cherokee out of the cramped parking lot, pulling to within fifteen feet of Stanley Stilwell, then headed back toward their home in Aspinwall.

"Show time," was all Stilwell said. He held out his hand as if it were his silenced semi-automatic and aimed it at the Cherokee before he pulled out into traffic. The two cars wound their way through the business district of Cheswick. Instead of heading up the steep hill to Route 28, Merlin continued on Freeport Road toward Harmarville. "Oh shit, where the hell are they going?"

*   *   *

"Hey, Merlin, where we are going?" Tory asked, not the only one surprised by the choice of route.

"The scenic route."

"Since when does Jack Merlin take the scenic route?"

"Well, to be totally truthful, I know a great little spot to park the car—"

"A makeout spot?" Tory enthused.

"Well . . . that's what the teenage Jack Merlin would call it."

Tory laughed out loud. "So what does the grown up Jack Merlin call it?"

"Romantic."

For a very long moment, Tory had nothing to say, and the two lovers drove in silence. It didn't take Tory long to figure out where they were headed. Merlin guided them on a circuitous route to the beginning of Squaw Run Road in Fox Chapel. This was absolutely Merlin's favorite stretch of roadway in all of Pittsburgh, a mile of country road winding through a thickly wooded park known locally as the Trillium Trail for the marvelous flowers that at one time bloomed each spring. There were several pull-off areas near a small creek, perfect places for hikers to park. They were also perfect for what Merlin had in mind.

Just as the Cherokee made the turn onto Squaw Run Road there was a roar. A car sped by him in such a rush it was no more than a blur. In an instant it had disappeared around a bend in the road. Neither Merlin nor Tory could tell what kind of car it was.

"What an asshole," Tory said.

"Oh, these women drivers," Merlin said, knowing full well the illegal maneuver they had just witnessed was most certainly a testosterone-propelled act. But it was an opportunity to tease.

Tory slugged him in the arm; he smiled. Just as he took his hand off the steering wheel to give Tory a tickle, it happened.

Phittt. Phittt.

That's all the noise the silencer allowed the Heckler and Koch to make. What with the music playing and the windows up neither Tory nor Merlin heard either of the two bullets being fired.

The first bullet missed its mark, whizzing past the front of the headlights across Squaw Run Road and lodging harmlessly in the trunk of a tree. But the second bullet hit its target: the front tire on the passenger side of the Cherokee.

Bang!

The front tire blew out with a blast. Devoid of air, the wheel no longer turned freely and forced the heavy car into an abrupt skid to the right.

"Jack!" Tory screamed, hearing what she thought was a gunshot and reacting to the car swerving wildly as Merlin fought to keep control. The tires screeched madly on the black asphalt, drowning out the music coming from the speakers.

In an instant, the Jeep was off the road, scattering gravel as it crossed the narrow shoulder, careening out of control toward an embankment that led down to a little creek.

Wap! Wap! Wap! Three slender saplings went down.

Reflexively, Merlin's foot hit the brake hard. The two passengers lurched forward before being restrained by the shoulder harnesses. In a horribly rapid moment of insanity, everything slowed down.

There was little time for panic or conscious planning for what would happen next. Merlin saw the overhanging branch less than a tenth of a second before the front windshield of the Jeep smacked right into it. "Close your eyes!" Merlin hollered. Then came the terrible crashing noise and the windshield shattered into a jigsaw puzzle of a million pieces. Miraculously, most of the glass stayed in place. Only a few shards separated from the puzzle, crumbling into a variety of sizes that peppered the passengers but left no wounds.

They experienced a brief period of weightlessness as the Jeep went over the shallow embankment. Merlin's stomach went up to his throat.

The front tires of the Jeep banged into the dirt on the side of the embankment. Abruptly the car was slowing down, branches and underbrush slapping against the car as it banged its way down to the creek and jerked to a halt in eight inches of cold water.

Then it was quiet.

The headlights remained on, illuminating half a dozen trees and some brush on the far side of the creek. But the car's engine was dead. "You okay?" Merlin asked.

"Yeah," Tory answered and swallowed hard before saying, "I heard a gunshot." Then she looked around, left and right, craning her neck to its very limits, desperate to see where the gunman was.

"Tory," Merlin insisted, "we just blew a tire. That's all."

But Tory wasn't listening. She had her leather bag on her lap and was frantically rummaging through it. "I'll feel better when I have my Beretta."

"I'm going to check things out. Wait here."

Tap. Tap. Tap.

The sound was coming from Tory's window.

Tory jumped. "Ahhh!" she blurted out and recoiled back into her seat. "There's someone out there."

The two passengers in the car froze at the sight of a hideous man standing next to Tory's door, bent over so that he was looking right into the window, his tight face only inches from hers, tapping the end of a very long silencer against her window.

Stanley Stilwell looked different enough not to be recognized immediately.

"Open the door," he commanded. *Tap. Tap. Tap.* He took a small step backward, lest Tory thrust the door open and bump him with it. "Slowly," he directed. "And shut the lights off."

Merlin obeyed and everything went dark. It would take more than several seconds for their eyes to adjust to the moonlight. "Go along with him," Merlin said under his breath. He spoke without moving any visible part of his mouth so the words came out slurred—*"Go along ith in. Do ut he says. Take you ag ith you,"* he whispered and Tory understood.

Working the handle of the door, Tory grasped her leather bag with her left hand and prepared to exit the vehicle.

"Okay, now get out. Slowly! I'll use this," Stilwell ordered, waving the tip of the silencer about in little circles to make his point. He was standing in water up past his ankles that was cold enough to numb his toes. "That's good," he told Tory as she stepped into the icy water. "Okay, now you, big shot."

Tory could feel her shoes sink half an inch into the brown muck. Somehow she didn't notice the cold. Tory held the leather bag in her left hand at the top of the sack, clutching it in front of her belly in the most timid way she could muster. The top of the bag hung open, waiting for her right hand to slip inside at the first opportunity.

Merlin stepped from the car and sloshed his way around the front.

"That's far enough, big shot."

"Hey, you damn near killed us. What are you after?

Money?" Merlin demanded in an arrogant tone, taking a few more steps toward Stilwell. "If money's what you want, here's my wallet."

Phitt. Stilwell put a round into the water not two feet from Merlin. An explosion of water and muddy silt splattered all over Merlin's clothes. "Hold it!" Stilwell snapped. "I don't want yer money."

Suddenly Tory recognized the voice. The most powerful feeling of doom pierced her stomach and squeezed hard until the frozen custard shot up her esophagus and singed the back of her throat. His face seemed different, even in the moonlight. Mostly it looked thinner. He was wearing a baseball cap that was fringed with fake-looking hair.

But she couldn't remember his name.

"Well, what is it you want?" Merlin asked as he moved away from where the bullet had entered the water. "You want the car? Drugs?"

"Shuddup is what I want," Stilwell demanded.

"Look, whatever it is you want just tell us."

Their eyes had adjusted. Even under the canopy of the woods they could see quite well in the moonlight. Realizing Stilwell was focusing on Merlin, waving the long silencer about as though it were a baton, Tory snaked her right hand into the opening at the top of her leather bag.

"One thing we don't want is trouble," Merlin was saying, trying to get into some sort of rhythm that would give Tory a few seconds to locate her gun. "And no one will ever find out about this. I mean, it was a smart move to have me turn out the lights. That way we have no idea what you look like so we can just go our separate ways."

Something caught Stilwell's eye. Or maybe he heard something in Tory's bag make a little noise, but he turned his head toward her. Tory's hand was buried up to her forearm. *Phitt.* He shot another bullet into the water, this one nearly catching Tory in the ankle.

A second eruption of icy water and mud now splattered the front of Tory's shirt. Involuntarily, she tore her hand from the bag and brought it to her chest as every muscle in her body froze like rigor mortis of the living.

A burst of light came from the road and all three turned to see a car cruising past them. For nearly a second, the headlights shined directly in their eyes, but the car didn't slow down. It was over so quickly, any hope the driver might have noticed what was going on fifty feet from the road vanished as the bright headlights quickly became disappearing red taillights.

"What do you got there?" Stilwell asked Tory.

"Nothing."

"Next bullet goes into your friend. Throw the bag over there, on the shore." Stilwell directed, using the silencer to point in the general direction of the far bank.

Reluctantly, Tory tossed her bag into the weeds.

"Let's see your hands," Stilwell said evenly, demonstrating his control of the situation.

Tory's breathing was deeper now and her heart hammering in her ears seemed to deafen all other sounds. Every movement was slow and deliberate. She did not want to startle the madman with the gun. Holding her hands in front of her chest and rotating them back and forth, she confirmed for Stilwell—and Merlin—that her hands were, indeed, empty.

"Okay, both of you. This way."

Stilwell followed them with his gun, slogging out of the water and up the embankment on the far side of the narrow creek, then directed them off into the woods. The ground was covered by a crunchy blanket of fallen leaves. Twigs snapped beneath their feet and small bushes scratched at their legs.

Suddenly Stilwell stopped walking. "There, that tree," he said, indicating a sturdy sapling with a thick branch coming off the trunk at eye level. Stilwell reached into his pocket and produced a pair of handcuffs. He flipped them toward Tory's feet. "Pick 'em up . . . good. Okay, Miss D.A., snap one of them cuffs on your wrist."

Tory looked at Merlin, then at the handcuffs. She had never touched handcuffs before. They were surprisingly heavy. It took several seconds of fumbling to fit the cuff on her right wrist, slipping the male piece into the female receptacle. *Clickclickclickclick.*

It hung from her wrist like a Rolex watch two sizes too big.

"Click it a couple more times."

Click. A Rolex one size too big. Tory paused.

Stilwell waved the end of the silencer back and forth, indicating she should keep on tightening the cuff.

Click . . . Click.

Now the restraint was tight, with no play between skin and steel.

"Okay," Stilwell continued, satisfied that Tory was properly shackled. "Up and over the branch."

"What?" Tory asked.

"Put your cuffed hand over the goddamn branch!"

Tory reached her hand up to the branch, shaking it several times until the other handcuff dangled free on the other side.

"Okay, big shot," Stilwell said, addressing Merlin. "Git yer hand in the cuff and gimme half a dozen clicks."

Merlin stood there knowing full well once he was cuffed there would be no chance of escape. Bargaining would be a waste of time. "What the hell do you want from us?"

"I want you in those cuffs, now! You want any chance of getting outta here alive, then put your fuckin' hand in the cuffs and close 'em!" Stilwell was breathing hard. As soon as he finished speaking he made a little sucking sound and pulled in some spit that dangled from his lip.

What are the possibilities? Think. Run your options. Merlin's brain was juggling so many messages that he was feeling dizzy. *Run. Make him go after you so Tory can get away. Duck and run.*

Phitt.

A bullet smacked in the ground in front of Merlin's feet. Instead of water exploding, this time dried leaves kicked up to his shins. "Don't even think about it. You run, I go after her. Put your goddamn bracelet on, close it tight, and be a good boy."

Reluctantly, Merlin turned and looked at Tory. Her outstretched arm made it look as if she were dangling from the branch. Their eyes met with such sadness and defeat that for a moment they were taken by a sudden urge to hug each other. But this was not the time.

Being five inches taller, it was quite a bit easier for Merlin to reach the waiting handcuff than it was for Tory to keep her arm aloft. He chose his left hand, slipping it into the steel cuff before using his right to click the jaws closed. Merlin recognized the only distinct advantage he had. It was dark, and Stilwell, in wanting to keep his distance from the couple, was about to allow him to put on the handcuffs by himself.

Unbeknownst even to Tory, Merlin was about to attempt one of the oldest sleights in the very long history of magic. But it was one that he only read about, never actually tried.

Clickclickclickclickclick. The terror set in. They felt trapped, at the mercy of this madman. It was hard, no, absolutely impossible, to control their breathing. Not trusting their rubbery legs to support them, they each gasped the branch for support.

And they waited. Waited for Stilwell to say or do something. Waited for the boss to decide on the agenda. Waited for the unthinkable to happen.

"Wiggle your hand around," Stilwell ordered.

Merlin complied, giving his hand a lackluster shake. The tight metal shackle barely moved.

Apparently Stilwell was satisfied because for the first time he lowered the H&K, aiming it down at the ground.

"Okay, now you've got our attention," Tory said, infused with an angry boldness that surprised Merlin. "What the hell do you want?"

"Betcha 'member me now, huh?" Stilwell said. When the thought hit him that he must look phenomenally different from the last time Tory saw him, he served up his best smile. "Too bad the light's not better. My own mother wouldn't recognize me. Which brings me to the reason I went to all this trouble to have this little meeting with you."

Tory stared at him with eyes full of hate. "Don't think a tuck job makes you into a new person."

Merlin was stone-faced.

"No one's gonna come charging through the door and rescue you this time."

While Tory debated with her captor, Merlin gave his arm a little twist and a gentle tug.

The handcuff moved, not a great distance, but enough. Not for an instant did Merlin direct his eyes upward toward the metal bracelet that fit as loosely as Tory's favorite gold bangle.

"What the hell were you doing out at Cutter's?" Stilwell continued, unaware of the escape artist quietly at work.

"You've *got* to be kidding. Is that what this is all about? I already told you when you had your hand around my neck. I was having a mole checked."

"You're from the D.A. Plain and simple. I have one question, and if I don't get an answer pretty quick, I shoot one of you in the foot. How'd the D.A. know I was there?"

Tory grew curious. "Who are you?"

Merlin prayed Tory didn't notice what he was doing. If she shifted her eyes even for a second, the ruse would be up. Ever so slowly, Merlin worked his slender wrist within the once-tight cuff, feeling the cold metal slide down his forearm where the distal ends of the radius and ulna flared.

"That's what I'm asking you, sis. Who told you? Cutter?"

Clunk. It was more a feeling than a noise, but when the steel of the handcuff bumped against the bones of the wrist, Merlin stopped. Now came the tricky part.

"I got nothing to lose. Killing the both of you doesn't change things for my future, so if you 'spect to walk outta here you best start talking."

Pulling gently, twisting subtly, Merlin's hand worked its way through the circle of metal. The exact moment he knew he'd done it—when he felt the base of his thumb clear the bracelet—he stopped, splaying his fingers wide enough to keep the shackle from moving further. And while Stilwell went on ranting, Merlin bided his time for anything that looked like an opportunity to yank his hand free and take Stilwell by storm.

Out of the very reaches of his peripheral vision, Merlin noticed a slight movement among the dark shadows off in the distance. They were not alone. Someone was moving through the woods. It was too dark to make out any details, but a dark silhouette was skulking about, working his way silently, stopping from time to time behind a tree or bush, making slow but relentless progress toward the little tree where Tory and Merlin were being held captive.

Maybe this would be the diversion Merlin was waiting for. Eventually, Stilwell would hear something behind him, some leaves crunching or a twig snapping underfoot. At that moment, when the lunatic turned to see where the noise was coming from, Merlin would make his move, lunging for the gun and taking the man down.

"Look, you dumb ass," Tory complained, "I don't know how to prove it to you, but I have a mole on my neck. That's all. You're paranoid. There's no conspiracy. No one is after you. Nothing is going on. Now throw the key on the ground and get out of here. We'll let you—"

"Let me what, go? Yeah, right. Either I get some answers or I put a slug in the big shot's leg." Once again Stilwell took aim with the powerful weapon.

Merlin directed his head in Stilwell's general direction, but his eyes were in hard lateral gaze to the right, watching the dark figure sneaking through the woods. Silently. Tree to tree. Waiting. Watching, as if a phantom were floating from tree to tree.

C'mon, make a noise, make a mistake, Merlin urged.

Tory did several little steps in place like a terrified child being approached by a large dog. Her terror now controlled her. Gone was the angry bravado that she possessed a few short seconds ago. "All right, let's calm down. Please. No one needs to get hurt." Her voice softened. "I know you think my being at Cutter's had something to do with you but I swear . . . on my mother's grave . . . that I was a patient just like you. Look, I don't know what you're afraid of, but no harm will come to you. Please . . . please unlock us and . . . and . . . I'll do what I can to help you."

Merlin's eyes were starting to hurt. *Keep going, Tory. Tell him whatever he wants to hear. Nice and smooth.*

The mysterious figure was close enough now for Merlin to make out some details. It was a man, and not some late-night hiker happening upon something going down in the woods. His presence and incredible stealth was anything but coincidental. He was no more than a dozen feet from Stilwell and by his posture—knees bent, arms held out from his sides—he was poised to make a surprise attack. Something was in the man's right hand, something long, a stick maybe. *A weapon. He's got a weapon.*

No ally of Stilwell's would arrive so covertly. Obviously this man intended to do harm to Stilwell. But what if Tory noticed the shadowy man? What if she suddenly reacted to his presence, let out a gasp or abruptly stopped talking, and Stilwell turned around and put a bullet into him? "C'mon Tory, enough. Tell the man what he wants to know and he'll leave us alone, right?" Merlin spoke loudly enough to muffle any noise the intruder might make.

Tory whipped her head to the right and shot a glance at Merlin, mostly in confusion, but Stilwell took it to mean she knew something she did not want to divulge.

Infused with a renewed anger, Stilwell stepped right up to Tory and got in her face. "Enough of your bullshit. Who's watching me? Someone in the D.A.?"

Now it was impossible for Tory to see anything beyond Stilwell's surgically tightened mug. Merlin's eyes went from the nose-to-nose conversation Tory was having with Stilwell to the intruder who had now moved even closer to the threesome.

Without warning the man covered the final distance to Stilwell with the stealth of a cat springing on a mouse.

Stepstepstep. And then he was there, raising his right hand above his head, wielding an eighteen-inch baton with which he clearly intended to smash Stilwell. In one brutal swipe he slammed Stilwell's right forearm, sending the semi-automatic to the leafy ground. The sound of Stilwell's arm being hit was grotesque, a hollow crunching noise as the baton smashed the bones of Stilwell's arm into enough pieces that a radiologist wouldn't even bother counting.

Before Stilwell could react to the pain, the man, who was wearing a dark mask, threw his weapon to the ground with a heavy thud and snapped a half-nelson on Stilwell.

"Betcha didn't expect to see me, asshole!" the man whispered into Stilwell's ear. "You been telling lies about all the dirty little things you've been doing, huh? You been shooting your mouth off?" The masked man's right hand went to his own waist, withdrawing something from a long, narrow holster. "You made the biggest mistake of your shitty life coming here tonight."

"Let me go, goddamnit," Stilwell demanded. Struggling was all but impossible. His left arm was trapped in a vise-like grip while his right dangled uselessly down by his side.

Merlin caught his first glimpse of what the masked man now held aloft in his hand. It was an ice pick. As the man used his left hand to flex Stilwell's head forward, he placed the tip of the pick up against the back of his neck, just below his skull.

"You like talking so much, let's hear what you've got to say now. Time for the wicked dance," the man whispered and slowly pierced Stilwell's thick skin with the sharp tip.

Stilwell screamed.

The ice pick nosed ahead, cutting a sure course through the paraspinal and trapezius muscles that attached to the bony spines of the vertebral column.

Tory recoiled at the sight, pulling against the handcuff

as she averted her eyes to get as far away from the torture as possible.

Stilwell was screaming and flailing about, but his desperate efforts were to no avail. The man's strength was far superior. He seemed to control Stilwell's movements quite easily and relentlessly continued to push the ice pick deeper and deeper. As it winged the highest vertebra, scraping the sensitive surface coating of the bone, Stilwell let out a piercing scream that made Tory clamp her eyes shut and suck in her breath, holding it as if it were the last one she was even going to have.

Now the tip of the pick was almost an inch beyond the surface of the skin, poised to pop through the rugged dura, a thick membrane that forms a protective barrier separating the critically important central nervous system from the rest of the body. The dura always gave the ice pick the most resistance, and the man in the black mask had to give it a little jab. His fingers knew the drill well. When he felt the pop as the pick jumped forward into the fluid-filled sub-arachnoid space, he paused to savor the feeling.

He knew the cold steel was about to enter dangerous, forbidden territory. Everything within the central nervous system—including spinal cord and brain—was extraordinarily delicate. Anything severed by the roving ice pick would be lost forever. But as important as everything within the brain and spinal cord was, the medulla, which controlled breathing and other basic bodily functions, might actually be the most vital. It was located at the very base of the brain, and was now precious millimeters from cold steel.

The man loved this moment between life and death. Stanley Stilwell's existence was completely in his own hands. Amazingly enough, there would be almost no bleeding. Slide the ice pick forward less than an inch and

Stilwell would die. Remove it now and he could walk
away with hardly the need for Extra Strength Excedrin.

The man urged the ice pick in a forward direction,
working the handle carefully. There was now no way to
know when he hit pay dirt by the feel of the ice pick. The
only way to know was to watch for the wicked dance.

Stilwell was keenly aware he had something sharp inside his neck. He stood absolutely still. He was pushed
down at the waist, hunched over like Quasimodo, lamely
staring down at the ground. The pain was barely noticeable but he sensed how precarious his situation was.
Every muscle in his body burned with lactic acid.

Millimeter by millimeter the ice pick cut forward. The
man no longer held the wooden handle of the ice pick
in the palm of his hand but now had it delicately in his
fingers the way a violinist would hold a bow caressing
the strings of a Stradivarius. It was time to make Stilwell
dance to his macabre music.

Without warning Stilwell's arms and legs exploded in
a frenetic series of thrustings and spastic flailings. The
tip of the ice pick was deep within the soft medulla,
destroying the various nerves that controlled the muscles
of the arms and legs. Each nerve fired one last time,
sending a meaningless message to the dozens of muscles
that flexed and extended the four extremities.

The man in the black mask knew how to prolong the
agony by wiggling the ice pick back and forth. Stilwell's
arms and legs relaxed only to return suddenly to full
extension, like those of a marionette in the hands of an
evil puppeteer.

The wicked dance lasted less than two seconds, but
went on much longer in Tory and Merlin's minds. Once
such a grisly scene had been witnessed it had the ability
to change a person forever.

When the dance was over Stilwell's arms and legs hung

limply at his side. Everything in his body was flaccid. His head flopped forward, his diaphragm stopped working, and when the man in the black mask let him go, he flopped to the ground in a crumpled heap. Though he was not yet dead, death would surely come quickly, in seconds or minutes. No one could survive a brain injury of that magnitude.

The man ignored Tory and Merlin as if they weren't there. Instead he bent over his helpless victim and used Stilwell's shirt to wipe the body fluids from his ice pick. Carefully sliding it back into its sheath and reaching down to retrieve his baton, he grabbed hold of Stilwell's flaccid arm and began pulling him to a sitting position.

Merlin and Tory watched in silence as the masked man, his feet almost a full yard apart for support, squatted down and looped Stilwell's arm around his neck, then grunted loudly as he straightened his legs and strained to hoist the dead weight up onto his shoulders. When he was as fully upright as he could manage and turned to head back through the woods, Merlin realized his only link to this terror was leaving on the back of a masked man. Jerking free of his handcuff, Merlin dashed back toward the embankment where Stilwell had thrown Tory's bag in order to retrieve her Beretta.

But the masked man heard Merlin's footsteps, turned for a moment, and instantly dumped his heavy load. As silently as he had come, he took off through the woods.

Chapter 6

Marshall Cutter stood in the kitchen of his Fox Chapel home, gazing out the window over the sink at the reflection of the full moon in Gumper Pond. His home was anything but a bachelor pad. Each night the plastic surgeon came home to a single-story white brick contemporary with a two-car garage, three bedrooms, and a study. The reason he'd bought the house was the den—a spacious room with fifteen-foot beamed ceilings, a stupendous slate fireplace, and huge windows that overlooked a six-acre pond named for the original owner of the property.

It was a minute or two before eleven o'clock. Cutter was just about to begin rinsing the dishes from dinner while a scrumptious woman named Daphne primped herself in the bathroom in anticipation of a romantic night.

Quite by habit Cutter had his little Sony television on as he pushed up the sleeves on his custom tailored shirt, donned thick rubber gloves, and rinsed each of the dishes before placing them in his dishwasher. They had dined on mesclun salad with a homemade raspberry vinaigrette dressing, marinated salmon seared on a fancy gas grill, asparagus with creamy garlic dressing, and dilled new potatoes. It was his traditional first-date meal, one that could be prepped the night before and thrown together for a very late-night supper without effort while he and his date sipped cocktails and enjoyed Gumper Pond.

"Can I convince you to let me finish those in the morning?" Daphne purred. She had strolled into the kitchen looking positively irresistible. Her silk blouse was now two buttons more décolleté, and she'd removed her jewelry to leave her body unencumbered for what was to happen next.

The temptation was too great. Cutter turned off the water, snapped off his rubber gloves, and turned away from his date while he fumbled with the remote control. The news had just begun. Daphne sauntered over to Cutter, slipped her arms around his chest, and started nibbling and licking his neck erotically. Just as he was about to give in to her tantalizing charms and zap the television into silence something else caught his attention.

Apparently it was a big news night because the station immediately went to a live remote in a wooded area brightly illuminated by artificial lights. The reporter, a black man in a beige sport coat, stood holding a microphone. "At this time details are sketchy, but what we know is this: several hours ago a bizarre assault occurred in the Fox Chapel area."

Fox Chapel. Any report of a bizarre assault in one's home community would cause a viewer to show more than passing interest. Marshall Cutter was no exception. By now Daphne had worked her pink tongue around to his earlobe and was caressing it like a butterfly on a flower. Her manicured fingernails were tickling his chest in those lazy little circles she was supposed to be making *after* they'd made love, right about the time she would murmur something about it being the best sex she'd ever had. But she knew the kind of message she was delivering and fully expected to hear the voices on the television disappear when Cutter could no longer control himself.

"I have with me Detective Daniel Deringer, City of Pittsburgh Police, who arrived on the scene a short time ago after local authorities had begun the investigation." The camera angle shifted to accommodate both the reporter and Detective Deringer in the shot. The detective was wearing a dark jacket with his badge displayed on the breast pocket. He had on a white shirt and his tie was pulled loose at the neck. By the way he frowned it seemed obvious he didn't want to be on camera. "Detective Deringer, can you lead us through what happened here this evening?"

"Yes," the detective began and paused to collect his thoughts. The camera pulled in for a close-up. Deringer appeared to be a no-nonsense sort of police officer. He looked like a hard man with his strong features, deep-set eyes, and the cleft in his chin. His eyes flicked down at a small notebook in his hand. "Sometime around eight-thirty as Dr. Jack Merlin and Tory Welch, both of Aspinwall, were driving down Squaw Run Road here in Fox Chapel, an unknown assailant shot out the front tire of their Jeep Cherokee. At gunpoint the couple was then forced from their car—"

Tory Welch! Oh my God. Cutter's tongue shot out and swiped across his lower lip to moisten his suddenly dry mouth. His breathing quickened, which Daphne took as a good sign and started tonguing the inside of his ear, whispering a short list of naughty things she intended to do to him just as soon as she got him in bed.

"—by a man who allegedly had a confrontation with Ms. Welch two days earlier at a plastic surgeon's office."

The remote control slipped from Cutter's fingers and clattered to the floor.

Daphne took this as an even better sign. She was busy

unbuttoning Cutter's silk shirt and kissing her way down his chest.

"After handcuffing the couple to a tree, the man threatened Ms. Welch with a gun."

"Oh my God!" Cutter blurted out.

Daphne was totally into it. "This what you like?" Her lips had captured one of Cutter's nipples, her tongue flicking across it wildly.

Off camera the reporter encouraged Deringer to continue. "And there was a second assailant?"

"That is correct. This is where the story becomes confusing. According to statements made by Dr. Merlin and Ms. Welch, a second man came out of the woods. He was dressed in black and his face was covered by a mask. He then overpowered the first assailant—the man with the gun—and stabbed him in the back of the neck with an ice pick–like device. This second assailant subsequently made a clean escape back into the woods, leaving his victim for dead."

By now Daphne had slithered her way down to her knees. Her tongue darted about his belly button like a moray eel rooting in an underwater cave for food. "Oh, Marshall," she purred.

"I don't believe this," Cutter whispered.

"Believe it, baby. I want it every way you can give it to me," Daphne whispered urgently. She pulled her head away just long enough to find his belt buckle, which she immediately began to work on.

Cutter couldn't pull his eyes away from the image of the news reporter standing in the woods. His mouth hung open in horrified disbelief. The erotic pleasures Daphne was offering were wasted. His chest tightened and it was difficult to swallow.

"Dr. Merlin, who is a surgeon at the Medical Center, somehow freed himself from the handcuff which attached him to the tree. Ms. Welch then summoned the authorities on a cell phone while Dr. Merlin performed CPR on the victim.

"Although the unknown man had apparently suffered life-threatening trauma to his brain, I'm told there was a heartbeat and that Dr. Merlin placed a breathing tube into the man's airway to assist with breathing.

"The ambulance left this wooded area almost an hour ago with Dr. Merlin." Detective Deringer turned around to look at the crime scene. The camera caught some footage of crime lab technicians kneeling on the ground hunting for evidence amongst yellow POLICE LINE DO NOT CROSS tape strung from tree to tree. At the far reaches of the scene Tory Welch could be spotted sitting alone on a fallen tree trunk, wrapped in what appeared to be a large trench coat.

"Oh, Marshall, I don't think I can wait," Daphne blurted out as she yanked his trousers to his knees and started smacking her lips greedily.

"Merlin," the emergency room nurse called out, breathless from her short hustle across the emergency room of the Pittsburgh University Medical Center. She approached Merlin and a cluster of physicians and nurses who were stabilizing the as yet unidentified patient. "Scanner's ready."

Merlin nodded and directed the trauma team as they readied his patient for the short elevator ride up to the CT scanner. Medical personnel had a tremendous need to call patients by name, so everyone in the ER had adopted the comatose patient as John Doe. Consensus was John Doe was in his early to mid-fifties.

The patient was in a deep coma, supine on a stretcher, IVs running here and there and his skin mottled as if he had been petrified into Italian marble. It was hard for some of the nurses to look at his face without getting sick. The skin on John Doe's nose had come loose and was hanging from one side. Most of the small blue sutures around his right ear had ripped open, leaving a gaping hole on one side of his face. It reminded Merlin of those old *Mission: Impossible* shows where a character would tear off a latex mask, starting at the ear and peeling it away from the face.

Mercifully, several squares of gauze were quickly taped over John Doe's flapping skin.

About the only part of John Doe's anatomy that seemed intact was his heart. Although the neurologic insult paralyzed the muscles used for breathing, the neurons connected to his heart had somehow remained untouched. For the past several hours, though, his heart rate had been slow and erratic, and required an IV infusion of enough cardiogenic drugs to open a small pharmacy. Dobutamine. Dopamine. Nitroprusside. Levophed.

Merlin was hell-bent on meticulously examining his patient through all the commotion. He flitted about the lifeless form with a perverse intensity the ER staff was not accustomed to seeing performed on a John Doe in the deepest of comas. First Merlin tried whacking him on the knee with a rubber hammer. There was not the slightest hint of leg movement. Then the surgeon took an ordinary house key from his pocket and scratched the sharp tip of it firmly on the sole of John Doe's foot. Starting at the heel and running all the way up to his toes, Merlin watched for the Babinski reflex. Normally, a key scratching the foot elicited a downward movement of the great toe. But when the neurologic connections controlling the muscles of the lower extremity were interrupted, the great toe moved in an upward direction, as if it was trying to distance itself from the stimulus. All the emergency room physicians and nurses jockeyed about to watch this little experiment, looking like a group of children gathered about a chicken's egg ready to hatch. As the key reached the toes everyone bent over at the waist so as not to miss anything. The patient's great toe flicked upward almost half an inch, eliciting a collective "Ooooh" from the gaggle of personnel.

An up-going toe was truly a bad sign. Even without the results from the CT scan it was obvious the damage had been severe.

Finally, Merlin searched for one of the most basic of all reflexes—the response to pain. Although the practice seemed grotesque to some of the spectators, Merlin used his thumb and forefinger to grab a thick wad of pink flesh below John Doe's left nipple. Pinching as hard as he could, his hand was shaking as if he had developed a tremor when he let go. The flesh under John Doe's nipple remained tented up for several seconds.

John Doe didn't react at all. He didn't flinch a muscle. His blood pressure and pulse remained steady. "Goddamnit! This can't be happening," Merlin exclaimed, and stormed away from his patient before he lost it completely.

The stretcher was manned by two nurses who moved the patient to the CT scanner. A respiratory therapist accompanied the ventilator and Merlin walked alongside the stretcher to keep an eye on his patient. By now it was obvious to all comers that John Doe most certainly would never talk again, but Merlin was certain he held secrets so dear, he was more than willing to do anything in his power in the dim hope that something might be revealed.

While the stretcher traveled by elevator to the third floor, Merlin reflected on what had happened in the woods after the man in the black mask had stolen off into the night. He had opted to attend to the crumpled remains of John Doe rather than chase after the masked man. The rest of the world ceased to exist. The only thing that mattered was saving the life of a man who most certainly would have killed the two of them had he not been attacked himself.

Every muscle in John Doe's body had gone flaccid. His arms and legs flopped about like dead fish as Merlin rolled him into a supine position. Surprisingly, Merlin was able to find a feeble pulse in the man's neck but there hadn't been any respiratory effort for almost three minutes. The clock was ticking, and with each passing second more and more brain cells were dying. Merlin estimated that in another ninety seconds the man would be dead.

Without hesitation Merlin initiated mouth-to-mouth resuscitation, blowing into the comatose man's mouth and sucking in fresh air until he was too dizzy to speak. He continued without interruption until the police and paramedics arrived nearly fourteen minutes after Tory's call.

Now they were ready to wheel John Doe into the CT suite. A small, dimly illuminated work area, brimming with control panels and computers, was separated by a glass window from the room where the scanner was located.

John Doe was lifted to a motorized table that was connected at one end to the monstrous doughnut-shaped scanner. The scanner room was cleared of the two nurses, the respiratory therapist, and Merlin. A neuro-radiologist sat down at the control panel and directed the patient slowly into the CT scanner.

Within seconds, the first cut appeared on the computer screen. It did not look good. The anatomy of the brain stem—the lowest part of the brain—had been macerated by the ice pick that had been shoved into John Doe's neck. What had been diagnosed by clinical exam was now graphically displayed in vivid black and white.

Merlin covered his eyes with his hands. His efforts would never be rewarded. Any other doctor in this hopeless situation would have picked himself up and gone home to bed.

Merlin chose to stay.

The absolute best John Doe could hope for was a quick death. It could happen in any number of ways. The easiest might be if his heart decided to stop responding to the complicated potion of cardiac drugs.

The worst fate for John Doe would be a chronic vegetative state hooked to a ventilator with a feeding tube going through his nose. It was impossible to know when to stop trying until it was too late. In the heat of the moment, with a patient crashing in the ER, it was routine to pull out all the stops and institute advanced life support systems in the hope that once the crisis passed, the patient would wake up and recover. Most times, fortunately, the patient did go on to a satisfactory recovery. But once the possibility of a reasonable prognosis had passed, the patient was stuck on a ventilator. At that point it became more of a moral than a medical dilemma.

Ventilators were easy to turn on. It was another story turning them off.

Merlin joined the others in the CT room to move John Doe from the motorized table back to the stretcher, the *wesssssh-wesssssh* of the ventilator and *beep-beep-beeping* of the heart monitor being the only sounds to break the silence. Everyone took up positions around the table, grabbing handfuls of the sheet on which the unconscious patient rested. But Merlin just stared at the heart monitor.

"Merlin," a fat nurse said gently, reminding him that he was needed to help move the patient. She had to say it three more times before he heard her.

*   *   *

Brian Trilby woke from a dead sleep, drenched in what medical textbooks call a night sweat. Repeated occurrences were usually associated with bona fide medical conditions such as infectious mononucleosis or cancer. Night sweats were quite horrible for patients. Bedclothes and pajamas became wringing wet, and a physical exhaustion set in akin to the fatigue associated with running a marathon. The only way to go back to sleep was to get up, change everything, and lie in the dark praying the night wouldn't inflict another.

Trilby, at age thirty-four, still took his job seriously enough to turn out the lights at ten-thirty each night so he wouldn't be yawning his way through the first case of the morning. He was losing his hair but was otherwise in excellent physical shape. Even though Cutter kept him busy, he forced himself to exercise daily.

This was the fourth time in thirteen days that Brian Trilby had been awakened by a night sweat. His health was perfect; he'd even been to his internist after the second one, but the tests came out clean and he was declared healthy.

Tonight, at least, Brian Trilby knew exactly why he had the night sweats. He'd had the dream. Every time he experienced one he ended up so drenched that his wife had to strip the bed while he stepped in the shower.

Tonight was the worst one of all, an order of magnitude more severe than the others combined. Only one person in the world had been trusted with even the most cursory explanation of the content of the nightmare.

He sat up, supporting himself from behind with his arms pushing against the pillow. He was breathing hard. Big fat drops of sweat rolled off his forehead, down his lean cheeks, then sped past the sharp angle of his jaw before racing down his neck. The room seemed hot and stuffy. Trilby badly needed fresh air, cool air to wake him up, as if he were at a ski resort sucking in the first whiff of a new day.

With a sweep of his hand he threw off the quilt and slowly rotated his body so that he could place his feet on the thick pile carpet. Everything in his body hurt. His head throbbed with the force of a vicious migraine. Each bone and joint in his upper extremities ached with a stiffness similar to rheumatoid arthritis. Absently he massaged his fingers, trying to rub some life back into them. And come to think of it, his heart was drumming some weird beat. Ba-dum, ba-dum, ba-dum, ba BA-DUM. *Jesus Christ.* He was throwing PVCs, premature ventricular contractions. Occasionally his powerful ventricles were beating too early, which caused the weird thumping sensation in his chest.

Air. I gotta get some air. Brian started to concentrate on his breathing and forced himself to do the slow Lamaze breathing technique his wife had practiced for months before they had their first baby. *Iiiiiiiiin . . . Ouuuuuuuut . . . Iiiiiiiiin . . . Ouuuuuuuut. That's it, slow it down. You're okay, hang in there.* Now that he was concentrating on the slow breathing he was able to get up from bed and walk over to open the window and put his dry lips right up to the dirty screen so that he could pull some delicious air in from the night. Ba-dum, ba BA-DUM. Damn! Another PVC. *C'mon, Brian, slow it down, take it real easy. You can do it, Brian. Iiiiiiiiin . . . Ouuuuuuuut . . . Iiiin . . . Ouuuut . . . Iin . . . Ouut . . . In . . . Out . . . In . . . Out . . . In . . . In . . . In . . . Out . . InOutInOutInOut.*

"Shit!" he exclaimed out loud, breathing so hard he was afraid he was going to wake his wife. He was losing control. The more he thought about the dream the worse it got. He clamped a hand to his mouth, cupping it over his lips to stifle the ridiculously chirpy sounds he was making as he desperately tried to calm his breathing.

That's when Brian Trilby picked up the phone, a fancy, gilded contraption that looked like something from a French whorehouse. He hated the phone, but his wife, Lori, had ordered it through a decorator who promised that the garish French brothel look was the next trend.

The dial wasn't lighted and the last thing he wanted at 11:26 at night was for Lori to wake up and want to know what the hell was going on. So he kept the lights off and slowly dialed the number, walking his fingers around the dial over and over.

"Doctor's answering service," an anonymous female voice said.

"Will you let the doctor know Brian Trilby is calling." Trilby worked hard at trying to use the same crisp tone of voice he would use had he been calling a medical colleague regarding a patient. But he was whispering in a barely audible voice and came off sounding like some sort of crank phone call.

"Is this an emergency?"

"Uhh," Trilby hesitated, wondering if it really was an emergency. Heart attacks and strokes were *true* emergencies, things no rational person—not even someone making minimum wage in the middle of the night at an answering service—would question. But waking up with a night sweat that had frightened his heart into throwing PVCs?

Yes. That made it an emergency. PVCs were nothing to mess with.

"Yes, this is an emergency. Please page my doctor, for crissakes."

Once she heard it was an emergency the pressure was off. She could safely wake the doctor, knowing she had secured the right answer when he barked into the phone, "Is it an emergency?" "Your callback number?"

As Brian whispered his telephone number he was grateful for one thing. Most shrinks didn't expect their patients to rattle off their most intimate thoughts to the answering service.

Then he hung up the phone and waited. At this hour he figured he would get a call back in less than two minutes. But it seemed to take forever. The first minute was an eternity. So long that he wondered if his bedside clock was broken. Just as he was reaching for it to see what was wrong, the time changed.

Ba BA-DUM. Ba BA-DUM. *Oh, shit!* Two in a row. When the hell was the phone going to ring?

Brian had to do something. He couldn't just sit there sweating it out. Now he did wish Lori would wake up so he'd at least have someone to talk to. Wiggling his upper torso like a dog shaking off a bath, he rocked the entire bed.

Despite the jostling Lori remained on her side, facing away from him, breathing so nice and relaxed, oblivious to her husband soaking the sheets with sweat and throwing PVCs to beat the band.

"God damn," he said and reached for the remote control. The big Sony television across the room in the heavy oak wardrobe came to life.

He was catching the last minutes of the eleven o'clock news. The anchor, a woman heavy on the lipstick and rouge, was recapping the top story. He caught her in mid-sentence, but what he heard made his heart seize. "—the man, as yet unknown, had recently undergone extensive cosmetic surgery at a Harmarville surgi-center operated by plastic surgeon Marshall Cutter. Of note is that the man had attacked Ms. Welch in the plastic surgery center and had apparently been following her since then—"

Ring.

Ba BA-DUM. Brian ignored the phone. What was being said on the news was impossible to ignore. He covered his face with his hands and just listened to the words.

"—a second man, also unidentified at this time, came out of the night and stabbed the assailant in the back of the neck with an ice pick—"

"Ahhhhh!" Trilby screamed out involuntarily.

Ring.

Ba BA-DUM

"Brian, the phone!" Lori snapped, jumping into her husband's middle-of-the-night nervous breakdown. Her tone of voice showed her irritation with the interruption of her own sleep. She was propped up on one arm, brushing stray hairs from her face and glaring back and forth between the television and her husband. "Bri-an."

Trilby reached for the phone. "Hello," he said, turning away from his wife to look toward the open window, hoping she would roll over and just go back to sleep. "Sorry to bother you but I think I need to talk with you. . . . Oh, just some stuff I've been worrying about," he continued. Trilby juggled the difficult task of admitting to his psychiatrist that he was at the brink of collapse while at the same time ensuring that his nosy wife wouldn't have the foggiest idea what he was talking about. "Oh, you know, what we've been talking about. . . . Right, just had another."

"Another what?" Lori wanted to know. "Bri-an, another *what*?"

Trilby waved her off with one hand, beckoning her to

be quiet. "Well, how's your schedule, say, tomorrow? . . . Okay, fine. . . . That's great." His doctor hung up the phone. The emergency appointment was scheduled. But Lori was still listening and he obliged her with just a bit more. "Yeah, I understand your problem, like I said, I had another one just now," he said to the dial tone.

"Another what?"

Brian put his other hand to the phone to block the mouthpiece. Then he turned around and whispered, "Idea. Another idea."

"Oh." She sounded confused and a little disappointed.

"Very good, tomorrow at lunch, and I think you'll like what I've come up with." Then he hung up the phone and slipped his feet beneath the covers. "It was Marshall," he said to his wife. "He wants to bring another surgeon in a couple of days a week but doesn't want a second anesthesiologist. I just had an idea about using a nurse anesthetist."

Lori propped her head up on one hand and stared at her husband in profile. "At eleven-thirty at night?"

"I had a brainstorm—"

"You having an affair I should know about?" she asked suddenly.

"What?"

"Are you having an affair?" This time Lori spoke slowly, so the import of her words would not be misunderstood.

"No."

"Then what's going on?"

"I already told you—"

"No you didn't. You're soaking wet. No way were you giving Marshall ideas about nurse anesthetists. If you're not having an affair, are you in some kind of trouble?" Lori sounded frightened now.

"I'm fine," Brian said and scooched over in the bed

to slip his arm reassuringly around Lori's shoulders. He looked at the clock and knew he would spend the next four hours thinking about what he had just heard on the news. *Was Stanley Stilwell dead or alive?*

Chapter 7

The crime scene on Squaw Run Road was crawling with uniformed cops even before the ambulance left for the Medical Center. No one, not even Detective Deringer, took much notice of the fact that John Doe was wearing black leather gloves. All of the attention was directed toward his heart and lungs, and toward trying to keep him alive until he could reach the Medical Center.

The police recovered his handgun with the silencer and the handcuffs. The Chrysler Concorde was impounded, and soon determined to be stolen, belonging to a man named Jonas Osterman. Despite Mr. Osterman's protestations, the car was towed to the Fox Chapel garage to be combed over by the techs from the crime lab in the morning.

John Doe had no identification. His pockets were empty—no wallet or even loose money.

There were footprints, not very good ones, in the leafy soil near the bank of the little stream. Plaster casts were taken in hopes of getting some sort of a handle on the man in the black mask, but Deringer shook his head and grumbled that it was a waste of time, what with the leaves.

The patient in the Medical Center was still being referred to as John Doe hours after his arrival. Neither Tory nor Merlin could remember Stilwell's name. While Tory was being driven home by Detective Deringer, several uniforms made the short drive across Fox Chapel to Marshall Cutter's home in search of some answers. The lights were out and no one answered the doorbell.

Cutter had left his driveway just in time. The very instant he heard the newscast he realized that Stanley Stilwell's death meant big trouble. Standing in his kitchen with the remote control on the floor and Daphne's mouth pumping him erotically, a gripping terror built in his chest like a coronary.

"Daphne," he said when he had his wits about him, "this isn't going to work."

Daphne continued lapping him up like a kitten working on a warm bowl of milk. Either she didn't hear him or she was determined to change his mind.

"Daphne!" he demanded, grabbing a handful of her hair and ripping her head away from him. "Aren't you listening? I said not now."

Initially, she was too stunned to pull her tongue back inside her mouth. As soon as she realized what was happening she recoiled, cursing quite loudly, but Cutter's pulse was hammering away in his ears and it sounded like so much gibberish to him. What Cutter needed was a chance to think. And a chance to make one very important phone call in order to arrange an emergency meeting.

By now Daphne had hissed out several more colorful insults, each a bit more caustic than the last. Adding to her fury was the realization that her rantings were going unanswered, and she found herself staring up at a man who was looking through her as if she weren't in the room.

She stood up and punched him in the stomach, hard. Immediately he doubled over and let out a loud grunt.

"I said, drive . . . me . . . home *NOW*!"

"Good," was the only thing Cutter could get out. As he worked himself back into an upright posture, Daphne headed into the den to collect her things. She was moving quickly, using the heavily exaggerated movements wives make when they're totally pissed off at their husbands for flirting with some blonde at the neighborhood Christmas party. With a furious swipe she yanked her fancy little purse off the coffee table and flung it over her shoulder. Then she exhaled loudly, a reminder to Cutter just in case he forgot how irate she was. A brief moment of silence followed as Daphne marched across the thick carpet toward the front door. Her heels clicked off the heavy ceramic tiles in the large foyer like a terse metronome gone mad. Cutter listened to her working the latch on the front door as if she didn't give a crap if she broke every one of her perfectly painted nails. Finally, he endured the awful thud the solid wood door made as it was thrown open, banging off the little metal door stop so forcefully that it would leave a permanent pockmark as a reminder of this moment.

Not wanting to make it look as if he had run out of the place, Cutter raced about turning off one light after another. As he pulled the heavy front door closed behind him he whipped his head around just in case an army of grim-faced men in somber suits was hiding in the bushes.

It was quite an effort reminding himself to stay calm. *Yes, I was quite shocked to hear about what happened. Of course I remember him. Starwell . . . no, wait, Stilwell! . . . That's it, Stanley Stilwell . . . strange fellow . . . apparently from lots of money . . . insisted on the whole surgi-center being cleared of patients . . . I should have discharged him as a patient when he locked himself in that room with Miss Welch.* Yep, that's exactly what he would say. And just to make certain he had the routine down pat, he repeated it as if it were a musical jingle that he couldn't get out of his mind.

The ride to Daphne's townhouse was the longest twenty-two minutes he could remember. He peeled out of his fancy brick driveway sounding more like a kid driving a GTO with a pack of Marlboros rolled up in his sleeve than a rich plastic surgeon wearing fifteen hundred dollars' worth of clothing in a sixty-thousand-dollar Mercedes. Stop signs and red lights meant nothing. When Cutter hit Route 28, a two-lane highway with a speed limit of fifty-five, he was already pushing seventy. Once on the open road, his right foot eased the gas pedal down and he really opened the German engine up.

Daphne's terrible anger was quickly replaced by gut-grabbing, sphincter-releasing horror. No longer was she furious—or embarrassed—by the way Cutter had pulled her away from him like she was some kind of slut. She swayed in her seat as Cutter powered by every sort of vehicle imaginable. "Slow down," she said when she'd finally found her voice. But it came out so tiny and weak that even in the opulent quiet of the Mercedes, Cutter had no idea she'd uttered a word.

If Cutter had taken a peek at the speedometer he would have seen that he was in triple digits, nearly double the limit. Bumps and dips in the road sent the generous suspension into a series of graceful waves, like a big cabin cruiser rolling on the tiny wake of a much smaller boat. Cutter had one thing and one thing only on his mind. He had to call Mannheim. That was the drill. If there was ever trouble, call Mannheim. Whatever would happen next he had no idea. That was for Mannheim to decide. Cutter's obligation was to make the call.

"Slow . . . down!" Daphne ordered, louder now. Her

eyes were fixed on the road in front of them. She had
one hand on the seat where the soft brown leather rolled
down toward the carpeted floor, white-knuckling it until
her nails were cutting into the leather with marks that
would last as long as the dent she had put in Cutter's
front door. Her other hand had somehow locked on to
her fancy little pocketbook and was putting a pretty significant dent in that, too. "Do you hear me? *Slow down!*"

But Cutter was too busy trying to keep the car on the
road while he silently rehearsed what he planned to say
to Mannheim right after he dropped Daphne off.

Who the hell attacked Stilwell? That was the burning
question. The more it ran through his mind, the faster
he urged the car to go. *Maybe it's someone from Stilwell's
past, someone he pissed off who's been following him.*
But Cutter reminded himself just how much care was
taken not to allow that to happen. *Maybe he pulled a
stunt since arriving in Pittsburgh. Yeah, that had to be it.
Stilwell pulled some shit that got somebody mad.*

Several seconds before the big Mercedes pulled to a
sudden stop in front of her building, Daphne had the car
door open and one foot waiting to hit the pavement. She
slammed the door and stormed away. There was no time
for Cutter to say goodnight or apologize for ruining the
evening.

Finally alone, Cutter snatched the cellular phone from
its black cradle and dialed a number he knew by heart.
As the connection went through he looked at his watch.
Eleven forty-eight. The ringing went on and on at least
thirty times before it was answered.

"Yes," a voice said crisply at the other end of the line.

"Mannheim, this is Cutter." There was a long silence
at Mannheim's end of the line. For a moment Cutter
even wondered if the phone had gone dead. Aware he
was starting to sweat, he wiped his brow with the palm

of his hand, then held it up so it would catch the light from Daphne's building. A shiny glaze of moisture coated his entire hand. "You there?"

"The thing on the news," Mannheim said evenly, giving no hint to what he might be thinking. "Your boy wasn't it?"

"Yes, but I had no idea—"

"Where are you?" Mannheim interrupted.

"My car."

"Don't go home. Drive around. Don't stay in any one place."

"Should I call you—"

Mannheim cut Cutter off. It was obvious who was calling the shots. "The usual place. One hour. I need to check into a few things."

Before Cutter could say a word, before he could ask what the hell did Mannheim think happened to Stilwell, the line went dead. Immediately he put the car in drive and pulled away from Daphne's building. He had no idea where he was going, but he was calmed by the fact that he had a set of directions to follow.

Every few seconds he was checking his rearview mirror looking for a police car to be following him. *Starwell . . . Starwell . . . no, wait, Stilwell! . . . That's it, Stanley Stilwell . . . strange fellow . . .* Then it struck him. Being interviewed by the police was the least of his worries. He knew the song and dance. He could play innocent and dumb with the best of them.

His tongue brushed across his lower lip when it dawned on him, *What if whoever shoved an ice pick into Stilwell's neck decides to do the same thing to me?*

Eventually Cutter took the bridge across the Monongahela River and headed up the P. J. McArdle Roadway, a gently curving street that climbed to the top of Mt.

Washington. Halfway up he drove under the Mon Incline, one of Pittsburgh's most famous landmarks, consisting of a pair of cars running on metal tracks that climb straight up the steep mountain, one going up precisely as the other went down, the transportation equivalent of a seesaw. Although once a vital system for commuters to come and go from the precipitous bluff, the inclines were now less for transportation than they were a way to entertain out-of-towners.

At the top he made a left onto Grandview Avenue, drove a quarter mile or so, turned again onto one of the dark little side streets where his Mercedes would be less conspicuous, and got out of his car and walked to a concrete observation deck that tourists flocked to for a breathtaking view of the city.

It was empty. Cutter checked his watch. One a.m. Grandview was empty. No pedestrians or cars. Slowly Cutter ventured onto the open air observation deck and went over to the railing. The vista was spectacular. He gazed down at the Monongahela River as it met the Allegheny River in the distance to form the Ohio. The City of Pittsburgh was tucked neatly between the two converging rivers.

"Cutter," a voice behind him said.

Cutter jumped and turned around. "Oh," he said, breathing out heavily, "it's you."

"Jumpy, huh?" It was Mannheim. A man in his early fifties, he wore a dark-blue running suit and black athletic shoes and reminded Cutter, as he always did, of an astronaut.

"A little."

"Briefly . . . tell me what you know."

Cutter took a moment to formulate his thoughts, worried that he had no idea how Mannheim would react. In fact, for all the years he had known Mannheim, he realized he knew practically nothing about the man. Beyond the physical aura of supreme fitness, Mannheim never showed a drop of emotion, nor did he ever let down his guard and offer even the tiniest glimpse into his own personal life. At the beginning of their six-year relationship, Mannheim's coolness had bugged Cutter. The plastic surgeon had invited him for dinner several times, but every invitation was politely turned down with a simple, "I have a conflict." Not "My kid's got a soccer game," or "My in-laws are coming over." So Cutter checked Mannheim out in the phone book: unlisted. He didn't even know his first name.

Who the hell is this guy I report to? Cutter had wondered. Then he had a clever idea. While on vacation in the Bahamas, Cutter used a credit card to telephone Mannheim in a phony panic about some minor aspect of the operation. True to form, Mannheim listened to Cutter's long-winded question, thought silently for almost a minute, then delivered a concise response.

When the credit card bill came, Cutter called the 800 number and said to the agent that he had no recollection of making any calls from Eleuthera to the States.

The operator promised to check into the number and in less than twenty-four hours he had his answer. The number he had used to call Mannheim was assigned to ABC Technology, which Cutter eventually determined was nothing more than a post office box. There was no way to know for certain who owned the phone.

Now Cutter was standing high above Pittsburgh on a little cement observation deck with a man about whom he knew absolutely nothing. Mannheim just stood there, watching the acrobatics of Cutter's facial muscles as he got ready to speak. "Two days ago . . . three now, it's past midnight . . . Stilwell was in for his surgery. Like I told you the other day on the phone, another patient,

Tory Welch, had been mis-scheduled for an initial appointment at the same time. Stilwell accidentally finds out she's in an adjoining examination room, takes it upon himself to lock himself in the room with her, and scares the crap out of her demanding to know why the hell she was there. Anyway, I controlled the situation, sent her on her way—she was just in for a routine mole examination—and the surgery on Stilwell went without a hitch. He thanked me, paid up in cash, and left. That's the last I heard of Stanley Stilwell until tonight." Cutter gave a little shrug with his shoulders to show he was done with his story.

Thinking about the enormous weight of the situation, Cutter expected Mannheim to pace around or put his hand to his mouth while he ruminated. But Mannheim just stood there, maintaining the same ramrod posture he always assumed. Finally he spoke, "Right now, Stilwell's alive, but hanging by a thread."

"How do you know that?" Cutter interrupted.

Mannheim ignored him. "Whatever was inserted into his neck destroyed his brain. He's going to go quickly so we don't have a lot of time. Let's go over our priorities. Above all, we must maintain the operation at all costs."

Immediately, Cutter reacted to the expression "at all costs." It sounded like something he had heard in a movie when an absolutely insane plan was about to be put in motion. "Look, I may be in danger. What the hell are you proposing to do?"

Mannheim paused again before speaking. "We'll get to that. Stilwell was a pro. I spent the last forty-five minutes going over his file. My hunch is he made no mistakes, which I believe works to our advantage. The police have already determined the car he was driving was stolen—"

"I heard that."

"—and one of the late reports I caught on the way over mentioned he was wearing gloves. Trust me. Those gloves he was wearing were no accident. With a little effort, Stanley Stilwell can become just some kook who paid a small fortune for new eyes and cheeks."

Cutter was stunned with the approach Mannheim was taking. "But the first thing the cops'll do is nose around, and when they find out he's bogus they'll want to know exactly who he was."

"And how long do you think that'll take?"

"How should I know?" Cutter blurted out.

"I figure less than twelve hours."

Cutter furrowed his brow and raked his fingers through his hair. "Okay, so time's running out. What are you going to do?"

"We'll get there. The police certainly are going to want to talk with you."

Cutter looked down at the ground. "I realize that. That's why I got out of the house so quickly."

"Soon as we're done, call them. Tell 'em you saw on the news what happened and you want to fill in whatever details you can. They'll want you to ID him. Don't overdo it."

Now Cutter was rubbing his forehead. "Oh my God," he exclaimed. He licked his lips nervously. "I don't like this."

Mannheim waited to be certain Cutter was done whining. "You're not supposed to *like* this. You knew the dangers when you signed on. You have to face a certain inescapable reality. Life cannot go back to the way it once was. There's no backing out now."

"I know! I know!" Cutter was getting irritated. He had extended his rubbing motions to include his entire face. "I don't want the notoriety, I mean, who wants to go to a plastic surgeon that gets involved with people like Stilwell? Privacy is what *my* kind of patients have come to—"

Mannheim held up his right hand in a signal to stop. When the surgeon quit rambling, Mannheim continued, "That's a discussion for next week. As I've told you, the operation is our primary concern. Now, what are you going to tell the police?"

Cutter went into a monotone, the same way he had as a child when asked to recite the Pledge of Allegiance for the zillionth time. "That Stilwell came to me for a new look, that he claimed to be a businessman with a hot young wife who wanted him to lose fifteen years, and that he demanded privacy—"

"—but that didn't strike you as terribly weird because many of your patients—"

"—are a little pathologic when it comes to privacy. Yeah, yeah, I remember the routine."

"Good. That's step one." Mannheim allowed Cutter to digest this for several seconds before continuing. "Step two. Stilwell's not been arrested . . . yet."

"How the hell do you know all this?" Cutter asked like a wide-eyed pre-schooler mesmerized by the vast body of knowledge his father possessed.

"Don't ask me how I do my job," Mannheim said flatly, not rudely or condescendingly, but with a strong showing of confidence. "Suffice it to say there wasn't time to arrest him. His condition was too critical. So, that brings us to when Stilwell dies."

"What if he doesn't?"

"We'll worry about that in about twelve hours. Let's think positive. He's *going* to die." Mannheim stopped speaking to let things sink in.

"Okay, okay. Stilwell dies like a good boy."

Over the years Mannheim had instilled a variety of emotions in Cutter. Mostly it was curiosity and frustration. Now it was resentment bordering on anger. What right did this cool, calm bastard have jerking him around like this? Cutter waited, tried to slow his breathing, and took to studying Mannheim's face. His eyes were so piercing that instinctively he knew never to engage in a staring contest with the man. His forehead had lines—everyone's did—but Mannheim's weren't nearly so deep as Cutter would expect for a man of his age. Cutter watched his cheeks to see if Mannheim was feeling the stress of the moment and clenching his jaw muscles. But Mannheim seemed totally at ease with himself. He looked to be under absolutely no strain at all.

Suddenly Cutter's anger got the best of him. "All right, Mannheim! You wanted this meeting, let's get on with it. Tell me what's going to happen when Stilwell dies so I can get the hell out of here, spill my guts to the cops, and get some godamn sleep before I operate in"—Cutter strained to see his watch—"seven and a half hours." When he was finished spewing his words he had a pang of doubt that maybe he had gone too far. After all, Mannheim, for all his unemotional bullshit, was more important to Cutter's life than he would care to admit.

A strong breeze blew over the observation deck and lifted up a wing of Cutter's perfectly styled hair. As the hours slipped past midnight the temperature had dropped, but neither man was cold. Mt. Washington was lonely at this hour. If a passing police cruiser had happened by, the officers would have slowed down to take a cursory look at the two men and continued on, because they were dressed too well to be any trouble for anybody.

When Mannheim finally spoke his voice was as calm as it had been throughout the conversation but there was an edge to his tone now. "After you talk with the police, they'll want to go on over to the Medical Center and ID him. He's somewhere in the ICU on a breathing machine. Plant yourself there and check him out. Talk with the docs. Drink some coffee. But you stay put, close enough to know when he checks out."

"And stand there doing what?"

"Nothing. You don't have to do anything. Just call me the moment he dies."

"Like hell I'm going to do that! I've got five cases scheduled. You have any idea what happens to someone in my profession when they get their name in the news for operating on some lowlife, then start canceling cases willy-nilly at the last minute?"

It didn't seem to bother Mannheim that Cutter was waving his arms about in spastic frustration. Mannheim wandered away from Cutter and stood at the railing on the other side of the deck, looking down the Ohio River.

Cutter watched Mannheim from a distance for several minutes and considered what was in store for him. Was he actually going to become part of the plan to keep the world from knowing who the hell Stanley Stilwell actually was? Maybe there was a simpler way out. Something so simple even the omniscient Mannheim hadn't considered. "Hey, Mannheim," Cutter called out.

Mannheim continued to gaze in a northwesterly direction down the Ohio, seemingly not caring what Cutter had to say.

Cutter was sick of the games. Begrudgingly he wandered over to the other side of the deck. "Hey, you ever consider the obvious?"

"You see those lights down there?" Mannheim asked when Cutter was close enough that he didn't have to raise his voice. "That's the state penitentiary. Took a tour of it once." Mannheim gave a little point of his index finger. They couldn't actually see the lights from the penitentiary where they stood on the observation deck, but Mannheim was pointing in the right direction and a little show and tell never hurt.

Cutter turned momentarily and saw lights every which way he looked. "So?"

"Pretty grim place." Mannheim watched Cutter swallow hard. "Every new inmate gets a tag, a prison nickname. Like Prettyboy." Mannheim raised his eyebrows.

Cutter swallowed again and licked his lips. "Wait a second . . . maybe there's a simple way out."

"Or maybe you're not lucky enough to end up there. Maybe you go off into the night and run as fast as your fancy Mercedes can take you." Mannheim cocked his head as though an important idea had just popped into it. "Oh, wait, not the Mercedes. That's what everyone'd be looking for. You'd better unload the Mercedes and get a Chevy or something. But you'd be smart to think of everything, because they won't stop coming after you. You might as well paint a target on your face." With that comment, Mannheim brought his index finger close to Cutter's face and outlined a circle in the air.

When Cutter finally spoke his voice seemed weak. "What about someone talking to the police? I mean there must be somebody in the department who you could . . . I don't know . . . trust to lose some papers?"

"No. The less people who know the better. Right now this is a nice, tight little operation. Each additional person who knows is a liability."

"It'll be one person. The paperwork gets lost and Stanley Stilwell is forgotten. Those lowlifes die every day. One creep knocking off another."

"Not every lowlife drops twenty grand to get a new face from a hot shot plastic surgeon."

Cutter let out a sigh. It was more like seventeen grand, but that wasn't the point. "Okay, Mannheim, you win. I clear my schedule for today and call you when he dies.

What makes you so goddamn sure Stilwell's going to go so fast?"

"They said on the news someone shoved an ice pick up into his brain, that it's practically a miracle his heart's still going, and that they've got him on so many fancy drugs the reporter couldn't remember whether it was four or fourteen. He's not long for this world."

"I hang out in the ICU until Stilwell dies," Cutter said, surprised with himself for agreeing to such a plan.

"Your excuse for canceling patients can be that with the trauma of what happened to you during the night, you thought it safest not to operate on anybody."

"I get it, Mannheim! I already told you, I'd handle it. Then what?"

"Call me the second he goes."

"Then what?"

"Then you go home and get some rest. Business as usual for Marshall Cutter, Inc." He didn't say "incorporated" but pronounced it "ink" for emphasis.

"What are you going to do?" Cutter asked quietly, almost to himself.

"You're officially dismissed from any further obligation."

"Wait a second. What about me? What if I get caught? Someone might put two and two together. Maybe the phone lines in the hospital are monitored. Who the hell knows?"

"No one will bat an eye. Stilwell was your patient. Who's gonna be suspicious if you show a little concern?"

"'But what if I do get caught?" Cutter repeated. "Then do you go to someone on the inside and make some kind of deal?" Cutter's voice was shrill.

"No," Mannheim said as calmly as he'd been throughout the entire conversation. "You get caught, you're on your own."

Cutter shot him a hard stare. He was grinding his

teeth, considering exactly how loyal he'd feel toward Mannheim if he got caught. Not very much, he decided.

"I know what you're thinking, Marshall. You get caught you spill your guts about the operation, cut some sort of a sweetheart deal. You try to turn against me you'll find out pretty quickly that I don't exist. And if I don't exist you've got nothing to hope for except an early parole.

"Right now I'm offering you in or out. You've known me long enough to be certain I'm not blowing smoke. You stay in, I'm with you. Get caught and I promise you I've left no trail. You jump town, you'll probably end up in a landfill someplace in Jersey."

"What about whoever got to Stilwell?"

The corners of Mannheim's mouth curled into a faint smile for only a moment. It was a good sign that Cutter had changed subjects. He had capitulated and was ready to proceed to the next problem. "I'm still working on that."

Cutter noticed that Mannheim didn't invoke an excuse like "Gimme a break. I only found out about this mess ninety minutes ago." As much as the mysterious Mannheim frustrated him and beat him down, Cutter was impressed with his swagger. "You think someone followed him into town?"

Mannheim shook his head back and forth a couple of times while he held out both hands, palm side up. "Don't know."

This disappointed Cutter, who had hoped for reassurance that whatever happened to Stilwell couldn't possibly happen to him. As horrible as the business of Stilwell was, the idea of being accosted physically and stabbed in the back of the neck was almost too much to bear. Cutter knew the answer even before he asked the next question, but he had to know what Mannheim thought. "You think

I need to be worried about my . . . physical safety? I mean, being the one who operated on him?"

Mannheim shook his head slowly. "Don't know." Business apparently being completed, Mannheim turned to walk off the little observatory and disappeared into the shadows of the night.

Chapter 8

The uniformed cop assigned to guard the patient in the ICU was out in the hallway pretending to be awake.

Three hours ago it had been decided to go no further with John Doe should his condition worsen. The official order to make him Do Not Resuscitate had not yet been written in the chart. Of course it had been discussed by the ICU staff, but without family members in attendance it would have necessitated a middle-of-the-night phone call to a magistrate for legal permission. Fortunately, an alternative was available. The ICU staff had the ability to pick and choose exactly which medical options and treatments would be offered should the need arise. The house officers affectionately referred to the options as the "code a la carte." In the event of a life-threatening event—or code—the physicians on hand would know in advance what level of medical care was appropriate. While not as all-inclusive as Do Not Resuscitate, it allowed the attending physician to decide just how far they would go with a hopelessly sick patient.

The responsibility for the decision had fallen to Merlin, who hadn't strayed much more than a dozen feet from his patient in the last seven hours. Once the decision had been made, Merlin sat down at the nursing station with the chart. He was accompanied by the nurse in charge of the ICU, a corpulent woman named Mary who reminded everyone of Miss Piggy, not only in her generous body proportions but in her self-absorbed manner. Mary was the type to shadow whichever doctor was in charge so that she was physically present the exact moment any decision of importance was made. Mary stood silently at her post next to Merlin, waiting to see what had been chosen from the code a la carte for John Doe.

"He's taking too many secrets with him," Merlin mumbled to no one in particular, but Mary assumed he was speaking to her.

"You did everything—more than everything—that you could," Mary responded.

Merlin wasn't in the mood for a middle-of-the-night ego massage. He absently watched two ICU nurses fuss over John Doe in bed space number four.

The last several hours had been spent in the Medical ICU on the eleventh floor of the Medical Center, a high-tech ward crammed with the sickest patients in Pittsburgh. There were no windows in the unit and no framed posters to take anyone's mind off the business that went on there.

Fourteen beds were arranged in a huge semi-circle around a central nursing station. Attached to the wall above the head of each bed was a sturdy shelf, two feet deep. A single piece of heavy monitoring equipment sat on the shelf, constantly displaying the patient's most important vital functions on a thirteen-inch screen. An EKG, with its sharp up and down complexes, represented each heartbeat in yellow. A continuous readout of the blood pressure—tightly packed sine waves—appeared in bright blue. And the respiratory pattern in white looked like an endless series of rolling hills that meandered slowly across the screen. A bundle of wires emerged from the base of the monitor and were connected to different parts of John Doe's body.

Tall IV stands were scattered about, sometimes three or more per bed space, their bags of intravenous fluids hanging penduously. Next to each bed were ventilators in a variety of shapes and sizes, creating their own special brand of white noise so that the ICU was never really quiet.

What first caught the eye of many visitors was the way the ICU dehumanized so many of its residents. Wires and tubes sprung from every part of the body in such a confusing array that patients were all too often rendered no more vital than androids. Many were in deep, painless comas and had no idea what was happening to them. Others were awake enough to feel the pain and whiled away the hours moaning, their eyes opened just enough to see an alien world that made no sense and terrified them. Some even thought that they had already died and floated off to heaven.

Then there was John Doe, still without an official name. On the little white card attached to the shelf above the head of his bed was written JOHN DOE in block letters. He remained flaccid and supine in the bed with only a sheet covering his naked torso. No matter how his body was violated with needles and tubes, he didn't move a muscle, his blood pressure not rising one millimeter of mercury. He was attached to a cardiac monitor, two IVs, one arterial line, a ventilator via an endotracheal tube in his mouth, a pulse oximetry monitor that made his finger glow, and a Foley catheter that crept out of his penis.

There was no sign anywhere to remind the staff about the code a la carte, but it was no secret. Each doctor assigned to the unit was made aware of it. The nurses and unit clerks overheard the conversations and knew what had been discussed. Even the guy who mopped the floor and dumped the trash seemed to take notice. *John Doe gets no more heart medication,* they would say to themselves, because there is something intensely dramatic about a patient who is so beyond a reasonable chance of survival that he is not to be aided should his body cry out for help. And it didn't seem to matter how many times one had seen a patient drift away, it had a certain grisly aspect that everyone remembered.

As the end was apparently drawing near, Merlin began to feel the tremendous effects of fatigue. He needed a shave and his oily hair was matted to his head. At times he felt chilled, only to become hot and sweaty ten minutes later. Everything that could be done for the patient had been. He stood quietly watching John Doe's chest rise and fall with the ventilator.

Just as Merlin was about to pull himself away from bed space number four so he could pour himself a cup of coffee, Marshall Cutter made his appearance in the ICU. He had come directly from the police station and was dressed in the same clothing he had been wearing all evening.

As a rule, plastic surgeons spend very little time in the ICU, so it took Cutter several seconds to get acclimated. The lighting was terrible. ICUs of the nineties seemed to prefer subdued lighting, hoping to create an atmosphere that kept the patients as calm and relaxed as possible.

There were always more staff in the unit than was apparent. With all the shadows, equipment, and floor-to-ceiling curtains that separated the beds, the ICU camouflaged people the way hidden pictures for children contained birds and bicycles disguised within the bark of a tree. The longer Cutter looked about, the more figures he spotted: a nurse in the corner, her scrubs indistinguishable from the curtain next to where she was standing; a respiratory tech practically in front of him, adjusting a ventilator, cloaked by a small grove of IV poles. Across the room he spotted a tiny collection of doctors and nurses huddled around bed space number four.

Nothing seemed to be happening. Everyone remained in precisely the same position, so that the little scene could have been something from Madame Tussaud's.

A feeling came over Cutter that he was not alone in the doorway. He turned his head quickly, thinking he was in someone's way. He came face-to-face with a uniformed policeman, not some fella from hospital security, but a city cop, rocking back and forth on his heels in a tempo that advertised how bored he was.

"Doctor," the officer said politely as though he were addressing a more senior officer in the squad room.

Cutter gave the officer a jittery smile, one that he wiped off his face as soon as it struck him he must look like some sort of idiot trying to play cool. He looked away. *Get the hell out of here while you can. Forget Mannheim and Stilwell. Look around like you don't see who you're looking for, then leave. Get in your car and drive a thousand miles. Go!* Cutter was getting himself totally worked up, his shoulders twitching away, his eyes darting back and forth with a look of guilt on his face anyone could have spotted across the room. It took every bit of reserve to remind himself he was in the ICU on official police business, not on a mission from a secretive bastard named Mannheim.

"Marshall!" called a voice from across the room. Cutter turned to see that Merlin had spotted him and was walking toward him. The surgeon had a serious look on his face. "I think we need to talk."

"There's a detective with me, should be up any minute," Cutter said quickly, just to let Merlin know whose side he was on. "They want me to ID him."

"I know, they called a little while ago."

"You and Tory okay?"

"Why don't you ID him, then we'll talk."

"How's he doing, anyway?" Cutter inquired as he and Merlin approached the bed space.

"He's waiting for the gates of hell to open up and suck him down." Merlin never talked like this, especially about one of his own patients, but he wanted to rattle Cutter.

It worked. Cutter stopped walking and turned sharply to look at Merlin. He didn't say a word but his tongue flicked away at his lower lip as if it had suddenly gone to parchment.

"So, what's his name?" Merlin asked, looking into Cutter's eyes, suspecting that he, too, might be holding secrets.

One glance at John Doe and Cutter uttered softly, "That's him. His name's Stilwell. Stanley Stilwell. There's no doubt. The detective will want to know."

"This time, your buddy almost killed us."

"Wait a second. What do you mean by 'my buddy'?" Cutter was on the defensive. "Let's clear a little something up before Detective Deringer arrives. I'm sorry I ever operated on that maniac. I should've thrown the bastard the hell out. End of story."

"What do you know about him? Was he under psychiatric care?"

"Look, all I know is that he came to me with a story about getting married to someone much younger, and he wanted privacy."

"I know all about plastic surgery patients and their privacy. But attacking another patient in the office is way beyond normal behavior."

"I realize that," Cutter said sincerely.

"I was a fool to let you get away with not calling the police."

Again, Cutter's tongue moistened his lower lip. "What difference would it have made?"

"You're talking to a surgeon. You know goddamn well you don't perform elective surgery on someone who is out of control. What forced you to operate?"

Just as Cutter was deciding on how to handle Merlin, Detective Deringer made his way across the ICU. He was wearing the same brown suit he had worn for his television interview, although it was now considerably more wrinkled.

"Sorry, Doc. I got beeped," he said to Cutter then dared a glance at Stilwell and cringed noticeably.

Grateful for the interruption, Cutter said, "Oh, Detective Deringer, you know Dr. Merlin." The detective gave a little nod of recognition. "It's him. It's Stilwell," Cutter said looking back at the patient's face as he spoke. "No question."

Detective Deringer said, "How is he, Doc?" This time he was speaking to Merlin, evidently using the term "Doc" generically for anyone with an MD.

"Unfortunately, he's stable."

The detective looked surprised. "Huh? So he's gonna make it?"

"His brain's been destroyed. CT shows massive damage to the brain stem. No reflexes. Nothing."

"So, what, he's never gonna wake up?" Detective Deringer said matter-of-factly.

Merlin wanted to rip into Cutter and place a big chunk of blame on him for what had happened. But instead he said, "No."

"Do me a favor. Keep us posted." The detective took

a single step closer to Stilwell's bed for a final look. "Jesus, what a mess." Then he turned to leave.

"Don't worry, Detective. It'll be a coroner's case when he goes."

Cutter was staring at Merlin.

Deringer directed his gaze not at Merlin, but at Marshall Cutter, studying his face with a puzzled glance as he digested what the surgeon had just said.

With the one piece of information Deringer had sought—a positive identification of the suspect and victim—he left as quickly as he had come.

When he had disappeared through the door, Merlin continued his conversation with Cutter. "Okay, Marshall, what else do you know about him?"

"Look, Merlin, I told you exactly what I told the cops. I thought the guy was crazy about privacy. What you didn't get to see was the remorse he demonstrated. He was as calm as any patient I've ever operated on ten minutes after you and Tory left."

"So you play the innocent bystander." Merlin was getting angry. "You've ID'ed him for the police, you've asked how Tory is, now get the hell out of here."

"I didn't come here for a lecture and I don't care for your tone of voice."

"You don't want to push me tonight, Marshall."

"Whether you like it or not, Stilwell is my patient, too. So how 'bout keeping your emotions to yourself and answer a few clinical questions for me."

Merlin was too angry to speak.

"How long can he go on like this?" Cutter pressed.

"Forever. It's easy putting him on the ventilator. Harder taking him off."

Oh my God! What if Stilwell didn't die as planned? What then? Suddenly Cutter got an acute case of the itchies. He was twitching all over, scratching here and there. What would Mannheim want him to do? Cutter looked around. He noted more staff than patients milling about. Would Mannheim expect something crazy? Cutter was working himself up into a lather. His hands found each other and he started wringing them together.

The only place he found where he could safely rest his eyes was on the monitor above Stilwell's bed. The yellow, blue, and white graphic readouts were hypnotic in their disappointing regularity. The yellow EKG complexes, coming at ninety-four times a minute, seemed textbook stable, and the respiratory pattern was more regular than the other patients' in the unit because Stilwell had absolutely no muscle function that could help or hinder the ventilator. *Wessssh-wesssssh.* One perfectly white rolling hill after another. *Wessssh-wesssssh.*

"You better be playing by the rules, Marshall, 'cause I'm not going away."

"Don't threaten me, Merlin." He spoke condescendingly, directing his attention to the monitors. Maybe he should call Mannheim and let him know Stilwell wasn't going to die as quickly as he thought. *Listen to me, Mannheim, you goddamn sonovabitch, I can't sit in the goddamn fucking ICU for the rest of my life. Why the hell don't you come up here and—*

He almost missed it. An aberrant EKG complex appeared on the screen that was twice as wide as the others. It looked to Cutter like a giant letter N, up-down-up. No mistaking it, but it was quickly moving from right to left and in several seconds would be gone.

Something was going wrong with Stilwell's heart. The electrical firing mechanism that produced a controlled pumping motion had gone absolutely haywire for one single solitary beat.

Cutter's own heart skipped a beat with anticipation. A brief smile crossed his lips and he got so excited he blurted out, "Take a look at the EKG!" Almost as soon as the words left his mouth he realized that his voice had a certain ecstatic quality that was terribly inappropriate for the situation.

Merlin glanced up at the monitor.

"There, you see it?" Cutter asked Merlin, trying to modulate his voice.

"So?" Merlin was unimpressed. "He's been throwing occasional PVCs all night. They don't seem to mean much. Never more than one on the screen at a time."

Before Merlin had finished what he was saying, a second PVC appeared on the screen, scrawled in bright yellow.

"There it goes again," Cutter said hurriedly.

"I see," Merlin said quietly. Then to Mary, who had taken up a position by the bedside, "You haven't changed any of his cardiac meds, have you?"

Mary hustled to check the various pumps sitting on a bedside table, each with a giant 50cc syringe loaded with one of a series of cardiac drugs that were maintaining Stilwell's heart. The pumps acted like giant vises, squeezing the syringes in such a precise manner that Stilwell received exact amounts of the medications. None was empty. "No, everything's fine," she announced crisply.

Two more PVCs floated across the screen like ducks at a shooting gallery.

"His BP's down, Merlin," Mary said in a strong voice as she read the blood pressure displayed numerically beneath the sine wave. "Had been one-ten over seventy. Now he's ninety over sixty."

Two more PVCs, then half a dozen regular complexes followed by three PVCs.

There was absolutely no change to the rolling hill respiratory pattern, which reflected the tireless effort of the mechanical ventilator, not Stanley Stilwell.

As the PVCs flowed, a crowd seemed to gather. Two more nurses and a respiratory therapist joined Merlin and Cutter in watching the EKG. Even the uniformed cop, realizing something was happening with the man he was supposed to be guarding, strolled over.

Now a string of PVCs appeared all at once. The electrocardiogram was zigzagging up and down in a series of interlocking Ns. With that came a shrill continuous alarm on the monitor, warning that Stilwell's heart rate was dangerously fast. "He's in ventricular tachycardia," Merlin observed, then stepped around toward Stilwell's head to press a button that silenced the alarm.

"What's that mean?" Cutter wanted to know, needing his suspicions confirmed.

No one answered.

A nurse said, "You want me to draw up some Lidocaine?"

"No," Merlin said grimly. "No cardiac meds."

Stanley Stilwell's face was turning ashen. His head was turned to one side, facing the ventilator to which he was attached by the plastic endotracheal tube. With his eyes closed and his chest moving up and down with the ventilator he appeared to be sleeping comfortably. But Stanley Stilwell's heart was not pumping in an organized fashion. The weaker, smaller atria, the sole purpose of which was to pump blood into the thicker-walled, powerful ventricles, were not participating.

The ventricles had taken over. An electrical mutiny was taking place. Instead of waiting patiently for the atria to contract first, pumping them full of blood, the ventricles were running the show and beating whenever the hell they felt like it. But without the atria to fill them to capacity, there was less blood being pumped out to the body and lungs.

As so often is the case, mutiny leads to chaos.

Stillwell's heart rate began to pick up speed. Now well above one hundred, the complexes began to change again. Instead of the jagged interconnected Ns, it became impossible to tell where one ended and the next one began.

"BP's dropping. Sixty over thirty. Heart rate is all over the place, Merlin," Mary said. An obvious tone of resignation had crept into her voice.

Marshall Cutter held one hand over his mouth. He stole a glance around the room and quickly focused on the nursing station. There were three phones available and no one was sitting near any of them. The closer the end came, the more acid churned in Cutter's stomach.

The yellow line was saw-toothed, meandering up and down like a drunk stumbling down the street. The blue line that represented Stilwell's blood pressure no longer continued in a perfect sine wave. The peaks and valleys had all but disappeared; the earthquake that was destroying the heart had flattened the peaks and filled in the valleys.

"V-fib," Merlin diagnosed. "This is it." Stilwell's heart had gone into ventricular fibrillation. If the doctors and nurses could peek inside his chest, the heart would appear to be quivering, not beating. Cardiac surgeons who had observed the human heart in ventricular fibrillation described it as a squirmy bag of worms. No blood was being pushed through the arteries of Stilwell's body.

"Blood pressure's not registering," Mary said, finding it difficult to watch a man dying and making no effort to help. It was comforting for her to do the play-by-play.

The drunken tracing of V-fib lasted less than a minute. The erratic yellow line softened and gradually became dead flat, no ripples, no tiny peaks or valleys. The ventilator chugged away, creating beautiful white rolling hills, but Stanley Stilwell's heart had stopped beating. He was dead.

Merlin looked at his wristwatch. "Four-oh-three," he said aloud to remind himself he would have to fill out the death certificate that required the exact time of death. "You can turn off the ventilator," Merlin instructed.

The respiratory therapist flipped a single switch, and Stanley Stilwell's chest stopped moving.

The monitor looked as if it, too, had died. No one bothered to look at it, but the complexes and sine waves and rolling hills were gone, replaced by three straight lines. Yellow. Blue. White.

Merlin was staring at Cutter, sizing him up, gauging what it would take to crack him open.

Call me the second he goes. Cutter could hear Mannheim's command as clearly in his head as if the man had been beside him whispering in his ear. He gave a quick glance over to the nursing station and declared, "Well, I guess I better shove off." For some reason he patted his chest nervously and cocked his head to one side, preparing to break away from the bedside. *Call me the second he goes.* Three phones were just sitting there.

Merlin bent over the body while he donned gloves to disconnect the endotracheal tube from the ventilator.

Cutter patted his chest some more and licked his lower lip. No one was anywhere near the nursing station. "Hey, Merlin?" Cutter finally said.

Merlin drew the white sheet over Stilwell's face. He stood to his full height. "Yeah?"

"The guy that got to Stilwell. You get any sort of a look at him?"

Merlin shook his head. "Big guy, 'bout your size. In good shape. Moved through the woods very quietly, but I didn't see his face. He was wearing a mask that covered his entire head. I couldn't even see his hair."

"He say anything?"

"A coarse whisper." Merlin watched Cutter moisten his lower lip and shrug his shoulder involuntarily. "What's got you twitching?"

Cutter swallowed while he collected his thoughts. "You think I know more than I do. What if whoever got Stilwell thinks I was involved with him?"

"You better do some serious thinking, Marshall."

Cutter's hand went to scratch the back of his neck. "Just stabbed him in the neck and bolted, huh?"

"Pithed him, like high school biology, only it wasn't a frog. You shoulda seen his arms and legs. Really hard to watch."

"My God."

"This wasn't a first-timer getting lucky with a needle. Come to think of it, I'd have to say the guy used surgical precision."

"Surgical precision?" Cutter repeated.

"For all I know he could have been a doctor." Merlin turned and walked away.

The three-ring chart with JOHN DOE written on the side was sitting right in front of Marshall Cutter when he sat down at the nursing station. At first he didn't see it. His eyes were everywhere around the room except the nursing station. For the moment he was alone. He grabbed the phone, punched nine to get an outside line, then scanned the room a second time.

All safe.

With seven quick jabs of his index finger he dialed Mannheim's cell phone.

Ring.

He noticed John Doe's chart. It was right there, opened up like a menu before him, and he couldn't help but notice his name right there on the first page in the second paragraph. The little hairs on the back of his neck stood up.

Ring.

He began reading silently. "No prior medical history is available. The patient underwent plastic surgery on the face, eyes, and neck three days prior to admission by Dr. Marshall Cutter." *That's not so bad.*

Before Cutter could read another word a voice next to him began to speak. "Hello, Operator, would you please get me the coroner's office? There's a special number you need to use at night." Merlin was sitting not three feet away, looking across the room at bed space four, making a telephone call of his own. "I'll hold on, thanks."

Ring.

A wave of panic tore at Cutter's stomach. His heart rate soared, thumping wildly in his chest so that it became a strain just to breathe quietly.

"Yes." For a moment Cutter didn't realize Mannheim had picked up the phone and was speaking to him. The receiver was to his ear, but he sat there, frozen with fear that what he was about to do was so evil and so obvious, Merlin would be able to see it on his face. "Yes!" This time Mannheim's voice grew louder.

"Oh, yes," Cutter said and swallowed loud enough to make a gulping noise that Merlin heard. "Hi, Carol, Marshall here," he said, using his voice-mail tone as though leaving a message for someone.

"Well?" Mannheim said into the phone.

Again Cutter didn't hear him. He was listening to Merlin say in a separate conversation, "Hello. This is Dr. Jack Merlin, Pittsburgh University Medical Center. I'm requesting pickup of a body for the coroner."

"Cutter? Can you talk?"

Merlin had stopped speaking. He turned his head and

looked over at Cutter, who was slack-jawed, staring back at him with a peculiar expression on his face.

Jerking his head around so his eyes were trained on the chart, Cutter cleared his thoughts. "Just wanted to let you know to cancel my schedule for tomorrow. Had a terrible night. Talk to you later."

"If he's dead say, 'I'll call you at noon,'" Mannheim instructed over Cutter's meaningless words.

Now Merlin was speaking. "Uh, Stanley Stilwell. S-T-I-L-W-E-L-L. Approximate age fifty-five. Stabbed in the brainstem by an unknown . . . That's right, saw the whole thing. Absolutely horrible. Julian can call me in the morning if he needs any information."

When Merlin stopped talking and started nodding his head as though he was being given some instructions, Cutter said, "Call you at noon," and quickly hung up the phone, practically dropping it in the receiver as though it was burning his hand.

"No," Merlin said, now smiling. "The cause of death is not in question. Don't you dare call Julian at this hour. We should have the chart copied and everything in order in about, say, ninety minutes. Thanks." Merlin hung up the phone and once again looked over at Cutter.

Chapter 9

Clyde Messingeiser cringed every time someone actually made the effort to pronounce his last name. Why the hell hadn't they just changed it on Ellis Island when his great-grandfather came over from the old country? Fortunately, sometime in the fourth grade the kids started calling him Goose and it stuck.

Goose was twenty-three years old, still trying to get his degree from City College of Allegheny County, working at night in the morgue at the Medical Center doing custodial work and signing in the bodies whenever they arrived. He was death-row skinny, proudly sporting a stringy excuse for a goatee. No matter what time of the night someone walked into the morgue, he was firmly planted in a small secretary's chair, as backward as the baseball cap on his head, reading from a biology textbook. He favored surfer talk and would regale anyone who would listen with ridiculous comments like, "Hey, dude, just checking out the xylem and phloem," murdering the pronunciation of any word not already in his vocabulary.

When the pretty nurse from the ICU pushed the door open twenty-seven minutes before five a.m., she wasn't surprised to see Goose sitting between the two empty

stainless steel autopsy tables on his little chair in a room
that was otherwise empty. He was twisting himself back
and forth with his feet, staring into his textbook.

"Hi, Goose," she said politely, squinting her eyes in
the harsh lighting of the morgue. The pretty nurse
smelled great, the fragrance of her perfume wafting its
way over to Goose almost as quickly as her voice.

Goose looked up and smiled. "Hey, Angela, what
gives?" Then he sniffed in the wonderful smell of Angela
from the ICU.

Angela was using one foot to hold the door as she
maneuvered the seven-foot-long stretcher carrying the
body of Stanley Stilwell. A white sheet neatly covered
his naked body. Wearing rubber gloves, she had spent
the last twenty minutes disconnecting every lead and
tube from his body. On the elevator ride down to the
basement she'd produced a small sample bottle of Estée
Lauder she kept in the back pocket of her scrubs for just
such an occasion. The stench of the morgue was horrible
and the lingering reek of death in her nose made her
gag long after she'd ascended back to the world of the
barely living. Therefore, she and the other nurses had
devised a slick little way of fooling themselves. A couple
of drops of their favorite cologne dabbed under their
noses was able to overwhelm their senses and make a
trip to the morgue slightly less obnoxious.

As Angela worked the stretcher between the two autopsy tables she said, "This is Stanley Stilwell. Merlin
said to tell you the coroner's office is on the way."

Goose was still breathing in Angela, which was the
one complication of the perfume-under-the-nose trick.
For the past six months he thought the nurses were
spritzing themselves with tantalizing scents just to turn
him on. The moment the erotic pheromones hit his olfac-
tory nerve he could hardly control himself. "Hey, An-

gela, you know Rusted Root? They're coming to Star Lake in—"

"Oh, Goose, I'm sorry," Angela said, not realizing she hadn't waited to hear when the concert was being held. "I can't. But thanks." After a fleeting pause she continued with, "Anyway, Merlin said you should get him ready."

Goose stood up and walked over to the covered body. He wanted to smell Angela a little closer. "Boy, you really smell good, Angela."

"Goose! C'mon, I have work to do, and you have to get him ready. They'll be here soon."

Goose looked at his watch. "Does Olsen know he's here?" he asked, finally getting back on track. He was referring to Jonathan Olsen, the chairman of pathology who ruled these domains as his private fiefdom. Goose knew only too well that Olsen didn't like it when things went on in his morgue without knowing about them.

"All I know is that he was murdered. Merlin said something about him getting pithed. You know what that is?"

Goose shook his head.

Angela shrugged. "Anyway, he's the one that's been on the news. Merlin said it's definitely a coroner's case."

"We don't get too many of these. I'd better call Olsen."

Angela was already walking over toward the door. "If there's any problem, just tell him to call Merlin. I'll see you, Goose."

"Bye, Angela," he said sadly. He took a few more whiffs of her lingering Estée Lauder, then picked up the phone. A few moments later the groggy voice of Jonathan Olsen filled his brain and erased the wonderful memory of Angela. "Uh, Dr. Olsen, this is Goo—uh, Clyde. Sorry to bother you but the ICU just sent down a body. . . . Oh, sorry, I didn't know Merlin called you. . . . I'll get him ready. I know where the body bags are. Don't worry. And Dr. Olsen, next time I'll call Merlin before I bother you again. Good night.''

For some reason Goose decided to get a look at the body after he hung up the phone. He figured he'd seen it all in the morgue, so he lifted up the white sheet and got an eyeful. The white gauze that had been taped over the area in front of Stilwell's right ear had become dislodged, presenting Goose with one of the most gruesome faces he had ever seen. He just stood there, holding the white sheet in one hand, breathing in noisily through his mouth, disgusted with the fact that he was going to have to wrestle the body into the bag all by himself.

The white Ford Econoline van pulled up to the Emergency Room entrance of the Medical Center and parked off to one side so as not to block the ambulances from coming and going. The driver was wearing blue pants and a white shirt under a dark blue windbreaker that said CORONER on the back in block yellow letters. He stepped out of the van to finish his cigarette. His black name tag said CRISNATOWSKI, and he was anything but in a rush. With one foot on the rear bumper of the big white van, he sucked down a Marlboro while he watched a crew that had arrived just minutes before unload someone from the back of an ambulance that still had the flashing red lights going.

The early morning air was deliciously cool. Once he'd enjoyed the final drag he dropped the butt on the driveway and used his black shoe to grind it out. He opened both back doors of the van and grabbed hold of the stretcher that was stowed in the back.

The stretcher was one of those ambulance-type contraptions with collapsible legs that were supposed to open up as the stretcher was rolled out of the vehicle. But this stretcher was new, and as he pulled it out of the van the legs didn't open automatically. Suddenly he was having a terrible time holding one end of it in the air with his left hand while balancing the other end on the back of the van. His right hand fiddled roughly with the lever that was supposed to drop the legs to the ground. Finally he gave up on the lever and gave it a good hard yank so that the stretcher suddenly pulled free of the van, the legs still tightly folded beneath it, and banged noisily to the cement driveway.

Crisnatowski would have liked to take a breather and have another cigarette, but he looked at his watch and figured he'd better get a move on. He squatted down and worked the lever again, discovering how simple it was to lift it first, then slide it. At last he was able to raise the stretcher. He pulled at his nylon windbreaker so that it wouldn't bunch up behind his neck, adjusted the seat belt–like straps that would keep the body from accidentally falling off, and headed around the parked ambulance on his way to the sliding glass doors of the Emergency Room.

The moment he crossed the threshold into the large, empty waiting room of the emergency department, he was greeted by a large black man in a hospital security uniform who politely inquired where he was going.

Crisnatowski stopped pushing the stretcher and adjusted one of the seat belts that really didn't need straightening. "To the morgue. Picking up a body," he said, then turned in an exaggerated way so that his back faced the security officer.

"Oh, coroner's. You want the silver elevators down on the left. Morgue's in the basement."

"I know," Crisnatowski said, sounding indignant as if he didn't need some third-shift security officer to tell him where the elevators were. As he went by the officer he shook his head back and forth, giving the officer a little attitude just in case he missed the putdown in his choice of tone.

While he waited for the silver elevators, Crisnatowski looked back down the hallway. The security guy was already sitting down in one of the waiting room chairs, his clumsy legs thrust out as if he was exhausted from another night pointing out the elevators to people who knew goddamn well where they were.

He rode the elevator down alone. When he hit the basement he was still thinking about the goof in the uniform who spent eight hours a night pretending to be a real cop. He pushed the stretcher off to the left and went about fifty yards before making a ninety-degree turn and heading down a second empty hallway. For two minutes he proceeded down one hall then another, as familiar with the route as if it was the second or third time he'd done it since midnight. Finally he came to the heavy metal door marked MORGUE and opened it, leaving the stretcher in the hallway.

"Coroner's office," Crisnatowski said to the skinny kid in the little chair with his nose in a book.

"Oh, yeah," Goose said. "Got him ready." For a second, Goose admired his handiwork on the stretcher. Stanley Stilwell was neatly stowed in a dark blue body bag, zipped up nice and tight so that no skin or flesh was visible.

"Crisnatowski. How ya doing? That Stilwell?"

"Yep." Then, remembering his manners, he said, "Goose. Call me Goose. They say he was murdered."

Crisnatowski reached for the door and re-opened it so that he could pull his stretcher inside. "They're still going on about it on the news."

"Oh yeah?" Goose said, hopping up to help line the two stretchers side by side.

"He got stabbed in the neck with an ice pick or something," Crisnatowski mentioned casually as he moved next to what appeared to be Stilwell's head by the shape of the body bag.

"Pithed," Goose was saying as he positioned himself at the feet.

"Huh?"

"It's a medical term or something."

"I ain't the coroner. I drive." Crisnatowski shrugged his shoulders. "They say that doctor—what's his name, Merlin, I think?—he was right there. Saw the whole thing." He nodded his head three times, counting down to lift off. With a pair of grunts, the body bag containing Stanley Stilwell was moved to the coroner's stretcher.

"Man, that must've been something." Goose held the door.

Crisnatowski reached inside his windbreaker and found a pen. Holding it aloft in his right hand he pretended to be scribbling in the air so Goose would notice. "So between you'n me, it takes the coroner to tell us this mug was murdered?"

Goose chuckled. "Over there," he directed, motioning with his head to a small desk with a clipboard containing the necessary paperwork. As Crisnatowski bent over the desk and signed the forms, Goose was commenting, "You take one look at this guy and there's no doubt he got it but good."

"Can't wait to get him back to the office and get a gander at him."

Goose helped while Crisnatowski pushed the stretcher out and began the circuitous trip back toward the silver elevators.

The security guard didn't appear to have moved an

inch by the time Crisnatowski headed out the sliding glass doors of the emergency room. A young woman had appeared, clutching a tiny baby who was heavily wrapped in blankets. She was waiting by the empty registration desk, holding the baby so tightly it was the picture of desperation.

Crisnatowski scowled and said to the guard, "If somebody's waiting to mug me in the parking lot will you still be awake?" The guard didn't budge. "Hey, pal, if you're not going to help me, at least see what you can do for her," Crisnatowski said, his words stinging the guard enough that he got up out of his chair, straightened his thick black belt, and shuffled over to the woman with the baby.

Again Crisnatowski shook his head as he wheeled Stilwell out to the white Ford Econoline. The ambulance was still waiting. It was dark outside and a quick glance around didn't reveal anyone in the vicinity. He opened both of the back doors, then took his position at one end of the stretcher. Pushing steadily, he directed the front end into the back of the Ford.

This time the design features of the stretcher worked without a hitch. As the legs of the stretcher hit the rear bumper they began to collapse, so that by the time Crisnatowski had worked all of Stanley Stilwell inside, the stretcher was all of ten inches tall, the wheels tucked up neatly underneath.

The two-man ambulance crew rolled through the sliding glass doors, loaded their empty stretcher into the back of their ambulance, watched Crisnatowski working alone for several seconds, and drove off.

Crisnatowski slammed the back doors of the van, took one final look around, then slipped into the driver's seat. As he drove away from the Medical Center, his right hand was shaking a pack of Marlboros up and down to coax a cigarette out. He rolled down the window, lit up his smoke, and turned right onto Fifth Avenue.

"Hey, Dr. Merlin," Goose said when he looked up from the world of biology. "Lemma ask you. What kind of a grade do you have to pull in Bio to get into med school?"

Merlin smiled. "I was lucky to get an A." He was holding a sheaf of papers about an inch thick and a big manila envelope filled with copies of the CT scan for the coroner. "Here're the records and films." He looked around. "Hey, where is he?"

"Stilwell? They already came for him."

"Oh, shit," Merlin said. "Didn't Angela say anything about not letting him go 'til I got everything copied?"

Goose stroked his goatee contemplatively, not wondering whether Angela actually said anything about waiting for the records, but pondering what the hell Olsen was going to do to him. "Gee, I don't think so. I woulda remembered that."

"No problem. Just call a cab and send all this down." Merlin snatched his wallet from his back pocket and pulled out a twenty. "Here, use this."

"Thanks. You probably saved my ass."

The door to the morgue opened and a man wearing a white shirt with a gold badge over the left breast and dark blue pants stepped inside. "Good morning."

"Hey," Goose said by way of greeting.

"Sorry it took so long. Had a flat." He looked around the room, noticing the twin stainless steel autopsy tables and the stretcher. All were empty. "You got everything ready?"

"You're late, pal. One of your buddies has come and gone." Goose smiled.

"Give me a goddamn break. You know what I been

through?" the man said. "Lemma use your phone," he continued and, not waiting for an answer, headed over to the little desk.

Merlin and Goose stood silently watching the man make his call.

"Hey, this is Koenig," the man said into the receiver. He was raising his voice, as if he were ready to chew someone out. "I'm over here at the Medical Center, and they say someone else made the pickup. What the fuck is going on? Why the hell didn't you call me and tell me someone else was making the pickup. . . . Huh? . . . You sure? . . . All of 'em, huh? . . . Yeah, goodbye."

Merlin's mouth went dry. For a long beat, all three of them were silent. Merlin and Goose had heard enough from their end of the conversation to know there was trouble.

The man with the white shirt and gold badge pulled out his picture ID and flashed it right in Goose's face. "Mark Koenig. Coroner's office. *Think* before you speak. What the hell did you do with the body of . . ." He pulled a sheet of paper from his shirt pocket, unfolded it, and read from it. "Stanley Stilwell?"

Goose's voice trembled as he spoke. "Someone from the coroner's office picked it up.

"Son, you screwed up big time. Where the goddamn hell is the paperwork?"

Goose looked back and forth between Koenig and Merlin, trying to find an ally. "You gotta believe me. The guy had on a jacket that said 'Coroner' on the back." Goose reached around to his own back and drew an imaginary line across it with his thumb.

"Where's the paperwork he signed?" Merlin asked softly.

"It's right on the desk. I swear, his name was some

long Polish thing. He only said it once. Critonski or something."

Koenig was still over at the desk, holding the clipboard as he read aloud from it. "Lawrence Cris-na-tow-ski. Never heard of him. Son, I wouldn't want to be you."

"I wouldn't do anything wrong. I *didn't* do anything. You guys gotta believe me."

"What happened that made you late?" Merlin asked Koenig.

"Like I said, I had to change a friggin' tire." Koenig looked back down at his hands and evidently spotted some grease because he worked his fingers against the fleshy part at the base of the thumb, lending some credibility to his story. "All three vans had flats at the same time."

Merlin flashed back to the woods. Why the hell had the masked man picked up Stilwell's body after inflicting a lethal injury to his brain? In an instant it seemed obvious who had stolen the body. Merlin was moving quickly over to the desk. As he grabbed the phone, Goose said, "Hospital security is four-four-five-one."

Instead Merlin punched just one button. "Operator," he said when the call went through, "this is an emergency. Get me the Pittsburgh Police."

Chapter 10

Detective Daniel Deringer was pissed off. He and Merlin were squeezed shoulder-to-shoulder into a stingy skimp of space so they could both get a view of the master video console in the security office of the Medical Center. Merlin couldn't decide whether the detective's foul temper was because an amateur was inserting himself squarely in the middle of the investigation, or because Stanley Stilwell's body had disappeared.

In any case, Deringer turned his head in Merlin's direction and frowned. His brown suit looked a good bit more rumpled than it had in the ICU. Already he had interviewed the bona fide driver from the coroner's office and the young man named Goose. There had been no revelations, not a piece of information that Merlin hadn't described for him on the telephone. The driver described the flat tire he'd changed and the now obvious sabotage that had knocked the other two vans out of commission. Once he'd been sent on his way, all attention turned to Goose, who sat backward in his favorite chair, so upset at the prospect of losing his job he could hardly form a coherent sentence. With generous prompting from Merlin, he described Crisnatowski as being in his late forties, wearing a uniform that *looked* like the uniform the drivers from the coroner's office wore, and having very long hair that he played with when he talked. Goose also noted Crisnatowski didn't know what the word "pithed" meant.

Now Deringer and Merlin were looking like Chang and Eng and could smell each other's body odor after a night that had gone on too long. Sitting in front of them was Chief of Security for the Medical Center, a perennially tired man everyone called Speed. Speed looked quite comfy in his big padded chair, writing out little white labels for half a dozen black video cassettes stacked up in front of him: EMERGENCY ROOM ENTRANCE, SILVER ELEVATOR #1, SILVER ELEVATOR #2, ADMISSIONS, MAIN ENTRANCE, and REGISTRATION. His stated age was fifty-five, but if he'd lied and added ten years no one would have been surprised. No matter what time of day, Speed worked in slow motion and drank coffee, sipping it out of a giant ceramic mug. Never mind that a body had been stolen right out of the morgue, every label had to be perfect before he would consider allowing his tapes to be viewed.

The little security office was dark. Typewritten notices were hung on every inch of wall space and might as well have been plastered down permanently as wallpaper. There were no windows, just the gargantuan video console brimming with monitors, twelve in all, three rows of four. Twenty-seven cameras were scattered about the Medical Center. The image on most of the monitors shifted every few seconds from one camera's view to another. Only six of the surveillance cameras were attached to videotape machines, and that was the reason Merlin and Deringer wedged themselves between Speed and the wall.

With Speed setting his eyes on the complicated video playback machine and spending some quality time with his coffee, Deringer reached over him for the phone. After he dialed he pulled the curly wire taut over Speed's shoulder. "Hey, Deringer here—got something for ya. That car that's up in the Fox Chapel garage needs printing. . . . No, right away. We need the identity of the driver. . . . Yeah, I know it was stolen. Look, I need London out of bed now and tell her I want her hot breath on every inch of that car," he said, then hung up the phone just as Speed hit the play button. A black-and-white image of the area just outside the sliding glass doors of the ER appeared on one of the monitors. From Merlin's view it looked like a still photograph, and he wondered if Speed had the tape on pause. But then he realized there were no people or cars driving by to bring the little scene to life. All they were studying was a black-and-white picture of the driveway and a cement wall thirty yards away.

"We think the body was taken about five a.m.," Merlin said.

"Okay, five a.m.," the security officer repeated in the kind of slow drawl one's grandfather might use when talking you into a checkers game. "Let's fast-forward." He pressed a button and sat back, holding his coffee in front of his chest with both hands. For the next thirty seconds the image on the screen remained the same, a still life of blacktop and concrete. Suddenly an ambulance materialized as if by magic right in front of the camera. *Poof!*

Speed reached out and slowed the tape, not to a real-time image, but a speed approximately three times normal so that the two drivers unloading the patient looked like something on an old turn-of-the-century film. The red flashing lights on top of the ambulance were blinking on and off so rapidly they looked like strobes. In an instant the two drivers had disappeared into the ER, walking underneath the camera as they disappeared from view.

Now the camera captured the waiting ambulance. The only evidence that the videotape was still playing was the pulsating light. Before anyone in the room could react, a second empty stretcher appeared on camera, coming around the back of the ambulance. It was being pushed by a man wearing a dark-colored windbreaker and pants. The man with the stretcher quickly slipped under the view of the camera.

"Hold it," Merlin exclaimed. "That's gotta be him."

Speed didn't say a word. He stopped the videotape and rewound it for several seconds. When he hit the play button, the tape resumed at normal speed. The image of the man pushing the stretcher was visible on the monitor for a total of about seven seconds. He had one hand on either side of the stretcher with his head bent down as if he were inspecting something on the empty stretcher.

"Christ, we can't see his face. Run it again . . . slowly," Deringer ordered.

This time when the video clip began, it was running in slow motion and took almost thirty seconds to view. Merlin and Deringer peered closely over Speed's shoulder so that he had to lean up on his elbows to keep from being mauled. The three of them focused on the man's face.

"Nothing!" Merlin said. "He's got dark hair and it's long. That's it."

"Hold your horses. Let's see what we've got of him coming out," Speed said unemotionally as he sped up the tape. Thirty seconds went by. A young-looking couple clutching a blanket appeared on the monitor with the ambulance still serving as a backdrop. They shot into the ER.

Less than twenty seconds later the man pushing the stretcher reappeared.

Once again, Speed repeated the process. He worked the buttons and turned a dial, rewinding the film and playing it at normal speed. This time the video image of the man pushing the stretcher lasted only five seconds. Apparently he was anxious to get back to his waiting vehicle, which Merlin, Deringer, and Speed had yet to see. His stretcher bulged with a body bag, dark in color, cinched tight with two substantial straps, one at either end. Unfortunately the camera only captured the back of his head and the word CORONER printed in bold block letters on his windbreaker.

When he disappeared from view the film was once again sped up until the ambulance crew was seen pushing their empty stretcher back outside. In several seconds they had it loaded into the back of the ambulance, stood for a moment watching something across the driveway, then drove away.

That's when they got their first look at it. With their view of the driveway unencumbered by the ambulance, Merlin, Deringer, and Speed spotted a large white Ford Econoline van. The vehicle was in profile. There was no writing of any kind on the side panel. Evidently, Crisnatowski had just closed the back doors because he was coming around from the rear of the vehicle, crossing right in front of the camera, his head turned just so, preventing the camera from catching a glimpse of his facial features. He seemed unhurried as he walked—the word "strolled" came to Merlin's mind—to the driver's side door.

"When he drives away watch for his license," Merlin said.

"See if you can slow it down just a bit," Deringer directed.

Speed twisted a knob on the console and the action slowed down. It took almost fifteen seconds for the man to get in the car and close the door.

A new image appeared on the screen. "Goddamn, what is *that* thing?" Deringer grumbled at the sight of something big standing right in front of the camera.

"That's one of the security officers," Speed said.

A huge man had walked out of the emergency room and was now planted right in front of the camera, hands on hips. Amazingly, he appeared to be watching Crisnatowski.

"That's Big John," Merlin announced. "He's a good guy."

"What the hell's he doing out there?" Deringer demanded.

Big John stood in front of the surveillance camera, blocking two thirds of the Ford van. Merlin, Deringer, and Speed watched as the vehicle slowly pulled away from the ER. As the Ford moved, so did Big John, turning his body and taking one or two steps as he tracked the path of the vehicle.

"Shit!" Deringer exploded. "That idiot got in the way."

Big John remained on camera for several seconds after the Ford had disappeared.

"Get that asshole down here, right away," Deringer barked.

While Speed was on the phone to the paging operator, he slipped the cassette labeled SILVER ELEVATOR #1 into the playback machine. It didn't take long to find the moment when Crisnatowski rolled the empty stretcher onto the elevator.

"Here he is," Merlin piped up expectantly as the first image appeared on the monitor.

Once again Crisnatowski's head was down, looking at

the empty stretcher. He remained in his neck-flexed position for the short ride. Not once did he look up. Not one feature of his face made it onto the video. It didn't need to be said, but Crisnatowski was obviously too smart to look up at a surveillance camera.

During the wait for Speed to find the segment where Crisnatowski re-boarded the elevator with the body bag, the only one to break the silence was Deringer. "You know what? We're wasting our time. This guy's obviously a pro."

When Speed located Crisnatowski for the fourth and what would be the final time once all the video was later studied in detail, the top of Crisnatowski's head was aimed perfectly at the camera. His face was not.

"Forget it," Deringer announced as he and Merlin were side-stepping their way out from behind the video console. "C'mon outside, I gotta grab a smoke." Then to Speed he added, "Send Big John outside," making it obvious that the chief of hospital security was nothing more than that, and wasn't invited outside to watch Deringer enjoying a cigarette.

"No way is this gonna get solved," Deringer was saying to Merlin as he rubbed the fatigue from his eyes. "No fucking way." The two were standing just outside the ER sliding doors. It hadn't been obvious how stale the air was in the tiny security office until they got a breath of what the morning air had to offer. "What do you think?" He eyed Merlin.

"Well, I assume that whoever killed Stilwell was also the one to steal his body."

"Oh, yeah? Lemme write that down." Deringer was spewing mock surprise.

"And whoever pulled this stunt off was phenomenally

well organized. This was no two-bit operation. The place
I'd start is with Cutter."

Deringer put up his hands as if he was directing traffic
to stop. "Okay, this is where *I* start. Enough already.
Listen up, pal. Apparently I never heard about you and
Miss Welch before, but everyone in the squad room
knew you. The two of you have reputations that pre-
cede you."

"I take it you mean that Tory and I—"

"Yeah, yeah, you got your names in the paper a couple
of times for solving some murders. Christ, I heard all
about it tonight. This cops and robbers stuff is sorta like
a hobby to you. Like collecting stamps or fishing."

Merlin bristled with his attitude. "You're scared to
death a couple of amateurs might show you up."

"I ain't scared a nothing. And I didn't say nothing in
there to embarrass you when you wanted to watch the
surveillance videos. But enough's enough. You know
what you are? A funsie. Detective work sounds *fun,* so
you want in. Right? I don't need a sidekick." Deringer
pulled a folded piece of paper from the inside pocket of
his jacket. "Okay, James Bond," he said sarcastically before reading from the piece of paper. "Stanley Stilwell.
One twenty-one Front Street, Pittsburgh. Zip, one-three-
two-two-two."

"Fake zip code," Merlin observed matter-of-factly,
knowing full well no Pittsburgh zip code started with 13.

"Oooo, you're sharp," Deringer said flippantly. "Op-
portunities are disappearing. And before you ask, there's
no Stanley Stilwell in the phone book."

"What about his insurance information?"

"Look, I don't have time for this. Everything about
the guy's fake. And before you ask, he listed himself as
a businessman, he had no previous medical problems,
and of course he was self-referred. Cutter says he was

paid exactly seventeen thousand dollars—in cash—and that's all he knows. The end."

"So," Merlin began, ignoring the putdown and beginning a summary of what they knew of Stilwell, "he goes berserk when he finds out Tory is in the office at the same time he's having his surgery. Then he tracks down Tory and threatens to kill us if we don't tell him what we knew about him, which of course was nothing. Before we know it, a masked man comes out of the night, stabs Stilwell in the back of the neck, and tries to take the body with him until I get loose. Then he drops the body and disappears. Stilwell dies and the body is neatly stolen. Of course we haven't the foggiest idea who Stilwell was in the first place. And that's the end?"

"That's it. Nothing. Nada. Zilch."

"It's the beginning. No operation is so tight it doesn't make mistakes."

Deringer heard the rumble of the sliding doors behind him and turned to recognize Big John from his video performance.

"Hey, chief said you wanted to ask me something." The short sleeves of Big John's uniform hugged his biceps like tourniquets. His shiny black head reflected the spotlights that illuminated the ER entrance. Big John had a scowl on his face as if he anticipated what might be coming. "Merlin," he said with a nod.

"John, this is Detective Deringer." The police officer offered no greeting of any kind. "Did Speed tell you what this is about?"

"I know what it's about."

"You know anything that might be helpful?"

"I talked with him."

"You talked with him?" Merlin said incredulously.

"Yeah . . . 'bout five . . . I was on duty in the ER when this guy with long hair"—Big John pretended to play with long hair he did not have—"came through those doors pushing a stretcher."

"Why'd you talk with him?" Deringer asked.

"That hour I pretty much check out everything coming in," he said.

Suddenly, Merlin cut in with, "He ask you for directions?"

"Un-unh. Matter of fact, he got annoyed when I asked if he knew how to get down there."

"So," Merlin said to Deringer, "he knew his way around the hospital."

"And the way to the morgue isn't obvious," Big John added. "One more thing, when he was coming back through the ER, say ten, fifteen minutes later, I was busy with something and he made a rude comment about not helping him. *Helping* him! Shit! That's his job, not mine." Big John lost his train of thought and had to stop for a second and collect himself. "So, anyway, soon as I was done with what I was doing I came out here to see. You know, being a nice guy and all that." He did not smile. "Right over there. He loaded the stretcher into a big white van. Ford, I think. That's all."

"Try to keep up. We *know* about the van." Deringer sounded irritated. "What the hell'd he look like?"

"Hey, don't be hitting me with that. I didn't fuck up, okay? You want me to help? Ask me nice, but lay off the try-to-keep-up bullshit." Big John crossed his huge arms across his chest and shut his mouth.

"All right, forget it. Whaddya know?" Deringer had gotten out a little pad of paper and was poised with a ballpoint pen.

"Okay," Big John said and hiked his belt up. "This guy pushing the stretcher was six feet tall, thin, good shape, wearing, you know, dark blue pants and that blue windbreaker with the word 'Coroner' across the back.

Long hair, like I said, no scars or distinguishing marks."
Big John looked off in the distance while he thought.
"And come to think about it he didn't seem in a rush.
You know? I mean if I was lifting a body you couldn't
photograph me. Oh yeah, he lit a cigarette as he drove
out the lot. That's it."

"You get the license plate, by any chance?"

Again Big John looked off into space, searching for
an answer that he knew he did not have, but not wanting
to answer too quickly and give Deringer ammunition
with which to criticize him. "Nah, didn't see it."

"Did the van have any writing on it? On the back
maybe?" Merlin asked.

This was something Big John should have been trained
to notice. Not wanting to come up short and look foolish,
he looked up at the sky one last time and closed his eyes
as tightly as if he had soap in them. "When he slammed
the doors shut I remember seeing the word 'Coroner.'
But I think it was on the back of his jacket. I . . . oh shit,"
he said to himself in exasperation. "I don't think so."

"Well, thanks," Deringer said sarcastically. He pulled
out one of the little cards the department had printed
up for him with his name and phone number and handed
it to Big John. "Now get outta here. I've spent too much
time looking at you already."

Big John pocketed the little card without reading it
and headed back into the Emergency Room.

"So, Barney Fife," Deringer said once they were alone
again. "That's the kind of moron I get to work with on
a daily basis. You still want to be a police officer?"

"See you around, Detective," Merlin said and turned
to walk away.

"Hey, I got an idea. Why don't we go one-on-one?
You know, see who strikes gold first. If you win I'll let
you shoot my gun." Deringer laughed.

Merlin didn't turn back to look at Deringer. There had been one critical part of his case summary that he had left out, and it was something he was going to discuss with Tory first.

Chapter 11

When Tory steered her two-year-old Honda Civic into the little parking lot next to the Fox Chapel Borough Building, she was operating on almost no sleep. While Merlin had been at the Medical Center with Stilwell, she'd been too keyed up to rest. Besides, the lingering thought of the masked man out there was rumbling through her brain. When she dared ask herself if he might come back into their lives, it was impossible to close her eyes and relax enough to sleep. So she'd kept the light on, made herself some cocoa, and watched one movie after another on cable.

Merlin had called three times, each conversation a quick update on Stilwell's condition. He arrived home by taxi just before seven a.m. and found Tory in the cramped kitchen of their two-story house. She was beating eggs in preparation for a cheese omelet, and when she saw Merlin she threw her arms around his shoulders and the two stood as one. Neither wanted the moment to end, but Merlin's stomach began to growl at the smell of breakfast.

"What an asshole," Merlin said when Tory mentioned Detective Deringer. "He challenged us to crack the case before he did. And he's not much of a cop, either. He didn't have the slightest idea which way to go from here."

Tory was tending to the eggs in a huge frying pan. As she stood by the white enamel stove she tore a slice of Swiss cheese into strips and dropped them onto the bubbling omelet. With the finesse of a short order cook she folded the omelet in two. "All right, a couple of questions."

Merlin beamed. It was terrific talking with someone whose mind was clicking away as fast as his.

"First of all, who killed Stilwell?"

"Easy. Stilwell's a man with a past. Fake name. Fake address. He was having plastic surgery to disappear. Whoever he was hiding from found him. Or . . ." Merlin stopped to think.

"Or?" Tory encouraged.

"Okay, what if Cutter was somehow in on it? Let's just say he does Stilwell a favor and changes his appearance. But Stilwell's a loose cannon—look at the way he freaked when he thought you were spying on him. After it's over Cutter has second thoughts. He doesn't want to get caught." Merlin was spreading cream cheese on a toasted bagel but stopped long enough to wave his hand around for emphasis as he spoke. "You know, he figures Stilwell's gonna get himself in trouble and turn the spotlight on the illustrious Marshall Cutter Cosmetic Surgery Center or whatever he calls it."

"So he kills him?"

"Why not? When rational people see their world crumbling around them, sometimes they can be pushed to do irrational things."

"Okay. So we know why Stilwell was at Marshall Cutter's office. He needed a fresh look to get away from somebody. But how do we know Cutter knew about Stilwell?" The cheese omelet was ready. Using the spatula,

Tory divided it in two and as she slid one of the halves onto a plate, a long string of cheese remained connected to the frying pan.

"Remember what Stilwell said when he had us in the woods?" Merlin asked.

"He asked if Cutter told us about him."

"Right. Stilwell was announcing that Cutter knew who he was. And Cutter didn't call the police when you were being attacked. So Cutter knew Stilwell was a phony *and* was protecting him." Merlin speared a chunk of omelet with a huge dollop of melted Swiss cheese in the middle. When the molten cheese hit the roof of his mouth he opened wide to suck in a cooling blast of air. "Deringer doesn't know about it, but it fits, doesn't it? But why run off with the body?"

"Maybe it was important his identity remain unknown."

"Deringer told me they'd run the car Stilwell drove for prints."

"Then that's my first stop of the day."

"How're you going to convince LaBove to free up your schedule?" Merlin was referring to Tory's boss, Frank La-Bove, the District Attorney of Allegheny County.

"When he hears how Stilwell kept asking me who at the D.A.'s office knew about him, that'll whet his appetite. He'll give me a couple of days to do the grunt work in hopes of a splash at one of his noontime press conferences."

They ate in silence for several bites. Finally Merlin observed, "You know, even if Cutter is involved, he couldn't have been working alone. He may have been the one who tipped off his partners when Stilwell died, but there must have been someone else who let the air out of the tires and drove the Ford."

After the cheese omelets and toasted bagels were gone Tory made the short drive to the small garage underneath the Fox Chapel police headquarters. It had two large white doors that ran up and down on motors and were nearly twice as tall as residential garage doors. Stilwell's Chrysler Concorde had been towed on a flatbed truck and was being stored inside. Now that Stilwell's identity was so much in question, the car was the most significant piece of evidence.

The inside of the garage was big enough for a dozen vehicles. This morning there were two, a dark green pickup truck that belonged to the borough, and the stolen Chrysler. Tory entered the building through a metal side door.

The Concorde had been parked several feet inside the garage. Instead of a team of uniformed crime lab technicians, the only person at work was a slender woman wearing freshly pressed blue jeans, tight enough to require quite a bit of wiggling just to get into them, and a man's tailored white button-down shirt tucked into the waist of her pants. She appeared to be in her early thirties with wavy brown hair that she had pulled into a thick, loose braid that ran halfway down her back. As she knelt beside the car Tory could see that she was wearing a pair of wire-rim glasses.

Tory approached the car and noticed the woman was using what looked exactly like a rouge brush on the paint along the top of the trunk, just where someone might put his hands to slam it shut.

"Please don't touch," the woman murmured softly as though she didn't want to breathe heavily on her work in progress. She obviously had caught Tory in her peripheral vision because her eyes never strayed from her work.

"This is the car brought in from Fox Chapel last night, right?" Tory asked. She'd taken a position far enough from the Concorde to show the examiner she was following orders.

"And you are?" she asked, again not turning her head to look directly at her visitor. She had delicate features, not the sort of face Tory would have expected for someone working in a dusty garage.

Tory quickly fished in her bag for her wallet, opened it up, and displayed her picture ID. "Tory Welch, D.A.'s office."

"D.A.'s office," the examiner repeated, over-emphasizing the D and the A to show how surprised she was. "I'm not supposed to talk to you." Her delicate lips curled into a tiny smile. "I'm London." Not once did she pull her eyes from her work or explain why she wasn't supposed to speak with Tory. Instead, London gently dabbed the camel hair brush on the gray velvet surface of a small round container she held in one hand. It was slightly larger than a tin of chewing tobacco and contained what she would describe as analytical gray fingerprint powder if asked.

"Is this a restricted crime scene?"

"No. Deringer called me and ordered me to keep you uninformed, especially if you stopped by." Gracefully, London leaned in close to her work, her mouth opened halfway. For a second Tory thought London was going to kiss the paint. Stopping just short of the shiny enamel, she huffed out a little puff of moist air. Instantly she frosted the surface with a subtle glaze of moisture. It looked like a gentler version of what people did just before wiping their glasses.

"So am I wasting my time?"

"Not at all. I can't stand the detective. If you ever want latents on Deringer, brush the right cheek on my butt." Without hesitation she pulled her head back and immediately began to stroke the delicate brush over the moisture. "What I'm doing here is the breath technique." She focused her dusting on a small oval area. As the moisture from London's breath evaporated, a gray fingerprint appeared on the paint. "Fingerprints are ninety-nine percent moisture. No sooner are they created than they begin to evaporate, slowly of course, and the older the print the more difficult it is to capture. My breath adds moisture to the fatty acids in the latent print, restoring it to what it looked like when it was created. You're the one who was attacked?"

"Yes," Tory answered.

"I heard the blow-by-blow on the radio. It must have been horrible."

"I haven't slept since."

London turned her head and looked at Tory for the first time. She smiled the way an old friend would have upon hearing the harrowing story. "There's a chair by the wall. Pull it up."

Tory smiled at London as she dragged an old folding chair across the cement floor and sat down.

London turned back to her work. "You have any idea why Deringer wants you out of the loop?"

"I'm stepping on his feet."

"He calls people like you funsies. When my department turns up something, do you think he ever gives us a lick of credit?"

Tory chuckled softly. Having London confide in her made her feel especially welcome. "Any prints?"

"Lots of them." She pursed her lips and blew most of the gray dust away. London's hand slipped into the breast pocket of her white shirt and pulled out a small rectangular magnifying glass. For several seconds she studied the print. "This is the ninth one. All the same." Then she reached for a tape dispenser on the floor and snapped off a pre-cut piece of transparent lifting tape. She carefully applied it to the fingerprint then rubbed the surface of it gently with her index finger.

"Great. How long until you know who they belong to?"

"I'm way ahead of you, Tory. I've got a match already." London turned her head and smiled, showing off a mouthful of incredibly white teeth. "I identified the very first one, about two hours ago. Belongs to a fellow named Jonas Osterman."

Tory whipped out her small leather notebook and began to scribble. "That's great. Jonas Osterman," she said. "O-S-T-E-R-?"

"Don't waste your time. Osterman was arrested in nineteen sixty-seven for possession of two ounces of marijuana." London's eyes returned to her work. Slowly, she grasped the lifting tape between her thumb and forefinger and gently peeled the tape off the surface of the car's trunk. No sooner had she removed it than she was reapplying it to a clear acetate card to create a record that could eventually be photographed. London held it aloft for Tory to see. A light gray fingerprint was perfectly displayed in the center of the card. London began to get up, but she'd been squatting so long her muscles were cramped and she had to push up on her knees to get to a standing position.

Tory stopped writing. She expected the marijuana arrest to be the first of many nefarious deeds Jonas Osterman, a.k.a. Stanley Stilwell, had committed.

"Osterman owns the car. His were the elimination fingerprints," London said, referring to the procedure of knowing which legitimate fingerprints should be on the car and eliminating them before the wrong person was needlessly arrested. "The car was reported stolen a couple of days ago. The police tracked Osterman down from the vehicle identification number. I ran Osterman's name in AFIS. You know what that is?"

"Automated Fingerprint Identification System. A computer registry in Harrisburg that has every fingerprint on file."

London was impressed with Tory and smiled. "We've got a terminal downtown. Osterman's prints are all over the place. The rearview mirror, steering wheel, door handles, trunk, radio."

"No other prints?" Tory sounded disappointed.

"Actually there were. All on the passenger side. Smaller prints that either came from a woman or a small-boned man."

Tory lifted her head slightly, showing off the purplish bruises that Stilwell's fingers had left on the side of her neck. "The guy I'm looking for had a hand this size."

London stepped close enough to Tory to get a good view. "Good Lord," she whispered, clearly sickened by what she saw. London's fingers went to her own neck and touched the skin softly. After an appropriate pause she said confidently, "Those are big fingers. The guy you want didn't leave the prints on the passenger side."

"So all the prints big enough to have been left by the man who did this belong to Osterman."

"Bingo. Let me tell you something, Tory," London said as she shook her head back and forth, "I'd sure as hell like to help you."

When Tanner Valdemar found Merlin, the surgeon was in the locker room changing into his blue scrubs. As much as Merlin would have liked to take the day off, his OR schedule simply would not permit it.

"Tanner, you make a wrong turn or something?" Merlin smiled at the sight of his psychiatric friend in the surgical suite.

Valdemar didn't return the smile. He was wearing his usual three-piece gray suit, off-white shirt, and patterned tie. "You okay?" he asked as he sat next to Merlin on one of the narrow benches between the rows of lockers.

"Yeah, I'm fine," Merlin reassured him.

"How about Tory?"

"She's already on the case. We're both a little shaken but we'll be okay."

"Listen. I've got to talk with you," Valdemar said abruptly. His eyes were so dark Merlin couldn't see his pupils.

Before he could say another word, two other surgeons strolled in, engaged in a loud discussion about a trade the Steelers were contemplating. Immediately they spotted Merlin and Valdemar and stopped talking. By this time, everyone in the Medical Center was talking about Merlin and the stolen body of the man who had almost killed him. Each of the television networks had sent a crew to the medical center to capture the intensity of the moment, and Merlin even had to sneak in through a service entrance to avoid being accosted.

"Hey, Merlin," one of the surgeons said. "Anything I can do for you today? See some of your post-ops?"

Merlin shook his head and smiled. He wondered if his colleague's offer was prompted by what he had heard on the news or the fact that it looked like Merlin was getting therapy just before heading into the OR. "I'm fine," he said. "Tanner's just refilling my Prozac, that's all."

Laughing nervously, the other surgeons left the small locker room quickly without bothering to change into scrubs.

When they were alone again, Merlin turned to Valdemar. "So . . . you okay?"

Valdemar looked around nervously, holding in whatever was troubling him until he was absolutely certain no one was around to eavesdrop. Twice his lips started to move without making any sound. Clearly he was uncomfortable. "This isn't easy," he whispered, his voice thick with emotion.

Merlin slid closer to Valdemar. "Tanner, are you in some kind of trouble?"

Valdemar shook his head. "No, I'm fine, but I'm walking the line, Merlin. This is really tough. Right on the edge. Look," he said, craning his neck around once again to make certain no one would overhear, "someone could walk in. Is there someplace else where we can talk?"

"Yeah, c'mon," Merlin said quickly and led the psychiatrist out of the locker room to the surgeons' lounge. Mercifully, it was empty. The television had not yet been fired up for the day. Merlin sat down on an overstuffed easy chair while Valdemar chose a sofa littered with medical journals and a copy of yesterday's *Wall Street Journal.* "So what's going on?"

"I'm in . . . uh . . . a situation I've never been in before. I need to ask—" He cut himself off. He shook his head back and forth as if he'd experienced a sudden chill, then pulled his lower lip between his teeth and bit down hard. Without warning he steeled his courage and blurted out, "I hope to God I'm wrong, but I think you still may be in danger."

"What?" Merlin said hoarsely. "You know Stilwell's dead."

Valdemar waved him off. "I know about Stilwell. I followed the news all night long. What I heard made me sick, but whoever the hell got him isn't finished."

Merlin's jaw dropped. "What do you know?"

Again his lower lip went between his teeth as Valdemar extended his neck so that he was looking up at the ceiling. Merlin thought he was about to cry.

"Tanner, is Tory the one in danger, or is it just me?"

"I don't know. Maybe it's just Tory," Valdemar said quietly.

Merlin sprang from his chair and walked the several steps across the room to join the psychiatrist on the sofa. "Look, Tanner, if Tory's in danger I need to know about it right away. Please tell me—what do you know?"

"I wish it was that simple."

Immediately panic took over and Merlin raised his voice. "It *is* that simple. If you know something, don't you dare keep it from me. For chrissake! Tory's out there right now. She's all by herself. I beg you, don't hold back on me!"

"Where is she?"

"What do you know, Tanner?"

"Merlin, we've got to do things my way. I'm walking the line, but I'm on your side. Where is she?"

"First she was checking out Stilwell's car." Merlin's voice quavered as he spoke. "Then she was going to Marshall Cutter's office."

Valdemar's eyes widened noticeably. "Stop her. Just stop her." The psychiatrist reached into his jacket and pulled out a small Nokia cellular phone. Handing it to Merlin he said, "Just to be safe."

"What? What the hell's going on? Have you been threatened or something?" Merlin cried out.

"No. No one even knows I'm talking with you. I thought I was ready for this conversation." By now Valdemar was breathing heavily, and he kept wiping the side of his face with his fingers as if sweat was pouring down. "Call her. Have her wait until I know more."

"Is Cutter behind all this somehow?"

Valdemar shook his head back and forth violently. "I don't know who's involved. I only know it's not over."

"What should I tell her?"

Valdemar was struggling to control his emotions. "Just make the call."

Merlin punched in the number for the cell phone Tory

carried in her leather bag. As it started to ring Valdemar finally spoke. "Meet me at ten of one today. Not in my office. Here," he said, looking around the sparsely decorated room.

The phone rang seven times. Then a familiar voice came on the line, but it wasn't Tory's. "I'm sorry, the cellular customer you have called is unavailable or has traveled outside the coverage area. Please try your call again later."

Merlin handed the phone back to the psychiatrist. "Ten of one?"

"We'll have ten minutes to talk." Valdemar bolted from the room as quickly as possible.

The waiting room at The Cutter Institute for Cosmetic Surgery was empty. The lights were on and the fish were swimming around in their tank. Classical music filled the room, and the glossy magazines were fanned out on the little coffee tables. But no one was waiting to see the doctor.

Tory hesitated next to the bubbly fish tank, looking down the lush carpeted hallway toward the examination room where Stanley Stilwell had attacked her. Absently she rubbed her neck. As seconds rolled into minutes Tory became aware of quiet activity in the business office. Several secretaries were silently at work, filing charts and doing paperwork. It was Carol who caught her attention, dressed in her pink scrubs and wearing a pair of half-glasses on her nose. She spoke on the phone in hushed tones while she typed something into the computer. Tory ventured closer and could hear Carol apologizing to someone on the phone, saying how sorry she was to cancel such an important appointment at the last minute.

When Carol realized someone was standing right in

front of her, she jumped, and for a moment was rendered mute by the sight of Tory. Evidently the person with whom she was speaking on the phone became irritated with Carol for ignoring her because all at once Carol started apologizing all over again. It took several minutes more for Carol to hang up the phone. "Miss Welch," Carol began, "we weren't expecting you."

"There wasn't time to call first. Is Dr. Cutter in?"

"I'm sorry. I'm afraid he's not seeing any patients today. In fact I've just been on the phone canceling his cases for the morning." Carol was pointing to her computer console when Tory interrupted her.

"Carol," Tory said and placed her hands on the counter as she segued into a modulated version of her courtroom voice, "I'm not here today as a patient. The reason I drove out has to do with what happened last night."

"Oh," Carol said in a tiny voice.

"You know about what happened?"

Carol stared at Tory as if trying to decide what was appropriate to say. Finally she admitted, "I heard about it on the news. It must have been terrible. I didn't discuss it with Marshall, though. I just couldn't."

"Is he here?"

Carol hesitated before looking over Tory's shoulder toward the hallway leading to Cutter's office. Her frosted hair bounced gently as she nodded in a reluctant way. "Yes."

"Please tell him I'm here."

Carol picked up the phone and pressed two buttons. Several seconds later she said in a whisper, "Dr. Cutter, there's someone . . . I know you did, but it's Miss Welch. . . . No, not for an appointment, it's about last night. She says she needs to talk with you." Then Carol sat obediently and listened for a while, nodding her head in agreement with whatever her boss was saying. Finally she hung up the phone and said, "Okay, you can go on back. His office is at the very end of the hallway."

The hallway was well lighted this time, but Tory barely noticed the bright watercolors displayed on both sides of her. When she reached the examination room where she had had her incident with Stanley Stilwell, she paused. The room was darkened and she could barely make out the small table with the crinkly paper.

The door to Marshall Cutter's office was closed. It was a heavy wooden door, the grain of the wood appearing as wandering black lines on a rich brown background. Tory hesitated for only a second before knocking firmly on it.

"Come in," came a muffled voice through the door.

Tory's hand went out for the knob precisely at the moment her cell phone began to ring. *Oh no, not now.* Working quickly she slipped a hand into her bag and found the little button to silence the ring. She pushed the door open and found Marshall Cutter sitting behind a stunning antique desk. Her first impression of him that morning was how small he looked, anything but the picture of one of the most celebrated plastic surgeons in the region. He was dressed in a deep blue button-down shirt without a tie. It appeared that he had been sitting at his desk all morning staring off into space because the leather blotter in front of him was absolutely empty. His office was larger than Tory expected, square in shape and probably twenty-five feet in each direction. Two large windows dominated the wall behind Cutter, offering a tempting view of his private garden. The desk that Cutter sat at was ornate, one that might have been a museum piece. It didn't appear to have any drawers beneath the writing surface. From her vantage point in the doorway, Tory could easily look under it and see the plastic surgeon's legs stretched out on the oriental rug, his feet crossed. The rest of the wall space, painted a salmon color, was sprinkled with beautiful impressionist art in lavish baroque frames.

"You wanted to see me?" Cutter asked once the door was fully opened. His voice sounded meek, just like Carol's.

"I'm sorry to barge in on you like this, but there are questions . . ." Tory didn't bother finishing her thought, thinking it was obvious what she was about to say. Leaving the door opened partway, she crossed the large oriental rug quickly and sat in one of two handsome wooden-backed chairs placed directly in front of the desk.

When she was seated Cutter asked sheepishly, "Did he hurt you last night?" He already knew the answer from his conversation with Merlin, but he took comfort in asking a question that might put the rest of their meeting in a more positive light.

"No."

"How about your neck, where he grabbed you?"

Tory's fingertips gently touched where she had been grabbed, where the purple bruises were partially hidden by an upturned collar. "I'm fine," she said confidently, hoping to end any further discussion of her own health.

"You know, I spent almost two hours with Detective Deringer early this morning," he said, not defensively but in a matter-of-fact way. He sat himself up so that he could reach the far side of his desk to grab a thin patient file, which he handed over to Tory. "Take a look if you like."

Tory reached out for the chart, read the typed label with the words STANLEY STILWELL in caps, and slowly sifted page by page through the file. The first two pages were the demographic sheets written in Stilwell's own handwriting, listing what was now known to be phony information. The handwriting was heavy. There was one thing Deringer hadn't seemed to notice, otherwise he might have mentioned it to Merlin. On the very first line, where the patient was supposed to print his name, Stilwell had evidently spelled his last name wrong on his first try, because something was crossed out so thoroughly it looked as if there had been a rectangular box that he had filled in completely.

The body of the chart contained several typewritten notes. The first was dated six days before the others, and was half a page in length. It began, "The patient is a fifty-two-year-old businessman about to remarry. He has requested surgery for a"—and this next part was in quotation marks, as though Stilwell's very words were being recorded faithfully—" 'fresher, more youthful, appearance.' " The body of the note described the various features of Stilwell's face that Cutter was going to work on.

The second note was Brian Trilby's two-sentence preoperative note. His dictation stated that Stilwell was in good health, had no allergies, was not taking any medications, and had never had problems with anesthesia before.

The longest note in the chart was Cutter's operative note. Taking up a full page and a half, it included a paragraph or two on each of the several procedures he had completed on Stilwell. Eye lift. Face-lift. Chin implant. Cheek implant. Much of it was quite technical, mentioning specifics of how the patient's skin was prepared for surgery, precisely what type of suture material was used, where the incisions were made, and what brand of chin and cheek implants were used. He finished by mentioning that blood loss was minimal, there were no complications, and the patient tolerated the procedure well.

Finally there was Trilby's anesthesia note. This was

much shorter than the operative dictation and mentioned the particulars of IV fluids used during surgery, what anesthetics had been given, and another specific mention of how well the patient tolerated the procedure.

One other thing caught Tory's eye. A single sentence at the end of Trilby's dictation seemed oddly out of place. Tory read it twice.

"So," Cutter began, "any insights?"

"How did Stilwell come to you?"

Cutter frowned as he composed his answer. "Don't know." He scrunched up his face and cocked his head to one side to emphasize that he was as much in the dark as everyone else.

"How often does a patient of yours demand—and get—your office to be shut down?"

"Oh, once in a while, I suppose. Usually some society matron who claims to want to surprise everyone at the club," Cutter said, not sounding the least bit surprised by the question. "I do something very different from what Merlin does. Believe it or not, I treat much more than droopy eyelids and saggy breasts. What I do keeps people out of the shrinks' offices. People want youth. That's what I provide. People want a fresh start with bigger breasts or more hair or a new face, and I give it to them. Stanley Stilwell came to me with a story about getting remarried. He wanted to look younger. I don't question that. Don't kid yourself. He's not the first one with a story like that. In every case when a middle-aged man says he wants to look younger for his new wife, she turns out to be *much* younger. It's a temporary shot from the fountain of youth. Sometimes it's more potent than Viagra."

"So it didn't seem odd when he insisted that the office be cleared of other patients?"

"I don't want to go 'round and 'round with you. I was

paid seventeen thousand dollars for my work on Stilwell. I know that sounds terribly crass, but that's a lot of money. More money than some people make in an entire year. I figured he was embarrassed by going to a plastic surgeon in the first place—the vast majority of this sort of work is performed on women—and I wanted to respect that."

"Dr. Cutter, why didn't you order someone to telephone the police when Stilwell went berserk and assaulted me in your examination room?" The tone of the conversation had taken a sharp turn. Tory had again slipped into her courtroom voice, this time to goad Cutter to answer specifics of his role in the situation.

Immediately Cutter pulled his feet under his chair and shifted his whole body. He sat up very straight and placed both hands on the desk surface, palm side down. His tongue shot out and swiped his lower lip while his legs crossed and uncrossed. He made a loud rumbling sound deep in his throat before he said, "I've answered that. Next question." He peered at Tory to see her reaction. The issue with the police was a sticky one and he was anxious to move on to another subject. Tory maintained her composure and waited silently. Finally, Cutter continued, "There've been many Stanley Stilwells in this office. Don't get hung up on the idea that he was one of a kind. And you know what? They're all scared. All of 'em. Scared the operation won't work. Scared because they robbed their pension plan to pay for it. Scared someone's gonna make fun of them. All of them, scared. And, goddamnit, that's exactly what Stanley Stilwell was. Now let's move on." Cutter pointed his index finger at Tory and thrust it forward to emphasize each word he was saying. "I knew if I could get into that room and talk with him I could calm him down. And I did."

"Things were out of hand, Dr. Cutter."

"It may not sound pretty, but I'm not going to throw this practice down the toilet for Stanley Stilwell. I know the Stanley Stilwells of this world and I knew I could control the situation. I'm not going to call the cops when they're not needed. I've got a reputation."

"Reputation?" Tory asked, leading her witness to focus on what he had just said in greater detail.

"Yeah. A reputation. Just like Merlin. That's what we live by. If people think I operate on . . . on . . . goddamn hooligans, do you think women are going to want to drive all the way up here to have me bob their noses or puff up their breasts? Hell, these are country club debs who wouldn't want to sit on one of my sofas if they thought Stanley Stilwell had been there first. There are more than a dozen plastic surgeons in this city that do what I do as well as I do it. But you know what? I do more work than anyone. Look at this place. Gardens. Artwork. Hell, my patients feel better just walking through the door. This is an atmosphere that people remember. They tell their friends about it." Cutter turned his head and stared out the windows. The little garden was a reminder to him of the perfection he sought for each of his patients. "That's all. End of discussion." Cutter did a little karate chop through the air with his hand.

He took several deep breaths. His eyes were still focused at the tulips, grape hyacinths, and dusty miller that dotted his private garden.

The quiet in the room was growing thick. Somewhere off in the distance a phone was ringing. A woman's voice silenced the ringing and spoke in hushed tones that couldn't be deciphered. With Cutter doing his best to ignore Tory, it was a nice reminder for her that they weren't alone.

Without warning, without so much as a sigh or comment, Cutter pushed himself up from his chair and walked around the desk toward Tory. Looking beyond her, he strolled right by the chair where she was sitting as if he were about to walk out into the hallway and leave her by herself. When he reached the door, he grabbed hold of the brass knob and turned it. As the latch disappeared, he gradually—and silently—pushed it closed.

From across the room he asked, "Now, what was it you *really* wanted to know?"

In the time it took for him to cross the room and close the door, he looked different. Tory saw it in his eyes. They were filled with a fury that made Cutter look like a feral animal.

Tory felt uncomfortable, not a panic or terror, but a twinge of something that made her twist around in her chair so that she could keep an eye on him while he walked back toward his desk. "Didn't it worry you to have such a mentally unstable patient?" Tory began, toning it back just a bit.

"Of course," Cutter said in that unhurried tone of someone feeling very much in charge. Instead of returning to his chair, Cutter stepped directly in front of Tory in a gesture so surprising that she recoiled immediately and pulled her head back to look directly into the plastic surgeon's eyes.

He had situated himself in the little space between her chair and the desk. With a perverse look of amusement, Cutter perched himself on the edge of his desk so that he was sitting a good sixteen inches higher than she was. It felt to Cutter as though the meeting was now being run according to his own rules.

The skin on his tanned face tightened. Every fiber in his body was on alert. "How dare you waltz in here and question one little moment in time as if everything hinged upon it. Why don't you take it up with Deringer?

I told him everything last night. Everything! And he didn't have a problem with it. So let's get it out in the open. You wondered about whether I thought it . . . odd . . . that Stilwell did what he did when he came upon you the day of his surgery. It's too goddamn easy to make a big deal out of something after the fact. Hell, why didn't *you* call the cops? What stopped you?" Cutter intensified his stare.

Tory remained mute, re-running the argument she'd had with Merlin on that very subject in her head.

Bolstered by Tory's silence, Cutter exploded. *"God-damnit, it was a judgment call! Leave it the hell alone!"* Cutter took a deep cleansing breath to calm himself down. "And don't you go judging how ridiculous it was for Stilwell to make a big stink about you knowing he was here. He just needed to know his trust in me was safe." Cutter leaned toward Tory, waggling one finger as if to admonish her. "Stillwell acted sanely for a man who saw his pitiful world crumbling beneath him. It may not have been nice or pretty, but he was desperate for something he'd wanted for a long time."

"Enough!" Tory interrupted. "Everything about him was phony and you should have known it. He couldn't even get his own zip code right. If all he was looking to do was please his new wife, why didn't he trust you with his name?"

"How the hell should I know? I don't run a Dun and Bradstreet on my patients. I trust them. I don't look at the zip code or the address. That's the kind of relationship I want. Hell, I don't even collect my fee until *after* the surgery. So the answer is no. No, I didn't think it odd or strange. Life is too easy for you. You can't possibly know what it was like to be Stanley Stilwell." Cutter's eyes wandered south from their lock on Tory's face and came to rest on her breasts.

Tory knew what Cutter was doing. Her cheeks flushed hot. Anything she might say to Cutter could be incendiary. But there was that one sentence in Brian Trilby's note. Tory opened the chart and leafed through the pages.

"Let me show you something," Cutter said as he leaned to the far side of his desk to grab an oversized photo album, one with a thick leather cover and gold leaf on the spine. Tory looked up from the chart. Cutter flipped through several of the stiff white pages. "Here," he announced when he spotted what he wanted. Then he turned the book around to show Tory a crisp five-by-seven color photograph. It was alone on the left-hand page, the before picture, perfectly centered as though the rest of the white page was its frame. The subject of the picture was a young woman staring straight into the camera with absolutely no expression on her face whatsoever. She had long greasy brown hair, parted in the middle. Her eyes were dreary and the corners of her tight-lipped mouth were turned down in an expression that showed her contempt for the reason she had visited Marshall Cutter. Even head on, her nose was tremendous. The bridge was wide enough that ordinary glasses designed for women wouldn't fit. And her enormous nostrils were upturned in such a way as to give the impression that somewhere in her ancestry was a relative of the porcine family.

Cutter gave Tory several seconds to take it all in. Then he shifted the book in order to show the after picture. Clearly it was the same woman, only this time her hair was shorter and styled, her eyes twinkled, and her nose was now this cute little button that she probably stared at in the mirror for hours, not believing how terrific she looked.

"She'd never had a date in her whole life. Three grand.

An hour and a half. And she's never been happier. I'm sure you look at your nose in the mirror a hundred times a day, Miss Welch. Nice little upturned thing. Makes you look adorable. Think how life would be with this behemoth plastered on your face," Cutter challenged.

Cutter was making his point by trying to embarrass her. So far it was working.

Working quickly Cutter found the next example he wanted to discuss. This time, the before photograph was that of a middle-aged woman's legs, ankle to thigh. Although her legs were slender and shapely, a series of prominent varicose veins bulged out as if a tiny gopher had burrowed its way up and down her gams.

Then with a shift of the weighty tome, the very same woman's legs were pictured after Marshall Cutter had worked his magic on her. She was wearing a pair of purple bikini panties and each and every one of her varicosities was gone.

"This one used to wear pants three hundred and sixty-five days of the year. Never went to the beach. Hated to have her husband see her undressed. She was desperate. Her marriage was in jeopardy and she came to me as a last hope." As Cutter looked down at Tory's legs he made no effort to conceal what he was doing.

Again Tory felt uncomfortable, as though she had forgotten to get dressed before her meeting. With one hand she gave her pleated skirt a little tug on the side to pull it down a bit farther, but it barely made it past her knees.

"You've made your point," she said. Her irritation was obvious.

"I don't know that I have," he countered. He turned the photo album back toward himself while he searched for another patient. "Ahh," he announced. Dramatically, he turned the book back so that Tory could see the before picture of a very attractive young woman in her late twenties. She was naked from the waist up and had the striking facial features of a fashion model. But the reason for her visit to Cutter was painfully obvious. Her chest was as flat as a pre-pubescent child. Two tiny pink nipples poked up from her skin like a couple of goosebumps.

Tory sensed what was coming next, and Cutter didn't disappoint. Balancing the heavy photo album on one knee, he shifted the book and showed off the after photo. This one looked like something out of a soft-core porn movie. The very same woman, now photographed at a forty-five-degree angle, looked over her shoulder at the camera. Her hair was tousled as if she had just finished a very randy dance and her back was arched suggestively. Her prominent breasts, augmented by the wonders of surgery, looked as if they would be able to defy gravity forever.

"She was a model before coming to me. Made quite a name for herself doing face work. Toothpaste ads, lipstick, that sort of stuff. But she was miserable. I gave her what she wanted, and now she's making a fortune. She cleaned out every penny of her savings for her implants, but ask her if it was worth it and she'll tell you 'Hell, yes.' "

Cutter's eyes drifted back to Tory, this time lingering on her chest long enough to piss her off. Before he could comment on how firm her breasts looked, or how well she must fill out a bikini, Tory decided she had had enough. Her hands were shaking as she noisily opened the Stilwell chart.

"What are you trying to do? Scare me off by leering at me? If you need a cold shower, I'll wait, but otherwise cut the crap!" She said the last part through clenched teeth and Cutter looked startled. Immediately she launched into what she had noticed in the chart. "If Stan-

ley Stilwell was acting in a rational manner, how come
Brian Trilby wrote that, quote, 'Prior to surgery Mr. Stilwell threatened another patient and locked himself in an
examination room for five minutes'?"

The room became deadly quiet. The skin on Cutter's
face became so tight it looked as if he had just had a
face-lift that went too far. Deliberately, as if he was using
every bit of self-control left in his body, he closed the
photo album and placed it on his desk. With one hand
he reached out for the chart that Tory was still holding
and quickly tugged it away from her.

He looked at Tory with a seething anger, and she felt
fearful that he might explode at any moment.

He didn't look at the chart. Instead he kept his eyes
on Tory, looking her up and down like a wolf stalking
its prey. Then he slid off the desk and towered over
Tory. His face was contorted as if he was going to vomit.

Get the Beretta. He's going to do something! Tory could
sense it. Adrenaline coursed through her body and a sudden panic gripped her. *Get the gun!* Without taking her
eyes off Cutter, she pulled her leather bag onto her lap
and her hands struggled to pull it open.

Marshall Cutter turned and walked around his desk.
Just like that, he returned to his chair, sat down in the
most gentle, refined manner, and slipped on a pair of
half-glasses. As he began to read he casually remarked,
"Hmmmm. Brian does comment on Stilwell's behavior.
Well, I guess you're going to just have to ask him why
he wrote that." Cutter didn't seem the least bit concerned. He held the chart open with one hand as if he
was in a choir as he picked up the phone and tapped
two numbers. While he waited, he passed the time reading Trilby's note a second time. "Oh, Carol, Miss Welch
would like a word or two with Brian. Can you ask—"
He stopped talking in mid-sentence. As he listened to

whatever Carol was saying he turned in his chair and looked out the window. "Oh." He was not able to conceal his surprise at what he was hearing. "I'll have Miss Welch talk to you on the way out to set up a time with Brian." He turned his attention back to Tory, nodding his head as if everything were under control.

"Is everything okay?" Tory asked.

"Of course. Brian's not in this morning. A doctor's appointment, I believe. I can have Carol set something up for you."

Tory's brain was racing. Something didn't fit. "How many anesthesiologists do you have?"

"Just the one."

"When I came in, Carol said she had just finished canceling your surgery for the day."

The color from Cutter's face disappeared in two beats of his heart. He clenched his jaw closed tightly. "Miss Welch, I trust Brian Trilby implicitly. If he has a doctor's appointment it must be damned important. I'm certain you'll call him on it when you meet him. Now, if you'll excuse me, I've got things to do."

Chapter 12

Merlin's day was a complete mess. For the first time in his career he did the unthinkable.

With young Tony Schaffer waiting to be wheeled into the OR, he postponed the surgery. This was something surgeons with a drug addiction did when they couldn't get their morning fix to stop their hands from shaking. Or it was the kind of stunt doctors pulled when they were running around with some young thing and had a hankering for a quickie and knew they wouldn't be able to concentrate on the surgery without it.

Merlin first spent several minutes with Tony's parents, looking them in the eye and explaining that he had a family emergency, forcing him to reschedule the operation.

Mrs. Schaffer said she realized the importance of the emergency because Merlin would never cancel at the last minute if it wasn't something big.

"What about Tony?" Mr. Schaffer asked.

"Leave him to me."

After Merlin explained to Tony what was happening, he pulled open a drawer and grabbed an empty bottle of Coca-Cola. It was an old fashioned glass bottle with the familiar hourglass shape. Bouncing around inside of it was a shiny fifty-cent piece. "Okay, Tony," Merlin said slyly, "here's something special for you. See the coin in the bottle?" Merlin shook the bottle and the fifty-cent piece rattled loudly. "Watch." The magician inverted the bottle, holding it in his right hand by the neck, and shook it firmly in a downward direction, the same maneuver one would use with a ketchup bottle. In three hard shakes the coin had apparently slipped through the narrow mouth of the bottle and was in Merlin's left hand. "Here, you get it back inside. The next time I see you I'm going to tell you the secret."

Merlin handed the boy a fifty-cent piece—not the one from the bottle, but one that had been palmed in his hand. The rigged coin was neatly slipped into his pocket. Although Merlin usually shunned gimmicky tricks, this one was a favorite. What had originally been a newly minted coin had been painstakingly cut into three pieces, the machinist artfully sawing around the figure's head to hide any marks left by the blade. A shallow groove had also been cut around the entire edge of the coin. That way, when the three pieces were reassembled, a small rubber band, similar to what orthodontists use to straighten crooked teeth, could be secured in the groove and the coin stayed together. But the rubber band didn't merely hold the coin together. Essentially it gave the coin hinges, allowing the three pieces to fold over one another the way the morning paper is rolled before being tossed onto the front stoop by the paper boy. Thus the fifty-cent piece could be rendered one-third its original size. It was simple to work the hinges and pre-insert the coin into an empty bottle. Once inside, it automatically opened to its original size.

The illusion was effected by the magician holding the neck of the bottle so the audience would not see the rigged coin fold up as it was shaken back through the narrow opening. All that was needed to complete the sleight was a real coin hidden in the magician's hand to be switched with the fake. The effect was tremendous.

While Tony eagerly accepted the bottle and fifty-cent piece and began in earnest to force the coin inside, Merlin dashed out to the tired Buick station wagon he had borrowed from his landlady while his Cherokee was in the shop. Seconds later, he bombed out of Oakland. Fortunately traffic was light. He pushed the engine until it moaned, the speedometer hitting 87 miles an hour on Route 28. Four minutes later he was tearing up the long driveway to The Cutter Institute for Cosmetic Surgery.

Coming down the driveway, traveling no faster than was appropriate for the sloping curves, was Tory in her Honda. Merlin hit the brakes hard, working the steering wheel back and forth to keep the Buick from swerving out of control.

"You okay?" Merlin called to Tory once the two cars were stopped next to each other.

"Don't you have a hernia to remove or something?"

"Is your phone working?" Merlin asked pointedly, his tone alerting Tory he was upset.

"Why?"

"Is your phone working?" He enunciated each of the words in a very deliberate way.

"Yes," Tory said softly. "I turned it off when I went in to interview Cutter."

"Goddamnit, I needed to reach you."

"I'm sorry."

"Don't you ever do that again!" Merlin snapped.

Tory studied Merlin's face and realized his behavior had something to do with Marshall Cutter. "Let's find someplace to get some coffee."

*　　*　　*

"Tory Welch, please. Tell her it's Detective Deringer."
He was standing in front of the reception desk on the
third floor of the County Court House. The rumpled
clothes were the same, but the strong smell of coffee
hung about him as if he'd been chugging it ever sine he
had left Merlin. Placing one of his little business cards
on the desk, he snapped it smartly with his thumb.

The receptionist looked up from her word processor.
She was a no-nonsense type, a lifelong receptionist who
took her job seriously. "I'm sorry, Detective," she said
crisply, "she just called in. Said she was on an investigation. I'll have her call you."

"Probably the same reason I'm here. Stanley Stilwell,
huh?"

"I believe that's right. She's interviewing that
doctor . . ." She stalled, trying to remember the name.

"Cutter? Dr. Marshall Cutter?"

"That's it. Marshall Cutter. You want me to have her
call you?"

Deringer's big hand tightened into a fist. "I don't friggin' believe this." Before he went any further he realized
the receptionist was sitting there wide eyed, watching his
little display of temper. Sheepishly, he added, "I just
wanted to coordinate things between our offices."

"I'll have her get in touch—"

"Forget it. Just forget it, okay? *I'll* call *her,*" Deringer
barked and brusquely turned toward the stairs.

At 12:45, after a nice lunch with Tory during which
they compared notes, Merlin left to wait for Tanner Valdemar in the surgical lounge. As he had promised, Valdemar arrived at precisely ten minutes before the hour. He
seemed quite relieved no one else was in the room.

The surgical lounge was never quiet during the day.
There were currently no doctors sprawled out on the

sofa watching CNN or reading the *Wall Street Journal,* but the noise from the hall filtered in through the door as if it wasn't there. The chirpy sounds of female nurses complaining about how slow the surgeons were and the muted sounds of physicians getting curbside consultations from one another filled the room with background clatter that Valdemar appreciated for what it was: white noise.

"Is Tory okay?" Valdemar asked once the two were seated on the sofa.

"She's fine. She met with Cutter before I could stop her. One curious thing. His anesthesiologist, a fellow named Brian Trilby, called in sick. Had a last-minute doctor's appointment even though he had no way to know Cutter canceled his OR schedule."

Valdemar sat quietly, digesting what he had just heard. His fingers played with his lower lip while his eyes glazed over. A long time ago Valdemar had developed the psychiatrist's ability to sit in one position endlessly. It proved useful while his patients went on about their neuroses and psychoses for fifty minutes at a stretch.

Merlin had carefully considered each word Valdemar had said to him. Every nuance was evaluated, every possibility run. While they ate lunch, he and Tory played out scenarios until they finally agreed what the psychiatrist really wanted to tell Merlin. The only thing that made sense was that a psychiatric patient of Valdemar's had also been a patient of Marshall Cutter's, and that the patient had seen something in the office that had to do with Stanley Stilwell.

What else could it be?

Finally Valdemar spoke. "Look Merlin, what I'm about to do may cross the line of professional conduct. I've been in psychiatry twenty-seven years and have never been in this position. But if something ever happened . . . I don't think I could live with myself."

"Something about one of your patients, isn't it?"

Valdemar nodded. "I figured my behavior would tip you off." He shrugged as if to say there was nothing he could do about Merlin reading him so well, then looked down at the floor. Without realizing it, Valdemar was doing precisely what his own patients did just before making a dramatic revelation. "The rules that govern my relationship with my patients are quite specific. If a session between a patient and a psychiatrist reveals a wrong-doing in the past, the patient's confidentiality is sacred. But if a patient reveals that a crime is *about* to be committed, then the psychiatrist has an obligation . . ." Tanner's voice trailed off. Merlin remained silent, allowing his friend to work through his feelings without interruption. "I've thought more on this subject in the past twelve hours than I have in my entire career. On a theoretical basis I am comfortable with the rules that govern the doctor-patient relationship. It's when it applies to me and one of my patients that I get lightheaded."

"Another murder is going to take place?"

Valdemar shook his head. "I'm not sure. If a patient blurted out that someone was going to be murdered, I'd have no trouble going to the police. This is different. It's what I've . . . deduced from information I have been told."

"Tanner, would you feel more comfortable if you told me what information you have without mentioning the patient's name?"

Valdemar studied Merlin's face. It was an easy face to look at. What patients seemed to remember most about the surgeon was his smile. He could deliver the most horrendous news to a family and do it with a reassuring smile that fostered optimism and courage.

Merlin's lips were closed, the corners of his mouth turned up almost imperceptibly in a reassuring grin, not one that made Valdemar feel foolish, but one that said they were in this together.

"Brian Trilby," Valdemar said simply. Then he knew enough to shut up and let Merlin digest the news.

"Trilby! He was there the day Stilwell attacked Tory in the office," Merlin exclaimed in a hushed tone.

"Now, Merlin, this is between us. I know I don't have to tell you that, but I'll sleep better if you say it."

"Of course it is. Just between us."

"Not even Tory," Valdemar added quietly. "It's not that I don't trust her. You know I don't question her integrity. It's just that she may be compelled to take action, that she might have no choice *but* to do something. I'm just not certain about the information I have. That's all. If I'm wrong, so be it. Then it's between the two of us and we bury it."

Even as Valdemar looked away from Merlin, the surgeon's eyes never left his friend's face. He was being asked to break new ground. Secrets were not part of his relationship with Tory. There was virtually nothing they could not share. Each had cried in the other's arms and had murmured the most intimate things in the darkness of their bedroom after they made love. Merlin knew that once that trust was threatened, their relationship would forever change. This was not a patient confidentiality issue that didn't affect Tory directly. She was very much in the arena. Withholding information could conceivably put her in danger. Reluctantly, Merlin responded, "Okay, we'll do it your way." He was afraid any other response could spook Valdemar.

"I've been seeing Trilby for almost a year. When I first started working with him he was having some marital problems. The usual things. His wife was spending a fortune on some remodeling. He was bored with the kind of work he was doing. Midlife crisis in his thirties. So I

saw him once a week for about six months. Then he
stopped coming.

"A couple weeks ago, he called me out of the blue.
He was experiencing horrible nightmares so I began
working with him again. Sometimes he was having more
than one a night. And they were always the same thing.
The Wizard of Oz is playing on TV—you know, Judy
Garland? Everything seems to be just the way it was in
the movie but Trilby is playing the Scarecrow. Remember how he would dance with his arms and legs moving
as if they were hardly attached to the body? Well, Trilby
is doing a wicked version of the Scarecrow's dance, his
arms flailing out in a hideous way, violently." As if he
was about to start calisthenics, Valdemar held both arms
out to the side. Slowly he flexed his arms, then shot
them out to full extension. Each time he repeated the
maneuver, his arms moved more violently. "Finally he
goes totally out of control and his arms shoot right out
of the sockets."

Just listening to the vivid description made Merlin's
heart race. He knew the wicked dance all too well.

"When I heard the way that guy Stilwell had his neck
pierced, it made me think of high school biology—"

"Pithing a frog with a needle," Merlin whispered. He
vividly remembered his own experience with a bullfrog,
holding it tightly in one hand while he inserted the needle into the amphibian's brain. As he worked the needle
back and forth, the nerves in the spinal cord were severed. Each of the muscles in the frog's legs contracted
in violent spasms that could never be forgotten. "Cutter
was asking me about it in the ICU. The color drained
from his face when I described what had happened."

"I may be way off, but it got me thinking."

"So where do we go from here?" Merlin asked.

"This morning, right after I spoke with you, I met with

Trilby for a short time. He feels he's losing his mind. He's desperate. Obviously I did not ask him if his dreams had anything to do with Stanley Stilwell, and he is absolutely adamant that he has no idea why he's having the nightmares." Merlin was nodding his head while Valdemar rambled on. "So he agreed to be hypnotized by me."

"You're kidding."

Valdemar checked his watch. "In about twenty minutes."

"There's an observation room next to your office. I've been in it," Merlin pointed out.

Valdemar gave Merlin one single nod. "Remember, I'm afraid you may be in danger, *that's* why I'm here."

"Let's go," Merlin said.

"There's one more thing." Valdemar hesitated and looked away from Merlin while he chose his words. "Trilby doesn't know about you. Be absolutely still."

The observation room should have been called the observation closet. It was a dark space, smelling of cigarettes and stale coffee, with only enough room for two plastic molded chairs placed side by side directly in front of a one-way mirror. There was no lighting of any kind. Even though patients were usually informed if their session was being observed, the darkness was a precaution against a thoughtless observer flipping a light switch and calling attention to the fact that someone was watching.

As the door closed behind him, Merlin immediately seated himself. Taped to the middle of the mirror was a three-by-five card with the word QUIET printed in black marker.

Merlin had an excellent view of Valdemar's empty office, nearly the same view the psychiatrist had when seated in his leather armchair during sessions. Although the office was quite well lighted, the view through the one-way mirror toned things down the way sunglasses mute the intense brightness of the beach on a sunny day. Across from Valdemar's chair, no more than three paces away, was a corduroy sofa. It was large enough for a couple to sit side by side, but was far too small for anyone to lie down on unless the patient had his legs hanging off the end. Off to the left of the sofa was an ordinary wooden office desk, the type a mid-level executive in a big company might have waiting for him on his first day at work. The walls were filled with diplomas and certificates in thin black frames.

Without warning the door on the far wall opened. Trilby, followed several seconds later by Valdemar, entered. He was dressed in dark pants, a white dress shirt open at the collar, and a plaid sport jacket with none of the buttons fastened. Trilby seemed to know the drill because he headed for the small sofa and seated himself without hesitation, crossing and uncrossing his legs several times before the psychiatrist had even reached his own chair.

Initially Valdemar said nothing. He appeared to be allowing Trilby to get comfortable. But the longer he waited the more Trilby couldn't seem to control his movements. He started fidgeting, holding one arm out at a time as if to straighten his sleeve, only to repeat the process over and over. His eyes started blinking, but not the brief little flicks that automatically happened thousands of times each day. Trilby was doing forceful blinks, scrunching up his face over and over as if he had something caught in his eye.

"Well, Brian, from what you mentioned this morning, you feel the dreams have gotten out of control."

"I can't sleep. I'm afraid to even try, the dreams are so . . . so . . . horrible." Blink, blink. Arm out, arm in.

"Worst thing you can imagine. You want me to tell you about them again?"

"I wonder if we should proceed with what we discussed this morning?"

"The hypnosis?"

"Brian, I want you to experience one of your dreams in a trance. Would you feel comfortable with that?"

Trilby shifted in his seat, rubbing his neck as if he were getting sweaty. "I have to do something. Anything. I can't go on like this."

Merlin noticed that each time Trilby stopped talking he was out of breath. Checking his watch he clocked the anesthesiologist at a brisk thirty-five breaths a minute.

"You can stop anytime you want," Valdemar reassured him.

"Oh, yeah?" Trilby sounded intrigued.

"It's not like general anesthesia." Valdemar was speaking slowly, his voice reassuringly smooth. "You're in control of everything that happens. If you want to stop, you open your eyes and stop. You tell me only what you want. This only works if you are comfortable with hypnosis. And with me."

"I've got to get some sleep."

"Shall we try?"

Trilby nodded and placed both hands out in front of him and gave them a little shake like an athlete warming up. Noisily, he pulled in a single deep breath and let it out slowly. A cleansing breath. "So what do I do? Lie down or what?" He eyed the short sofa.

Valdemar began. "Why don't you start by closing your eyes? That's it, just sit back against the cushion and take some slow deep breaths. Concentrate on your breathing. Inhale . . . exhale." Valdemar had slowed his speech pattern, relaxing the way his words came out so they floated in the air like little clouds before they disappeared.

There was a narrow windowsill on Merlin's side of the one-way mirror. His arms were planted on the sill as he leaned forward. No longer did he bother looking at the back of Valdemar's head. He focused only on Brian Trilby as he took one deep cleansing breath after another. Gradually, the twitching slowed. Trilby's legs finally stopped crossing and came to rest in a comfortable position, both feet on the floor.

"That's good. Your breathing is perfect. Take another breath . . . hold it . . . let it out. This is a good way to relax, thinking about your breathing. Sense each breath, and think about how the air goes into your body and then flows out again. The more you think about your breathing, the more relaxed you feel. Now I want you to focus on the muscles in your chest. Think about those muscles and how they make you breathe in and out. Inhale . . . exhale . . ."

Merlin was fascinated with what was happening. The change that had come over Brian was remarkable. His breathing rate had slowed to about twenty breaths a minute and he seemed to be enjoying a light sleep, his head bent forward slightly, his eyes closed peacefully.

For the next several minutes Valdemar kept up his focused rambling, reminding Trilby in a variety of ways how easy it was for him to relax. Gradually, almost imperceptibly, the psychiatrist changed direction. "The more relaxed you feel, the more comfortable you will become. Comfortable and smooth. Think of something smooth. Silky smooth. A blanket of white snow in the morning. The surface of a sleepy pond. Fresh ice on a skating rink."

Valdemar continued, guiding Trilby through the systematic relaxation of his shoulders, arms, legs, hands, and

feet. There was no rush. Each part of the body was lav-
ished with gentle persuasion.

About six minutes into the process Valdemar noticed
a brief fluttering beneath Trilby's eyelids, a clinical indication his patient was well into a trance.

"Brian, how do you feel?"

Trilby spoke slowly. "I feel fine."

"Would you like to explore your imagination with
me?"

"Yes."

"I want you to think about the terrible dreams you've
been having." Trilby was nodding his head in a subtle
way, and Valdemar sensed that the nightmare was coming into focus for his patient. "Tell me your dream."

"The shirt is stuffed with fresh hay. The Scarecrow's
chest is puffy. He's dancing with Dorothy on the yellow
brick road. Happy dancing. Arms and legs swing about
as the Scarecrow glides and dances on the yellow brick
road."

"Is anyone else on the yellow brick road?"

"No, just Dorothy and the Scarecrow." Trilby seemed
comfortable to re-live what was evidently the happy part
of his dream. Both hands remained in his lap, his fingers
relaxed and motionless. "Wait . . . there is someone else.
A witch. A horrible witch is watching the dancing. Her
face is covered, but I know it's the wicked witch. I know
it." This was new, an element Trilby had never before
revealed.

"What is she doing, Brian?"

"The wicked witch is grabbing the Scarecrow from behind. She's putting her arm under the Scarecrow's arm
and then up to grab his neck. The Scarecrow is trapped."

The room was silent for several seconds. Valdemar
counted his own pulse, *two, three, four, five, six, seven,*

eight, nine, ten. When it seemed Trilby had stalled, he gently prodded, "Tell me what she is doing now."

"The witch has her broom in the other hand. It's above her head like a spear." Trilby's breathing quickened. "The wooden handle is touching the back of the Scarecrow's neck. But it's sharp, not rounded like it should be. It's sharp like a pencil. It's touching the back of his neck. She's pushing it inside." Trilby stopped talking. He was out of breath now and it seemed that he needed a rest before continuing.

"Brian, concentrate for a moment on your breathing. Inhale . . . exhale. That's better. Let yourself feel relaxed. That's good. Now, what happens next in your dream?"

"It hurts. The handle pokes through the skin. She's pushing it inside. Ahhhhhh! Arms are going out. Harder and harder. The happy dance is gone. The arms are going faster. Harder and harder, they shoot all the way out and then all the way in. Faster and faster. Make it stop. Please, make it stop!"

"Brian, you can make it stop right now. Concentrate on your breathing and it will stop. Focus all of your energy. You can stop the pain."

Trilby's eyes remained closed. With each breath he seemed to allow himself to relax.

"Brian, before we stop, I wonder whether you'd be willing to go back and use your imagination again for me." Trilby made no effort at response. Valdemar wasn't certain whether his request had been heard. Nevertheless, he tried one final question. "Tell me about the broom, Brian. Why did you think of a broom?"

"The broom is sharp. Pointy as a pencil."

"I know your dream has a broom, Brian. But what about your life made you think of a broom. Tell me why it's sharp like a pencil?"

"I don't know."

"Yes, Brian, you do know. Focus your thoughts on your breathing and become totally and thoroughly relaxed. Every part of you is relaxed. Your scalp. Your neck muscles, think about your neck muscles and they will become smooth and relaxed. Breathe in. Breathe out."

As Valdemar's soothing voice talked him once again into a deeper and deeper trance, Trilby started to nod his head, a series of tiny rhythmic oscillations that the psychiatrist noticed but went unseen by Merlin, still watching through the one-way mirror.

"An ice pick," Trilby said quietly.

Merlin went bolt upright. "Holy shit," he whispered loudly.

In no discernible way did Valdemar react. He waited a few seconds to see if Trilby had anything more to say, then said, "Tell me about the ice pick."

"An old ice pick with a wooden handle. It's long. The blade is clean and shiny, not rusty." Trilby's fingers were no longer idle. His thumbs were working against the tips of his other fingers as if he were feeling a piece of fabric.

"Let's think about your breathing," Valdemar tried, but it was too late.

All at once Trilby opened his eyes and lifted up his head. His breathing was loud and both hands immediately shot to his face and cupped his cheeks to support his head. Both eyelids were blinking away, and he had a frightened expression on his face. "I gotta go."

Before Valdemar could say a word, Trilby had pushed himself up from the sofa and was heading for the door in long purposeful strides. "Brian," Valdemar said, not moving from his position in the leather armchair, "we need to talk. Our work's just beginning."

Trilby never turned around. Yanking the door open as if he were escaping from something horrific, he put one hand in the air and gave a single curt wave over his shoulder before pulling the door closed behind him.

Merlin was already on his feet, ready to race out the door of the little closet.

Valdemar assumed that Merlin was already on his feet ready to hit the hallway but feared that Trilby might have a change of heart and open the door unexpectedly. He held his hand out in the air, motioning to Merlin through the glass to stay put. But Trilby did not return.

"Did you notice—" Merlin said as he raced into Valdemar's office and sat in the same sofa Trilby had just vacated.

Valdemar was nodding. "That he never said *he* was the Scarecrow. Yes."

"He could just as easily be the witch."

"I was suspicious of that. Was he describing the weapon that was used on Stilwell?"

"I couldn't see the handle, but it was an ice pick. That's the kind of puncture mark it made on Stilwell's neck. But he's describing exactly what I saw last night. The masked man got Stilwell in a half-nelson, totally overpowered him, then took what looked like an ice pick and inserted it in his neck. Either Trilby was there watching—and I don't think there was anyone else in the woods—or he was wearing the mask. You had to be there to know that kind of detail. We're making some progress."

"The information is useless," Valdemar said flatly.

Merlin was stunned. "What? We can't just ignore what he said."

"Even if he admitted to the crime, we can't do anything. It's privileged information and you know it. The only reason I got you involved was because I was worried Tory might be next."

"Right. So we've got to go to the police. I'm not going to let her walk into danger. No way."

"Let the police handle the investigation themselves. Convince Tory to pull herself off the case."

"Be reasonable, Tanner. I can't get her to drop the case and not tell her why."

"I don't like this any more than you do. Information obtained under hypnosis about a crime that has *already* been committed is privileged. The exception is if information comes out about a crime that is *going* to be committed. He didn't say anything about the future."

Merlin stood up and paced back and forth. "Okay, okay, Tory stays on the case, and I act as her guardian angel."

"Don't take advantage of this situation, Merlin."

"Tory was going to interview Trilby anyway. I told you that before I even knew Trilby was your patient. There's no reason he can't be checked out. Cutter, too. I'll just have to run interference."

Chapter 13

". . . it's an old trick Houdini used to get out of real police handcuffs," Merlin was saying to an older woman named Marilyn. They were sitting in the medical staff office, a small room on the second floor of the Medical Center that was devoted to the needs of the physicians in the hospital. Marilyn was a one-woman operation, taking responsibility for arranging the yearly golf outing and Christmas party, sending out the quarterly announcements for the business meetings, and, most important, collecting the voluminous re-appointment applications that each physician had to submit every two years in order to retain staff privileges. It was in this regard that she came to be so well known to each physician. She checked every piece of information sent to her to be absolutely certain the doctors had attended the required number of continuing medical education hours, and had a license that was up to date. She also scanned every line of the eight-page applications, on which the queries ranged from local addresses and year of graduation from medical school to boldly asked questions concerning use of drugs and arrests for felonies.

Marilyn looked like a bug. She was in her early sixties and wore tight-fitting designer glasses that were so ridiculously huge it was the first thing anyone noticed when they walked into the office. She was seated behind a metal desk that was festooned with small glass figurines and a mug from Disneyland picturing the Magic Kingdom in all its spired glory. Against one wall was a photocopier and a fax machine, with two tall file cabinets pushed up against the other. The file cabinets contained the alphabetized applications from each and every physician on staff, and were the reason Merlin had happened by the office instead of dictating charts as he was supposed to be doing.

"It's easier than you'd think." Merlin was sitting in a chair next to Marilyn's desk regaling her with a vivid rendition of what happened when Stanley Stilwell captured them in the woods. "Remember, Stilwell had me put them on myself. I held my arm like this," Merlin said and extended his arm pointed toward Marilyn, his radius and ulna parallel to the ground, so that she had an excellent view of his hand but little perspective on the wrist and forearm. "And I made a little fist so that the muscles in my forearm would bulge out." He made a tight fist. "Then I placed the handcuffs around my forearm, not my wrist." To demonstrate, he looped his thumb and first finger around his forearm so that it fashioned a crude handcuff that clung snugly to him. "When I relaxed my fist and pulled my hand away, there was just enough play. . . ." And with that he gave his arm a swift pull, sloppily freeing himself from the makeshift handcuff, his hand sweeping across Marilyn's desk.

It was an innocent mistake—at least that's the way it appeared to bug-eyed Marilyn. Merlin's hand collided with the white Styrofoam cup of coffee the staff secretary had been sipping for the past ten minutes, spilling the last ounce or two right onto her lap.

"Oh, how clumsy!" Merlin berated himself as the two

jumped up to survey the damage. Marilyn's cream-colored dress now had a small brown stain just below her waist. "Where can I get a paper towel?" he asked, heading for the door.

"That's okay, Merlin. I'll just go to the ladies' room," Marilyn said in a less than cheery voice and scurried from the room.

Finally, Merlin was alone. He was at the file cabinets before the clicking of Marilyn's shoes faded from the hallway. He pulled open two drawers, the one marked A–C and the other T–V.

When Marilyn returned to her metal desk, the brown coffee stain had been replaced by a much larger wet spot, but at least the dress was clean. There was, of course, no way for Marilyn ever to know two of her precious files had been temporarily removed from the cabinet, Xeroxed, and the copies stashed between the pages of the *Pittsburgh Post-Gazette* Merlin was carrying when he left her office.

Marshall Cutter was standing in the business office of his surgi-center, peeking through one of the windows as Carol unlocked her car, slipped on a pair of sunglasses, and drove down the long driveway.

A single patient chart was in his hand.

At last, he was alone. Carol hadn't seemed the least bit surprised when he had emerged from his office and announced they should knock off early. The rest of the small staff didn't need to be asked twice. Jackets and bags were grabbed and the parking lot emptied so quickly, a little cloud of dust and exhaust fumes lingered behind as a wispy reminder of the shortened workday. Unlike the others, Carol was in no rush. In fact, she seemed quite concerned about her boss, even offering to stay and keep him company if he wanted her to. But

Cutter had insisted, saying, "No, I'm fine, I just need some time alone," and directed her to put the answering service on and enjoy the rest of the day.

He found the switch to the CD player that was playing softly in the background and silenced it.

Once Cutter had time to reflect on the recent turn of events, everything began to make sense.

Except one thing.

The nagging question wouldn't go away. It terrified him, playing over and over in his mind in a confusing hum. *Who was the man in the black mask who killed Stilwell?* Who wanted Stilwell dead? Was it as simple as Mannheim made it sound? In the short time he was in town, could Stanley Stilwell be so stupid as to piss off someone enough to want to kill him? No, Cutter decided. Stilwell was killed because of what he had done *before* arriving in Pittsburgh.

Another thought popped into his head: Brian Trilby hadn't shown up for work because of a doctor's appointment. That got Cutter thinking about how odd it was for his anesthesiologist not to bother calling to inform him.

Deep in thought, Cutter headed down the carpeted hallway. A terrible hum that only he could hear deafened him. Just before he reached the threshold to his own office, he turned left, opened a door, and stepped into Brian Trilby's office.

The room was nothing more than a cubicle. The desk and bookshelves seemed to have been crammed into a space that was more suited to be a storage closet. Trilby did have a window, though, one that looked out on the very edge of Cutter's private little garden.

The desk was quite ordinary, hardly big enough for the telephone and framed photographs of his wife and young children Trilby had placed in a little cluster on one of the far corners. There were six charts stacked up in a little wooden bin waiting for signatures. Otherwise, Trilby had left his desk clean.

Cutter placed the one chart he had been carrying in the middle of the pile in the wooden bin, then promptly helped himself to a seat in the uncomfortable chair behind Trilby's desk. First he opened the pencil drawer, finding four cheap ball-point pens advertising a new drug used for anesthesia, a dozen Hershey's Kisses in a cellophane bag, an old photograph of his children, and a bottle of Valium.

Cutter examined the Valium, noting that Brian Trilby was both the patient and the prescribing physician.

The desk had three other drawers running down its left side. The top two drawers were overstuffed with junk: certificates of attendance from medical meetings, a couple of calculators, a Pittsburgh phone book, a pocket text describing current medications used in anesthesia, and several copies of the journal *Anesthesia,* still in the clear wrapping.

The bottom drawer, in addition to several more unread copies of *Anesthesia,* contained more than one item of interest. In the back of the drawer, tucked neatly behind the medical journals, was a can of pepper spray and a brown envelope containing a gun permit dated nine days earlier. There was also a flat, black plastic box. In small raised lettering on the top of the box were the words "Safe Action Pistol." He popped the lid. Inside was a 9-mm Glock semi-automatic with a stippled handle. It looked new, the black matte finish absolutely perfect, with no scratches or oily fingerprints marring its surface.

Cutter felt his throat tighten. Suddenly aware of what he was doing, he looked first out into the hallway, then took a second peek over his shoulder out the window.

No one was spying on him.

Licking his lower lip, he took the Glock in his hand

for a moment. It felt surprisingly comfortable, not at all heavy, certainly less than two pounds. And it was so compact and sleek in design, Cutter couldn't resist turning his hand this way and that to admire how it looked. He examined the matte black clip and counted ten bullets already packed in. Holding the tip of the barrel to his nose in a way he had seen countless times in movies and television shows, he took a sniff. The smell of gun metal and oil was readily apparent. If the Glock had ever been shot, Cutter could not tell. Replacing both the gun and clip in the flat box, Cutter stowed the box exactly where he had found it.

Then he examined the last item in the desk. Brian Trilby kept a small blue leatherette book with gold colored lettering on the cover that simply read "Addresses."

Cutter heard a sound. Instantly he froze and closed his eyes to block out all other stimuli so he could concentrate. He held his breath until the pulse in his neck banged out a furious cadence. He threw a quick look over his shoulder, then another before taking a brief walk to the doorway. But there was nothing. His mind was playing with him.

Then he went back to Trilby's phone book. Starting with A, Cutter read aloud each name in the book. Immediately, the process was more confusing than useful. Every time he came upon a name he didn't recognize, which was often, he asked himself, "Who's Abrams? Who's Alderman?"

This was an exercise in futility. Cutter couldn't even be certain what he was looking for. On a hunch he flipped the pages to the section marked with a blue S. His eyes quickly scanned down the handwritten names looking for Stanley Stilwell. Even though Stilwell was not the man's name, maybe his pseudonym had found its way into Trilby's book as a reminder. Cutter held his breath. Sarver. Shapp. Shiffman. Shipper. Silverman. Skalski. Stark. Swank.

But no Stilwell.

Almost afraid of what he might find, he turned to the page containing names beginning with the letter V and searched for a name he had not dared to let cross his lips: Philip Vorkman.

Two names were on the page and he read them quickly, certain he would find the name Vorkman.

Van Sant Auto Body and Valdemar. No Vorkman.

Valdemar! Cutter knew Tanner Valdemar from an occasional patient whose mental needs weren't fixed with a cute little nose or a bouncy pair of breasts.

Valdemar. The phone number had the right exchange for the Medical Center. It had to be the same one. *What the hell is going on with Trilby?* Cutter skimmed each of the remaining pages. Not one surprise or useful piece of information was tucked away. Just as he closed the book and replaced it, a voice cut through the quiet.

"What are you doing?"

It was Trilby. He was standing in the doorway to his office glaring across the room.

There was no way for Cutter to determine how long he had been standing there.

"Brian, I didn't hear you."

"I asked you, what are you doing?" Trilby stepped inside his office. His face was red and both fists were balled up, ready. As he clenched his jaws shut, the little muscles in his cheeks flared out. The way he was standing there, feet splayed apart, torso bent forward, made him look like a boxer waiting for the bell.

Cutter innocently leaned over the desk as if he were just about to reach for the stack of charts. "Don't get yourself worked up, Brian. Just looking for the Stilwell chart. Do you have it?" Cutter's voice came out an octave too high, but he managed to get the words out more smoothly than he expected.

"You were going through my drawers. I saw you!" Trilby barked.

Cutter held his hands out, trying to calm Trilby. "Hey, we're all on the same team here."

"Tell me something, Marshall." This last word he said with utter disdain. "What the hell have you gotten me into?"

"*You* into? Look, Brian, I know this Stilwell thing has everyone rattled, but I'm as much in the dark as you."

"You're full of crap!"

"What do you think I did?"

"What was Stilwell about?"

"Like I told the detective and the D.A., he's a guy who wanted to look better for his hot new wife. And fuck you if you don't believe me."

"Don't lie to me. I know exactly what's happening. Stilwell was like all the others, hard guys with suitcases full of wrinkled money who walked out of here with a new face so no one would ever recognize them again. Only Stilwell was crazy. That's what made him different."

"You're paranoid. I'm just looking for Stilwell's chart."

Trilby took two steps toward the visitor's side of the desk. He rummaged through the little stack of charts. "Here," he said, whipping one chart free and flipping it on the desk for Cutter to pick up.

"Aha, Carol must have stuck it there. I copied it during the night to take to the police, but it disappeared from my desk."

"I never keep charts in my desk drawer," Trilby said, sounding angry.

Cutter stood and headed for his own office. As he

came around the small desk he stopped in front of the anesthesiologist. "Carol said you had a doctor's appointment this morning. What if I hadn't been too tired to operate?"

Trilby stood there considering where the conversation was going. "Don't change the subject. We haven't finished with Stilwell."

"Yes we have, Brian. I'm done talking about him!" Cutter's voice was raised now. "I want to know where you were that you skipped out on me!"

"I had a doctor's appointment—an emergency."

"What *kind* of doctor's appointment?"

"Do I need a written excuse, Marshall? What is this? Third grade?"

Cutter started walking toward the door. "You need some time off, just let me know. Otherwise I expect you on time."

"Are you surprised I know what's going on?"

Cutter took a single step back toward Trilby and screamed, "All he told me was he was doing this for his new wife and didn't want anybody to know! End of story! By the way, Tory Welch from the D.A.'s office wanted to speak with you."

Trilby's lips quivered. "Huh?" he said hoarsely.

"Something about why you didn't show up for work."

"So?"

"I think you better give her a call," was the last thing Cutter said before he strode from the room.

Chapter 14

It was four-thirty when Tory drove out to Cutter's surgi-center for the second time that day. The drive had become automatic. Leaving the city, Tory turned onto Route 28 near the monstrous brick Heinz factory with its imposing columnar smokestacks. Her brief telephone conversation with Brian Trilby crept into her thoughts. He had called not fifteen minutes earlier, a lonely, frightened voice catching her at the end of a hectic day. "This is Brian Trilby," he had meekly said. "You wanted to speak to me?"

Brian Trilby sounded like a man genuinely fearful of something.

As she drove north along the Allegheny River toward Harmarville she forced herself to ask the question, *What are first impressions worth, anyway?*

She told Trilby she needed to speak with him about the Stanley Stilwell situation, which prompted an uncomfortably long silence at Trilby's end of the line. Information traversed telephone lines intact; emotions were impossible to interpret. *What are first impressions worth, anyway?*

"Well . . . I guess I could answer a couple of questions, maybe we could just do it over the phone?" That's when she knew a face-to-face was mandatory. Tory stated how important it was for them to sit down together and Trilby said, "Oh," in a voice so small Tory wondered if he had put the phone down and walked away. "We probably should do it now," he eventually said in a barely audible whisper. "Marshall canceled surgery for the next few days. I may be . . . uh . . . heading out of town for a couple of days."

Once Tory checked her watch and realized how late it was, she grabbed her bag and flew past her secretary, who had to race down the hall with Tory just to find out where she was headed in such a hurry.

Suddenly, with the Highland Park Bridge in her rearview mirror and less than five minutes from Cutter's office, Tory had her first pang of doubt. There wasn't one damned thing she knew about Brian Trilby. *Don't forget how surprised Marshall Cutter was when he heard Trilby hadn't shown up for work. Where the hell was Trilby? Did something about Stanley Stilwell have to do with Trilby's absence? But it was Trilby who had thought to write something in the medical record about Stilwell. Why? What if the frightened and confused Dr. Trilby turned out to be Dr. Jekyll? Could Mr. Hyde be far away?* Absently, Tory began to massage her neck where the purple fingerprints from Stanley Stilwell were just starting to fade away. *What are first impressions worth, anyway?*

Deep in thought, Tory didn't register driving the last few miles. Mindlessly, she got off Route 28 and headed toward the entrance of the long driveway that climbed to the surgi-center. What snapped Tory back to reality was the sight of Jack Merlin, leaning up against the battered station wagon that had become his temporary means of transportation.

There was only one other car parked there, a late-model BMW.

Tory rolled the window down. "What are you doing here?" she asked Merlin before pulling her Honda into a parking space.

"I'm coming with you," he said simply, hoping there would be no further need for discussion.

"How'd you even know I was here?" Tory questioned through her open window.

"I called your office just after you left."

The district attorney in Tory clicked. Something didn't fit. She pulled the Honda into a space and stepped out of the car. "I want to know *why* you're here." She used her stern courtroom voice on Merlin for the first time ever.

He smiled, pretending he was enjoying the cross-examination, but he was really buying time to think. "Tor, I'm as much a part of this as you are—"

"Cut the crap." Tory was angry. "Do you have any idea why I'm here?"

"No," Merlin answered defensively.

Tory's anger flared. "So you have *no* idea why I'm here, but you just decided to show up. What a coincidence!"

"That's right."

Tory opened her leather bag and rummaged about for several seconds before locating her cellular phone. She had her secretary on the line before Merlin realized what she was doing. "Valerie, hi, it's me. When Merlin called—" Tory was cut off in mid-sentence. While she listened she eyed Merlin. "Oh, I see. . . . Don't be silly, I don't care. . . . And you told him who I was meeting? . . . You did. . . . No, no problem. I'll see you tomorrow, bye." Tory shot Merlin a sharp glance, no different from what she would do in a courtroom when catching some defendant in a lie. "You didn't call her, she called you. You looking to sleep on the couch again?" Tory demanded quietly, keeping her temper under control.

"Look, I don't know what's going on in there, or that it's even safe—"

"You had my secretary spying on me. You know exactly what's going on in there. You always know what the hell's going on. Now," she said and made a motion with her fingers as if she were calling a dog over to be stroked. "What do you know about Brian Trilby?"

Merlin swallowed hard and had trouble looking at Tory. The wind had picked up and was making a soft whistling noise as it swept past his ears. His promises to Tanner Valdemar banged around in his head. The privileged relationship between doctors and patients was sacrosanct to Merlin, but what he had with Tory was more important to him than anything. It didn't take Merlin long to order his priorities and describe for Tory exactly what he had seen when Brian Trilby was in a trance. Finally he drew her close and whispered, "I was trying to protect you."

She hugged him back and whispered, "No more spying, okay?"

From where they were parked, Tory had a pretty good view of the waiting room through the front doors. There was absolutely no activity inside and it seemed even darker than she remembered from her encounter with Stanley Stilwell. That got her thinking about the attack. She could still see his eyes, angry reptilian slits only inches from her face as he spat out question after question at her. His breath was horrible and just thinking about it made her gag.

Tory and Merlin walked past the lush garden, not

wasting time admiring the Venus de Milo. Inside, the waiting room was completely empty, no music was playing. Tory took one deep whiff of the coffee smell lingering in the air and turned to scope out the business office, expecting—hoping—some lone secretary would be toiling away at one of the computers.

It was empty.

"Hello," she said quietly, but the only other sound in the waiting room was the bubbling of the fish tank. Her voice cut through the quiet like a scream in a cathedral. "Dr. Trilby?"

Immediately Tory and Merlin heard a voice from the hallway that led back to the examination rooms and offices.

"Miss Welch?"

Merlin turned to look down the hallway and instantly recognized Brian Trilby standing there in the same clothing he had been wearing for his session with Valdemar. He did not smile as he approached. Strangely, he walked with one hand extended as if he expected to shake hands.

Even in the dim lighting he looked pasty. There was a noticeable swelling under his eyes that looked like a pair of tiny saddlebags. It was evident that sleep was a luxury Brian Trilby wasn't enjoying. "Hello," she said in a professional tone. "Tory Welch." She added this last part not because Trilby might not remember her name, but because she was nervous and wanted to establish who was in charge from the start. "You remember Jack Merlin."

"We've met." For a moment, as they briefly shook hands, Trilby eyed Tory's neck. The fading bruises were a graphic reminder of the Stanley Stilwell incident and it was hard for Trilby to do anything but stare. "Coffee?" he finally said and turned to lead Tory and Merlin down the darkened hallway to his own office, which was marked by a splash of light on the dark carpet.

In an instant, the tightness that had been in Tory's shoulders since Merlin described Trilby's *Wizard of Oz* dream eased and her posture relaxed noticeably. Just hearing Trilby's offer of coffee was reassuring. First impressions do mean something. "It's so dark," she commented. With all of the lights turned off, it would have seemed odd not to remark on it.

"Before Marshall leaves he goes around turning off the lights like my miserly father used to do."

Even though Tory thought what he said was funny, Trilby hadn't turned around to look at her while he spoke. He shuffled down the hallway making a scuffing sound on the carpet, hunched forward as if he'd rather be padding up the stairs to bed. When he got to his office he made an abrupt turn and disappeared inside.

Tory stood in the doorway, taking in the room before officially crossing the threshold. What a contrast from Cutter's office. The little wall space Trilby's office offered was crammed with diplomas and certificates and unframed artwork by his young children.

Trilby assumed Tory was making a comparison. "This is The *Marshall Cutter* Institute for Cosmetic Surgery. Brian Trilby works out of a cubicle." He didn't smile as he dropped his frame into the functional chair behind his desk.

"It's bigger than my office," Tory said pleasantly.

"Well, we might as well sit down and get started." Trilby pointed to two straight-backed chairs on the other side of the desk. "Oh, coffee?" he asked, but he said it with such little enthusiasm the only reply Tory and Merlin could possibly make was to decline.

Merlin hadn't said much to this point, figuring he was

there to ride shotgun, not interview Trilby. He shook his head.

"I'm fine," Tory answered once she got settled and stowed her leather bag down by her feet. "Well," she said as Trilby sucked some coffee from a mug decorated with NUMBER ONE DAD, "I wanted to find out what you know about Stanley Stilwell."

Trilby shook his head several times and pursed his lips. His eyes narrowed to sleepy slits and his jaw clenched down hard enough to make his teeth click. "I saw that cop on TV. The one in charge of the investigation. How come you need to meet with me and he hasn't, uhhh, you know, tried to find me?"

"I don't know." Tory shrugged. "I assume he'll be in contact with you eventually."

"I put the guy under, that's all."

"Stilwell?" Tory asked, confused for a moment exactly who Trilby was talking about.

Trilby shot a harsh look across at her. "Yes! I never even met the guy until fifteen minutes before your little incident. I spent about two minutes asking him about allergies and his past medical history. Never heard of him before." Then he added with a trace of irony, "Patients don't come here to see me, you know. They come for Marshall. It's his show."

"I noticed in your anesthesia note that you made mention of the incident Stilwell had with me."

Trilby thought for a moment before answering. "Why is that such a big deal?" Both corners of his mouth turned down.

"I don't know that it is." Tory tried to sound matter-of-fact. "Stilwell's body disappeared into thin air. I'm just trying to get a handle on him."

"As I said, this whole operation is pretty much Mar-

shall's show. You should begin by talking with him."
Trilby turned his head and gazed at his wall of diplomas.
An angry scowl had replaced the look of irritation on
his face.

In a matter of seconds Trilby had made the transformation from reluctant host to an irate suspect. Watching
the rapid change in Trilby's expression gave Tory and
Merlin pause to think. Could this man fly off the handle
at a moment's notice? The office was otherwise empty.
In the small room, they both felt vulnerable.

Tory decided that maybe this was a good time to thank
Trilby for his time and get the hell out of there before
he directed his anger toward them. "Well . . ." Tory said
as she leaned forward and reached down for her bag.

Trilby snapped his head around to stare at his visitors. "The guy was nuts! Okay?" The frown remained
in place, and though his voice was no louder, it had a
honed edge to it. "Simple as that. Stilwell was dangerous. Look what he did to your neck. I don't know what
the hell Marshall might have told you already, but I recommended that we cancel surgery that day. Period. And
I was overruled. So what the hell do you want me to
say?"

Tory looked at Merlin, signaling him with a subtlety
that was supposed to tell him it was time to leave. "Well,
thank you for clearing that up—"

"Hold it!" Trilby banged his hand on his desk. "You
come all the way out here just to ask me that? I could
have told you that on the phone. What's going on here?"

Now it was Tory's turn to sit and think. *Grab your
bag and get out of here.* But something made her start
talking. "Dr. Cutter seemed quite surprised this morning
when he buzzed out to the front desk and found out that
you didn't show up for work."

"I had a doctor's appointment," he muttered loudly, as though tired of having to account for his whereabouts.

"I see," Tory responded quickly, almost sounding pat.

Suddenly Trilby stood up behind his desk. "Just hold on for a second," he ordered. The anger in his voice was growing louder. Evidently he had something to say and he wasn't going to let the meeting end without making his point. "I want to make sure no one's listening."

Maybe there *was* someone else in the office. Expecting Trilby to stick his head out the door, Tory and Merlin watched as Trilby took four quick strides. But instead of putting one hand on each side of the door frame and leaning out into the hallway, he dashed out of his little office, turned, and disappeared momentarily into Cutter's office. Then, before Tory had any idea what was happening, he shot down the hallway in the direction of the waiting room and business office.

Tory turned to Merlin and whispered, "He's gonna explode. We've got to get out of here." Before Merlin could respond she heard it.

Click. Click.

The metallic sound of the lock being worked in the front door. Tory's emotions turned on a dime. No longer was she a fool for overstaying her welcome. She was downright scared.

Merlin had stood up and turned around to wait for Trilby to re-enter the room. He shook his hands at his sides in preparation for whatever might happen next.

While straining to hear what Trilby was up to, Tory reached down and grabbed hold of her leather bag to move it to her lap. Trilby's footsteps could be heard coming back toward his office. The scuffing sound of his shuffling gait was replaced by the crisper sound of feet moving rapidly on carpet.

The Beretta.

Tory's hand shot inside the opening of her bag.

"Sorry," Trilby said, coming into the room quickly. Just as he had been when he dashed out of the room, he was empty handed as he strode directly to his chair. He didn't seem to notice Merlin was standing because he seated himself and immediately began speaking. "Look, Miss Welch, I've been under tremendous pressure lately. Marshall's practice is so busy it's totally out of control. And this Stilwell thing really upset me. But there's more than that." He made a fist and banged it off the desk. "Goddamnit."

As Trilby continued talking about Marshall Cutter, he didn't seem terribly threatening, so Merlin took the opportunity to sit back down.

"Somehow—and don't ask me *how* I know this—I'm caught in the middle of something. I don't know what the hell it is, but I'm smack dab in the middle." Little droplets of sweat were forming on his brow.

"What do you mean?"

"C'mon, it doesn't take a goddamn genius to smell something's wrong. Who in their right mind would operate on a patient after they pulled a psychotic stunt like that?" For the first time Trilby brought Merlin into the conversation. "You're a surgeon. Would you do elective, cosmetic surgery on a psycho under those circumstances?" he asked loud enough to be heard in the waiting room.

"No," Merlin said simply and said no more, hoping Trilby would keep going.

"But Cutter insisted, said it had to get done!" Trilby continued, his voice quickly growing louder. "I don't know the game Cutter is playing but look at the consequences."

"Dr. Trilby, if you're in trouble, I can help you," Tory said. *Keep the situation calm.*

"Before you hear it from Cutter, I want to show you something." His hands were visibly shaking as he reached down and slid open his third drawer. "I caught Cutter going through my drawers when I came back to the office just before I called you. I don't know what he was looking for. But he's gonna use the fact I have this against me, I just know it." Trilby pulled out the black plastic case that contained his Glock and slammed it directly in front of him on the desk.

Time seemed to slow. Somehow, both Merlin and Tory sensed what was inside the case. Trilby's fingers fumbled with the plastic box, trying to pop open the lid.

Tory sat up straight, her fingers grasping the small handle of the Beretta while her index finger located the trigger. "Put that away! Now!" she demanded.

Merlin quickly scanned the room, searching for options. There was nothing that could double as a weapon.

Trilby ignored Tory's order. The lid made a loud snapping noise as its edges became free, revealing the contents of the box.

One look at the black handgun sitting in the molded foam padding and Tory's entire lung capacity emptied in a loud whoosh. "Don't!" she screamed. In one quick move Tory stood straight up. The Beretta had become ensnared on something inside the bag. "Put your hands on your head!" She shook her hand back and forth until the weapon pulled free from her bag.

Trilby was hyperventilating and didn't seem to hear the command. "Don't worry, it's not even loaded," he mumbled. And in one quick move he snatched the Glock from the box and thrust it into the air.

In a move of absolute desperation, Merlin grabbed the front edge of the desk. As his legs pushed him to a standing position, he lifted the light desk, hefting it toward Trilby.

Before Trilby processed what was happening, the black plastic gun box slid onto his lap. Reflexively, his hands shot out to prevent the weight of the desk from landing on top of him, but it was too late. The momentum of the desk carried it onto the stunned anesthesiologist. The Glock fell harmlessly to the floor.

"Run!" Merlin shouted to Tory. Without thinking, Tory grabbed her leather bag and the two sprinted from the room.

They were at the front door quickly. Tory hoped to have several seconds before Trilby came out into the hallway. While Merlin desperately fumbled with the lock on the door, Tory trained her weapon in the direction of Trilby's office. But her pupils had already constricted from the last sunshine of the day shining brightly through the glass doors. The hallway was a black hole. It was impossible to determine whether Trilby was standing ten yards away waiting to fire his weapon or had not yet left his office.

"Shit! You need a key," Merlin whispered loudly when he realized what type of lock it was.

They were trapped.

Tory squinted her eyes in an effort to adjust to the darkened hallway where she feared Brian Trilby was lurking.

"The gun's not loaded. It's never even been shot." Trilby's voice called out, but it sounded distant as though he hadn't yet ventured into the carpeted hallway.

Not wanting to get into any sort of debate about the gun in the black plastic case, Merlin turned sideways and gave the heavy glass door a good shot with his shoulder. The door rattled as it was banged around. But the lock held firm.

Tory didn't look away from the hallway. She could tell

by the sound that Merlin had been unsuccessful in busting them out.

Trilby heard the sound, too. "It's locked. I have to unlock it with my key."

The splash of light coming from Trilby's office was finally coming into Tory's focus. "Stay right where you are, Trilby. I'll use my gun if I have to." Backing away from the door, she scanned the waiting room. At the far end of the room was a series of three windows. It was worth a sprint across the luxuriously appointed room to see if they could provide an escape route.

"Please don't shoot," Trilby's voice said. "I'm coming out."

Before Tory could react, before she could flatten herself to the ground and take aim, Trilby tossed something out of his office so that it landed with a heavy thud on the carpet. *Is that the gun? Is it his stapler?*

Immediately Tory and Merlin dropped to the floor in the prone position. Tory maintained her small Beretta in the direction of Trilby's doorway. Although the Beretta was a relatively light weapon, most women needed a two-handed grip to stabilize the gun for an accurate shot. "Hold it, Trilby. When you come out I want to see your hands held out to the side," she said pointedly.

"Just don't shoot."

"Walk slowly."

Brian Trilby obeyed. He stepped into the hallway, turned, and stood facing Tory. As instructed, he held his arms straight out to the side, and he rotated his hands several times to show them to be empty. Initially Tory and Merlin were below his line of sight and he rotated his head back and forth several times looking for them. "The gun's on the floor. I'm unarmed."

"Put your hands on your head," Tory demanded.

Trilby lowered his head to look down at the floor

where Tory's voice was coming from. Moving in a slow, exaggerated way, he placed both hands on his head and interlocked his fingers.

"Now start walking toward me. Slowly!"

One step, a pause, another step, a pause. Trilby seemed to disappear when he left the light from his office and descended into darkness. "I'll unlock the door," he said softly. His anger had broken.

"I want to see everything you do. No sudden moves."

Step, pause, step, pause. "I just wanted to show you the gun. That's all. You can check it out. It's new. I want to put an end to what's been going on just as much as you do." Step, pause, step, pause. "Cutter gave me the third degree today. Now this."

Trilby was less than fifteen away. His face was shiny with sweat.

"Hold it right there," Tory directed. "Do exactly what I tell you. Turn around very slowly. I want to see your back."

Trilby took a series of little steps as he made a single revolution. "May I get my keys? They're in my right pocket."

"Why didn't Cutter know you were going to miss work today?"

"I had a doctor's appointment, like I said. I'm seeing a psychiatrist. I told you I've been under a tremendous amount of pressure lately. His name's Tanner Valdemar. Call him. He'll verify it for you."

Tory felt some momentum building. Even though she knew much more about Trilby's visit with Valdemar than she could ever say, this was an opportunity to bring it out in the open. "Did your session have anything to do with Stanley Stilwell?"

After a pause, Trilby answered, "I've been having horrible dreams."

"Was it the Stanley Stilwell thing getting to you?"

"Maybe. The way he got killed, getting it in the neck that way."

"Did you ever have contact with Stilwell other than when you met him in the office?"

"No, I told you—"

"Who was Stilwell?"

"Someone who needed to disappear."

"Did you know Stilwell was about to kill us when he was stabbed?"

"Yes, I heard—"

"Then why was it so upsetting to you that he was stabbed in the back of the neck?"

"Just the thought of it, I guess."

"Are you withholding any information about Stilwell?"

Trilby took several deep breaths. "I have something for you."

Tory looked at Merlin for a second before saying anything. "What?"

"I downloaded Cutter's files from the system. I've got floppies of all his patients. Names, addresses, everything."

"Why is that so important?"

"I don't know. Maybe there's some connection."

"With what? Was Stilwell here before?"

"No, but . . ." Trilby's mouth went absolutely dry. He lifted his chin to make it easier to swallow. "There've been others."

"Other what?"

"Scary people. Dirtballs. Men who would kill you if they didn't like you, only not as crazy as Stilwell."

"How many others?" Tory wanted to know.

Trilby's mouth was moving but he was stumbling over his words and incoherent. Just when Tory was about to say something, he said, "I'll give you the floppies."

"Where are they?"

"Tomorrow night. I'll give you my address."

"You come to my office."

"No. I know you don't trust me. But I'm not coming to your office. Come to my house tomorrow night. Bring a cop if you like, I don't care. I'll have them then."

"Which pocket are the keys in?"

"My right."

"Get them. Slowly."

Trilby lowered his right hand, sending two fingers into his pocket and tugging gently before pulling out a key ring with half a dozen keys. "You can check to make sure the gun is registered if you like. It's in my name. I've got paperwork and everything."

"Keep your left hand on your head. Unlock the door."

Trilby approached the door and slipped one of the keys into the lock. Tory could hear the mechanism working as he unlocked the door. He even pushed the door open about six inches to show there was nothing tricky about what he'd just done.

"Okay, Trilby, walk outside. Leave your keys in the door."

Trilby pushed the door wide open and stepped outside. Without being asked, he placed his right hand back on his head and relaced his fingers.

Taking their cue when they saw Trilby step away from the door, Tory and Merlin got to their feet and followed the anesthesiologist outside. Before letting the door go, however, Merlin propped it open with his foot and removed Trilby's keys. Tory was already outside, holding the Beretta more casually now, aiming it at the anesthesiologist's feet. Merlin examined the keys. The one he was looking for was the biggest on the ring, the one with the BMW logo in the middle.

"Go over by the statue," Merlin ordered. He watched

Trilby step off the driveway and onto the thick grass. "When I start to drive, walk down the driveway. Your keys will be in the garden under the sign. We'll see you tomorrow night."

Chapter 15

It was just about to rain. Marshall Cutter took the most circuitous route he could devise to the top of Mount Washington. First he cruised all over Fox Chapel, logging thirteen miles on his odometer, scooting in and out of the winding, tree-lined roads, checking his rearview mirror every hundred yards. Knowing the back roads as well as he did, it would be impossible for someone to have followed him. It wasn't until his headlights had been on for almost fifteen minutes and the evening mist had started to bead up on his windshield that he ventured anywhere near Route 28. Then he drove south toward Pittsburgh for his late-night meeting.

It was well after nine when he parked his car on Grandview Avenue. The street was mostly empty and he rolled into a space right in front of the observation deck. He didn't get out of the car immediately. The mist was thickening, progressing to a light drizzle. As soon as the wipes were turned off, the windshield became wet. The light from the street lamp refracted as it shone through the droplets, bursting in a thousand directions.

Cutter yawned. He hadn't slept in more than thirty-six hours. Fatigue was making it hard to think. While he closed his eyes, he had a clear vision of Daphne on her knees when he heard the news on television. It was the exact moment that things began to spin out of control. The romantic dinner with Daphne had been nothing more than a kick-off party for the nightmare he was living.

With a violent shake of his head to wake himself up, Cutter reminded himself what he wanted from Mannheim. Something had to be done about Trilby. He was asking too many questions. And why did he have that gun? If Mannheim could engineer the heist of a body from the Medical Center, then he sure as hell could do something about Trilby.

That was it. Mannheim had to handle Brian Trilby.

He popped the trunk before he got out of the car. The cool drizzle felt wonderful, like a brisk shower at the end of a long day in the OR. He raised his face to the clouds and waited for his skin to get wet enough for the water to trickle down his cheek. He then rummaged around in the trunk of the Mercedes for a collapsible umbrella and popped it open before venturing out to the observation deck.

Dressed in the same clothing he had been wearing the entire day, Cutter could have easily been a waiter from one of the restaurants on Grandview taking a cigarette break.

At this hour the observation deck was empty. The rain was picking up, rapidly changing from a refreshing spring drizzle to a hard rain that sounded like a drum as it threw fat drops against his umbrella. Cutter strolled out to the railing and gazed down at Pittsburgh floating in the distance where the Allegheny and Monongahela Rivers converged. With the rain, it looked as though a sheer curtain had been pulled across the individual lights of the city.

Mannheim was late. *Goddamn, he's* always *late.*

Steadily, the weather grew worse. In a matter of minutes the hard rain evolved into an icy storm that felt like a stinging spray spewing from a water-saving shower head in a cheap motel. The wind whipped over Mount Washington so hard it blew the rain sideways. Holding the umbrella directly over his head did nothing to keep him dry. Cutter angled it into the wind and, for a few seconds, enjoyed not being pelted with the freezing droplets.

Suddenly the wind shifted. *Whomp!* The gust was too strong for the flimsy umbrella and it flopped inside out, leaving the plastic surgeon unprotected from the elements. After a brief fight, Cutter was able to fix the umbrella, but it hardly seemed worth the effort. His shirt was soaked. Only his nipples seemed hardy enough to stand up to the rain, poking through the slick cotton as if to remind him just how cold he was.

He looked at his watch, then toward Grandview Avenue. Where the hell was Mannheim? The bastard was always late. *Why the hell does he think he can keep me waiting all the time?* Tonight was no different. He was freezing. The rain had made it through his pants and his underwear was sopping. Cutter wanted to say "Fuck it!" and hop back in his car and drive home. But there was one very important reason to stay for this meeting.

The situation had become totally out of hand. Not the business with Stilwell. Cutter had followed the news and knew the body had been lifted successfully. Not one single print—not even a partial—had been recovered. Mannheim had been right. The Stilwell thing was fixable.

Trilby was another story. The self-prescribed Valium. And the handgun. That was the big one. Could Brian Trilby somehow have played a role in killing Stilwell? Even as Cutter dared to consider the possibility, he shuddered with the thought.

Could Trilby be some vigilante working on his own? There were too many questions.

Another idea jumped into Cutter's head. What if Trilby was working for Mannheim? Maybe Trilby was a mole planted in his office just to keep an eye on him. Was it conceivable that Mannheim *ordered* Trilby to silence Stilwell before he called attention to the whole operation?

Whomp! The umbrella inverted again, violently flipping out of shape. "Shit," Cutter hissed and heaved the black umbrella over the railing into the vast darkness of the hillside. Not bothering to watch it fall, he swiped at his forehead to whisk a wet clump of hair out of his face. The wind was blowing harder and harder. The rain was pelting him, falling in huge sheets that moved with the shifting wind. Pittsburgh had become a distant smudge of light. Cutter was so cold he started stomping his feet on the ground and rubbing his hands together to keep warm. A quick look at his watch told him he'd been waiting twenty-seven minutes. "Forget it," he said angrily and started to march back in the direction of the Mercedes.

Off in the distance, though his vision was blurred by a slow drip of rain falling from his eyelashes, Cutter could just make out a man walking on the other side of Grandview. He was headed toward the observation deck, dressed in a dark trench coat without a hat or an umbrella. As he passed under a streetlamp the light reflected off his wet hair. Amazingly, he seemed no more in a hurry than if he had been out for a stroll after dinner.

Mannheim. Finally.

Goddamn it, Mannheim. I'm sick and tired of your goddamn bullshit. You want my cooperation, how about a little fucking cooperation from you. Next time I call a meeting have the goddamn decency to show up on time.

The words sounded right, and Cutter planned to hit him with it right away, before Mannheim had a chance to get a word in. He'd let him have it, right in the face. Cutter smiled, an inappropriate toothy smile that made him look crazed. *Mannheim, you're up to your ears in shit, so why don't you listen to the voice of sanity.* Maybe Cutter would need to remind Mannheim who arranged to steal Stilwell's body.

Now Mannheim was getting closer, continuing to walk slowly. When he was no more than thirty yards away, he turned to cross the street. Before he ventured off the curb he turned and looked both ways, like a Boy Scout being extra careful because of the weather. *Christ almighty, the asshole thinks we've got all night.*

Cutter had trouble controlling his temper. *The bastard doesn't know what he's in for.* He started walking toward Mannheim with broad strides, ready to launch a laser-guided diatribe.

In one terrifying heartbeat, Marshall Cutter froze. His hands didn't move, his feet remained planted on the concrete in mid-stride. Water dripped off his forehead but he didn't seem to notice. Was this a dream? Was he caught in a nightmare so horrible nothing could possibly make sense?

"Oh my God." The words lingered in the air, but Cutter barely recognized he was the one who said them.

It wasn't Mannheim strolling onto the concrete observation deck. It was Detective Deringer.

"Thought it was you," Deringer said. His brown trench coat was shiny with rain, and he was squinting to keep the rain out of his eyes.

"Detective!" Cutter exclaimed, too stunned to even attempt to cover up his shock.

"Surprised to see me?"

"I'm surprised to see anybody out on a night like this."

"This ain't really a night for sightseeing. What are you doing up here?"

"This is where I come to think. With all that's happened, you can understand—"

"Were you expecting someone?" Deringer interrupted.

"Expecting someone? No. Why?"

"As I was crossing the street I got the distinct impression you were looking at me like you were expecting someone. The way you lifted your head and started walking toward me."

"It wasn't that at all. It's dark and when I saw you I didn't know who you were. I was worried you might be planning to mug me or something."

"Nah. It looked like you were walking toward me, as if you thought you knew me. Someone who thinks he's about to get mugged runs *away*, you know what I mean?" Deringer had a way of asking questions that made Cutter feel like a cornered animal. Once he locked eyes on Cutter he refused to let him go.

Cutter pulled at his ear. "Look, Detective, I want to go home. I'm wet and I'm cold. The last thing I want to do is stand here in the rain and debate which way I was walking. If that's all you wanted to chat about—"

"Okay, Doc, have it your way. You're up here in the pouring rain without a raincoat or umbrella to clear your head, and I'm taking an after-dinner walk to help digest my food. Now that we're both done lying, I'm gonna ask you a couple questions. Saves me a trip out to see you tomorrow."

"Have you been following me?"

"Right now, you're about all I got to jump-start this case. So I want you to level with me. Tell me what you know."

"I spent two hours with you last night. I don't know anything else."

"You know how Stilwell was killed?"

"Yes."

"Doc Merlin watched the whole thing. This morning he told me the guy grabbed Stilwell and pithed him with an ice pick." Deringer pretended to have an ice pick in his hand and he pushed it through the air toward Cutter, twisting it back and forth suggestively. "It would have been so much easier using a gun or smashing Stilwell's skull with a crowbar. So that got me to thinking how hard it would be to know exactly where to put that needle." Deringer paused to wipe his face.

Cutter was staring at Deringer with his jaw hung open, rain cascading down his face, his chest heaving with each breath as if he was ten years old and hearing a ghost story for the first time.

"Anyway," the detective continued, "I wondered if the person we're looking for might have had some medical background or something. What do you think?"

Medical background? That brought Cutter back to reality. "Detective, if you're insinuating that I had anything to do with what happened to Stilwell, I have a perfectly good alibi for the time it happened. I was on my way to pick up my date for the evening."

"What about your anesthesiologist?"

Cutter looked like a hooked fish. "You'd have to ask him yourself."

"I plan to do just that and see what Brian Trilby knows. If you're as innocent as you seem to be, you'd be smart to help me as much as possible. A killer's lurking about. I wouldn't want you to be next. You know what I mean?" Deringer saw Cutter's shocked facial expression and knew his little speech had gotten to him. The man was terrified. "So you met with that assistant district attorney today. You're not playing favorites, are you?"

"Detective, I don't know what you're talking about."

"I talked with your girl in pink, Carol. Told me you canceled your entire OR schedule today." Deringer pulled out a little spiral notebook from his pocket and flipped it open. He held it close to his body to protect it from the rain. Squinting so that he could see in the dim light from a distant streetlamp, he read aloud, "Karen Myers, blepharoplasty. What's that?"

"Eye lift."

"Oh. Michael Kessel Drenru, mole. Roberta Robak, mole. Alan Lantzy, mole. A lot of moles."

"That's how I relax between more complicated cases."

"Okay," Deringer said, eyeing the surgeon suspiciously. "Jeanne Shaffalo, rhinoplasty. That's a nose job, huh?"

Cutter nodded.

"Two more—Laurie McKennan, blepharoplasty. And . . ." Deringer held the pad up toward the streetlamp to improve the lighting. His entire face contorted as he struggled to read. "Somebody Vorkman, a mole."

"Huh?" Cutter blurted out.

"It looks like Vorkman, maybe not."

Cutter felt his pulse hammering away in his temples. The thought crossed his mind that his blood pressure was soaring and maybe he would end up with a stroke and have to be put on a ventilator like Stanley Stilwell. "I know my patients. There was no one by that name on the schedule. Never heard of him."

Deringer brought the little spiral pad closer to his face and squinted hard. "It's hard to see. Maybe you're right. York. Yeah, that's it, Joel York. Where the hell'd I get Vorkman from? Writing musta smeared. Anyway, so what's with your boy Trilby? I hear he's been acting strange. He have anything to do with Stilwell's murder?" Before Cutter could answer, Deringer hit him with another question. "How long you known Trilby?"

"A little over a year."

"You know him well?"

"Just through the office."

"Watch your back, Doc. Things are evil out your way." The two stood in the rain not saying anything, the cop watching Cutter's face for some sign that what he'd said had registered. Finally Deringer went on, "Look, I got a sixth sense about this kind of stuff. I got a feeling maybe there's something you could tell me, save me some running around." He paused. "You look scared. Maybe you think you're in some kind of danger. Don't go this one alone."

"Look Detective, there's nothing else."

"Well, if there's nothing you want to discuss with me, I better be getting home. Be careful." The detective turned to leave.

"I found a gun in Trilby's desk." The words cut through the sound of the rain on the concrete and the howl of the wind. When Cutter heard the words he was surprised at himself. But Deringer stopped and turned around abruptly.

"A gun, huh? That changes things. You have any reason to believe Trilby knew Stilwell?"

Cutter shrugged.

Deringer nodded. "You got some serious shit going on. Hey, that gets me to thinking. What if I wanted to take a look at your patient files?"

"My office files?" Cutter squeaked out.

"Yeah, names and addresses, that sort of stuff. Maybe something'll click."

"I suppose that would be okay, considering the circumstances. I can have one of the girls make a copy for you on disk."

Deringer nodded as though the meeting were a triumph for his side. "Tell Carol maybe I'll stop by tomorrow. Meantime, you better dry off." He turned and walked away.

Chapter 16

"He's covering his ass. I can't believe it, Merlin. He's giving up already." Tory was sitting up in bed, pulling her hair away from her face while she aimed the remote control at the television to make it louder. It was nearly seven, and the morning light was filtering into their bedroom, dappling the white sheets on their bed. She had pulled away from Merlin the moment she realized who was being interviewed. The man's face filled the screen, his hair slicked back as if it had been rubbed with Vitalis, his dark necktie cinched tightly at the neck. His ruddy complexion didn't photograph well so it looked more like a grainy mug shot. At the bottom of the screen, in yellow writing, was Detective Daniel Deringer, City of Pittsburgh Police Department.

"Right now we've got nothing to go on," Deringer was saying with a somber expression on his face. "So far the two crime scenes—the one in Fox Chapel where Stanley Stilwell was attacked and the Medical Center where his body was stolen—have not yielded any evidence to give our department any leads." He shrugged.

When Deringer finished his statement, the interviewer, the back of whose head barely made it on screen, questioned, "I'm told the name Stanley Stilwell was an alias. Any progress in identifying who he really was?"

"No. Like I said, no fingerprints were recovered. We still have several interviews to complete, but as it stands, Stilwell's killer remains at large."

With a zap of the remote Tory turned off the television. "It's ours for the taking."

By the time coffee was on and bagels were in the toaster, Merlin was sitting at the small butcher block table in the kitchen, poring over the medical staff re-appointment forms.

The storm that had dumped two and a half inches of water on Pittsburgh had moved on and was now pelting the central part of the state. A thick cloud cover lingered as a reminder of the rain that had fallen during the night. From the window above the sink Tory could see a puddle in their small yard that was big enough for a family of ducks.

"All right, Merlin, what do we really have to go on?" Tory asked as she stood at the counter spreading cream cheese on a hot bagel.

Merlin reached for his mug of coffee. "Who do you want me to start with?"

"Trilby."

"Okay, forgetting your little cross-examination of the witness while you had him at gunpoint, under hypnosis he gave an incredibly accurate account of pithing."

"On the positive side, he offered to supply a list of all of Cutter's patients."

"Counselor, how do we know it's not an abridged list?"

There was no satisfactory answer for that question. Tory sipped her coffee and wondered how crazy it was to consider going to Trilby's house without a police escort. "And everyone you called last night said the same thing about him, right? That he's not involved in anything dirty."

Merlin thought about the three telephone conversations to various colleagues he had made while they had waited for a pizza to be delivered. People who knew Trilby all vouched for him. He was solid, not the sort to go around ice-picking people in the middle of the night. "Okay . . . what about Cutter? No one seems to know much about him before he arrived in Pittsburgh six years ago. He doesn't see the other plastic surgeons socially—which doesn't necessarily mean anything. He went to Columbia for medical school, graduated in seventy-eight, and did his plastic surgery residency at Penn."

A hard knock on the front door interrupted their analysis. Merlin headed out of the kitchen while Tory munched her bagel.

Crossing the small living room, Merlin immediately spotted Detective Deringer's big head through the front door window. He looked the same way he had on television only his cheeks weren't so red. He was wearing what was evidently his trademark, a brown trench coat. With his fly-away collar askew and his tie pulled to one side, his sartorial statement screamed that if he had to wear a suit he didn't give a shit how he looked.

"Detective," Merlin said as he pulled open the front door.

"Your girlfriend here, too? I gotta talk with the both of you." Immediately he sniffed the air a couple of times and added, "I could use some coffee. Black."

Merlin didn't care for the idea of Deringer dropping by unannounced. He made a face that should have prompted Deringer to say something like, "Am I interrupting something?" but the detective didn't, pointing his nose in the direction of the kitchen, which made it impossible for Merlin to do anything but lead the detective to the back of the house where Tory was already pouring a steaming cup.

"How you doing?" the detective said. "Sorry to barge in on the both of you, but we gotta chat." Without being invited, Deringer pulled out one of the padded chairs and helped himself to a seat.

Once they were all settled, Deringer on one side of the square table, Tory and Merlin on the other, Merlin said, "We caught you on the news."

Deringer waved his hand back and forth as if clearing the air of a noxious odor. "That's all bullshit. Those reporters are so stupid. I can spoon feed them anything and they'll buy it. We tell 'em what they already know, but it sounds better coming from a detective standing in the woods. They lap it right up and repackage it over and over. You know what I mean?" He paused for a second and watched a smile play across Tory's lips. "No matter what's gone down—it don't matter if it's a murder, plane crash, scandal, you name it—we're always about three days ahead of the media." He leaned back. "Counselor, did you learn *anything* from what I said on TV?"

"No," Tory said through her smile.

"Exactly. I didn't say one fucking—'scuse me—one friggin' thing that wasn't on the news *yesterday*."

"It sounds like Stilwell, whoever he was, disappeared into the night without a trace."

"Bullshit he did. See, this is why I work alone. I've already passed Go, and the two of you are still home making coffee." He took a sip. "Good coffee, by the way." He sounded triumphant and leaned way back in his chair again so he could reach inside the big pocket on the side of his trench coat. He pulled out a piece of paper that had been neatly folded into a small rectangle. He took his time unfolding it, then smoothed it on the table with his hand. It was a Xerox copy of a set of mug shots, both straight-on and side views of a man, but the reproduction was bad and Tory and Merlin had no idea who it was. Deringer took a moment to regard the photocopy in a thoughtful manner, one hand stroking his chin, before sliding it in front of Tory. "You recognize this ugly face?"

Tory took one look and drew in her breath. "Hey, that's Stilwell." She slid the paper toward Merlin, who picked it up and studied it.

"No, it's not," Deringer said proudly. "It's Paul Vorkman." The detective took a loud slurp of coffee.

Tory noticed that he had puffed up his chest and was beaming.

"Where'd you get this?" Merlin asked.

"After the lamebrains from fingerprints turned up zilch on the car *and* the gun, I said, 'wait a fucking minute.'" This time he did not correct himself in his choice of words. "There's no way in hell Stilwell's that smart. So I said, start over, I don't give a crap if it takes all night, just start the fuck over. I even had 'em break the gun down and check *inside* for prints. And you know what was in there? A partial. Probably left when he cleaned his gun." Deringer looked like a giant rooster strutting his stuff. "Came through last night. Paul Vorkman, a.k.a. Stanley Stilwell."

"What do you know about him?"

"A rap sheet out to here," Deringer bragged as he extended one arm above the table as an indication of how long Vorkman's nefarious accomplishments were. "What do you want to know? He's an out-of-towner. Never even been arrested in Pennsylvania, but shit, he's been busier 'n hell in a couple other states. Armed robbery, drugs, racketeering, you name it. In ninety-three he somehow escaped from a courthouse in Dallas and hasn't been heard from since."

"Makes sense. He had to disappear," Tory said. "The important question is, did he set up things with Cutter or did someone do it for him?"

"That's what *I* gotta find out." The way he said it made it sound like the whole reason he had shown up for breakfast was to mark his territory. He picked up the photocopy and folded it before slipping it back into his pocket.

"So, who else in Pittsburgh knows?" Tory wondered aloud.

"I don't believe you. Are you *really* that naive? Cutter knows, all the way. Has to. And I bet Stilwell's not the first. That's why I don't want you spooking him into closing down his operation."

Tory eyed Merlin across the table as she asked, "Have you spoken to Brian Trilby?"

"Yeah, for about a minute. He doesn't know squat."

Merlin entered the conversation. "When we visited him yesterday he gave us a good scare when he showed off his gun."

"A gun?" The detective perked up and sounded interested, as if he was learning this for the first time. "What kind of gun?"

"I didn't get much of a look. It was black—"

"Ooooh. A *black* gun," Deringer cooed sarcastically.

Tory gave Deringer a hard stare. "It loaded from the bottom of the handle with a clip."

"Okay, lemme tell you what it is. It's a Glock, semi-automatic. And he got a permit for it two weeks ago. I do my homework."

"You saw it?" Tory sounded amazed.

Deringer chewed his lip before saying, "Nah. Just forget it." Again he waved his hand around. "I talked with the guy. He's a scared puppy, twitching all over the place when I asked him a couple of questions."

"One thing he said to me—" Tory added, ready to reveal that Trilby wanted to share Cutter's patient file with them, but Deringer cut her off.

"Like I told you, he's a frightened little puppy. Forget him. Cutter's the man. Can't you see that? Last night, in the rain, I tailed the fucker. Drove all the hell over the place before heading up to Mount Washington. You know that little observation deck at the top of the incline?" Deringer waited for Tory and Merlin to nod. "He just stands there in the monsoon, no raincoat or nothing, getting soaked. I figure he's waiting for someone so I hang out behind a mini-van and get pretty wet myself. When I can't stand it no more, I go strolling up and he comes tearing up to me like I'm some long-lost buddy of his."

"What did he say?" Tory asked.

"Not much. I scared the crap outta him when I pulled out a list with the names of all the patients he canceled for the day." Deringer let out a deep belly laugh when he recalled what had happened. "So I start reading them one by one. You know, Smith, Jones, Davidson. Those kinda names. And it's raining like there's no tomorrow and Cutter's sort of nodding his head as I say each of the names and bingo, I slip in the name Vorkman. It was classic. He looked like he was gonna get sick. You know, like he was tasting some puke in the back of his mouth." Deringer laughed at the thought. "Anyway, he gets all flustered and mumbles something about how he knows his patients like the back of his hand and there was no Vorkman. But he knew. He fucking knew."

Tory looked over at Merlin. She was impressed. "So what're you going to do?" Tory asked.

Deringer nodded. "I like the way you think. *I'm* gonna

watch him. You see, I don't think Stilwell's the only one who's been to Dr. Cutter for a new face."

"Let me interrupt you," Merlin said.

"What?" Deringer responded. He was annoyed that the surgeon was spoiling his momentum.

"I'm not disagreeing with you, but I don't think we should just forget about Trilby," Merlin said.

"Not *we,* pal. There is no we." Deringer trained his eyes on Tory and Merlin one at a time, letting the news sink in. "Trilby's a minor player. Even if he's involved—and I don't really think he is—he's not the one. Cutter's the man. Let me ask you something, Doc. Give me an explanation why Cutter would be up on Mount Washington in the friggin' rain in the middle of the night?"

"You got me."

"He's meeting someone he doesn't want to call on the phone or have anyone know about. He's plain dirty. Okay?" Deringer was talking rough so it would be clear to Merlin not to question anything else. "Lemme ask you another question. You know anything 'bout Trilby I should know?"

Merlin shook his head. "All right. Let's say Stilwell—uh, Vorkman—came to Cutter as part of some scheme to change his looks so the feds don't grab him. Then who killed Vorkman?"

"Cutter," Deringer said right away. "With the way Vorkman attacked Tory in the office, Cutter bumped him off before the jerk pulled another stunt and blew apart the whole gig."

"When I was talking with Trilby he offered to make a copy of Cutter's patients," Tory said.

"Oh yeah?" Deringer sounded surprised.

Merlin added, "Maybe he knows there've been others and—"

"Calm down, you two. Before you start patting yourself on the back, I already extracted the same promise from Cutter. Fact is, I'm gonna stop over his office later today and pick it up."

"Well, Detective, I wouldn't want you to be late. Thanks for stopping by," Merlin said and pushed his chair back from the table so that it squeaked loudly, hoping that Deringer would get the hint that breakfast was over.

"One more thing. The reason I came over in the first place. I get the sense you two aren't gonna take no for an answer. You wanna play cops and robbers. Am I right?"

"You don't own this investigation, Detective. If you've got a point to make, let's hear it," Tory stated.

"Like I told your boyfriend the other night, I work alone. I don't need a sidekick or a buddy. Stay clear outta my way." Deringer swept his finger across the surface of the table. "You wanna play? Fine. Just stay on your side of the line. Hey, I know. I'm officially deputizing the both of you." He held out his index finger and pretended to touch each of them on the shoulder as if they were being knighted. "You are both specialists in Brian Trilby. Be my guest." He considered what he had just said and appeared to be happy with the suggestion. "Yeah, why not? You do some background checking, interview him, whatever. I don't give a shit."

Tory glared across the table at the detective. "Then why did you come over here and show us Vorkman's picture. Was that just to brag?"

"Un-unh. I don't need to brag. I wanted you to know I got this case under my thumb. Don't you dare fuck it up for me. I want a promise from the both of you. What I shared with you goes nowhere. Think of it as a little test." His voice got louder. "If I hear Vorkman's name blasted out on KDKA or anywhere else, I'll know where to look for the leak. And don't expect me to be so nice next time. If Cutter is up to his eyeballs in shit, I don't want you blowing it for me."

"I hear you," Tory said.

Deringer then turned to take a look at Merlin. "I know I ain't stopping you from digging around. But I'm not leaving here until I know you'n I are on the same wavelength. Whaddya say, Doc? You got something to say, gimme a call. I'm the one who feeds the press."

"No problem."

Deringer took one last mouthful of coffee before leaving.

Chapter 17

"Hey, Mike," Merlin said as he strolled into the operating room. The surgical team standing at the table was swathed in yards of sterile blue-green cloth, huddled over the open abdomen of an obese woman with an ovarian cyst the size of a honeydew melon. Although camouflaged in scrub cap and mask, everyone knew it was Merlin who'd come in. He wore standard-issue light blue scrubs and a pair of white Nike running shoes.

Mike Slater, a general surgeon fourteen years Merlin's senior and a close friend since Merlin's internship, didn't pull his eyes away from his work. "How's Tory?"

Merlin chuckled. "Hey, I was handcuffed, too, and the gun was pointed in my direction once or twice," he said with mock jealousy.

"Who cares about you? Now that you're out of training, you're competition. I just as soon the guy popped you. I'd be able to send my kid to Cornell." Everyone laughed appreciatively.

Good-natured ribbing, even bordering on the macabre, was de rigueur in the operating room once the patient was unconscious. The scrub nurse giggled while the anesthesiologist stood at the patient's head, pleased not to be the recipient of any comments from the surgeon. This was Mike's OR, so protocol called for him to be the master of ceremonies, the one with all the put-downs. Merlin also smiled gamely through his paper mask, knowing that if Mike ever dared to drop by when he was operating, he would skewer the guy mercilessly.

Mike lifted his head several inches, not turning away from his patient, but pausing for a moment. "So, how is Tory?"

"She's just fine. I'll tell her you asked."

"So you stopped by for comic relief?"

"Actually, I wanted to pump you for some information."

"See that bleeder?" Mike was talking to the scrub nurse in a more serious, quieter tone. "Let me zap it." While Mike was handed the electric Bovie, which cauterized bleeding blood vessels with a buzz of electricity, Merlin waited patiently. "Good," he said to the scrub nurse, then a bit louder to Merlin, "What's up?"

"Marshall Cutter."

For several seconds the room went absolutely silent.

"What about him?" Then Mike, realizing he hadn't poked fun at someone for almost thirty seconds, turned to his scrub nurse and said, "You been Marshalled yet?" What little of her skin could be seen between her mask and cap turned red.

"How well do you know him?"

"He's a good doc. Gets great results and has a killer bedside manner. Probably's the best facial guy in the city." Mike looked first at his scrub nurse then the anesthesiologist. "Either of you quote me on that, I'll deny ever saying it."

"What about socially?"

"Just at hospital functions. Did you see him at the Christmas party last year?" Mike stopped operating for a moment and turned his head to look at Merlin. "You know what I heard?"

"What?" Merlin asked expectantly, as if Mike were about to reveal some truth about Cutter that had up until now gone unnoticed.

"Each year he plays Pygmalion—picks some babe, comps her for breasts and whatever else he can think of just so he'll have the best-looking honey on his arm for all the big parties."

"Anything else?"

Mike was still laughing at his own tall tale. "Nope."

"Where'd you do your residency? At Penn?"

"Yes. I finished up in Philly in eighty-four."

"Did you know Cutter at Penn?"

Mike straightened up and pulled his shoulders back to ease the tension in the muscles that ran down his spine. After several seconds of much-needed stretching, Mike grabbed hold of the retractors and adjusted them to improve the exposure of the cyst. "Penn? Un-unh. He wasn't at Penn."

"You sure?"

"Merlin, it's a small program. I know who I trained with."

"How much did the general surgeons and the plastics guys intermingle?"

"All the time. Just like here. When you were a resident, how many of the plastic surgery residents did you know?"

The room fell silent again.

"Merlin?" Mike said over his shoulder as he began his dissection of the cyst. "Merlin, you there?"

The scrub nurse standing across the table from Mike lifted her eyes to look for Merlin. She caught the last second of the door closing and said, "He's gone."

*   *   *

At nine-fifteen a.m., Marshall Cutter should have been on his way to the surgi-center. Instead, patients were being canceled five days in advance. He had business more pressing than the wrath of big-nosed girls who wanted a trim before the Medallion Ball.

Cutter had replayed every minute of what had happened the whole soggy way home from his Mount Washington meeting with Detective Deringer. At first he was ridiculously grateful that Mannheim was always late. The thought of Deringer coming upon the two of them might have scared Mannheim into cutting him loose. Or worse.

It wasn't until he was turning into his driveway that it hit him. Mannheim wasn't late. Somehow he knew that Cutter had been followed and bagged the meeting. That was it. Mannheim was one step ahead of the cops. *What a relief.*

Indeed, when Cutter arrived home in the middle of the night there was a fax waiting in his machine:

CALL ME FROM A SECURE PHONE AT 9:15 A.M. *DON'T* GET FOLLOWED THIS TIME.

The message was typed, not signed, and there was no tiny printing across the top of the page listing the name and number of the sender.

He'd slept miserably after that. Now he was driving around Fox Chapel for the second time in twelve hours, cruising past bus stops and carpools, driving around in endless circles, spending more time looking in his rear-view mirror than through the windshield. Finally, when he couldn't take the monotony for one more second, he pulled into a gas station on a busy road near a strip mall. Running down the center of the road, where the white line was supposed to be, was a low cement divider no more than six inches high, painted bright yellow so no one would dare make a left hand turn and block traffic. The gas station was hardly busy, just a Chevy Suburban with a woman wearing a warm-up suit pumping her own gas. The pay phones were situated away from the pumps, along the side of the lot by four empty parked cars. At precisely the predetermined hour, Marshall Cutter picked up the phone.

As he dialed Mannheim's number he moved in as close to the telephone as he could, using his torso to block anyone's view of the keypad should they be using binoculars. As he punched in the last number he craned his neck around. Detective Deringer—or anyone else—was nowhere in sight. "It's me."

"You let yourself be followed last night," Mannheim said evenly.

"I took precautions."

"I hope you were more careful this morning. What'd the cop want?"

Cutter had spent several sleepless hours debating whether to mention the business about Deringer mispronouncing Joel York's name. He finally rationalized that as direct as Deringer was, if he knew Stilwell's identity, he would have come right out with it. Just as Mannheim had reassured him several nights earlier, there was no way anyone could know who Stanley Stilwell was. "He tried to rattle me, that's all. Then he asked for a list of the patients in the practice."

"And that's not a problem, right?"

"Nope. I'll double-check to make certain Stilwell's listed."

"Good."

"Speaking of problems, though—"

There was no hesitation on Mannheim's part. "Drive for ten minutes and find another phone." Click.

The line went dead. A pang of fear shot through Cutter. *I was followed.*

Merlin had gone straight back to his office, locked the door, and opened Cutter's re-appointment application form on his desk. More and more it appeared that Deringer was correct. Cutter was the key to the case. Running his finger down the page, not stopping until he reached the space where Cutter had written down where he had completed his internship and residency, he then read aloud, "University of Pennsylvania Hospitals." *What the hell is going on?* "All right, Marshall, let's go back one step further. Let's see if you even went to medical school in the first place." His eyes drifted up the page and soon found the space where Cutter had declared he had graduated from Columbia's College of Physicians and Surgeons in 1978.

Several minutes later, Merlin had the alumni office of Columbia on the phone.

"Hello, this is Wendy, how can I help you?" Wendy spoke slowly in a mellifluous tone of voice as if her work load was light and she was eager for something to do. She sounded like a concierge in a four-star hotel. *Yes, Dr. Merlin, I've taken care of the reservations at the Four Seasons and the limousine will pick you and Ms. Welch up at six o'clock.*

"I'm wondering if you would give me some biographical information on a graduate of yours."

"Yessir. May I have your name, please?" Wendy had the ability to ask *who the hell are you, wanting to know about one of our grads?* without sounding the least bit obnoxious. She obviously had every intention of helping Merlin and asking his name was merely a formality.

"Certainly. My name's Dr. Jack Merlin. I'm a surgeon in Pittsburgh and I'm interviewing a candidate for the department of surgery at the Medical Center. Will you check on Dr. Marshall Cutter, class of seventy-eight?" Almost immediately, Merlin could hear the sound of keys being tapped as Wendy dutifully began her search.

"I'm sorry to keep you, Dr. Merlin, for some reason our computer's slow as molasses today," Wendy apologized, knowing how busy doctors are. Somewhere along the line Wendy had been taught to make a special effort to use the caller's name in as many sentences as possible. "Ahh, here we are, Dr. Merlin, class of nineteen seventy-eight. Now, you said Marshall Cutter, didn't you?"

"Yes. You do have him listed, don't you?" Merlin heard Wendy's fingers tap dance over the keys.

"M-A-R-S-H-A-L-L C-U-T-T-E-R?" Merlin detected a subtle change in Wendy's tone of voice. No longer smooth and relaxed, Wendy said each of the letters in a staccato fashion, as though she were suddenly in a hurry.

"I believe that's how he spells it. Class of seventy-eight."

"And he's applying for a job with you?" The change in Wendy's tone was now unmistakable. Gone was the concierge ready to find scattered singles for the two o'clock performance of *The Lion King*. Wendy had become the assistant principal in charge of discipline. *And where do you think you're heading, Mr. Merlin? Aren't you supposed to be in algebra?*

"Yes," Merlin replied with some annoyance. "Do you have him listed?"

"Yes, please hold, sir." The transformation had gone full circle in a matter of seconds. Concierge to disciplinarian to girl working the intercom at McDonald's. *No, you can't get onion rings with the Happy Meal. That'll be six eighteen. Drive around.*

Merlin was baffled. He'd expected a similar answer to the one Mike had given him in the operating room—that they had no record of Cutter. Several minutes went by. Wendy had evidently been so quick to interrupt her conversation with Merlin that she didn't bother to put him on hold. Instead of piped-in light rock tunes dipped in powdered sugar, Merlin was treated to snippets of conversation that he couldn't hear well enough to make any sense of.

"Hello," Concierge Wendy said when she came back on the line, sounding a little out of breath but making an obvious effort to effuse calm. "I must apologize, Dr. Merlin. My computer's absolutely on the fritz. Would you mind terribly if I get your number and get back to you right away?"

Merlin dictated his office number then said, "Wendy, I couldn't help but notice that the name Marshall Cutter seems to be a problem. Is everything okay?"

"Everything is fine, Dr. Merlin. Just a computer glitch. Actually, I'm just a secretary in the alumni office. I'm going to make sure Andrea calls you back—she's the director of alumni services. Thank you for your patience, and have a good day."

Cutter whipped his head around, first to the left, then the right. He didn't know where to look, so his eyes flitted everywhere, bouncing around in their bony sockets until he had a headache, starting in his temples and viciously ripping to the back of his head. Cars were speeding by the gas station, going way too fast to pay any attention to someone on the pay phone. Two cars were at the pumps now. A red Pontiac minivan with a bike rack was in the self-serve island, being filled by a middle-aged woman wearing a tennis outfit. The second was a Buick sedan, parked in full-serve. One of the attendants, a young kid wearing an oversized shirt that was untucked and unbuttoned, was halfheartedly using a squeegee on the front windshield. Cutter had a head-on view of the Buick's driver, a man with dark hair, a mustache, and sunglasses. But his head was bent forward as if he were looking inside his wallet so he could pay the attendant.

Cutter's hands were now shaking. He'd been followed again. The situation was obviously much more grave than he had believed it to be. Determined not to allow the man in the Buick to follow him out of the gas station, Cutter threw himself into his car, thrust the engine into drive, and floored it before he even had the door closed. The tires spun wildly, screeching out a piercing whine that would alert anyone not already aware that the Mercedes was making a hasty departure. The car whipped across the blacktop of the gas station, racing toward the road. A little sign, located where the parking lot sloped down to meet the street, reminded drivers: RIGHT TURN ONLY. First Cutter looked to his left. All clear. Then to the right. Forty yards away, an eighteen-wheel tractor-trailer was barreling toward him. Cutter gunned the engine, sending the Mercedes hurtling down the sloping driveway and straight across the road.

Cutter had his head turned toward the eighteen-wheeler when his front tires hit the cement divider. The Mercedes jumped into the air several inches so that turning the steering wheel had absolutely no effect whatsoever. With panic twisting his intestines, there was a horrible lurch as the tires crashed back into the blacktop on the other side of the low barrier.

At thirty-five miles an hour, it took the back tires less than a tenth of a second to pop the barrier. By this time Cutter had the wheels turned all the way to the left.

When the driver of the eighteen-wheeler saw the Mercedes, he let out a blast from his air horn. He was approaching way too quickly to slam on the brakes.

Cutter didn't need to look at the big rig to know how close it was to him. The squeal of the Mercedes's tires was drowned out by the deafening air horn. It sounded as if it were coming from his back seat. The eighteen-wheeler was no more than six feet from Cutter when the tires finally gripped the road and the Mercedes sped off.

Leaving the eighteen-wheeler behind, Cutter allowed himself a brief look in the mirror. The Buick remained at the pump. Cutter smiled. At this point, whatever it took to be safe, he was willing to do it.

In twenty minutes he found a pay phone outside a supermarket. It was not in a booth that he could step inside, but a plastic shell that housed the phone and afforded privacy only if the caller leaned inside as if he were a clam in the shell.

"I lost him," Cutter said after Mannheim picked up the call.

"Who, Deringer?"

"No, some guy in a Buick. Glasses and a mustache. How'd you know he was following me?"

"I have no idea if you were followed." Mannheim sounded annoyed. "I just wanted you to move to a new location before you described the problem. You sure someone was following you?"

Cutter stood silently as his cheeks flushed red and the skin on his face went tight as dry leather. He remained mute until he was certain he could control his temper. When he dared to speak he said, "Absolutely. The guy was watching me like a hawk. Don't worry, I lost him."

"Good. You said you have a problem."

The first thing Cutter noticed was that Mannheim didn't pursue any more information about the man who had been tailing him. It wasn't like Mannheim to let something go that could have an effect on the operation. Mannheim must have known Cutter's bravado was bullshit. "Trilby."

"He start asking you questions?"

"Yes. He knows what's going on. He's seen the men with suitcases full of money. Christ, his behavior is so bizarre. I mean, the day after Stilwell's murder he doesn't even show up for work, giving me some crap about a doctor's appointment."

"Has he ever done that before?"

"For chrissake, no!"

"Keep talking," Mannheim said as if he needed to be convinced.

"All right. He's got a gun in his drawer." Cutter's voice had suddenly gotten loud.

"Calm down, Marshall, you don't want to attract any attention. What kind of gun is it?"

Cutter leaned close enough to the phone to smell the filthy plastic. "Don't tell me to calm down! He walked in on me, goddamnit. I didn't get a chance to read the manual. What the hell difference does it make what kind of gun he has? It's a gun, for chrissake! Trilby's got a gun in my office."

"Anything else?"

Cutter was all set to mention finding Valdemar's name in Trilby's phone book, but was afraid it would sound anticlimactic. "This is your arena, Mannheim. You gotta do something 'cause I don't feel safe with him in my own goddamn office."

Mannheim didn't say a word. He made Cutter wait. "What do you want me to do?"

"I want you to take care of him."

As usual Mannheim spoke without emotion. "What do you mean, 'take care of him'?"

"Goddamnit, Mannheim! This isn't some sort of a

game. This cloak-and-dagger shit is killing me. You're my contact and I don't even know your friggin' name! Help me before I get killed. Give me a straight answer. Did you play any sort of a role in what happened to Stilwell in the woods that night?"

Again, Mannheim didn't answer right away. Cutter needed to cool down. The wait would do him good. "I want you to listen to me very carefully, Marshall. I want you to hear every word that I'm about to say. You understand?"

"Yes," Cutter hissed.

"I have no intention of being cross-examined by you, now or ever. If you think for one second I'm in the business of eliminating people who scare you, think again. I'll consider alternative options for handling Trilby, and that's all you need to know. As far as what you are to do—"

"No, Mannheim, you listen to me!" Cutter screamed. His face was red and he was so furious he didn't bother turning around to see if his outburst had attracted attention. "We're in trouble. But you're in the shadows and I'm about to get my head blown off. I *demand* that you take some action."

"Marshall, you do not demand anything from me. You want out, give me the word." Mannheim waited for Cutter to say something. When there was nothing from the other end of the line he calmly continued, "You were foolish to allow yourself to be followed last night. But that's in the past. Now it's time to get back into a routine. I don't see that you're in any immediate danger. You're being watched by the police. So don't give them anything to see. Start seeing patients. Go back into the operating room. Keep your eyes open. If you come up with anything on Trilby, call me from a secure phone."

"Did you have anything to do with Stilwell? Answer me!"

"And if I were to say no, would you believe me?"

"Tell . . . me . . . the . . . truth," he said, reigning in his anger.

"What do you want from me, Marshall? You want me to say I killed Stilwell so you can relax. Is that all it takes? If I killed Stilwell then Trilby isn't a murderer. Is that what this is all about?"

Cutter looked up to the sky and took several deep breaths. He decided to change directions. "Please," he pleaded. "I have to know."

"I'm not on your witness stand."

"Fuck you! I'm not going to wait around while you ignore what's going on. What if Trilby killed Stilwell? Then what?" Cutter's face distorted with anger. He was not going to be defeated by Mannheim again.

"Then we've got our hands full."

Cutter pulled the receiver away from his ear and began smashing it against the metal phone. Over and over he lashed out at Mannheim in the only way he could, but the line had already gone dead.

Merlin was seeing his last patient of the morning, Tony Schaffer, who was having a routine postoperative check. The two had become pals, and all Tony could talk about was the coin in the bottle trick. Mrs. Schaffer was sitting on a chair in the corner enjoying the relationship the two had developed.

When Merlin's secretary poked her head inside the little examination room and whispered that he had a long-distance phone call, the surgeon pulled open a drawer and grabbed a deck of cards. Merlin quickly shuffled them and held the deck facedown. "Okay, Tony, pay attention." Merlin executed a flawless double-lift, turning over the top two cars on the deck as if they were one. Although this particular sleight was second nature to anyone who called himself a magician, few performed it well. Merlin didn't hold his hands in a peculiar way or stare at the cards as if he expected to make a mistake. He merely caught the top two cards with his thumb and turned them over, dropping them back on the deck. Nothing flashy but a bit of legerdemain that was pure magic. "Jack of spades. That's your card." Merlin repeated his double-lift, flipping the two cards over again so the jack of spades appeared to be the first card in the deck. "Let's take the jack of spades," he said as he slid only the top card off the deck, "and place it somewhere in the middle of the deck."

Tony was paying close attention, beaming at his new best friend.

While Merlin shuffled the deck and cut twice, he relied on finesse and misdirection so that the jack of spades never moved from its position. "No way to know where your card is, right?"

Tony nodded.

"How 'bout if I throw the deck of cards up into the air and your card, the jack of spades, sticks to the ceiling?"

The deck was still in Merlin's hand, but Tony couldn't resist a quick look at the ceiling to see where his card was going to be. That's when the back of the top card got a dab of sticky magician's wax that had been waiting on the tip of Merlin's finger ever since he grabbed the cards from the drawer.

Once Tony's eyes settled back on the cards Merlin was ready. He held the deck in his right hand and threw it straight up in the air so that the cards would not spin or roll. *Smack!* All fifty-two cards collided with the ceiling tiles and the magician's wax held tight. Fifty-one cards began to flutter around the room in every direction so that for several seconds Tony and Merlin were in a dense storm.

"It worked!" Tony enthused. "Look!" Indeed the rigged jack was now clinging to the ceiling.

"Do me a favor. Clean up the cards while I'm on the phone and I'll teach you how to do it when I get back." Merlin winked at Mrs. Schaffer.

When he reached his office, Merlin closed the door and snatched the phone from its cradle. "This is Dr. Merlin."

"Hello," a business-like female voice responded crisply. "This is Andrea. I'm the director of alumni affairs at the College of Physicians and Surgeons. You made an inquiry about one of our graduates earlier today."

"Is there some kind of a problem?"

"Wendy explained to me that Marshall Cutter, P and S seventy-eight, was applying for a job with you."

"That's correct. I get the sense there's some kind of problem."

"Doctor, I need to ask you: Is this some kind of prank?"

"Of course not," Merlin answered. "What's going on?"

"We've checked the several sources we have in our office. Unless some dreadful mistake has been made, the Marshall Cutter you're referring to died in nineteen eighty-one."

"Say that again."

"According to the Columbia College of Physicians and Surgeons alumni magazine, the Marshall Cutter who graduated in seventy-eight died from a brain tumor three years later."

"I see." Merlin swallowed hard.

"As I said, I checked several sources and . . ." Andrea prattled on about Marshall Cutter, but Merlin heard very little of what she had to say.

Ultimately, Merlin ended the conversation by saying,

"I must be the one someone's playing a joke on," and hung up.

Just before returning to Tony, Merlin picked up the phone and called Tory. "You and I are about to cross Deringer's line."

Chapter 18

London drove by the big house on Gumper Pond just before noon. Tory wasn't at all certain about the legality of what they were about to do, so the meeting spot was arranged a couple hundred yards down Old Mill Road. This way, there wouldn't be any cars parked in front of Cutter's house in case he should drive up.

As there were no sidewalks on Old Mill, London, Tory, and Merlin tramped down the shoulder of the road. London was in jeans and a white tailored shirt with her long hair pulled back in a thick ponytail. Merlin and Tory wore their usual workday outfits.

"I feel really conspicuous," London finally said as she admired the expensive homes set back from the road. She was carrying her equipment stowed in a black case that looked like a fancy overnight bag. "No one's home, right?"

"I called just before you drove up." Tory looked at Merlin as if to ask if this was too crazy a plan, but he was busy searching through the thick foliage at Cutter's home.

"And you can't see where I'll be working from the road?" London asked.

"Right. There's a couple of big bushes in front of the

door. Merlin will stand lookout by the road and call to us if anyone should turn into the driveway. London, how long do you think it will take?"

"If I find a couple of good prints, ten minutes, max."

The plan to fingerprint Cutter without his knowledge had been hatched minutes after Merlin had hung up with the alumni office at Columbia's College of Physicians and Surgeons. Merlin had suggested to Tory that if Cutter was the type to assume such an alias, then the odds seemed to favor that at some point he had been arrested for a crime worthy of a set of fingerprints.

In several minutes, Merlin was hunkered down among the flowering azaleas, watching every car that sped along Old Mill Road. The air smelled wonderful, full of the perfumes of spring. All the traffic seemed local—women driving monstrous Suburbans and Range Rovers to ferry their small children to soccer practice, teenagers zipping around in their parents' luxury sedans, and a rumbling pickup filled with lawnmowers and sweaty men on their way to another acre of fresh grass.

Not one Mercedes Benz traveled the road.

Tory and London had reached the front door of Cutter's house. Immediately London liked what she saw. The door handle looked new, an impressive brass affair with a curved vertical handle to grasp while using the thumb to depress an appropriately sized piece just above it.

London went down on one knee and brought her open mouth to within an inch of the thumb piece and gently huffed out a breath.

"By the way, I see what you mean about Deringer."

"What do you mean?" London asked casually, while using her camel hair brush and powder to dust the area before it had time to dry.

"Well, he dropped by for breakfast and gloated about the prints on the Stilwell case."

London looked up at Tory and frowned. "Gloated? That doesn't make any sense."

"After what you told me in the garage, it didn't surprise me."

"It was totally routine." London sounded irritated as she turned her attention back to the thumb plate. "Hey, we're in luck. This looks like a good one." Using a precut piece of clear tape, she lifted the print and affixed it to a card to make a permanent record. "Let's do another on the back door, just to be sure."

The view of Gumper Pond as they came around the house caught the fingerprint examiner's attention. "Wow," London enthused as she knelt down to open her bag. The back door led into the magnificent family room Cutter used to entertain guests and sported a more traditional round doorknob. This was also shiny brass and was ideal for lifting prints. London was able to obtain two more latents. With a magnifying glass the prints appeared to be from the same person, and by the size London felt reasonably certain they were left by a man.

The whole thing took about twelve minutes.

As the three of them were walking back to their cars, Tory asked, "How long do you think it'll take to get a match?"

"It all depends on when I can get on the system. If there's an emergency waiting for me when I get back, it could take a day. Could be as quick as a couple of hours."

Tory nodded. "That'll be great. Is there any way you'd be willing to call me first, before you send the results over to Deringer?"

"He really gloated, huh?" London shook her head.

"You should have heard him, bragging how he insisted that Stilwell's gun be broken down for prints."

London stopped walking. "What? Don't believe that

crap for one second. I've been doing this for a lot longer than Deringer's been in Pittsburgh. I don't need that slezoid to remind me to break down a gun. Every gun—handgun or rifle—is broken down in the lab. Stilwell's was clean, inside and out."

"What?"

"Clean. Stilwell knew what he was doing. There wasn't even a partial on one of the bullets."

Tory looked at Merlin. "Wait a second," Tory said suspiciously. "Deringer showed up at our house with mug shots of Stilwell. That's how we found out his real name."

"You know his real name?"

"Paul Vorkman."

The color in London's face seemed to disappear. "Tory, the gun was clean. I checked it inside and out myself," London said softly as if she knew a silence was about to follow.

"Is it possible that someone else—maybe someone in your department—went over it again and found something?" Tory was careful not to say, "something that *you* overlooked."

"No. My eyes review every case. Believe it or not, Pittsburgh's small enough that there's only one finger-print examiner."

"How easy is it to run a print?"

"When we lift a print, a photograph of it is placed into the AFIS computer. Anyone in the department can input data. But the computer doesn't find an exact match, only a relatively small series of *likely* candidates. It's my job to make the final identification visually. The last part is never done without me."

"So how the hell could Deringer come up with a fin-gerprint identification?"

London swept her hand over her hair as she considered the question. "If he didn't trust my work he could have always requested a second opinion from a different department in another city. But even if that happened, I would know about it."

"What about someone else in the department going behind your back, rechecking the weapon, entering the data into the AFIS computer, and doing the visual check without you knowing it?"

London shook her head. "No one in my department is trained to do it. Comparing prints is not as easy as the movies make it look."

"So Deringer's got another source."

London smiled. "I think you need to have a little heart-to-heart with the good detective. And don't worry, I'll put your number on my speed dial."

"Right here, right now, I want to know what the hell's going on!" Tory demanded in a raised voice. She'd just marched through the police headquarters and directly into Detective Deringer's cluttered office without knocking and was standing next to his desk, looking down at him.

Deringer had been reading his mail. He seemed more surprised than annoyed at the interruption. "Hey, calm down, missy." His voice was soothing, almost syrupy, as if he had placed Tory in the same category as someone on a bridge who was threatening to jump. "You don't want to pop an ovary, do you?" Deringer said jovially. "C'mon, take a load off and siddown. What's gotten you so cranky?"

Tory noticed the detective was looking past her and into the hallway and assumed he was expecting her outburst to attract an audience. "I'll stand. And don't you dare patronize me. I want to know why you lied to me."

"Okay, counselor, be cool." Deringer was holding his

hands toward Tory, palms out, in a conciliatory gesture.
"Let me just close the door and we'll talk this thing
through." Deringer was smiling at Tory now, a phony
sort of smirk he'd plastered on his face for show. His
chair had wheels on the legs, and he remained seated
while his feet walked across the floor, pulling his seated
frame behind him. The door to his office had a large
window in the upper half with DETECTIVE DANIEL DERIN-
GER printed across it in black letters. He gave the door
a hard shove with one hand and it slammed with a bang
loud enough to be heard throughout the station.

Before he had wheeled himself back behind his desk
Tory started in at him. "There weren't any prints on
Stilwell's gun. You've been jerking me around. Where
the hell do you come off—"

"All right, that's enough! Just shut your yap!" Deringer's demeanor changed abruptly. Without warning his
lips curled into an ugly snarl. He looked like an angry
rottweiler, baring his teeth as he spat out his words. His
face was almost purple and there was a bulging vein on
the side of his forehead that looked as if it might burst.
"Don't you *ever* come into this office again without being
invited." He waved a finger at Tory. "I've had about all
I can take of you and your goofy boyfriend. Where the
hell do *you* come off charging in here and demanding
anything from me? You're a nothing. You're a babe in
the woods who wouldn't know what's going down even
if it bit you on your tight little ass."

"You've deliberately kept me in the dark."

"You're goddamn right I have! Do you have any idea
what you're investigating?" Without waiting for Tory to
answer he continued. "I don't think so. Well let me break
some sad news to you. This case is too goddamn big to
let a couple of gee-whiz kids blow it for me. This is real
police stuff. But you wouldn't take a hint. So I fed you

a little bitsy piece of juice about Stilwell that made you think you were in the loop, and you were hungry enough to bite. All I wanted you to do was stay the fuck out of my way."

Tory was too mad to think straight. "You bastard. If this case was so big all you had to do was have your captain call the D.A. and I would have been pulled off."

"Oh, Mommy, Mommy," Deringer teased, using a squeaky voice that made him sound as if he was about to cry. "Someone from the D.A.'s office is being really, really mean to me. Make her stop." Quickly he reverted back to his own angry voice. "Now you know something about us cops. We handle our own problems in our own way. I've been investigating Cutter for six months. I didn't need Vorkman's prints to know who the hell he was. I knew he was coming to town three weeks before you ever heard of him. So tone down your ego and let me do my job. What Cutter's into is going to be stopped . . . by me."

"Exactly where'd you get your information about Stilwell?" Tory's voice was strong.

"Say please," Deringer chided.

Tory was seething. She was ready to storm out of the office, but didn't want to let Deringer have the last word. "This isn't over," she promised.

"Why is it so important to you, Counselor? You're a D.A., for chrissake. Go push some paper. Let me do my job. Then I'll turn everything over to you when I bust this thing open so you can have your little noontime press conference and smile pretty for the cameras."

Tory sat down on a metal chair. "He had his hand around my neck. He handcuffed me to a tree. He nearly killed Merlin and me. That's why it's so important to me."

"You're not going to let go, are you?" he said gruffly

as he pulled out a ring of keys and unlocked a big drawer on his desk. As he rummaged through a series of files, he mumbled, "I'll fuckin' strangle the both of you if you blow this for me . . . aha! Here it is." He pulled a file from the drawer and held it aloft. It was thin, no more than a quarter of an inch. Reading from the handwritten label for dramatic effect he stated, "Paul Vorkman. Makes good bathroom reading."

Deringer stood and walked around his desk. He dropped the file on Tory's lap. As she picked it up and opened the manila cover, the detective headed for the door. "Take all the time you want, Counselor. I've got a case to work."

After Deringer was gone, after he had once again slammed the door, so hard this time that the glass cracked and two uniformed cops hurried over to see what was wrong, Tory opened the file. There were two sets of black-and-white mug shots, a series of candid photographs taken with a telephoto lens, and a typewritten list of Vorkman's crimes, eleven items in all. Tory read the rap sheet three times. Something didn't make sense. After a quick glance out the cracked glass in the door to see if either of the two uniforms was still lurking about, she folded the sheet and furtively slipped it into her bag.

Not taking Mannheim's advice, Marshall Cutter did not re-schedule patients for the OR when he returned to his office. In fact, he canceled surgery for the next two weeks. The thought of spending time in an OR with Brian Trilby was too much for him. Instead he had the girls at the front desk move patients around, and Cutter enjoyed an afternoon of relative calm seeing an endless series of consultations. Each of his patients came with something specific in mind, some with photos torn from magazines, other with pictures in their minds of how they wanted to look. "I want a nose like Demi Moore's." "Strip my varicose veins so my legs look like a dancer's." "A long graceful neck like a swan. Here, look at this picture of Gwyneth Paltrow."

But as he entered the room of his last patient of the day, the nagging image of Brian Trilby with a gun was grimly bobbing just below the surface of his conscious thoughts.

Claudia Beckman was perched on the examination table with the crinkly paper, wearing the little cloth gown in what she must have thought was a fetching way. At twenty-four years old, Claudia was already a perfect little Barbie doll about to endure a divorce. A new pair of breasts was a present to herself, courtesy of her husband's cleaned-out checking account.

"Mrs. Beckman, I'm Dr. Cutter." The surgeon took his seat on the little secretary-type chair so that he was forced to look up in order to see his patient's pretty face.

"Yes, I know," she said coquettishly and giggled.

"I understand you are interested in breast augmentation."

"Yes." Her cheeks flushed in a most appealing way.

Cutter's eyes made a cursory examination of Claudia's ample chest through the flimsy gown. "Tell me why you want larger breasts." This was a question that Cutter always asked, a routine that competent surgeons followed that was no different from questioning patients about allergies to medication before they were prescribed.

"Since I'm getting divorced from my shit of a husband, I'm arranging for him to give me a beautiful new pair of breasts before he becomes my ex."

"How old are you, Claudia?"

"Don't worry, Dr. Cutter, I've really, really thought

this through. I want you to make 'em nice and big. But not so big I need to have them out in a year, you know what I mean? Once everything heals and he's dying to take 'em for a spin, I'm gonna throw the bastard out."

This is why Cutter asked the question in the first place. Now came the tricky part, when the plastic surgeon became psychiatrist. "Claudia, do you think a decision like this should be made when you're so upset about a relationship?"

"Absolutely," Claudia affirmed and pouted prettily. "He's been terrible to me and this is just what . . . you see, he's been bugging me ever since we started dating to get a boob job."

"Why don't you let me examine you?" Cutter said.

Instantly, Claudia hunched her shoulders forward so that the little cloth gown fell from her torso and landed in a delicate heap on her lap. The way she had disrobed without having to reach behind her neck to undo the ties suggested a premeditated plan. Claudia did not look down at the objects under discussion. Instead she smiled coyly, as if she was allowing a lover to see her naked for the first time.

Claudia's breasts were full enough to nicely fill out a bikini or décolleté evening gown. "Claudia, there's nothing wrong with your breasts," Cutter spoke gently, as a father would to an ugly duckling daughter who didn't have a date for the big dance. "In fact, they are in perfect proportion to your body. Quite frankly, I don't think surgery is what you need right now."

"What do I need?"

"You've got a relationship problem. If you don't want to be with your husband anymore, do something about it."

Claudia pulled the gown up to cover herself. This time

she reached behind and tied it at her nape. "But I need a fresh start."

"Surgery's not the way to a fresh start. Maybe you need a new hobby, or take a class at Pitt."

"No, that takes too long. I wanted something, I don't know . . . quick." She wiped a tear from her eye. "I don't know what to do. I feel so alone."

"Maybe you should talk with someone."

"I tried talking to my husband."

"I was thinking of someone else. Maybe a girlfriend. Or even a—"

"A shrink. That's what you were going to say, isn't it?"

"Well, if you're feeling lost, sometimes a psychiatrist is a good place to start." *Valdemar!* The name popped into his head just like that. One second Cutter was the good doctor trying to do right by a patient, the next he was fixated on Tanner Valdemar. *He's got the answer.*

"Oh, I don't know."

"Look, I'll make a deal with you. Let me give you the names of several excellent psychiatrists. Get your husband problems out of the way, and if you *still* want to consider bigger breasts, come back and see me." *Tanner Valdemar. If Mannheim's going to leave you hanging, do it on your own.*

Claudia sniffed and slid off the table to look for her clothes. "I guess you're right, Doctor."

"Stop by the front desk. I'll have one of the girls type up a list for you."

Before Claudia had hooked her bra, Marshall Cutter was in his Mercedes heading toward Oakland.

Chapter 19

Marshall Cutter had known Tanner Valdemar since he had first come to Pittsburgh. By no means were the two of them friends, but they had certainly become colleagues, and if there was one thing colleagues could expect from one another, it was off-the-record consultations.

At three-thirty p.m. the hallways of the Medical Center were still crowded. As Cutter rode the elevator to the eighth floor, he rehearsed what he intended to say. Of the many possibilities he considered, approaching Brian Trilby from a professional liability standpoint seemed to be his best bet.

The eighth floor housed psychiatry and social services. Valdemar's office began with a cramped anteroom that served both as a waiting area and a place for his secretary's little desk. Patients bided their time until Valdemar could see them on a small sofa that should have been replaced years earlier.

Cutter opened the door and was surprised to see that the anteroom was completely empty. Not even his secretary was around. No background music could be heard. Although the ceiling lights were still on, the computer screen on the secretary's desk was dark. His first impulse was to turn around and head back to the elevators, but then Cutter noticed that the door leading to Valdemar's office was ajar. He was reluctant to push the door open for a peek into the psychiatrist's lair. Psychiatrists were especially picky about patient confidentiality issues. Getting caught sneaking into the office would blow any possibility that Valdemar would grant the favor Cutter was seeking.

But his curiosity overwhelmed his sense of propriety. There was light on the other side of the door, that much he could see, but Valdemar was not visible. *Why didn't I call first?*

Suddenly, the door opened in a sweeping motion and Cutter was standing face-to-face with Tanner Valdemar. The psychiatrist smiled. "Marshall, what are you doing sneaking about? C'mon in. What brings you here?"

As Cutter followed Valdemar into his office he remarked in the most offhand way he could muster, "By the way, I referred you a patient today."

"You did?" Valdemar sounded surprised, not by the fact that he had been referred a patient but that Cutter had stopped by to tell him about it.

"Young girl, pretty. Major guy problems, though. Wanted a new set of breasts to get at her hubby. I gave her your name."

"As always, thank you. Hey, where're my manners?" Valdemar said. "Sit down." With a motion of his arm he directed his guest to the couch.

Cutter looked around, taking an appropriately long moment to admire the artwork on the walls, the mahogany desk in one corner, and the grand mirror behind Valdemar's seat. As he sank into the couch, the same one Brian Trilby had occupied when he told of his *Wizard of Oz* nightmares, he tried to say something casual. "How do you make do without a window, Tanner?"

"I guess they figured that without a window, I wouldn't have any jumpers." The two men shared a laugh.

"No bridges either," Cutter said, suddenly in a good humor. "Well, that's not the reason I wanted to speak to you."

The psychiatrist nodded his head. "What's up?"

"Well . . . this whole thing with that patient who attacked Merlin and his girlfriend."

"I figured as much. Stilwell was his name, I believe."

"Yes, Stilwell." Cutter tried to sound exasperated and exhaled loudly.

"How are you feeling about it?"

"Oh no, it's not that, Tanner. I can handle my end of it." Cutter chuckled knowingly. "Actually I'm worried about one of the people in my office. Brian Trilby." Cutter studied the psychiatrist's face for some sign of recognition.

Valdemar sat in his chair, the reflection of the back of his head in the one-way mirror behind him, his legs crossed and appearing supremely serene. Not one of the muscles in his face flinched. Neither of his pupils dilated, his fingers remained perfectly still, and his Adam's apple did not bob in response to a hard swallow. This was a situation Valdemar knew how to handle.

"Anyway, I'm aware he's been a patient of yours for some time now, and with Brian handling all the anesthesia for me—"

"Marshall, let me interrupt you. I hope you won't take this the wrong way, but understand that since I went into practice, I've never discussed anything about my patients without their explicit written permission. In fact, I don't even *identify* who my patients are to anyone."

"Tanner, I understand this is strictly confidential. I'm not here for my benefit, you see. It's my patients I'm

concerned about. If Brian's unstable, then . . ." Cutter
let his voice drift off.

"Look, if you have concerns about someone you work
with, you have an obligation to handle the problem definitively yourself."

Cutter stood and began to pace around the room. Valdemar noticed that the wooden armrest where the plastic
surgeon had placed his hand was shiny with perspiration.
Cutter walked over to the mirror behind Valdemar.
"One-way, huh," he said and placed a hand on the clean
surface as he brought his face close enough to it to create
a shadow, hoping to see inside.

"The room's empty. Is there anything else on your
mind?"

"Look, Tanner, I *know* Trilby is one of your patients.
He told me so. You don't have to confirm it."

Valdemar did not respond verbally. He shrugged both
shoulders, letting Cutter know he was free to draw whatever conclusions he desired.

"Okay, okay, Tanner. Hypothetically, if someone was
one of your patients and you knew he was doing something illegal, you'd have to inform the police, right?"

"I have an obligation to *prevent* a crime that has not
yet happened. That is correct."

"Does that mean that Trilby—"

"I already explained—"

Cutter waved him off. "I know what you said. But
we've known each other for too long. We're colleagues,
for crissake. I refer you patients. You refer me patients.
We have a certain understanding. We respect each other.
Let's just agree on the fact that Trilby's one of your
patients."

"Marshall, I'm not getting spun into a web of logic.
Deduce what you want, but please move on to another
subject."

Cutter strode to the other side of the room and randomly grabbed a tall glass figurine from Valdemar's desk and crudely held it in his sweaty hands. The thought struck him that Valdemar was handling him in much the same way Mannheim did. "Goddamnit, Tanner. We're friends. I come here looking for help and you sit there like you don't know what's going on."

"What *is* going on, Marshall?" Valdemar interjected, hoping to encourage his colleague to open up.

"Oh, I know what you're doing. Everything I say gets flipped into a question. Right? I know the routine. I'm in on the psychoanalytical tricks." He put the figurine back in its place and walked over to the couch. "Okay, we're having a privileged conversation here, right?" Cutter was getting angry, and his head bobbed when he spoke.

"If you mean will I afford it the same confidentiality I do my patients, the answer is yes."

Cutter forced himself to be still and looked Valdemar directly in the eyes. "Tanner, I'm terrified for my life." The words hung in the air for several seconds before he went on. "This Stilwell thing . . ."

"Ahhh, Stilwell. What kind of trouble are you in?"

"Big time. I'm in so deep there's no way to get out." He swallowed.

"Would you like to tell me what's going on?"

Cutter shook his head hard. "I can't. It's too dangerous."

"What do you mean?"

"It's so goddamn frustrating! Someone's out there. I don't know who, but someone's there. I think they may be after me." Cutter peered at Valdemar to see if he was going to jump into the conversation. When he said nothing, merely nodding his head in an encouraging way, Cutter continued. "Look, like I said, this is privileged. . . .

I'm terrified Trilby has something to do with this whole Stilwell thing. You know? I went through his desk. Guess what? He has a gun, some fancy thing in a black case. I never thought Trilby was the sort to go around with a gun in the office. So I'm asking you as a colleague—I'm begging you as a goddamn friend—am I in danger?" He clenched his teeth together and spoke softly. "Am I working with the guy responsible for killing one of my patients? And before you say a word, I promise—I swear on my dead mother's grave—I won't say a word to anyone. I just have to know if I'm in danger."

"You've got some real concerns, Marshall. And I have some advice for you. Before we go any further, you've got to get control of yourself." Valdemar had reverted to the tone he reserved for unstable patients, calming yet not condescending. "Okay, I want you to take several deep cleansing breaths. Do them with me."

"No! You're not going to hypnotize me. No way."

"Marshall, I never hypnotize anyone without his permission. Either you allow me to help you calm down or we can't go any further." Valdemar studied Cutter sitting forward, face on fire, hair matted to the sides of his head with sweat. "Now, sit back against the cushions and take some deep breaths."

Reluctantly, Cutter obeyed, leaning himself back and taking a few showy deep breaths. "Okay, Tanner, I'm okay," he finally said, taking care to modulate his voice in the calmest way possible. "Tell me what you know."

"You're not listening to me. What I want to tell you is based on everything you just told me. If someone you work with is behaving strangely and has a gun, you must go to the police at once."

"Is he unstable?"

"You just told me there is reason to believe Trilby is dangerous. That's all. Just go to the police."

"It's not that simple." Cutter kicked his voice up a couple of decibels. "I can't afford to be wrong. If Trilby's not the one, then I know who it is. Do you understand? It's one of two people. But I need some goddamned help right now and you're the only one who can help me."

"Marshall, listen to what you're saying. Somehow you've gotten yourself in trouble. You may be in some kind of peril—"

"Aha! So I *am* in danger. I get it."

Valdemar ignored this last comment. "So you don't need me. Go to the police."

"And what am I gonna do, guess? If I'm wrong, I'm a dead man." Cutter studied Valdemar's face, hoping to see a spark of sympathy. Realizing he wasn't budging the psychiatrist he said, "Screw you," with a sneer.

"Marshall, I think we're about done. You wanted my counsel, I gave it to you. But you're out of control." Valdemar rose from his chair as a directive to Cutter to do the same. Holding out his left hand toward the door, Valdemar began walking slowly so his guest would remain in front of him until he was safely in the anteroom.

Cutter obediently headed toward the door, head down as if he was humiliated by the experience. But he was more desperate than humiliated, prolonging the time he was with Valdemar, forcing himself to think of some last-ditch effort to extract the information he desperately needed.

They had reached the other side of the room and Valdemar was just opening the door for him when the plastic surgeon said, "Tanner, please, just give me a nod. You can trust me."

"When you have a chance to think about what I've said—maybe sleep on it if you're not ready to go to the police yet—I'm certain you'll make the right decision." He patted his colleague on the shoulder.

Cutter yanked his shoulder away petulantly so that Valdemar's hand was left in the air. "Get the hell away from me!" He spat out his words and gave Valdemar a tremendous two-handed shove away from him, catching him squarely in the chest.

The psychiatrist was caught off guard. As he stumbled backward, the sound of air rushing from his lungs filled the room. His outstretched arms began to flail about in desperate circular motions to catch himself. One, two, three, four, five steps, and with each one he fell back a little closer to his big desk.

Cutter had the feeling everything was happening in slow motion. He had time to experience every detail, every bit of nuance that was unfolding before him. For an instant he could see both Valdemar and the psychiatrist's reflection in the one-way mirror. There was the smell of peppermint in the air, which he wouldn't realize until later was the sweet smell of Valdemar's Altoid-freshened breath. Cutter even noticed the way the psychiatrist's tie, a bright red one with blotches of blue that looked like a Rorschach test, flew up into his face as his fall accelerated, his feet pedaling faster and faster. Most of all, Cutter visualized himself standing there, watching the tragedy that he caused unfolding as both hands came up to his face in horror.

Bang!

Valdemar smacked the edge of the desk with the back of his head, making a sick hollow sound.

Valdemar fell straight to the ground. His arms did not come up to grab his head. His feet did not kick in response to the pain. His vocal cords were strangely silent.

Cutter had not yet moved from the doorway. "You okay?" he called out. Already he was thinking of an excuse and an apology for what had happened. "Tanner? Hey, you okay?"

        *   *   *

"In the seventies he was arrested twice for auto theft and once for selling marijuana."

Merlin was in scrubs, drinking coffee as he listened to Tory read from the rap sheet. They were in the surgical lounge, sitting together on one end of the sofa, speaking in hushed tones so the two cardiac surgeons checking the stock market on CNN wouldn't overhear their conversation.

"In eighty-two he was convicted of selling stolen guns and did nine months in prison. Eighty-six, DUI, lost his license. Eighty-seven, driving without a license. Two armed robberies, more drugs, assaulting a police officer. In ninety-three he was arrested with two kilos of cocaine and escaped from a courthouse in Dallas." Tory then handed Merlin the rap sheet so he could see for himself.

"So he's a bona fide creep." Merlin scratched his cheek and began to read Vorkman's history a second time.

"That's the point. Vorkman was just a creep, not a murderer."

"Biggest thing he ever did was escape from the courthouse in Dallas. And that was five years ago."

"So why didn't he get his new face then? His face was probably on the news, he was a wanted man, but now . . ." Tory's voice trailed off.

"He's not the sort anyone cares about anymore. So why lay out seventeen grand to change his face?"

"Maybe he's into something new, and the cops are looking for him."

Merlin scratched his cheek again as he thought. "Wouldn't the file make some mention of that?"

"And even if he got a new face, his fingerprints are on file. The second he got arrested for DUI, he would be at risk for being discovered."

"It doesn't fit. Deringer's telling us half the story. He's trying to slow us down."

"Who do you know in the department who can do a little snooping?"

"No one. But I bet London does."

Valdemar was on the oriental rug, lying on his side with one arm under his torso. He looked like an old drunk who had fallen asleep in a gutter. Seconds ticked by without so much as a twitch.

Cutter inched closer to the fallen man. "Tanner, it was an accident. Wake up. Please, wake up." Another step. "This isn't funny anymore." Cutter turned around and checked to see if the door was closed behind him.

It was halfway opened, wide enough for anyone in the anteroom to view the grim scene. A quick glance back toward Valdemar, then he sprang to the door and slammed it closed.

Cutter pushed the little button in the center of the knob and locked the door. Once again he walked in the direction of his colleague. A minute and a half had gone by. No movement. No groans. "Oh, God! Oh, God!" he was whispering to himself as he towered over the body.

When he realized he was thinking of Valdemar as a body, and no longer as a person, he shuddered.

Cutter squatted down and checked for blood. Valdemar's head was turned sideways, his left cheek to the floor. There was a small crimson stain on the carpet, as if it were a shadow under his head. As time slipped by, Cutter studied the stain to see if it was growing. Sluggishly it expanded, moving away from Valdemar's face.

Cutter took a single deep breath. His throat felt as if it were blocked and beginning to strangle him. The windsor knot at his neck was too tight. Cutter clawed at it until he had yanked it six inches down his chest. "Tanner!" He desperately reached out for Valdemar's shoulder and gave him a good hard shake while he pleaded, "Wake up! This was an accident. That's all, an accident. I was . . . I was upset. You knew I was upset. Of course you knew. You're a shrink. Say something." Cutter stopped shaking and let him go.

Valdemar did not respond.

Cutter reached for Valdemar's thin wrist and felt for a pulse. Immediately he palpated a beat that was strong and fast. It was racing along at a hundred thirty beats per minute, pounding away ferociously. The plastic surgeon frowned. This was not the thready pulse of a man near death. Cutter had been taking his own pulse. He worked at it for several minutes, trying to isolate his own rhythm so that he could find one on Valdemar. "Shit!" he hissed when he was forced to the realization that there was no evidence Valdemar's heart was still beating.

His first instinct was to scream for help. Things were out of hand. He saw a phone on the desk and reached for it. *Wait!* His brain shot into ghost-of-Christmas-future mode. Detective Deringer's voice played clearly in his head. *So Doctor, what were you doing in Valdemar's office? . . . How often did you say you stopped by just to talk? . . . And you told the hospital police there was some sort of an accident? What happened, you pushed him? . . . Well, what was going on that you got so mad?*

"No way," Cutter blurted out.

An even more frightening thought popped into Cutter's head: What if someone had been watching? What if someone had been in the dark little observation room and had seen the whole thing? Springing to his feet, Cutter dashed across the room to the one-way mirror. He saw how disheveled he looked in his reflection. Sweat was pouring from his face in huge droplets that was turning the collar of his shirt three shades darker. Strands of hair were matted down to his forehead and his eyes had a glazed, brutal look that made him feel as if he didn't know himself. No longer was he the handsome, confident doctor the medical community knew him to be. Something was different about his eyes, something he couldn't quite put into words. Maybe it was the way he held his lids at half-mast as if he was hiding behind them. Or was it the truculence with which he glared back at himself? It didn't matter. He had seen it before. Men like Stanley Stilwell had it, hard men who handled their problems with a swiftness that defied reason. And now Marshall Cutter had it, too.

He cupped his hands around his eyes and leaned on the cool surface of the mirror. Working his fingers to block out all the light in the room, Cutter desperately tried to peer into the absolute darkness. He couldn't see a thing.

Cutter pulled back and examined himself. It was hard to look at his own image.

Oh my God! He licked his lips. *What if I'm wrong? What if Valdemar still has a spark of life?*

In four quick strides he was back, kneeling over Valdemar so that no part of his clothing would come in contact with the body. He turned his head and brought his ear up against Valdemar's mouth. Closing his eyes so that he could concentrate on nothing but the sound of air moving across Valdemar's lips, Cutter held his breath.

Utter quiet. Valdemar didn't have a pulse and he wasn't breathing. He was dead. And Cutter was responsible.

The terror of what had just happened seized him. He pushed himself away from the body then thrust himself clumsily across the floor to get as far away from the scene as he possibly could. In the process, his shirt pulled free from his pants and one of his pants legs shimmied halfway up his calf, exposing a swath of white skin above his socks. He had no energy left to do anything but sit on the floor and press the palms of his hands against his tightly closed eyes. *You pushed him. . . . What the hell's wrong with you?* The powerful urge to vomit grabbed him. Bitter bile singed the back of his mouth, and Cutter quickly responded with deep breaths through his nose as he struggled to contain the nausea. *Oh, God, please help me. Don't let me get sick. Not now.* Every bit of energy was focused on keeping his gastric contents safely inside his stomach. He pulled air in and out through his nose so forcefully he made an agonal noise that sounded as if he might be headed toward respiratory failure. He had maneuvered himself into a sitting position, leaning forward in a failed attempt to get comfortable.

Get out of here! a voice screamed inside his head. But his brain was so jumbled with noisy thoughts it was hard to single out any one voice and respond to it. *Run!*

Deep breath in. Deep breath out.

Over and over he reminded himself to suck air in and blow it out until the nausea passed, and he could look at the dead man lying eight feet away without feeling faint.

Cutter studied Valdemar. The body was in the same position it had assumed when it hit the floor. Other than the trauma to the head Cutter reasoned that the body would show no signs of a struggle. Who was to say what had actually happened in the office after everyone else had left for the day? *Run! Get the hell out of here as fast as you can and run for your life!*

"No. I need to think," Cutter said aloud to calm himself. "Just like Mannheim. Stay cool and think this out." He pushed himself to his feet, noticing how wobbly his legs felt. Working his hand like a crude comb he smoothed his hair, sweeping it off his forehead and back toward his ears. Then he readjusted the windsor knot and stuffed his shirt back into his pants.

Suddenly there was a perverse confidence to his manner as he moved across the room to the door. His eyes remained focused on where he was going. Tanner Valdemar had some sort of stroke and hit his head when he fell. That was the story. Cutter was as clean as an altar boy.

"When they find him in the morning it'll look like an unfortunate accident." Hearing his own voice was tonic for his madness, instilling him with an even greater sense of self-reliance. "Just open the door and you're on your way home. You need some dinner, maybe even a glass of scotch and a good night's rest. This is every man for himself."

Cutter grasped the doorknob and twisted it.

"Shit," he whispered, the confident facade disappearing as quickly as it had come. "Fingerprints." Desperately, his eyes searched the room. Valdemar's desk. The bookshelf. The little table next to the sofa. Finally he spotted a box of Kleenex, a blue box with an unimaginative design on it so that it wouldn't look like a box of tissues.

He checked his watch as he took several long steps to the sofa. Pulling tissue after tissue from the box until he had a huge wad in his hand, Cutter started retracing where he had been in the room. "The arm of the couch," he reminded himself as he wiped the wooden surfaces of the couch with broad strokes. "Maybe the table." A few swipes of the end table where the Kleenex box sat. Then he wiped down the mirror and headed for the glass statue he had been holding. The ball of tissues seemed to be shrinking in Cutter's sweaty hand. Before handling the statue, Cutter peeled apart the moist glob of tissues in his hand, teasing off a single Kleenex with which he picked up the figurine. Then he used the rest of the wad to wipe down the statue before replacing it on the desk.

"Couch, table, mirror, statue." Tanner Valdemar's lifeless body was inches from his feet. Cutter stood at the desk doing a clumsy little pirouette as he reviewed his whereabouts in the room. Finally, when he was satisfied he had been absolutely thorough, he crept gently over the oriental carpet, wiped down the doorknob, opened the door using the last of the Kleenex, and walked out of Tanner Valdemar's office.

Chapter 20

The man responsible for terrorizing Marshall Cutter had left the plastic surgeon on the eighth floor of the Medical Center and made the forty-minute drive out to Cranberry Township. He was now comfortably ensconced in a plush sofa in the Trilbys' family room off the kitchen, looking out the bay window that was framed by puffy curtains. The sofa had been recommended by the same designer who had suggested the fancy end tables in the bedroom. In the glossy catalogue the interior decorator provided, this particular piece of furniture had looked absolutely stunning. Its cushions were covered with a bold striped fabric creating the kind of piece people would be certain to notice. At least that's what the decorator had said while Lori was making up her mind.

Once it was delivered and Lori sat herself on it, striking the type of pose women are supposed to assume when they are sitting on an expensive piece of furniture, she realized it was the most hideous thing she could imagine. But it had cost almost two grand and the decorator never said it was attractive, only that people would notice it, so in the end, Lori decided to keep it.

The man who had pithed Stanley Stilwell was now lounging on it, leaning back on the expensive cushions as he sipped a Diet Coke from a can. He'd decided against a beer because he had a lot to do and wanted to keep his wits about him.

A copy of *Country Living* was sitting on the end table. He reached out for it and leafed through the slick pages as he passed the time.

He had arrived almost an hour earlier, just after Lori Trilby returned from the Giant Eagle with the back of her Land Rover brimming with bags of groceries.

As he made his way to the house, he rooted through the three remaining bags. There were all the usual items; tuna fish, mayonnaise, salsa, cereal. Evidently Lori was planning on making spaghetti sauce. Not only was there a box of Barilla pasta, there was also a twenty-eight-ounce can of crushed tomatoes. Neglecting to remove the bags from the car, he grabbed the can and held it in his hand, admiring its considerable heft.

Now he was making himself at home, taking it easy while he waited. Since he'd arrived from the Medical Center he'd been on the Gateway computer in the family room, going through every file, and had spent nearly fifteen minutes rifling through the dressers in the master bedroom. There was a small study off the bedroom, one of those men-only rooms with dark green wallpaper, plaid carpet on the floor, and walls crammed with meaningless awards and certificates with every imaginable type of embossed seal. The desk was compulsively neat. He examined everything. A series of slots recessed into the wall held every bill that had been sent to the house in the last three weeks. A ceramic mug was stuffed with pens and pencils. Three drawers contained Trilby's checkbooks and boxes of envelopes stuffed with photographs that begged to be placed in albums. And there were bookshelves, an entire wall of them, three-quarter-inch wooden planks straining under the weight of dozens of medical texts. Each book was opened and thrown onto the floor after it was confirmed to be empty.

The one thing he had been unable to find was what he had demanded Brian Trilby get for him. It was hidden somewhere in the house. The man was certain of it. There was no way Trilby had ignored the demand; once he had heard the description of the wicked dance, the anesthesiologist had nearly wet his pants.

So now the man with the ice pick strapped to his leg had plunked himself down on the designer sofa, wearing the same pair of surgical gloves he had donned in the driveway so that he wouldn't have to wipe down the twenty-eight-ounce can of crushed tomatoes he had used to put Lori Trilby out of commission before dragging her down to the basement. To assure her absolute silence, he had tied her up and gagged her with more than a yard of duct tape.

His black ski mask sat next to him on the couch. Once Lori had been stowed away in the basement, he'd removed it because it got itchy and hot. Besides, he'd have plenty of time to put it on once Brian Trilby pulled into the driveway. All he had to do was wait.

The plan was set at dinner. Merlin and Tori would travel to Brian Trilby's house together—without any cops in tow—and wait at the front door while he retrieved the information he had promised to Tory. There was no reason to actually go inside the house.

Even with such a simple plan, Merlin could not shake the vivid description Trilby had given of inserting a needle into someone's brain. The more Tory thought about what had transpired during her interview with the anesthesiologist, the more frightened and confused she had become.

The trip out to Cranberry Township took thirty minutes, two exits west on the Pennsylvania Turnpike and another ten minutes on the side roads looking for Winding Lane. It turned out to be an appropriately named street full of new construction. Houses were in the four-hundred-thousand-dollar range, sitting on three-quarter acre lots with skinny saplings that were two decades away from throwing any real shade on the yards.

Trilby lived right in the middle of the block in a sprawling clapboard that looked as if it belonged on the New England coastline. Two cars were in the driveway; a Land Rover and a BMW directly behind it. Several of the mailboxes on Winding Lane proclaimed something about the personality of its owner. One was festooned with pictures of ducks, another had a series of real golf balls attached to it, and there was even one that was a detailed replica of a steam locomotive. What gave the Trilby mailbox character was that the standard-issue, hardware store unit had been cleverly inserted into what looked like a miniature version of the home in which the family lived. It was the kind of thing that encouraged Lori Trilby's friends to remark, "Oh, isn't that cute," whenever they arrived for their weekly bridge games.

The neighborhood was full of energy. Children played outside, milking the last minutes of play from the darkening sky. A man was walking his dog. Young couples strolled with their babies.

Merlin parked the car by the curb and the two of them headed up the flagstone walk toward the heavily lacquered front door. There were rhododendrons not yet in bloom and azaleas bursting with pinks and reds planted in fresh mulch. Hanging from the doorknob on a cluster of metal hangers was a bunch of Brian Trilby's dress shirts, recently dropped off by the dry-cleaning service. Four decorative windows shaped like big keyholes spanned the door at eye level. Two more windows, side lights nearly the same height as the door, flanked the entrance like watchful sentries. Each was covered with a hanging drape. The one on the knob side of the door had a small crease in the middle where it had evidently been pushed aside by a child too short to see through the keyhole-shaped windows when checking who was at the door before opening it.

Merlin rang the doorbell and stepped back to wait. A gentle breeze caught the plastic wrap on the shirts, ballooning them up so that they resembled a Portuguese man-of-war dangling from the door. Three children shot down the street on bicycles in a frantic race to the end of the block.

Tory caught Merlin's eye, then raised her eyebrows and made a face as if to say, *You think anyone's home?* Merlin rang the bell again. This time Merlin stood directly in front of the door, raising himself up on the balls of his feet to catch his first glimpse of the Trilby household through the windows.

Light could be seen coming from the back of the house, but the front of the house, including the foyer on the other side of the door, was dark. Details were difficult to make out and Merlin could only discern the white spindles supporting the banister heading to the second floor and an ornate chandelier hanging in the middle of the foyer.

"You think he's home?" Tory asked.

"There's light on in back," Merlin said. "Two cars in the driveway. I wonder if he's ducking us."

It felt odd tramping across the yard to the side of the house uninvited. They walked quickly in front of the dining room before reaching the driveway. Merlin stopped by Lori Trilby's Land Rover and noticed the rear door was opened partway. Three bags of groceries still sat in the back.

The kitchen door, constructed with nearly equal parts glass and pine, was a short distance from where the Land Rover was parked. It, too, was not completely closed. All the lights were on in the kitchen.

"Someone's got to be home," Tory said.

Merlin bounded up the two wooden steps to the small painted porch and knocked firmly on the door's pane. The door began to open. "Hello!" Merlin called into the house. Groceries covered one end of the counter, still in the plastic bags from the Giant Eagle. When he didn't get a response he grabbed hold of the brass knob and held the door firm so he could make some real noise when he banged his fist hard against the wood.

Something was wrong. Cars were in the driveway. Groceries needed to be put away. And the door was left open.

Merlin pushed the kitchen door all the way open.

"What are you doing?" Tory whispered nervously. She was looking over her shoulder to see if any neighbors were watching. "Don't go in there. This could be some kind of trap."

Merlin didn't hesitate. He took one step inside the kitchen while Tory plunged her hand inside her leather bag in search of the Beretta.

Merlin was walking slowly, taking several steps then stopping to look around and listen. The house was deadly quiet. Merlin peered inside several of the bags on the counter, seeing one with a container of Häagen-Dazs ice cream and a box of Popsicles. A reddish-orange liquid that had once been frozen to a sliver of wood was now a puddle at the bottom of the bag. The container of cookies & cream oozed creamy goo.

Merlin held his index finger in front of his closed lips. Tory nodded and slowly slid her leather bag off her shoulder and placed it on the floor by the door. The Beretta was chest high, ready to fire.

Their eyes were on high alert, scanning about the room. The only thing out of place was a twenty-eight-ounce can of crushed tomatoes on the floor underneath the sink in the toe-space.

Two doors led from the kitchen—one to the dining room, the other to the family room. Both rooms were dark.

Merlin led the way. Tory stayed right behind him, oscillating her head back and forth, expecting someone to burst out of the shadows.

Sliding his hands up the silk wallpaper of the dining room Merlin found the light switch. A grand chandelier, several orders of magnitude more ornate than the one in the foyer, burst into brilliant white light. The room was rectangular and spotlessly neat. A second door, across the room from the kitchen, led out to the foyer. Oriental carpet covered the floor, each strand of fringe lined up perfectly as if Mrs. Trilby had her cleaning woman comb it once a week. A handsome wooden table was surrounded by half a dozen chairs, each costing twice what the table had. A huge sideboard displayed a silver tea service.

"Unnnnnh. Unnnh."

A muffled sound tore through the silence. It came from another part of the house but startled them as if it had been a Klaxon. Tory snapped into a ready position, legs apart, arms at full extention. First she directed the weapon toward the darkened foyer. Then she whipped around a full 180 degrees and looked back into the kitchen.

"Unh. Unnnn."

"What is that?" Tory coarsely whispered, quickly tucking her hair behind one ear.

Merlin shook his head. He pointed back toward the kitchen and the two retreated there. The muffled voice continued to call out, becoming louder as they left the dining room.

Moving cautiously, they crossed through the kitchen and headed into the family room. Merlin found the lights. The room was heavily decorated with furniture that looked like it belonged in a fashion magazine, along with cream-colored carpet and huge, billowed curtains. The only thing out of place here was a copy of *Country Living* magazine on the floor in front of the striped sofa.

"Unnnh. Unnnnnh. Unnnnnn!"

The muffled cries were growing more urgent now. Merlin and Tory strained to locate the voice, which seemed to be coming from a closed door directly to their left.

"Merlin," Tory whispered, "this could be a trap. Let's call the police."

He looked at Tory. Six feet separated him from the door. Using hand signals he backed Tory off so that if Trilby burst through the door he wouldn't be within striking distance of both of them.

"Unnnh. Unnnnnh."

Merlin's breathing was measured. As gently as possible he turned the knob and pulled the door open. No lights were on. A carpeted staircase led down to the basement.

"Unnnnh. Unnh." Someone was in the basement. The muffled pleas were impossible to understand, but conveyed the fear of someone struggling to get free.

"Don't go down there, Merlin," Tory pleaded quietly.

"You stay up here. If there's any trouble I'll call up to you."

"Take it," she said, offering him the Beretta.

Merlin waved her off. With a flip of the light switch

he could see the corner of a pool table in the basement.
The cries became more insistent.

Step by step he descended the stairs, one hand on the
wooden railing. At the bottom he paused and looked
around before moving out of Tory's line of sight.

Most of the basement was fixed up handsomely, with
knotty-pine wood paneling on the walls, a velvet pool
table, and a big screen television set flanked by two old
sofas. Plush carpeting dampened the sound of Merlin's
footsteps. The cries were coming from a different part
of the basement, an unfurnished area with cinder-block
walls and a bare floor of poured concrete. It was the
laundry room, tucked unobtrusively behind the stairs, a
part of the house for the cleaning woman to do Mrs.
Trilby's wash and ironing. A single light fixture dangled
from the ceiling but Merlin couldn't find a switch.

In the darkness Merlin could see three people on the
floor beneath the wash sink, a woman and two young
boys, lashed to the pipes with yards of tape. Their
mouths were bound with layers of duct tape. The woman
was struggling to free herself, crying out through the gag.

Merlin whirled around, both hands clenched in tight
fists, ready for a fight if the intruder was waiting behind
him. There was no one else in the room. "Tory, call the
police!" Merlin screamed out over his shoulder as he
dropped to his knees and began to peel off the sticky
tape from Lori's mouth.

Tory was startled by the sound of urgency in Merlin's
voice. Running to the top of the stairs she yelled,
"You okay?"

"Fine. Just go call the police."

Tory's head swiveled back and forth frantically looking
for a phone. As she turned toward the kitchen she spot-

ted a light blue cordless model sitting on one of the matching end tables on the far side of the striped sofa. Hurrying across the thick carpet, something caught Tory's eye: a pair of men's shoes behind the sofa. The toes were pointing toward the ceiling, standing up like those of the Wicked Witch of the East after Dorothy's house landed on her.

Tory slowed her gait and treaded across the carpet cautiously, as if she were on a thinly frozen pond and each step brought new danger of breaking through the ice. A man was attached to the shoes, dressed in nice slacks and a sport shirt. She saw blood pooled on the carpet near his head.

Immediately, she recognized Brian Trilby lying supine, arms at his side, his sport shirt bunched up where it had pulled free from his pants.

Tory took a single deep breath and covered her mouth with one hand. Her muscles felt leaden, unable to allow her the ability to do anything but stand there and gawk. The Beretta hung uselessly down by her side in her right hand. Her finger wasn't even on the trigger.

Without warning Trilby's right arm twitched, lifting up from the carpet for a moment before dropping back to the floor. The rest of him didn't budge. He made absolutely no sound.

"Trilby?" Tory inched closer. Coming around to his side she knelt down and reached out for his hand. It felt cold. She gave it a little shake back and forth. Tory was about to call out for Merlin when she heard a woman's voice scream from the basement. She was shrieking out her husband's name.

Tory reached for the phone. As she punched in 911, she stood up and looked about the room. That's when she realized she wasn't alone. The intruder was still in the house, not ten feet away from her. Although she couldn't see or hear him, one of the puffy curtains framing the bay window started to move back and forth. At the bottom, where the curtains were hemmed to within an inch of the carpet, she could make out the toe of a dark shoe peeking out like a frightened kitten.

Tory never knew what gave her away. Whether it was the sound of the cordless phone slipping from her fingers and bouncing off the floor, or the way she gasped when she spotted the curtains moving, somehow the man behind the curtains sensed that she knew he was there. Her vocal cords were frozen and she hesitated for the briefest moment before realizing the Beretta was in her hand.

The curtains exploded. In an instant the room filled with the furious energy of a man dressed entirely in black, a ski mask tightly covering his head. He was upon her at once, grabbing her with powerful hands wrapped in blue surgical gloves. Before she could react he had snapped a hand over her mouth and ripped the Beretta from her hand.

Tory kicked and clawed at the man but she was no match for him. He controlled her easily, clamping her in a tight bear hear from behind and dragging her to the top of the stairs to the basement.

Once the masked man had maneuvered Tory into the doorway, he gave one quick shove. Tory was caught off guard. Her arms flailed about for something to grab onto, but it was too late. She tumbled down the basement stairs, letting out a scream as she fell.

It was over quickly, and Tory lay in a heap on the floor.

Marshall Cutter forced himself to stay awake for the eleven o'clock news. Dressed in the same sweaty clothing he'd worn to the Medical Center for his session with Valdemar, he hadn't moved from the brown leather sofa in his family room for three hours. He never bothered to have dinner or that glass of scotch he'd promised himself. All he could see in his brain was the flaccid, doll-like way Tanner Valdemar's arms moved when he shook him. As he sat on his couch, he contemplated his own mortality. How long could this madness go on? One thing he knew for sure: Mannheim must never find out about the accident. *Tanner Valdemar died of an unfortunate mishap. I heard all about it.* It was a rationalization he was using to package the horror of what he had done in his own mind. *No one must ever know,* he reminded himself over and over. He even took to rehearsing what he would say in the morning when he made rounds. "Isn't that awful about Tanner? I'm just sick about it. He truly had a gift. By the way, when is the funeral?"

A box of saltine crackers sat unopened on the coffee table in front of him. There was also a glass of ice water, but the ice had melted long ago and even the sweat on the outside of the glass was gone.

At ten o'clock a fifteen-second promo for the late news ran between two commercials. The news anchor, a handsome woman with heavy makeup and rosy lips, looked into the camera as if she had the weight of the world on her shoulders and said, "A local doctor is brutally murdered. Is this connected with the bizarre story of Stanley Stilwell? I'm Sylvia Brookstone, join me at eleven for this and more."

A high-pitched whine escape from Cutter's open mouth. "Oh my God," he stammered over and over when his tongue finally began working. "Murdered! How's that possible? How the hell do they know?"

Cutter's head began to throb. *Could someone have been in the observation room behind the one-way mirror?* His brain was moving too quickly to accomplish any logical thinking. He hopped to his feet and tore through the house and into his little study. He stole a look out of the window at Old Mill Road. No police. No cars waiting at the top of his driveway.

He paced from room to room with such a feeling of dread that he debated calling Mannheim and pleading for help. Suddenly, in a brilliant burst of inspiration, he remembered that another station aired the news at ten o'clock. Running back to the family room he aimed the remote control and jabbed away with his index finger until he succeeded in finding the correct channel. It had already dispensed with the lead stories and was on to a human interest feature about a boy who was dedicating his little league season to his brother who had cancer.

"Jesus Christ!" he bellowed and whipped the remote control across the room in the direction of the fireplace.

At precisely eleven o'clock Cutter walked over to his thirty-six-inch-screen Panasonic and located one of the stations about to broadcast the news. He sat on the floor right in front of the set, cross-legged, like a kid watching Barney.

"Good evening," the news anchor greeted him.

"Yeah, yeah, yeah. Get on with it. What the hell happened?" He barked at the TV.

"I'm Sylvia Brookstone. A local doctor is brutally murdered. Could this be the next casualty in the mind-numbing case of Stanley Stilwell? That's our top story, join me and the entire news team after these words."

"No! Goddamnit, what happened?" Cutter pleaded. He rose to his knees and shook the television as if he could coax Sylvia back.

He had to endure a series of commercials powered by boppy music and happy people with impossibly white teeth. *If someone knew I pushed Valdemar, the cops would be here already,* he told himself enough times to believe it.

"A tragedy tonight in Cranberry Township. A masked intruder entered the home of Brian Trilby earlier this evening, beat his wife, Lori, and tied her up along with their young sons. When Dr. Brian Trilby, an anesthesiologist who works almost exclusively with Dr. Marshall Cutter, came home he was attacked in his family room and stabbed in the back of the neck much the same way Stanley Stilwell was murdered several days ago. The body was found . . ."

Marshall Cutter stopped listening. He wiped a single tear of joy from his eye and smiled. One word crossed his lips. "Mannheim." He said it with a tone of reverence and admiration. But there was also a hint of fear in his voice. He had a strong sense deep in his gut about the man with whom he was dealing. It was almost as if he was praying to some all-powerful God, one who could bring swift salvation to the needy. But this was not a God to cross. One misstep and Marshall Cutter knew what fate he could expect.

Chapter 21

"What the hell happened to you?" London asked in her soft-spoken voice. She was sitting at her cramped desk in the County Office Building. A half-eaten bagel with a smear of cream cheese and a slice of tomato hanging out the side waited on a small paper plate.

"I got pushed down some stairs," Tory said as she turned her head to the side to show off a purple shiner below her right eye.

"At Trilby's house?" London waited for Tory to nod before continuing. "You better be careful. Unfortunately, I don't have very good news." She picked up a photograph of the latent fingerprints lifted from Marshall Cutter's house. "Cutter's not in the computer."

"All that means is he was never arrested in Pennsylvania. He's got to have a record somewhere. What about the FBI's computer in Washington? How quickly can we access that?"

London smiled at Tory's grasp of the steps needed for identification of fingerprints. Although not widely known outside law enforcement circles, each of the fifty states had its own separate system. Running fingerprints in Pennsylvania identified only those individuals who had ever been arrested in the Keystone State. Therefore, someone could be arrested in New Jersey for a string of crimes, but once that individual crossed the Delaware River, he could leave fingerprints wherever he wanted. Unless the seriousness of the crime warranted a further look, the only way to track him down would be through the main system the FBI maintained in Washington. Their data base was infinitely larger and covered the entire nation. "I already contacted the local fibbies and explained the situation. Photos of the prints were couriered over to them an hour ago. They'll get them to Washington before five."

"Thanks, London. You know how to reach me."

"The guy that pushed you down the stairs—was it Cutter?" London studied Tory's face.

"It happened too quickly to tell. But it was someone strong."

Merlin was making rounds when he ran into Marshall Cutter. He had just come from the surgical locker room where he had taken a long hot shower to wash the grime of a night's work from his tired body. This had been the second long night in the ICU Merlin had endured in the past week.

Cutter looked splendid. He was wearing a double-breasted, chocolate brown suit over a custom-made powder blue shirt and a bright yellow tie. With his hair combed neatly and held in place with a dollop of mousse, his confidence was renewed. It didn't take a practiced eye to notice a jaunty bounce to his step.

"And a good morning to you, Merlin," the plastic surgeon called out to his colleague as if they were neighbors greeting each other across the hedges.

"Marshall," Merlin answered as cooly as possible. "Tragedy about Trilby."

"I'm just sick about it," Cutter replied as an appropriately sad expression came across his face. "I've got to get a hold of Lori, see what I can do. Whatever's the world coming to? Two in one night."

"Two?"

"Didn't you hear about Tanner?" Cutter asked incredulously, but there was also a hint of glee in his voice that he would be the one to tell Merlin about his fallen comrade. "You knew him, didn't you?"

Merlin got a suspicious look on his face. "Of course," he said slowly.

"I heard Trilby's funeral is Thursday. Do you know when Valdemar's is? I've got to clear my schedule."

"Valdemar's? What are you talking about?"

"My God, and I thought I was always the last to know. He died."

Merlin's heart skipped a beat. "I was in the shower. I didn't—"

"Happened sometime last night."

"Last night? I was with him the entire night. Unless he died in the last half hour . . . he's been on life support in a light coma."

"What?" Cutter whispered hoarsely. Images of Valdemar lying on the floor flashed through his brain. "Coma? He's okay . . . right?"

"I don't know. The cleaning people found him in his office unconscious. He'd fallen and hit his head. I didn't find out about it until later, after the CT. He had a subdural bleed that neurosurgery drained around midnight. The rest of the brain looked okay. He's still in a coma, though. Next day or two should be the critical time."

"He say anything?" Cutter studied Merlin's face.

"Marshall, he's in a coma on a ventilator." Merlin studied Cutter's face. Something in the way Cutter was reacting seemed somehow inappropriate.

"Oh, that's right. A ventilator," he mumbled. Cutter

couldn't believe what he was hearing. *Get control of yourself. Think.* "Well, I guess I better go on up and see him. My God." His tongue darted out of his mouth and whipped across his lips. "I just referred him a patient yesterday."

Merlin wasn't ready to let Cutter go just yet. "I'm headed up there myself. I'll walk with you."

No pulse. He wasn't breathing. Goddamn. He was dead! Cutter rode up to the ICU with Merlin in the elevator, not saying anything, fixing his eyes on the numbers above the elevator door just to have somewhere to look. Sweat was soaking through his shirt and he seemed to be wiping his slick palms on his pants leg every time Merlin looked at him.

When they reached the ICU, Merlin walked straight to Valdemar's bedside. Cutter lagged behind near the nursing station. A nurse wearing rubber gloves was drawing blood from Valdemar's arm while a respiratory technician was making an adjustment to the ventilator that had assumed responsibility for the unconscious man's breathing. The usual assortment of monitors displayed the vital information about the patient.

Cutter's mouth was dry. His fingers were tingling. Mechanically he went to one of the stainless steel sinks and got himself a paper cup of water. He gulped it down quickly and filled the cup several times. It was impossible to quench his thirst. After filling the cup for a fifth time, he hesitantly walked over to join Merlin.

Valdemar was covered by a thin, white sheet. Only his pale arms and head were visible. IVs ushered clear fluid into both arms. An endotracheal tube was taped to his face and someone had made the effort to comb his hair to one side. Unlike Stanley Stilwell with his recently tinted, greasy hair plastered to his scalp like a bad toupee, Valdemar looked as if he were on the road to recovery. More important, his tidy appearance gave the impression that everyone in the ICU was pulling for Tanner Valdemar to make it.

Cutter stood at the foot of the bed. A thousand sessions of psychotherapy couldn't bring him to describe the emotions he was feeling. Looking at Valdemar made him feel sick. To keep from vomiting he averted his eyes, looking everywhere but at the patient. It was safer to focus his attention on the monitors and pretend he was checking the vital signs. First he followed the EKG with its peppy up and down tracing. The rhythm was relentlessly regular. No PVCs. And each of the other tracings, the blue blood pressure and the white rolling hills of the ventilator-driven respiratory pattern, seemed textbook perfect.

Cutter spied about the room. Fourteen bed spaces and more than sixteen nurses, technicians, and doctors. Everyone looked busy, the nurses fluttering around the beds giving medications and recording bits of data on flowsheets. Almost all of the patients were being maintained on ventilators, keeping the respiratory technicians beating a path from one bed space to another. The ICU staff, a small team of physicians who wore scrubs and running shoes, never actually seemed to do anything but were always lurking close by, waiting for a disaster to strike.

While Merlin was busy speaking to one of the nurses about Valdemar's medications, Cutter was lost in thought. Only from the far reaches of his peripheral vision did he dare look at Valdemar. He looked peacefully asleep, as if a good hard shake might just wake up the psychiatrist. From time to time small eye movements, similar to the rapid eye movements of dreams, could be seen through his lids. Cutter imagined the first coherent words the psychiatrist would speak. *It was Marshall Cutter. He pushed me. We were speaking in my office, and he became very angry and pushed me.* That's what he would say. *It was Marshall Cutter. It was Marshall Cutter. It was Marshall Cutter.*

How long would it take for Detective Deringer to come looking for him? Ten minutes? Cutter knew there was no goddamn explanation in the world he could make up to explain his horrible behavior. Even if he could convince Deringer that the incident was a terrible accident, he was guilty of leaving Valdemar for dead. He would be arrested for sure. Mannheim would cut him loose. His picture would be in newspapers across the country. And with the way his luck was running, someone would take notice of his past life.

"Excuse me, Dr. Cutter," a young nurse in scrubs said deferentially as she maneuvered around the plastic surgeon in order to reach one of the IVs that needed some attention.

Cutter didn't budge. He was resting the paper cup of water on the railing at the foot of the bed with one hand while he white-knuckled it with his other as though he was riding the Thunderbolt roller coaster at Kennywood.

"Doctor," the nurse said a bit louder this time, but he did not seem to hear what she was saying.

"Marshall," Merlin called, tapping the plastic surgeon on the shoulder.

Cutter startled, spilling the remaining water in his cup onto Valdemar's legs. When he realized what he had done he shook his head. "Huh? Oh, sorry."

"That's okay, Dr. Cutter. I'll change his sheet after I give him his meds. No problem."

"We're in the way. Let's get some coffee." Merlin patted Cutter on the shoulder. He wanted to get Cutter alone. "I'll be on beeper if there's any change," Merlin reminded the nurse, but she was busy injecting a syringe full of the broad spectrum antibiotic ceftazidime into the IV and nodded without looking up.

Cutter seemed reluctant to leave the bedside. His good name was on the line, and he felt as though he needed to stay and defend it. "You think he's going to pull through or what?"

Merlin paused briefly before answering. "Yeah. I've got a good feeling." Then he said, "C'mon, I want to talk with you." But his tone had changed, sounding more serious, and Cutter noticed it.

"I think I'm just going to stay here for a while." The plastic surgeon turned to resume his vigil by Valdemar's bedside.

Merlin moved close enough to Cutter so that no one else in the ICU could hear what he was about to say. "I can help you."

Cutter remained intent on the monitors above the bed. Whatever Merlin was offering, Cutter was not buying.

Merlin tried again. "I know you're in some kind of trouble. Let me help you, Marshall."

Cutter turned toward Merlin. His lips were tightly closed and his eyeballs froze like ice. He said not one word.

"What are we dealing with?"

Slowly, Cutter shook his head back and forth.

"I don't get you. Stilwell attacks one of your patients, then gets killed. His body gets swiped. Your anesthesiologist is murdered. And you hardly bat an eye. Yet Tanner hits his head—and is probably going to be fine—and you get so choked up you can hardly function. What the hell's going on?"

Cutter stared at Merlin with a sudden flash of anger. "Trilby was bad news," he hissed. "Like I told the cops, it didn't take a genius to see it. He got himself mixed up in something and what happened to him is none of my business. For all I know he's the one who killed Stilwell."

"That doesn't make sense. Stilwell and Trilby were both pithed. They died by the same hand."

Cutter was stunned. He hadn't yet considered the obvious. "Pithed," he said, but his voice was distant as if he were considering other scenarios while his mouth went on automatic pilot. "So the same killer got to both of them."

"What do *you* have to do with it?"

That brought Cutter back into the conversation. His lips curled into an ugly frown. "I'm not going to dignify that with an answer. Excuse me." He took one side step and proceeded to walk around Merlin on his way out of the ICU.

Merlin did not stop him. "I'm not going away, Marshall. I'm digging. And I'll dig deeper and deeper until I know what you're about."

Cutter whipped around to face Merlin. He took two steps toward the surgeon and raised his voice so that everyone in the ICU could hear him. "You don't know what you're talking about. You don't know what you're getting yourself into. This is bigger than you or your girlfriend or Deringer. And don't keep pestering me, because I don't have any answers. I have no more idea what's going on than you do. But let me give you some friendly advice. Don't mess where you don't belong. Whatever the hell Trilby did to deserve what happened, I don't want to know. But this thing is going to bite anyone who gets close enough."

"What's behind all this?"

"Maybe if we just get back into our routines—"

"Did you know Stilwell's real name was Paul Vorkman?"

Cutter's lips formed a big circle and a guttural noise came out of his mouth.

"What was so special about him that his body was stolen?"

"Stop it! Stop asking me these questions. I don't know. I'm as frightened as you."

"I'm not frightened. When I first saw you today you acted as if you didn't have a worry in the world. You thought Trilby and Valdemar were dead. As soon as I told you Valdemar was alive you fell apart."

"You asshole." Cutter made a fist and took a swing at Merlin, a sucker punch that was delivered without warning of any kind.

But Merlin had been expecting something to come from their heated exchange. He caught Cutter's balled-up hand out of the corner of his eye and with a deft move of his head he eluded the plastic surgeon's punch. Cutter's fist shot through the air harmlessly.

As Cutter stumbled to catch his balance, Merlin said in the calmest of voices, "If you only remember one thing about today, remember this: I'm not going to stop."

Cutter looked around and realized he was the center of attention. "Then don't say I didn't warn you."

Merlin stood his ground until Cutter walked past him and out of the ICU.

Chapter 22

"I just had it out with Cutter in the middle of the ICU. Can you believe he took a swing at me? I've got to get him."

"Was he visiting Tanner?" Tory asked softly. She was eating lunch at her desk and put her turkey sandwich back down on a piece of Reynold's Wrap.

"He was, but he acted like a grieving widow the way he stared at him. We need to talk with London ASAP."

Tory looked at her watch. "Why not?" She re-wrapped her sandwich and pushed herself to her feet.

The walk took less than ten minutes. The door to London's small office was open and the fingerprint examiner was at her desk. As soon as London spotted the two of them she said, "I was just going to give you a call. We got it."

"So who is he?" Merlin exclaimed.

Tory sat down on a metal chair in front of the crowded desk. She pulled out a little pad from her bag and searched for a pen.

"His name is Raymond Lord Phillips. But there's one thing that's sort of odd. The only time he was ever arrested was in Boston. He was an undergrad at Harvard. Drunk driving. Nineteen seventy-two."

"That's all?" Tory wanted to know.

"Otherwise he's clean in all fifty states."

Merlin hit himself in the forehead. "I betcha anything he went to med school at Columbia—"

Tory completed his thought. "—and the real Marshall Cutter was someone he knew, maybe even a friend who wouldn't mind lending his good name."

"But what the hell is he hiding from?" Merlin asked.

Tory was already standing. "Looks like you've put us back in the game," she said to London.

The medical library on the tenth floor of the Medical Center was a seemingly endless series of rooms. Virtually any medical question could be researched definitively. What started as a one-room affair fifty years earlier had grown in a piecemeal fashion, overtaking offices on either side until it housed over 100,000 textbooks and leather-bound copies of several hundred different scientific journals. Virtually every bit of wall space was lined with bookshelves that kept three full-time librarians very busy.

In one section there was a series of three-sided wooden cubicles in what was referred to as the stacks; a dense forest of floor-to-ceiling metal shelves crammed full of journals that dated back to the infancy of medical research. Marshall Cutter had ensconced himself in one of those cubicles, armed with a cup of coffee and his two-strap leather briefcase. Once satisfied that he would be able to work without being disturbed, he made his way back to the library and retrieved a thick textbook entitled *Forsensic Medicine* and three years' worth of *The American Journal of Forensic Medicine*. Each of the editions of *AJFM* was three inches thick, bound in red leather with the title on the spine in gold. Six months of the journal were packaged in each volume. One by one, starting with the textbook, he scanned indexes and tables of contents. When he had finished with those volumes he returned them and retrieved another batch. In thirty minutes he had gone through ten years of *AJFM* and switched to more current volumes of *Scientific Forensic Medicine,* going backward three years at a time. It was in his second batch of *SFM* that he found what he was looking for. In the May 1995 edition he found an article entitled "Toxicology Evaluation, Scientific and Practical Limits." The article was boring and went on for a dozen pages. In it, the authors discussed the complete approach for the evaluation of toxicology in suspected homicides. In tiny print that required not only his half-glasses but a significant amount of squinting, he scanned the listing of all the toxins routinely tested when a toxicology screen was ordered by the coroner's office. He was searching for one particular drug. It was not listed. This brought a smile to Cutter's lips.

The first part of his research was finished.

Then he pulled a well-worn copy of what was called Kruger and Klein. Actually it was the most widely used pharmacology text in the country, properly called *Pharmacology in Medical Therapeutics,* but as was customary in academic circles, it was known not by its title but by the names of the lead authors. For the next forty-five minutes he sipped cold coffee and carefully read parts of the chapter on cardiac drugs, paying particular attention to one of the oldest drugs in the pharmacopoeia, the same one whose name had been conspicuously absent from the toxin list in *Scientific Forensic Medicine.* Three pages of Kruger and Klein were photocopied before the tome was returned to the shelf.

For Cutter's last bit of research, he went online on a computer that accessed not only a medical exchange of information but the Internet as well. He typed four letters—DMSO—into one of the search engines and instantly had a listing of dozens of references. Several clicks of the mouse later and the ink-jet printer whirred to life and spit out a six-page article.

Huddled in his cubicle he poured over the text twice. DMSO, the chemical shorthand for dimethyl sulfoxide, was a fascinating industrial solvent with almost mythical medical properties that had captivated a small cadre of mainstream medical personnel for the past several decades. Not only did its reputed properties include more rapid healing of burns, reduction of arthritis symptoms, and control of intracranial pressure after head trauma, but there was another particular property of DMSO, one that Marshall Cutter remembered from a lecture in organic chemistry that dated back to his junior year in college.

DMSO had the ability to deliver medications directly through the skin.

Oblivious to his surroundings, Cutter held both hands out in front of him like a pianist about to play. He admired how still he could hold them. No tremors or excess movements. He was now a man in control. His plan was coming together. For the first time, in the face of a tremendously dangerous situation, he felt a strange sense of calm.

He went into the main room of the library and retrieved a copy of the Greater Pittsburgh *Yellow Pages*. He quickly located what he wanted and returned to the stacks where he found a wall-mounted phone in an uninhabited corner of the large room. Confidently he dialed the number.

A voice came on the line quickly. "Sewickley Tack and Bridle."

"How late are you open?"

"Six o'clock, sir."

After writing down directions, Cutter hung up the phone and wandered back to his lonely little cubicle. His half-full Styrofoam cup of coffee was the only item left on the desk. Cutter looked around. He was alone. He slowly picked up the coffee and held it casually, the way doctors did when they made rounds, just to the right of his belly. Again he admired the steadiness of his hand. The surface of the dark liquid was black glimmer glass.

He began to flex and contract the muscles of his forearm. The surface of the coffee began to ripple, sloshing back and forth, reaching higher and higher on the side of the cup. His hand got into the act, shaking back and forth in tiny oscillations that brought tiny whitecaps to the java. Then his whole arm was trembling as if he was going to have some sort of seizure and he suddenly let go of the cup. It dropped into the cubicle and splashed all over the place. Cutter quickly covered his mouth with his hand as if he was shocked to see the damage he had deliberately caused. "Oh, sorry," he mumbled.

He lowered his hand. "Oh my God!" His lips were sticky. "What a mess. Let me clean it up." He smiled. "That'll play in Pittsburgh. Let me clean it up."

Merlin and Tory were out back of their Aspinwall home. They were sitting in bright red adirondak chairs, sipping Iron City beer from the bottle and snacking on little chunks of smoked cheddar cheese while they waited for the charcoal briquettes in their black Weber to glow red. It was getting dark and with the wind blowing it was downright chilly. Tory had on a thick cotton sweater with a colorful beach scene that began in the front and ran down one arm. The cold was getting to her, though, and she hunched her shoulders forward and hugged herself to stay warm. Merlin was wearing a dark blue windbreaker with the collar of his green shirt poking out at the neck. He was one beer ahead of Tory and, for the first time that day, feeling good, even if it was the artificial floating that came with a bottle and a half of brew.

As soon as Tory could feel the heat from the fire warm her body, she took a long swig of beer and headed into the kitchen to put the water on for the corn and bring out the platter of marinated swordfish. Merlin spread the coals and carefully placed the cast iron grate on the grill.

"You want another beer?" Tory called out through the screen door.

Before Merlin could answer, another voice in the yard answered, "Sure, better get one for Merlin, too." Detective Deringer was strolling across the little slip of backyard grass in his brown trench coat and scuffed up wingtips.

"Detective," Merlin said unenthusiastically. He had been looking forward to a quiet evening with Tory and didn't want to endure another debate with the officer. "Don't you ever go home?"

"Nah," Deringer said and dropped his big frame into the adirondak chair Tory had been occupying. It creaked under his weight. "This case's got a lot of white meat on it. I want to be there when it's carving time, you know what I mean? So what have the two of you been up to?"

"I spent most of the day in the ICU with a friend who had emergency neurosurgery last night. I ran into Marshall Cutter, though."

Ignoring whatever Merlin might have to say about Marshall Cutter he asked, "Who's your friend?"

Merlin wanted to say to Deringer that it was none of his business, but it was easier to reply, "A psychiatrist named Tanner Valdemar."

"Valdemar, Valdemar, Valdemar," Deringer said to himself, trying to place the name.

"You ever hear of him?"

"Sounds familiar . . . Valdemar."

"He fell in his office and hit his head last night. Had an internal bleed," Merlin continued.

"Is he okay?" Deringer said, sounding genuinely concerned.

"Hopefully," Merlin answered, his tone of voice improving once Deringer showed a smidgen of interest. "He was starting to move one of his arms by the time I left the hospital."

Deringer's hand came up to his mouth and he nibbled on his thumbnail contemplatively. "I guess that's good for your friend."

Tory came through the screen door with the beers and waited at the top of the stairs for Merlin to take them so she could go back in the kitchen for the food. "You want a glass, Detective?" Tory asked, knowing full well what the answer would be.

"Nah, outta the bottle's fine, then I gotta be shoving off."

Tory disappeared into the kitchen for a moment and returned with a platter that held two fillets of swordfish. Merlin placed the fish on the hot grill, which gave off a loud hiss as a delicious aroma filled the air.

As Tory sat in one of the chairs and sipped her beer, Deringer drained half of his with one swallow. "Did Merlin tell you about Cutter?" she asked the detective.

"I was just getting to that," Merlin said. "I had a talk with him up in the ICU. We were both visiting Tanner Valdemar."

"Cutter was visiting Valdemar?" Deringer asked, rubbing his hand across his chin.

"They know each other."

"So what'd you two talk about?"

"We went back and forth a little about the Stilwell case. I gotta tell you, he's got the look," Merlin said.

"What look?" the detective questioned. Suddenly he seemed to have lost interest in his beer and rested it on the arm of the chair.

"Guilt. It's in his eyes."

No one said anything for several seconds. Deringer exchanged hard looks with Merlin first, then Tory. "I thought you two were specializing in Brian Trilby. I thought *he* was the one."

Tory jumped into the conversation. "Maybe if we were cooperating with one another, Brian Trilby wouldn't be dead right now."

"Don't give me that crap. There was no way to predict that."

"So who killed him?" Tory asked.

"You seem to have all the answers. Why don't you tell me?"

"Stilwell—Vorkman—had a short fuse. After the surgery Cutter got cold feet when he realized Stilwell was going to go out and get into trouble and expose him. So Cutter kills him."

"And steals the body so no one can fingerprint Stilwell and find out his true identity," Merlin added.

"So who killed Trilby?" Deringer asked.

"Maybe Trilby knew about it. When things heated up he got cold feet and was threatening to go to the cops," Merlin continued. "He was scared shitless. He had a gun. You remember he even offered to turn over the patient demographics, that's why we were over his house last night. Maybe Cutter knew what he was up to and felt he had no choice but to silence him."

Deringer now had a broad smile on his face. He took a slug of beer. "You two are a real treat after a long day. You got another beer?" Deringer waited while Tory went back into the kitchen and fetched another Iron City. He seemed to be really enjoying their little back-

yard conversation. "Thanks," he said when Tory handed
him the bottle and held it up briefly as if he were toasting
her. Instead he got right back to business. "Sounds like
you want to lynch the bastard. Nice try. One problem
with that little scenario that'll get the case thrown right
out of court." Deringer lifted his bottle to his lips and
took a long pull of the frothy brew.

Merlin used a spatula that hung on a hook off the side
of the grill to turn the fish over, while giving Deringer a
puzzled look.

"You see, Cutter didn't kill Trilby," he said as he
pulled his closed lips into a forced smile. It was obvious
he liked being able to shut Merlin down.

"Have you looked the man in the eye?"

"I have."

Merlin curled his hand into a tight fist. "He's dirty. I
know it."

"Take a cold shower. Like I told you the first time I
met you, your reputation precedes you. You've had your
chance to play cops and robbers, but now it's time for
the pros to take over." Then Deringer turned to Tory
and added, "With all due respect, Counselor, enough is
enough. You got to rein your boy in. Cutter didn't kill
Trilby. Why? Because I was following Cutter. I was doing
real police work. Trilby was killed sometime between
four-thirty and six. I followed Cutter from his office into
Oakland 'bout three-thirty. He parked his car in the garage and it was there more'n an hour. Then he drove
home. He didn't do it. So let's not run out and arrest
him for nothing."

Merlin stood by the grill, ignoring a plume of white
smoke billowing out of the Weber. "You were *with*
him?"

"He don't know it, but yeah. I was on his ass from

the moment he hit Route 28 until he pulled into the parking garage. He didn't have the slightest idea."

"But he had that *look*. I know what I saw," Merlin said softly. Now it was Merlin's turn to nibble on his thumbnail.

"Yeah, well, don't beat yourself up over it. We still got some real police work to do. But don't worry, I'm on it. Cutter ain't going no place." Deringer drained his beer and stood up as if he were about to leave. "I'm not trying to be ignorant or nothing. I want this case as much as you do— maybe more. But I still don't want you blowing it." He took a step toward Merlin and lowered his voice. "So stay outta my way." He turned to walk away.

"Marshall Cutter isn't his real name," Merlin said flatly.

Deringer stopped walking and turned to stare back at Merlin. He didn't say a word. His eyes filled with hate and he looked as if he were struggling to contain himself from punching Merlin in the face.

Merlin had the feeling that with that one revelation, everything changed. No longer were they adversaries. Now they were enemies.

"I accidentally stumbled onto some information," Merlin continued. "When I called Columbia, where Cutter was supposed to have gone to med school, I found out that the Marshall Cutter who graduated was deceased." Merlin looked at Tory. "So Tory and I got a set of the bogus Cutter's prints, ran them through London, and found out his real name."

"Raymond Lord Phillips," Tory said, expecting more of a reaction from Deringer than a mechanical turn of his head and a hard stare.

"The three of us agreed we wouldn't step on each other." Deringer sounded as though he was working hard to control his temper. "We divided things up. Cutter is mine. Trilby was yours. Thanks for the info. First thing tomorrow I'll run the name and see what I come up with."

"It's already been started. We tracked Phillips to a residency in plastic surgery at UCLA. After that he spent almost fourteen years in private practice in Miami. That's all we got so far."

Deringer rubbed his stubbly face, making a sound like coarse sandpaper. A guttural sound rumbled out through his clenched teeth. "All right, you did good, you two. Now back off. You almost got Tory killed last night. Let's not forget that." Deringer looked back and forth at Tory and Merlin for several seconds, making his point. "Don't make me go above your head. If I get the feeling you're gonna blow the case, I'll go to my captain and he'll have the D.A. on the phone in about two seconds. Stay the fuck outta my way." When Deringer saw the way Merlin was staring back at him he shook his head and scowled. "Okay, Doc, you ever have a gun pointed in your face?" Deringer took two steps closer to Merlin so that he was close enough to grab him by the shirt if he wanted to. The detective extended his hand, making it look like it was a pistol and thrust it in Merlin's face. "Let's say you decide to keep playing cops and robbers. And let's suppose things get out of hand and someone pulls a piece on you. What are *you* gonna do when you're staring down a one-eyed roscoe? Huh? Lemme see you knock this gun outta your face." Deringer grabbed his own wrist as if steadying it before he squeezed off a round.

Merlin slowly took a breath. It was obvious Deringer wanted him to do something stupid.

"C'mon, don't stand there like a pussy. Lemme see what you'd do," the detective taunted. Several uncomfortable seconds ticked by. Deringer sniffed the air and made a face as if he'd caught a whiff of a foul odor. "Just like I thought. You'd fucking crap your pants. Now don't go where you don't belong if you can't handle the rough stuff." He turned to Tory and nodded once. "Thanks for the beers," he said and strode out of the yard as if he had some important unfinished business to attend to.

Marshall Cutter drove straight out to Sewickley Heights from the Medical Center. Traffic was clogged with commuters trying to get home for dinner. Sewickley was one of Pittsburgh's most prestigious communities. Private homes sat elegantly on sprawling plots of land that were lovingly tended by swarms of landscapers. Magnificent stone walls surrounded many of the homes. White wooden fences, the type associated with top horse farms, ran the perimeter of others.

Sewickley Tack and Bridle was a small wooden structure that sat by itself on one of the many country roads that crisscrossed through the sylvan community. When Marshall Cutter stepped inside the store the first thing he noticed was the wonderfully rich smell of saddle leather. The shop was fashioned from wood beams and planks, sanded and varnished to give the impression one had just entered a private hunting lodge. The trappings of typical business establishments were absent. There was no cash register and no visible telephone. The walls were lined with sturdy wooden shelves and cases for the various liniments and harnesses that could be purchased. Several ornate saddles were displayed on heavy stands constructed of pine that appeared rugged enough for someone to mount in case he wanted to try out the saddle before dropping twenty-five hundred bucks.

The woman at the counter had a look about her that screamed family money. Her hair was country club casual—short, and cut in such a way that allowed her to ride her horses, then take a quick shower and blow dry her locks before heading out for supper. She was dressed in a riding outfit, chocolate brown jodhpurs and a simple white shirt tucked in tightly at the waist and ballooning out nicely to show her ample breasts. She wore several pieces of diamond and gold jewelry but obviously wasn't the type to go for dangly earrings in the shape of horses or cowboy boots. Cutter immediately assumed this was no costume. The woman had evidently taken her ride earlier in the day, or was about to once she closed the shop. She was standing on the customer side of the wooden counter, working the leather straps of an old bridle. If she heard the door close behind Cutter she didn't react to it.

"Excuse me," Cutter said as he shuffled his feet on the wooden floor. "I called before—"

Immediately the woman looked up. "Yes, I spoke with you. What can I help you with?"

She was very pretty, in her late thirties, perfect skin and beautiful eyes. "I was looking for a bottle of DMSO."

"Right over here," the woman said as she led Cutter past an exquisite hand-tooled saddle that was too beautiful to put on a horse. She reached for a plastic bottle and handed it to Cutter. "Dr. Cutter?"

He swallowed hard. Whenever a pretty woman recognized him it meant one of two things. Either she was a former lover, or one of his patients. Yet she had called him doctor, so it meant she was one of the Barbie dolls. His mouth went numb while his eyes scanned her face and neck for a clue as to how he knew her. Unfortunately his work was so good it was impossible to find scars after the fact without excellent lighting and his little half-glasses. "I'm sorry . . ." he said and allowed his voice to trail off so that she would fill in the space with her name.

The thought that this woman would surely want to know what the hell he wanted with DMSO hadn't hit him yet.

"Sally Dunmire." Her eyes lowered momentarily, looking down at her chest.

Aha! Bosom Barbie. "Of course, Sally, and in that outfit"—he stepped back so that he could pretend to admire his work—"you look absolutely terrific." Then it hit him. Once the polite admiration of Sally's breasts had taken place there would be little left to talk about. The ice had been broken, and he had less than two seconds to prepare for her next question.

"Do you ride?"

Cutter gave an automatic smile. "Oh, no. It's for a woman I'm dating."

"Oh, maybe I know her—"

"Carolyn McPherson," he said quickly, borrowing the name of a ninety-year-old patient from whom he had recently removed a series of basal cell carcinomas.

"Carolyn McPherson," she repeated, mulling it over in her mind, trying to place the name. "I don't think I know her. Where does she stable?"

"Uhhh, up in Butler," he said, attempting to put an end to the conversation.

"Hmmmm, I'll bet it's at Cross Pines, it's the best one out that way." Sally sensed the cocktail party conversation was nearing its end. Gesturing toward the plastic bottle of clear liquid Sally enthused, "It's amazing stuff."

"So I hear." Cutter picked up the bottle with one hand as his other slipped into his back pocket and fished out his wallet. "Carolyn's horse has some sort of rheumatism."

"You know, Dr. Cutter," Sally said in the same sort of voice she might use when slipping her arm around the tuxedo-clad arm of someone at a charity ball, "you've absolutely got to wear gloves when working with this stuff."

"Oh, really?" Cutter said with a trace of awe in his voice, turning the bottle in his hand to admire it.

"DMSO can penetrate the skin like a sponge. Put a couple of drops on your hand and you can taste it in the back of your mouth."

"Wow," Cutter said like a wide-eyed kid hearing a tall tale.

"DMSO is absolutely phenomenal, but somehow it's escaped the medical community. Here's the best part: This stuff can pull *other* drugs through the skin and *into* the bloodstream. Imagine just rubbing medication onto the skin and . . . maybe kids wouldn't have to get shots. That would be something, wouldn't it?"

"I ought to read up on it." Although already quite knowledgeable about the chemical properties of DMSO, Cutter managed to sound genuinely interested in what Sally was saying.

"You won't find much. No one really understands the pharmacology of how it works. And in the United States it's only sold for veterinary use."

"Thanks for the tip," Cutter said.

"Hey, how come you came all the way out here? I can't believe Butler Tack Shop wouldn't have DMSO."

"Well . . . I was at Sewickley Hospital giving a lecture on plastic surgery, and I was on the phone with Carolyn as I was heading home and she said to stop by here if I could."

Sally smiled. "Well I'm glad to see you again. You know I've sent several of my friends to see you."

"Wonderful," his mouth said, but his brain was replaying their conversation to determine if he sounded like a complete idiot.

"That will be twelve-fifty." Sally leaned over the counter so that the peaks of her perfect breasts brushed the wood. Raising way up on one foot in the sexiest way, Sally reached for something under the other side of the counter. What she pulled out was a small calculator. As she began to punch the little buttons to determine what tax Cutter owed on his purchase, he placed fifteen dollars on the table.

"Why don't you just keep it," he said trying to sound like a good guy rather than someone who wanted to get the hell out of there before Sally suggested a get together with Carolyn McPherson to have cocktails and chat about horses.

On his way home, Cutter stopped by his office. Not even bothering to turn off the Mercedes's engine, he disappeared into the darkened building for less than one minute. When he returned he was carrying the little black box that contained Trilby's Glock. Why not? he thought. It wouldn't do Brian Trilby much good at this point. Maybe it would come in handy.

Chapter 23

Cutter was up early. Already he'd downed three cups of coffee while he assembled what was needed for a clinical trial. Everything was lined up on the blue-gray granite countertop in his kitchen. The bottle of DMSO had not yet been opened. Next to it was a small test tube of methylene blue, an intense blue dye used in the microbiology department of the Medical Center. Methylene blue was so dark that it could be mistaken for india ink. Only when Cutter picked up the test tube, causing the dye to splash around and leave a thin coating on the sides of the glass did it appear cobalt. Although capable of causing serious poisonings, in a low dose the dye was quite safe and a traditional source of college frat humor. Pledges were forced to swallow methylene blue tablets that quickly turned the freshman's urine an eye-opening color as it was flushed out of the system by the kidneys.

Cutter spread layers and layers of the *Post-Gazette* over the entire island. He opened the bottle of DMSO and sniffed the mouth of the plastic pint container. It had the faint odor of something familiar, maybe one of the spices in his pantry. He couldn't be sure. The properties of DMSO, glorified in the article he'd pulled off the Internet and the rave review by Sally Dunmire, seemed almost magical. Cutter, like many of his colleagues in mainstream medicine, found it hard to believe that DMSO could do all that was claimed of it, which was in large part why it hadn't been licensed in the United States for non-veterinary use.

The scientist in him needed proof of what it could do.

He poured an ounce of the clear DMSO into a skinny little glass, the type restaurants used to serve three gulps of orange juice before breakfast. It looked like a shot of gin or vodka. Next, he uncorked the test tube and carefully added a splash of the methylene blue to the glass.

Cutter took a whiff of the thin, blue liquid a second time. He grabbed a paper towel, folded it several times until it was a thick, sponge-like square and carefully poured as much of the concoction as the absorbent material could hold. Taking care to work over the newspaper so nothing would drip, he stained the entire surface of both his forearms a shade of blue that permitted no hint of his skin color underneath. In the process, his hands appeared cyanotic from holding the paper towel, although they were not nearly as dark as his arms. For a few seconds he thought about how long it would take a nurse to get around to changing the sheets on Valdemar's bed in the ICU. He decided about five minutes and went to the digital timer on his oven to set it, holding several fresh paper towels in his hand so he wouldn't stain the knob on the timer. Then he stood by the island, holding his arms straight out in front of him, expectantly watching his glistening skin as if the blue would suddenly disappear on its way into his bloodstream. But it was like watching paint dry. Nothing seemed to be happening.

He let his mind wander. In the past few days he had visited the ICU three times. Each time he discovered there was rarely a moment when Valdemar was left unattended. Nurses played with his IVs and recorded data from the monitors constantly. Respiratory therapists adjusted his ventilator. And physicians performed neurological examinations almost hourly. Valdemar was not receiving special attention. Every patient in the ICU watched this closely. Once patients didn't require the constant monitoring they were discharged to one of the floors.

Cutter had a recurring thought. It always began with a clear image of Valdemar's eyelids fluttering lightly and opening just the way Rip Van Winkle might after his long sleep. Then the psychiatrist would look about to see where he was. Everyone in the ICU would crowd around his bed space to hear the first words he would utter. When he began to speak his voice would not be rusty but loud and confident. "Marshall Cutter did this. He tried to kill me! *Marshall Cutter. Marshall Cutter. Marshall Cutter.*"

That's the way it would happen. And every time this horrible little scenario played back in his mind he shuddered at the thought. Life as he knew it would shut down.

Suddenly he became aware of his forearms. Two minutes on the clock, and, although still blue, there seemed to be less color on his skin. Dark blue had given way to deep azure. Something was happening.

He allowed himself the satisfied smile of someone who had followed directions and was enjoying the fruits of his labor. Again his thoughts drifted to the afternoon in Valdemar's office and the moment he had reached out with both hands and pushed the psychiatrist. How stupid he had been to allow himself to lose his temper like that.

With Mannheim taking care of Trilby, all of his worries should have disappeared.

Ding. Ding. Ding. The timer on the oven sounded. Immediately Cutter held his light blue forearms under a hard spray of water from the faucet. Then he used several paper towels saturated with rubbing alcohol to scrub his arms and hands clean. He didn't stop working until every trace of blue was washed away.

He became aware of a faint taste in the back of his mouth. Clicking his tongue off the roof of his mouth, he tried to identify the flavor. A spice, definitely a spice. He smiled. What was once an odor in a test tube was now in the back of his mouth.

The musical ring of his fax machine sounded in the little study off his bedroom. Slowly, Cutter shook his head back and forth. It didn't take much imagination to figure out who was faxing him. Reluctantly, Cutter headed into his little study and gently tugged on the piece of paper as it slowly rolled out of the machine. There were three words typed in the center of the page. CALL ME. MANNHEIM. Just seeing the name frightened him more than he expected and he thought about the Glock. He didn't want Mannheim anywhere around him right now. He didn't even want the name Mannheim in his house. With trembling fingers he tore the piece of paper into small squares the size of business cards, then threw them into a trash can, saving only the scrap with the three words on it. He tore this piece over and over until he had a handful of confetti that couldn't possibly be reassembled. Cutter walked the short distance to his guest bathroom and flushed them down the toilet.

"I'm sorry, I never checked my fax machine. From now on I'll check it before I leave the house every time," Cutter said aloud as he peeked out one of the windows that faced Old Mill Road to make certain Mannheim wasn't sitting in the driveway.

The little black box he had taken from Trilby's office was sitting on his desk. Cutter removed the lid and put it aside. Even upon a second viewing, the weapon was impressive. Before he dared to touch it he found the little booklet and read it, learning how to load the clip and pop it into the handle, where the safety was located, and how to rack the slide. Taking the weapon in his hand he held it reverently. He slid the clip up into the handle and gave it a smack with the palm of his hand to secure it.

It was the first time in his life he had held a loaded pistol. It seemed heavy. He felt strangely uncomfortable knowing it didn't belong to him. *I wonder what kind of a kick it has?*

Cutter dropped the weapon down to his side and walked back through his kitchen and down the creaky wooden stairs into his basement. It was an unfinished room with exposed joists in the ceiling and walls of unpainted cinder blocks. The room had a set of built-in wooden shelves, some rolled-up carpeting, and in the far corner, a hideous orange sofa and two easy chairs.

He placed the loaded weapon on one of the shelves, then removed the three seat cushions from the sofa and stacked them up, placing them upright on one of the easy chairs so that they provided a barrier that was more than a foot thick. He placed the rolled-up carpet behind the chair as added protection against a bullet ricocheting around the room.

Finally he was ready. With Trilby's Glock in one hand he positioned himself ten feet from the easy chair. He racked the slide and took aim, but his hand was shaking, the end of the barrel moving about in a frenetic way. Using his left hand to support his right wrist, he held his breath, settled down, and took aim at a point in the center of the cushion. There was a tingling in his loins and suddenly he had the urge to pee. *Concentrate,* he told himself. *Squeeze the trigger.*

Bang! The sound was absolutely deafening. Immediately the smell of gunpowder filled his nostrils and Cutter noticed that the gun was not pointing at the easy chair but at the ceiling. For a frightening moment he looked up for a bullet hole, thinking he had missed his mark completely.

The wood was intact.

It's just the kick of the gun, you idiot. Sheepishly he approached the easy chair. In the center of the first cushion from the sofa was a small hole, no bigger than the tip of his little finger, what you might expect from a cigarette burn, only the edges weren't charred.

He smiled and pulled the cushion away from the others so he could admire the hole in the next one and the next one and finally in the cushion on the back of the chair itself. Scattering the cushions on the floor, he kneeled on the seat cushion and leaned over the back of the chair to examine the rolled up carpet. It, too, had a hole in it, wider than the one in the first cushion, which Cutter understood to mean that the bullet had changed shape as it had pierced the cushions and back of the chair.

He regarded the weapon. No longer did he feel uncomfortable with a borrowed gun. It felt good and safe. He sat himself down on the easy chair and stroked the gun with his hand.

After ten minutes, he ascended the creaky old stairs quickly, heading for the little guest bathroom where he had flushed Mannheim's message down the toilet. Placing the weapon on the sink next to the little ceramic dish where he kept decorative soaps for his guests, he stood at the toilet and began to pee.

A jolt shot through his body. Not since he was a kid had he been so fascinated with the process of urination. What a wonderful surprise it was to see the toilet being filled with urine that was the prettiest color green he had ever seen. *Yellow plus blue makes green.* Any grade school child knows that.

A short while later, Marshall Cutter stood at the desk in the little study off his bedroom, dialing the phone. "Yes, this is Dr. Cutter. I wondered if I might speak with the nurse taking care of Tanner Valdemar. . . . Hello, this is Marshall Cutter. How's Tanner today? . . . He is? . . . Moving both arms or just the one? . . . Oh yeah? That's-that's great. . . . Well, it sounds like he's starting to get better. . . . I'll try'n stop by later. . . . Thank you."

He gently placed the phone back in its cradle, almost absentmindedly. "Shit!" he finally whispered after he had the chance to think through his options.

Chapter 24

Merlin arrived at the back door of his Aspinwall house just as the front doorbell rang. Even though it sounded nothing like the ring from the phone, his adrenaline was pumping and he tore into the kitchen and grabbed the phone. "Hello."

A dial tone was the only thing he heard.

He looked at the handset. The doorbell rang a second time.

Merlin was frazzled. All day he had been on the phone, long distance, to Miami. First he had reached the Dade County Medical Society and discovered that Raymond Phillips was a member in good standing until approximately four months prior to his arrival in Pittsburgh as Marshall Cutter.

After that he had called the Dade County police department. Merlin identified himself not as a physician, but as an ADA from Pittsburgh. After inquiring about Raymond Phillips he was placed on hold for almost twenty minutes. Finally, the desk sergeant returned. "There's an old warrant for his arrest issued in September nineteen ninety-four."

"What was it for?" Merlin asked.

"Who are you again? Maybe you ought to talk with

the captain." That's when Merlin thanked the sergeant for all her help and left to see half a dozen post-op patients. Later he telephoned the *Miami Herald*. That's when he got lucky. The intern who had answered the phone promised to pull what he could from September 1994 and call Merlin back around dinnertime.

Now Merlin headed out of the kitchen and through the living room, throwing his briefcase on the sofa. Without taking time to peak through the window, he pulled open the door and came face-to-face with a man he had never seen before. The way the man was standing, with perfect posture, shoulders back, and an expressionless face with strong features, made Merlin think he was military. This was the way he had always imagined the ROTCs in college grew up. However, the man was dressed in a suit, not a uniform, and it fit him perfectly. Merlin couldn't decide whether it was an expensive suit crafted by a tailor or whether the man had one of those terrific bodies that wore off-the-rack well. His shirt was white, and even at the end of the day, the collar looked as though it was crisply starched. Merlin noticed how tightly his tie was pulled at the neck, and, although Merlin couldn't see his collar button, there was little doubt it was still fastened.

"Can I help you?" Merlin asked with a measured tone of voice. It had been a long day on the phone and he was anxious to take off his own tie and relax.

"Is this where Tory Welch lives?"

"Yes," Merlin answered crisply, indicating to his visitor to get to the point.

"Is she home?"

"I don't know. Just walked in myself." Merlin looked the man over. The skin on his face was tight, marred only by a single deep furrow that ran vertically for almost an inch between his dark eyebrows. This was a man who knew how to take care of himself. He was someone who probably never had to raise his voice or use all sorts of foul language to make people listen to him when he spoke. At the same time, it was impossible to imagine him smiling. His dark eyes, set deeply within their sockets, stared out at Merlin as if they had the power to hypnotize. There was nothing soft about this man. "Who are you?"

London was sitting at a table in the back of Billy Shears Tavern having a beer. It was a small table that wiggled anytime an elbow was placed on it, but at least it was a good distance away from the bar and the noisy after-work crowd that was loudly toasting the end of another day. She was not drinking alone.

"Hey, glad you called," Tory said as she slipped into a wooden chair and rocked the table back and forth.

"Tory, this is my friend, Alex Langley. He's the detective who does me favors once in a while."

Tory smiled at Detective Langley. In his early forties, he was overweight and had a bushy mustache that captured enough foam from his beer that after every sip he had to swipe his fingers over it.

Before Tory could utter a word she was interrupted.

"What can I get you?" It was the deep voice of a waiter.

"I'm going to have a beer," Tory answered. "Whatever you have on tap."

"We have Molson, IC, IC Light—"

"Why don't you surprise her," London said, cutting him off before he could finish his list. There was an urgency to her voice that surprised Tory.

When the waiter was out of earshot, Tory turned to Langley. "London told me on the phone you were looking into this Stilwell thing. Thank you."

Langley stroked his mustache before speaking. "This is off the record, right?"

"Certainly."

"First of all, about Stilwell. Before London showed me his rap sheet I figured he was some Mafia type who was paying big time for a new lease on life." He paused to take a sip of beer. "No way he needed a new face because no one was looking for him. He was just a two-bit lowlife." He wiped some foam from his mustache.

"One beer, I hope you're surprised," the waiter said sarcastically and placed the frosty glass on the table hard enough to slosh some of the foamy head down the side.

London glared at the waiter as he turned and walked way.

While Tory took a sip, Langley went on. "It made no sense, so I asked myself why would Deringer even *know* that Stilwell was coming to town three weeks before he arrived? So I did some digging. There's no investigation of Cutter going on in our department. Everything begins and ends the night Stilwell was attacked."

"What?" Tory's mind raced. "Could Deringer be working on something secretly?"

Langley looked down at his beer. "No."

"How do you know?"

London entered the conversation for the first time. "A friend of a friend in the department."

Langley nodded. "Deringer's not on the fast track. No way in the world does he get chosen for a plum assignment."

"You sure?"

"Yep." Langley sounded confident.

Tory sipped her beer as she considered her options. "What would you do right now if you were me?"

"Go to the D.A. Tell him what you know."

"You've got suspicions about what's going on. Tell me."

London put her hand on the table and spoke very quietly. "Tory, Alex does have suspicions but that's all they are . . . suspicions. He can't go any further."

"Deringer's doing something illegal, isn't he?"

"Miss Welch, you have any idea what happens to cops who go to Internal Affairs with *suspicions*? No one *ever* trusts them again. Go to the D.A. That's all I can tell you." With that, Langley got up from the table and walked out of Billy Shears.

"David Rames, Department of Justice." He produced a small, black leather wallet and held it open to show a five-point gold badge and an ID card with his photograph on it. "It's urgent that I speak with her. I've just been to her office and she wasn't there. I took a chance and decided to stop by."

Department of Justice? "Come in," Merlin said, his tone improving now that he knew the visitor was stopping by on official business. As Agent Rames stepped into the small foyer and looked about the first floor of their home, Merlin turned his head in the direction of the stairs and called out, "Tory, you home?" No answer. "Sorry," Merlin said and held out his hand toward the living room. "Maybe you want to wait." Immediately Merlin regretted his hospitality. He looked at his watch and made a face. It was after six. His call would be coming any minute. Now he would have to make idle conversation.

"Thanks," Rames said and walked over to the sofa and seated himself. He kept both feet on the floor and his erect back barely touched the rear cushion. "You're Jack Merlin, aren't you?"

"Yeah. Have we met?" Merlin headed out of the room to the refrigerator. "Beer?"

"Might as well," Rames answered. "This is the end of my day. Anyway, I've been following this whole mess that started with Stanley Stilwell and knew you were involved from all the media coverage. He put you two through the ringer." Agent Rames had pivoted himself so that he was speaking in the direction of the kitchen. As he heard the refrigerator door close, he said, "Any idea when Ms. Welch might get home?"

"If she wasn't in her office, it shouldn't be long. She may have stopped off at the store," Merlin said as he came back into the living room and delivered a bottle of beer to his guest.

Agent Rames checked his watch. "Maybe a couple of minutes more, then I'll get out of your hair." He looked Merlin over like a pathologist examining a body before the first cut. He took a drink of beer, not a little sip, but a good hard slug. Agent Rames knew how to drink, and Merlin could see him putting away three or four without even starting to slur his speech. The agent balanced the bottle on one knee. "You know, there's lots of people looking into this case."

With the information Merlin now had about Cutter, his mind was already questioning why the Justice Department was involved. "If I might ask, what's your interest in Stanley Stilwell?"

Rames made a face, almost as if he were wincing. "Stanley Stilwell is yesterday's news."

"Are you aware that Stilwell's real name is Paul Vorkman?"

"Ahhh, you'n Ms. Welch have done well. I know all about Vorkman. Juvenile delinquent in Ohio. Big time in Florida. Trust me, I know Vorkman."

Merlin was intrigued. "So let me ask you. Why was Vorkman so special?"

"He wasn't. He was a rank and file crook, that's all."

"There's gotta be more. Someone stole his body to keep his identity a secret. What is it about him that's so important?"

"As I said, I'm not interested in Vorkman. Listen, Dr. Merlin, I don't mean to be impolite." He held up his beer. "I appreciate your hospitality and all, but the information I have is classified. I probably ought to speak with Ms. Welch."

"I understand," Merlin said and at that moment the conversation died. Agent Rames drained his beer while Merlin sipped at his. During the lull, Agent Rames looked about the living room politely, coming close to a smile when his eyes stopped to examine the pictures of Tory and Merlin's families on the white mantel above the fireplace. Merlin listened for the sound of Tory's car and looked out the front window, hoping she was about to arrive.

Finally the silence got to be too much for either of them. It was Rames who spoke first. He looked at his watch for the second time and shook his head as though he was on a tight schedule. "Maybe I ought to go. I don't mean to impose."

"Can I have Tory call you?"

"Tell you what, have her meet me tomorrow in her office, say two o'clock. You know if that works for her?"

"Tomorrow's Saturday."

"I know. But this is important. Otherwise I wouldn't come all the way out here. I know the D.A.'s office is dead on Saturdays, but it's still open. If it's a problem meeting me, have her call me."

The phone started to ring in the kitchen. Merlin's head

turned in the direction of the sound. Immediately he stood up.

"Go ahead, answer the phone. I'll let myself out." Rames reached his hand inside his jacket and pulled out a white business card that he handed to Merlin. As Rames got up to leave, he dropped a bombshell. "Let her know it's about Marshall Cutter."

The phone was ringing, but what Agent Rames said almost made Merlin forget about the helpful intern in Miami who was calling long distance. *Let her know it's about Marshall Cutter? So the Justice Department has focused on Cutter.* It was as if Rames had revealed his hand as an insurance policy that Tory Welch would show up in her office at the appointed time on Saturday.

"Give her the message, will you?"

"No wait, let me just get this call and I'll be right back," Merlin said emphatically. As he dashed off toward the kitchen he could hear Agent Rames saying, "And thanks for the beer."

When Merlin returned to the living room, Rames had already left.

Chapter 25

Two more faxes came in from Mannheim during the night. Cutter ignored both of them.

It was the ringing of the phone that finally woke him. Sunlight was streaming through the window. The Glock rested on the bedside table. He waited for the machine in his study to pick up the call. Once the recording of his voice finished instructing his caller to leave a message, Cutter recognized Mannheim's voice. "Marshall, I need to speak with you immediately. Call me when you get this message."

Cutter reached for the Glock. It just felt good in his hand, as if the danger that was in the air would disappear. There was no going back to sleep.

Everything was all ready and laid out on the island in Cutter's kitchen. The DMSO. A hammer. Waxed paper. And a small amber-colored bottle of digoxin tablets, a half-milligram per tablet, forty tablets in all. Cutter had learned more about digoxin in the last two days than he had known in medical school when he had studied it in pharmacology. His research all but ignored the therapeutic effects of digoxin on the heart. Cutter remembered that the drug had the ability to make a weak heart beat more strongly. The usual dose was quite small, many patients being maintained on a quarter of a milligram per day.

Five grams—twenty times the usual dose—would make most patients sick.

Ten grams was lethal, typically causing fatal cardiac arrhythmias.

Cutter was prepared to deliver twenty.

The square of waxed paper was spread out on the smooth granite surface of the island. All forty digoxin tablets were dumped in a pile in the center of the waxed paper. After covering the white tablets with a second sheet, Cutter used the hammer to tap the tablets, pulverizing them into smaller and smaller pieces. Without a mortar and pestle it was tedious work, but Cutter was patient, pausing more than once to pull off the top sheet of paper and use the edge of a butter knife to bring the gritty powder into one neat pile before resuming with the hammer. With time, the little chunks of the crushed digoxin turned into a fine dust, no different from the consistency of confectioner's sugar.

Once the work was done he transferred the powdered digoxin to a wide-mouthed drinking glass, then added two ounces of the DMSO. Cutter stirred the mixture for several minutes with an ordinary tablespoon. Most of the digoxin dissolved into the DMSO, but despite his best efforts, every last bit of the heart medication did not disappear. He expected this would happen, and used a clean dish towel to filter the solution. It was rendered clear after only one pass.

The resulting liquid was decanted into a small, freshly washed Grey Poupon jar with a screw-top lid. The gravity of what he intended to do struck him. Just thinking about it made his hands shake and a pruritic heat seemed to spread over his skin until he clawed at himself. Cutter closed his eyes. His hands came together finger to finger and he placed them up to his mouth and nose as if he was praying.

Murder. That's what he was planning. Murder. *I'm going to kill him. I have no choice. If he does not die, then my life is over.*

Cutter rubbed his eyes until he saw shapes and colors behind his closed lids. The phone rang again. Cutter continued his ocular massage as he stumbled his way into his little study. Too much was happening to sort out which way the danger was coming from.

The machine picked up the call. "C'mon, c'mon, c'mon." He urged the recorded voice to finish with the pleasantries quickly so he could hear Mannheim's voice. Impatiently, before his friendly speech ended, he changed his mind and snatched the phone from it's cradle. "Hello!" he barked.

"Marshall?"

Cutter recognized the voice immediately. "What do you want, Mannheim?"

"Haven't you gotten my messages?"

"What do you want?"

"We need to meet."

"Look, I'm not traipsing all over the city." Cutter was raising his voice and he spoke more quickly as his anger grew. "You're probably spying on me right now for all I know!"

"Marshall." Mannheim remained true to form and was utterly calm. Just the way he said "Marshall" without having to raise his voice a single decibel cut through Cutter's ranting decisively. "I'll come to your house. I know where you live."

"What? What'd you say?" Cutter whispered hoarsely. He was stunned. Meetings with Mannheim were always in some out of the way public location. Spy and dagger stuff was how he referred to the secrecy in the beginning. Bullshit was what he was calling it now.

"I'll come to you."

"Why?" Cutter said, but it came out through a throat so dry it sounded like a wheeze.

"Let's stay in focus. We're on the same side. Things are temporarily out of control. We need to close the operation down. I'll come by around one to talk. Okay?"

"I want to know what's going on."

"That district attorney's nipping at your heels."

"Jack Merlin, too. What the hell am I supposed to do?"

"You've done what was agreed upon. It's not your fault," Mannheim said soothingly, like a priest giving counsel. "Stilwell ruined everything. There's no way to salvage the operation. That's why I want to come over and engineer a plan to close things down. I'll see you at one."

Cutter hesitated. "I don't know."

Mannheim gave Cutter a moment to think before he continued. "Listen to me," he said in a relaxed tone of voice. "Once upon a time you asked me whether I had anything to do with Stanley Stilwell's death."

"Did you?"

"No, I did not. That make you feel any better?"

Cutter was so frightened he couldn't decide what he felt. "What about Trilby? I was scared after all those things I said to you. When I told you to take care of him—"

"Marshall, listen to me. I had nothing to do with Trilby, either. You wanted me to do something, but before I could look into what Trilby might have been up to, he was killed."

"Then who's behind all this?"

"I don't know. That's why I need to meet with you.

You're probably in danger. You're *my* responsibility. I want to close things down and move you someplace safe."

That sounded good. "You want me to just—" He cut himself off. He was about to say, "get in my car and get out of town" when he remembered Tanner Valdemar.

"You there?"

"Yeah," Cutter said quietly.

"Just stay put." Mannheim waited for Cutter to say something. "Marshall, do you have a gun?"

The question stunned Cutter. *Where'd that come from?* "Uhhhhh," he said to fill the silence as his brain struggled to answer the question.

Without realizing it, Cutter had answered Mannheim's question. "Do you know how to use it, Marshall?"

"Of course. It's a Glock, semi-automatic," he managed to say.

"Good, that's good. Keep it with you if it makes you feel more comfortable, but don't do anything stupid, okay?"

"I'm okay."

"I'll see you at one. Take it easy."

Cutter hung up the phone. One part of him didn't trust anything Mannheim said. Another part desperately wanted to believe he had an ally that would help him. First things first, he reminded himself. If Tanner Valdemar ever woke up, it really wouldn't matter whose side Mannheim was on. He had to get to the ICU and home before one o'clock. He checked his watch. He had less than two and a half hours.

Cutter was pulling into the parking garage at the Medical Center when he remembered the Grey Poupon bottle was still on the granite top of the island in his kitchen.

All the time he was showering and dressing he was

thinking about the Glock. Where would he put it? Of
course he needed to take it with him in the car. That
decision was easy. But should he carry it with him into
the hospital? What about in his briefcase? No, that
wouldn't do. There would be no way to get at it in an
emergency. So once he was dressed in a sport coat and
slacks, Cutter posed in front of the full length mirror in
his huge walk-in closet and tried to tuck the weapon into
the waist of his pants on the side where he usually wore
his beeper. But unless he kept his arm plastered down
against his side as if he were stricken with some sort of
palsy, it was impossible to hide the bulge. So he opted
for the small of his back. Without a holster, though, he
had to be careful how he moved. If he bent over too
quickly the grip chafed against his skin. When he sat
down the Glock had a tendency to shift position. Ultimately he tightened his belt a notch and put up with the
annoyance of having his skin irritated.

Everything had been Glock, Glock, Glock. He felt it
rubbing each time he took a step on his way to the garage so he walked stiffly, like a cadet. Getting into the
driver's seat was an effort, but he eased himself in slowly
and finally headed off to Oakland. It was a beautiful
Saturday morning and many of his neighbors were outside, puttering in their gardens or loading kids into giant
Suburbans. Cutter noticed none of this activity. He was
too busy shifting himself around in the deep leather seat
trying to get comfortable.

The Highland Park Bridge was nearly empty, and Cutter soon was speeding up Washington Boulevard to Fifth
Avenue on his way to the Medical Center. When he
pulled into the parking garage it hit him all at once, and
he slammed on his brakes and smacked his hand against
the steering wheel, screaming out the most vile language

he knew. Somehow the Glock didn't seem quite so annoying anymore.

Twenty minutes later he pulled back into his driveway and strode across the lawn toward the kitchen door. That's when he noticed something on the back step. At first he thought it was a giant metal syringe of some sort, maybe something used by the gardener to spray the plants.

He looked around but didn't see the red pickup truck his gardener drove. Approaching the strange object, Cutter noticed there was something attached to the end of the contraption. As he bent over he immediately realized what it was: the brass cylinder from the lock on his kitchen door.

Cutter looked up at the doorknob. There was a gaping hole in the center where the cylinder was supposed to be.

Mannheim! Cutter wasn't nearly as surprised as he thought he would be. This was an opportunity for him after all. Mannheim had broken into his house and it would be perfectly natural for Cutter to defend himself against intruders. His hand slipped under the tail of his jacket and found the Glock. He clicked the safety off and quietly racked the slide.

Fortunately the hinges on the kitchen door were well oiled and it opened silently. Cutter's outstretched Glock was first into the room. The kitchen was empty, the Grey Poupon jar exactly where he had left it.

He heard a noise coming from another part of the house. Instantly Cutter assumed a semi-crouched position. He listened intently for the sound. After several seconds he heard it again. It was his computer, playing that friendly jingle Windows 95 seranaded him with every time he booted up his IBM.

Mannheim was in the study. Cutter moved through his kitchen quickly, leading with the Glock, crossing through the dining room and front hall on his way to the other side of the house where the master bedroom and his study were. He knew his house well—where the creaky floorboards were, where he could hide without being seen, and just how far he could venture down the hall before Mannheim would be able to detect him.

Cutter waited outside the door to his study for several minutes. He wasn't able to see Mannheim at his desk, but he could hear the sound of the mouse clicking away.

Cutter's first instinct was to sneak into the room slowly, the way a child might get into a cold swimming pool, dipping one toe first, then another, taking forever to get wet. But he realized how important the element of surprise would be. All at once he jumped over the threshold, landing on two feet and screaming as loud as he could, *"Freeze! I'll shoot if you so much as move an inch!"*

Detective Deringer was sitting in the desk chair, his back to Cutter, staring intently at the computer. When he heard Cutter scream he jumped and made an involuntary noise that sounded like a loud grunt. He was wearing dark pants and a heavy black sweatshirt that made him look thick like a football player. A black ski mask lay on the desk.

Where the hell was Mannheim? "Deringer! What the hell . . . Put your hands on your head. Now! Now! Do it now!" Cutter screamed.

Deringer responded in slow deliberate movements. "No reason to get upset, Marshall. I'll do what you want. Let's stay calm—"

"Shut up! Keep your mouth shut!"

"I did want to talk with you. I probably should have come through the front door with a search warrant. My mistake."

"Shut up, I said! I've got to think."

"Go ahead, Marshall, think all you want. I'm going to stand up now. Shoot me if you must," Deringer said and slowly rose from the desk chair, keeping his fingers laced on the top of his head.

"You have a gun?" Cutter barked out while he waved the Glock around wildly in the air.

"Nope." Deringer pivoted left and right to show he had no gun.

"What is that thing?" Cutter had spotted something hanging from the belt on Deringer's right hip.

"This? It's nothing." Slowly, Deringer lowered his right hand and grasped the old wooden handle, spinning it around seductively.

"Let me see it," Cutter said.

Deringer unsheathed the ice pick and held it up.

The blade caught a ray of sunshine and momentarily blinded Cutter. "Oh my God," he whispered.

"Don't be shocked—once it's inside the brain there's no pain. Just the dance."

Cutter spoke through clenched teeth. "Put that away. Now."

Deringer sheathed the ice pick. "As far as I'm concerned, you're under arrest. A warrant's been out for you in Florida ever since the night you snuck out. If you kill me you won't get away. That D.A. and her boyfriend are on your ass like a big pimple. Go ahead, shoot."

Cutter looked around his study. There was his beloved antique desk and the beautiful tan carpet. The shelves were cluttered with knickknacks that he adored. He didn't want blood splattering over everything.

"I was goddamned relieved when you stole Stilwell's body. It was you, wasn't it? I mean, I was gonna take him with me that night so you could keep your little operation going and I could pick off the creeps you were working on one by one."

"Enough!"

"I was just going through your computer. Seeing who else you've done. Stilwell was number seven, wasn't he? I bet you've got records of every scumbag you've cut and restored. Why don't you just give me the list and I'll give you my word no one ever bothers you again. You got me on a little B and E. There are quite a few people who would love to know who you really are. Wanna trade?"

"Who are you working for?"

"The City of Pittsburgh Police Department."

"Goddamnit! Who are you working for?"

"You're not listening—"

"Go to hell."

"Hey, you don't believe me, there's the phone. Why don't you call the cops? You think I work for someone else, make a call."

"Forget it. You'll turn everything around. It was you who killed Stilwell."

"He deserved to die. He was a friggin' murderer. A big-mouth, blabbermouth scum of the earth."

A realization hit Cutter. "Then Trilby was working with you, too, wasn't he?"

"Trilby? That chicken-shit wimp? No fuckin' way. He died because he woulda gone to the cops."

"But he didn't know anything."

"He had access to your files."

"There are no files, you idiot! You think I'm stupid enough to keep their real names?"

"He was part of it, whether he knew it or not. Once I contacted him I couldn't very well let him go, now could I?"

"You've got nothing on me."

Deringer laughed out loud.

"Show me one thing I've done that's against the law."

"Okay, I stopped by my favorite little shop up in Sewickley the other day. I say to the girl working there—she's got a rack-and-a-half, by the way—'Hey, who was that guy I just saw leave? He looked so familiar.' And she says, 'Oh, that's Marshall Cutter, the plastic surgeon.' And I go, 'Oh, yeah, he did my wife's tits'—actually I said breasts, she didn't seem like the tit type, if you know what I mean. Anyway, she starts yapping on about her breasts and I finally ask her what a big shot plastic surgeon was doing way up in Sewickley in a horse store. That's when she starts telling me about how something called DMSO can go right through the skin and even make things mixed with it zap into the body. So I start thinking, hey, Cutter don't have a horse or nothing, so it makes me wonder what the hell you wanted it for."

"It's for somebody else. A friend."

"Oh, yeah? Well you better inform your little friend to clean up the mess he made in your kitchen with the DMSO. And I found an empty bottle of digoxin. That's heart medicine, right? My daddy used to take it. Took too much one time and got sick."

Cutter thought about this little turn of events for several seconds. He and Detective Deringer had reached a point of no return. Motioning back and forth with the Glock, he instructed, "That's it. No more chit-chat. Get your hands on your head. Walk slowly."

"So you gonna clue me in on the DMSO or what?"

"Start walking."

"Ahhh, got you rattled. Hey, where're we going?"

"Outside."

"Outside it is. I could use some fresh air. By the way, you don't have a silencer on that thing. What is it, a Glock?" Deringer said, trying to sound helpful.

"I don't need a silencer."

"With a Glock you need a silencer. Glocks are so

fuckin' loud. Man, that thing goes off, you got a heap of explaining to do. We better talk here."

Maybe Deringer was right, Cutter thought. Maybe they should stay inside to muffle the noise. But, then again, maybe it was Brer Rabbit talking. "Let's go."

Cutter kept his distance as the two wound their way to the family room. He never got within four feet of the detective and he never lowered the Glock.

"All right," Cutter said when they reached the back door, "use your right hand and open the door. No quick moves. Okay, now put your hand back where it was. Walk out on the patio."

Deringer did as he was told and even looked about the flagstone patio admiringly as though he were a guest at a gourmet dinner party being shown around while drinks were being served.

"Keep moving. Walk down toward the water."

"Nice place. No matter what you do with me you're gonna give it up."

"Shut up."

"You don't think you're gonna be left alone, do you?"

Cutter didn't answer.

"Nah, you ice me, they'll bring somebody in by Tuesday. You're history, man."

Suddenly Cutter realized something was missing. "Hey, where's your car?"

"Maybe I got dropped off. Maybe somebody's coming back . . . soon. Maybe you should cut a deal with me while you still can."

"No way. You don't get dropped off to break into a house. As long as your car doesn't turn up here I don't care. Keep walking."

"Hey, you 'member that pretty secretary you had? What was her name?"

Cutter stopped walking. "You mean Gretchen?"

"Yeah. Man, she had a rack-and-a-half on her. No scars, either. Was she the real deal or what? Almost got her to tap into your computer but you installed that friggin' new software and she didn't have two brain cells in her head and couldn't run it. Idiot."

"She's on vacation."

"Yeah. Vacation," Deringer said with a chuckle.

"Why didn't you just leave these people alone?"

"Who? Trilby and Gretchen? Or Stilwell? 'Cause if you think Stanley Stilwell, a.k.a. Stanley the Stoolie, a.k.a. Paul Vorkman, deserves to be alive after flapping his mouth the way he did on the stand, you got your head halfway up your ass."

Cutter's backyard sloped down toward Gumper Pond gracefully. A wall of enormous pine trees on either side of Cutter's two acres afforded them considerable privacy. As they neared the end of the grass, Deringer stopped at the edge of what looked to be a small cliff about twelve feet above the water. One towering pine tree grew out of the edge of the embankment, its magnificent branches extending more than a dozen feet from the trunk at the bottom.

"So what do we do now? You gonna make me jump?" Deringer turned around and looked down at the water.

"You broke into my house. I surprised you and chased you all the way out here and I panicked when I thought you were going to get away. Conveniently, you're wearing the murder weapon for Trilby and Stilwell."

"And Gretchen. Don't forget about Gretchen. Woooo, she was nice."

"Shut up!"

"Oh, you and the rack have a little something going on the side?"

"I said shut up." Cutter took aim.

"Hey, one last thing. After you kill me, don't breathe a

word about shooting me to that pesky D.A. You wouldn't want the authorities poking around down here."

"What the hell?" Cutter looked confused.

"You wouldn't want 'em to find Gretchen's body, now would you?"

Cutter's eyes darted about, under the pine, down in the water. Was Gretchen really back there? "You didn't—"

Deringer forced a laugh. "Take a chance."

"Pretty soon I'm history around here. I've got more socked away than you can imagine. Some property, too."

Deringer continued. "Not fifty feet from where you're standing. They find poor old Gretchen, naked and stabbed in the neck, who knows what that D.A.'s gonna think. You'll have one hell of a time convincing them you didn't strap this baby to me after you blew me away." Deringer dropped his hands and reached for the wooden handle of the ice pick. "That's exactly what the D.A.'s gonna think."

"They already know about you," Cutter lied.

"Bullshit."

"Bullshit? Mannheim saw you up on Mt. Washington. He's been following you and he'll make sure everyone in the D.A.'s office finds out what you did."

"Following me?"

"For days," Cutter lied again.

"Then he must know about you'n the shrink, too."

Cutter went silent.

"I liked the way you cupped your hands and leaned right up to the mirror. Like you wanted to French kiss me. Terrible thing what happened to him, by the way. He's the one who's gonna put you away. I hear he's doing better, starting to move his arms and legs. Hey, I just thought of something," Deringer said as he slowly pulled his hands apart and lowered them to his side.

"Those digoxin pills and that bottle of DMSO don't have anything to do with the shrink, now, do they?"

Bang! The Glock went off with a report so loud it echoed in Cutter's ears for more than a minute. Deringer shot backward over the edge of the little cliff, and for a moment seemed like he was floating in the air. Cutter watched the whole thing unfold in slow motion. Deringer's body went into a lazy roll that looked like a sloppy version of a back dive with a half-twist. When he finally hit the water the splash was enormous, as if what was supposed to be a graceful dive had turned into a disastrous belly flop.

Cutter looked around at the two walls of pine trees to see if any of his neighbors would be nosy enough to poke their heads through and see what was going on. He just stood there helplessly, the gun down at his side, waiting for the ringing in his ears to stop. The Glock slipped out of his fingers and fell silently to the grass beneath his feet. As he made his way to the edge of the little cliff, he dreaded what he would see. Gumper Pond would probably be red, and he had no idea whatsoever how long the blood would linger there. Of course he would have to bury the body, but that was going to take time. The whole thing with Tanner Valdemar was going to have to be put on hold.

When he peered over the precipice there was no blood to be seen, just the last glimpse of Deringer's body as it sank in the murky water. Deringer went down quickly. Now Cutter would have to put on his hip waders and get a rake or something and find the body. *Shit! Can I get one goddamn break?* Again he craned his neck from side to side, convincing himself he was alone. He scanned the surface of Gumper Pond where the ripples from the splash were settling down. The body was gone. He would definitely have to get the hip waders.

Time was running out. *Shit!* He'd have to bury the body after dark.

Cutter dashed up to the house and into the den. His hip waders were stored in the basement on the wooden shelves, but before he made it to the kitchen the doorbell sounded. He took a careful inventory of himself. His clothing was relatively clean and his hands had not yet gotten muddy. Smoothing his hair as he walked in the direction of the front door, he tried to slow his breathing.

He looked through one of the side lights. It was Mannheim standing there in a suit. "I got an early start," was all he said when the door was pulled open. Without being invited he walked into the house.

A terrible thought flashed through Cutter's mind. *Maybe I got dropped off. Maybe somebody's coming back . . . soon.* He swallowed hard and stepped out of the doorway so Mannheim could get by him. "I wasn't expecting you this soon."

"I wanted to make sure you didn't pull a Florida on me."

"I'm not going anywhere." Cutter sounded shaky, as if he was fighting to keep from crying. He was thinking about the Glock lying somewhere on the lawn near Gumper Pond. *What if Mannheim and Deringer are in this together? What if this is a conspiracy to set me up as the fall guy?*

"Where can we sit down?"

Cutter stared at Mannheim as if he were speaking a foreign language.

"Cutter!" This time Mannheim raised his voice.

"What?" Cutter responded, backing away from Mannheim.

"Don't fall apart on me now."

"I'm just a little unnerved. That's all. Let's go into the family room," Cutter offered and led Mannheim to the rear of the house.

When the two were seated, Mannheim on the leather sofa and Cutter sitting stiffly in an easy chair, Mannheim was the first to speak. "We're closing down the operation. I spoke with the D.A.'s office."

"Thank God," Cutter blurted out.

"You and I are meeting with Tory Welch in an hour."

"What about the cops?"

"I've left several messages for Detective Deringer, but so far we haven't hooked up."

As if a switch had been turned on, Cutter was breathing easier. "So it's over. That's it. Oh my God!" He smiled.

"I still don't know who was responsible for the murders."

"Who cares? Leave it to the cops, for Godsake. I did everything you've asked of me. Now you need to let me go."

"We're going to relocate you."

"No way. Enough of your relocations. I've been a good boy. You owe me."

"What do you want?"

"I want to disappear. Vanish."

Mannheim nodded his head. "I'll sell it. How 'bout a hotel room where we can have somebody watch you for tonight?"

"Tonight?" Cutter thought about Deringer's body floating to the surface of Gumper Pond. "No . . . no . . . I'm okay here. I've got things to do before I go."

"There's still a killer on the loose."

"No!" he said firmly. "I'd rather stay here tonight. I disappear tomorrow."

Mannheim looked at Cutter strangely. "That's up to you." He looked at his watch. "We'd better leave now if we're going to make that meeting."

Chapter 26

"You must be Agent Rames," Tory said as the man known to Marshall Cutter as Mannheim walked into her small office. She was dressed casually in slacks and a blazer, standing next to her government issue desk that held a computer and was also a repository for stacks of papers. There were two framed photos of Merlin on one corner of her desk along with a ceramic vase with a red rose in full bloom.

A reflection of sunshine streamed through one of her two windows, catching Rames in the eye and causing him to squint. Cutter was right behind the agent. Instead of looking at Tory, he was checking his watch. Tory was quite surprised to see him walking in with Rames. She had expected Cutter would be in handcuffs the next time she saw him and did not greet him verbally, offering the surgeon only a surprised nod.

David Rames flipped open the leather wallet with his badge and photo ID, paying no mind to the curt expression on Tory's face. "I'm sorry to bring you in on a Saturday, but things have come to a head." When they were seated, with Cutter settling down next to David Rames on the visitor side of Tory's desk, the agent began. "We probably should have had this conversation a while ago. Things got out of hand, and, well . . ."

"I believe I pretty much know what's been going on," Tory said.

"Tell me what you know."

"Well, Dr. Cutter has been practicing medicine for the past six years under an assumed name. His real name is Raymond Phillips, and a warrant exists in Florida for his arrest in connection with the murder of his anesthesiologist."

"Do you have any idea what he has been doing in Pittsburgh?"

"I believe Dr. Cutter has been performing plastic surgery on known criminals so the police can't recognize them."

"Close," Rames said and smiled. He looked at Cutter, expecting him to be smiling too, enjoying the moment of truth with him. Paying no attention, Cutter had his sleeve pulled up and was checking his watch. Rames looked back at Tory. "At one time Raymond Phillips was in Florida doing precisely that: operating on mobsters. Apparently he fell into that line of work quite by accident. In the early nineties he had quite an operation going down there, changing the faces of some of the most wanted people in the United States. When he was caught," Rames looked over at Cutter, "he worked out a deal whereby he would begin a pilot program for the Witness Protection Program. The theory was that when people entered the program, their safety would be assured if they didn't look like their mug shots.

"So, in exchange for his freedom, Raymond Phillips started working for the Justice Department in Florida. He began operating on underworld figures who had cooperated with the Justice Department and needed to disappear. Unfortunately, he got found out by someone who

didn't take kindly to his working for us. When his anesthesiologist was murdered, Raymond Phillips disappeared and Marshall Cutter was born. We set him up
here in Pittsburgh with his new identity and for almost
six years everything went great."

"Until Stanley Stilwell entered the Witness Protection
Program," Tory said.

"Initially, we had no idea Marshall was found out. For
all we knew, Stilwell shot off his mouth before coming
to town and he was followed. I don't have any idea who
killed Stilwell. Just for the record, Stilwell was instrumen-
tal in breaking up a Colombian drug smuggling cartel."

Everything came into crystal focus. "Wait a second! I
know exactly who killed him," Tory said. "Detective
Deringer."

"What?" Rames said.

Cutter sat on his hands.

"Not until this very moment did it all come together.
Deringer claimed to have a fingerprint analysis from Stilwell when there were no latents on the weapon. He
bragged that he was *investigating* Cutter, but sources in
the police department have no record of any investigation. He claimed he knew all about Stilwell, that he was
a wanted man who had come to Pittsburgh to have his
face changed."

"He told you that?"

"He was working me the whole time so he could get
to Cutter first."

"Well that's a relief," Cutter said and blew out his
breath noisily. "All you have to do is track down
Deringer."

"What a slick plan," Tory mused. "Hire a cop to shut
down the Witness Protection Program."

"Tory," Cutter said, his voice taking on a sincere tone.
"Now that you understand what's been going on, I hope

you can forgive me for everything. It was killing me not to level with you and Merlin."

"Apology accepted." Then to Rames, she said, "There has to be some sort of closure. You can't very well have Dr. Cutter disappear from Pittsburgh like he did in Florida."

"I agree. Exactly how his departure is handled will be coordinated by the Justice Department."

"So what happens now?" Tory asked Rames.

"We're going to nail Detective Deringer."

Cutter nodded, perhaps a bit too enthusiastically.

Traffic was light and Tory made it home quickly. She felt an incredible sense of relief now that the ordeal was over. She had telephoned Merlin twice, once from her office just after Cutter and Mannheim left and again from her car, but the machine picked up both times.

Tory hopped out of her Honda and walked to the back door of her house with a happy bounce to her step. She bounded up the stairs and stopped suddenly.

Something was wrong with the doorknob. There was a hole in the center. The part where the key was supposed to go was missing.

The downy hairs on the back of her neck stood at attention. Slowly she pushed the door open so that she had a view through the kitchen and out toward the living room. "Hello? Merlin?" There was no answer. Tory stepped across the threshold. A burning sensation in her chest warned her that things were not right. "Merlin?" she called a second time.

A soft, muffled sound came from the living room. "Mmmmmmm. Mmmmm."

Without having to think about it, her hand slipped into her leather bag and found the Beretta. She racked the slide.

"Mmmmmm. Mmmmmmm."

Tory could feel her pulse exploding in her throat. Holding the weapon cup-and-saucer style, Tory managed her first step toward the living room.

Just as she moved away from the kitchen door, it happened without warning, and it was over before she had a chance to think. A man grabbed her, one arm clamping around her chest as he held the cold barrel of a large handgun to her neck. "Let go of your gun right now. I don't have a lot of time, and neither does Merlin. I don't mind killing you." He jerked her body in the air for emphasis.

She was no match for the much stronger man. His voice was familiar, but with the adrenaline making her head scream she couldn't be sure. He smelled terrible, that much she noticed, like swamp gas. Not having any choice, Tory did as she was told, opening her hand and shaking the Beretta loose from her sticky fingers so that it dropped to the linoleum floor with a metallic *clunk*.

"Good. I'm glad you know how to behave. Now git!" he hissed into her ear and shoved her through the doorway into the living room.

Before she could turn around to identify the intruder, she spotted Merlin on the floor, both of his hands cuffed to the radiator in the corner and tightly gagged with a length of cloth tied around his head. The anger and fear she spotted in his eyes terrified her. "Oh, Merlin," she said softly and tears flowed down her cheeks. Then she turned around. Detective Deringer looked at her with an obnoxious grin, a victorious smile hideously smeared across his face. His gloved hand was brandishing a black, semi-automatic Glock. He was dressed entirely in black, his filthy hair pasted down to his head, but Tory's eyes were drawn to the thin leather sheath he wore on his hip with the narrow wooden handle protruding from the top.

"Sit down on the couch," he commanded.

"You okay, Merlin?" she asked, turning away from Deringer.

"He's fine. This time I made sure he couldn't pull his magic shit with the handcuffs."

Merlin nodded and motioned with his head toward the couch so that Tory would sit down before being hurt.

"I said sit!"

Tory turned back to the detective. Her jaws were clenched tightly together and in her fury she pulled her lips back slightly and exposed her teeth.

"Cutter probably didn't tell you he threw a bullet at me." He patted his chest with the side of his hand. "Bulletproof vest. All cops wear 'em. That's what Cutter forgot when he shot me."

"What are you doing here?" Tory demanded.

"Cutter didn't call the cops, did he?"

"What are you talking about?"

"Cutter caught me in his house, brought me down to the water, and shot me like a dog. He thinks I'm floating at the bottom of his pond, but I don't think he wants the crime lab going over to his house right now."

"So why come here?"

"Tying up loose ends. It was the fingerprint on Stilwell, wasn't it?"

"You're a fool."

"You're the fool, sweetheart. You jerks had no idea what you stumbled into. You were just playing cops and robbers."

"If Cutter thinks you're dead—"

"You got too smart," Deringer interrupted. "I shoulda done you at Trilby's. You with your, 'Hey, how did you get Stilwell's print when London never saw it?' I know your type. You wouldn't be satisfied that I suddenly disappeared from the world. You would have kept looking and looking and looking." Deringer's voice grew louder and angrier.

"And every cop in Pittsburgh will figure out you're still alive when you kill us."

"Not with Cutter's gun doing the dirty work." Deringer held up the Glock and admired it. "His prints are all over this thing. Everything comes back to Cutter. It's perfect." Deringer began to walk toward Tory. "I want you on the couch. Now!" he repeated. He pointed the Glock at Tory's face as he approached.

"Cutter told me *and* the agent from the Department of Justice that he shot you. There're probably a dozen cops dragging the lake. There won't be a hiding place anywhere in the world you can squeeze into."

Deringer stopped walking. "You're fulla shit. I know a little something about Cutter. The last thing he wants is a buncha cops running around his house."

Tory had a quizzical look on her face and her eyes flitted about as if she were searching for an answer. "What are you talking about?"

"We're done talking. It's time to go downstairs."

Downstairs. How could one word sound so horribly frightening. "No," Tory said defiantly. "You get the hell out of here. Handcuff me if you want, but you have nothing to gain by killing us."

"Turn around or I put a bullet in his head right now!" A little spray of saliva shot out in Tory's direction as he spoke.

Reluctantly, Tory did as she was told. Before she got any ideas, Deringer quickly came up behind her and grabbed her around the neck. "Ahhhhh," she gasped as his choke hold tightened, making each breath a precious commodity. As Deringer dragged her backward through the kitchen, toward the door that led down to the basement, Tory's right hand reached behind her and miraculously found the wooden handle of the ice pick. In one slick movement she unsheathed it and held it down by her side. The best she could manage from this position was to stab his leg and that was unlikely to do much more than piss him off even more. She would have to wait.

"You stuck your nose where it shouldn't be. I got no choice." When Deringer had manipulated Tory near the door to the basement he ordered, "Open the door," propping her up so she could reach it. As she momentarily regained her balance, Deringer relaxed his grip around her neck. Tory reached for the door with her empty hand. Deringer loosened his grip even more as she turned the knob. Tory pulled the door open and Deringer momentarily let go as he prepared to push her down the wooden stairs.

The opportunity had arrived. Tory spun around quickly and screamed out in fury as she plunged the ice pick deeply into Deringer's chest. Amazingly, the sharp tip of the ice pick easily pierced the Kevlar fibers of the bulletproof vest. While Kevlar was widely touted by police forces everywhere as being able to stop bullets, it had almost no ability to stop a knife. In fact, some high end—and significantly heavier—vests were equipped with a series of thin steel plates. Not only did these vests stop bullets, they also prevented stabbings.

Detective Deringer wasn't lucky enough to be wearing a steel-plated vest. But his reflexes had not been dulled by the events of the day. With a classic karate move he chopped at Tory's hand, knocking the ice pick to the floor. "Shit!" he screamed and smacked Tory down to the floor with one hand. "Goddamnit, you bitch!" he said as he towered over her. "Now your boyfriend's gonna get it!" he screamed. "Get up! I want you to watch." Deringer reached down and grabbed hold of Tory's blazer,

yanking her to her feet. Once again he spun her around
and clamped his hand around her neck. Immediately he
stormed toward the living room, Tory's feet dragging between his. He had the Glock jammed against Tory's tem-
ple, digging it into her flesh.

"See? See what she did? She stabbed me! It's gonna
make killing you easy."

When he was halfway to the radiator where Merlin
was handcuffed, he realized he was out of breath. For a
second he had to stop dead in his tracks and take two
deep breaths. It was hard, as if he had asthma and
couldn't get air in and out of his lungs. And his chest
was hurting, not where he felt the stinging prick of the
ice pick, but all over. The term "heart attack" crossed
his mind.

Deringer swallowed hard. He pursed his lips and
sucked in as much as his tight chest would allow, but
with each breath less and less air was moving. Sweat
beaded up on his forehead and neck, and the skin on his
face had now almost turned purple. Looking around the
room, he blinked several times to clear his head. The
room was becoming darker. It was nearly impossible to
see the back of Tory's head, and Merlin had disappeared
in the growing shadows. All he could visualize were the
windows, bright rectangles of white on a background that
was rapidly going from gray to brown to black.

He maintained the grip on his Glock through it all,
not wanting to believe whatever was grabbing him wasn't
going to let go. The pain in his chest was ferocious, a
deep, thumping pain that made him dizzy. *It's a heart
attack. I'm having a heart attack. I'm going to die.*
"Help," he managed to croak, but his voice had been
reduced to a faint whisper. "Hel . . . help." His voice
deteriorated into little noises, gurgles and high-pitched
grunts.

Deringer released his grip on Tory and reached out like a blind man for the sofa no more than three feet from where he was standing. It might as well have been in the next room. Its image had vanished from his oxygen-starved brain that was no longer able to distinguish colors or shapes. He bent over at the waist and his arms groped out as if he were playing Pin the Tail on the Donkey. Each of his steps shuffled aimlessly across the carpet. The pain in his chest was crushing and he could only manage tiny little gasps that didn't move the air far enough down his trachea to reach his lungs.

He was suffocating.

Increasingly desperate to lie down, he flailed about in search of the elusive sofa and stumbled onto the floor. The Glock flew out from his hand in the direction of Merlin, who quickly shot out a foot and brought the weapon toward him so he could hide it under his leg.

Deringer landed on his side like a dead dog, then kicked out his legs and wound up on his back. The detective's hands were at his neck, clawing the flesh between his head and shoulders as if he could open it up and ease his effort at breathing.

His arms flopped away from his neck and twitched several times. Without warning everything went still. Merlin watched him intently. He could see the ashen pallor that swept over his skin and the bulging veins in his neck.

Tory hurried over and untied Merlin's gag. "You okay?" she asked breathlessly.

"He's unconscious. Don't worry. Just get the keys to the cuffs. Try his pants pocket."

"What happened to him?"

As Tory frisked the unconscious detective, Merlin explained that Detective Deringer wasn't having a heart attack; but was probably dying from a tension pneumothorax.

As the tip of the ice pick pierced his chest wall, it had nicked the pleural lining of the lung—a thin casing no thicker than Saran Wrap that enveloped each of the two lungs. Although only a tiny hole, it had become a one-way valve that allowed air to escape from the lung with each inhalation. Several breaths later the air filling the space between the rigid chest wall and the sponge-like lung caused the lung to collapse. The tremendous pressure of the free air began to force the mid-line structures in the chest over to the opposite side. As the heart and its major blood vessels shifted, blood flow through them was restricted, and the various organs of the body, most notably the brain, couldn't receive enough oxygen to function. It was no different than a garden hose kinking up in the backyard.

The left side of Deringer's chest was now nearly empty of vital lung tissue and the heart. The right side of his chest was packed to the gills with the trachea, the right lung, the heart, aorta and vena cavas.

As soon as he was free, Merlin immediately knelt next to Deringer and felt for a pulse in his neck. "He's still alive." Merlin tore at Deringer's sweatshirt, lifting it up to expose the smock-like bulletproof vest that had saved him from Cutter's bullet. The front panel of the vest was held in place with large Velcro straps over the shoulder and around the sides. With a loud ripping noise, Merlin pulled the vest apart and exposed a white T-shirt. Once this was lifted, Merlin and Tory got a look at the purple bruise from the bullet. It was several inches in diameter and located on the right side, nowhere near the detective's heart. "Where'd you stab him?"

"His left side."

Merlin placed his left hand on the left side of Deringer's chest, lining up his fingers like the wooden bars on a xylophone. Using his right index finger, flexed slightly so that it could act like a mallet, he struck his left index finger repeatedly and thumped out a hollow note. Then he shifted his hand to Deringer's right side, placing it in the same position. He repeated the percussion, this time sounding out a note that was distinctly different—not full and hollow, but dull and lifeless. "Hear that?" he asked Tory, and went back and forth one more time for emphasis. "The left side of his chest is empty. It's definitely a tension pneumothorax. Let's see, get me a paring knife, the one with the black handle. Then a Bic pen, and one of those balloons left over from New Year's. Oh yeah, and a rubber band."

Tory was back with the paring knife quickly. The blade was two and a half inches long and the tip was quite sharp. Merlin positioned the tip of the knife at a point on Deringer's left chest that was above his nipple and several inches below the center of his collar bone. This was the second rib. Using steady pressure, Merlin pierced the skin, taking care to guide the blade over the top of the rib to avoid the delicate artery and vein that ran in a groove below the bone. The blade was more difficult to work than a scalpel and required considerably more pressure. He cut through skin and muscle, the fascia and the outer layer of pleura, and into the empty chest.

Wssssssssssssssssh! A rush of air escaped from the puncture Merlin had created as he withdrew the paring knife. Within seconds Deringer could be seen taking shallow breaths. His skin was gray, but the pressure had been released and the mid-line structures had shifted back to where they belonged so that he could breathe normally once again.

Tory returned with the other items. Merlin twisted the Bic's ink supply and extracted it from the plastic housing.

The hollow tube was then slipped into the wound so that it created a tunnel leading directly into Deringer's chest. Although air could escape from the chest, nothing prevented it from coming back each time Deringer breathed. What Merlin needed to create was his own one-way valve. This was neatly accomplished with the deflated balloon. It was several inches long, the type that looked like a miniature version of a condom, only this one said Happy New Year on it in white letters. Merlin used the paring knife to make a tiny slit in the far end of it, then slipped the open end over the plastic tube of the Bic pen. The rubber band was wound around the coupling to keep things secure. Each time Deringer exhaled he forced air through the plastic tube and out the balloon. But when he breathed in, the balloon collapsed so that air could not reach the plastic tube and enter the chest.

Deringer was breathing better, the color now slowly returning to his face. Merlin took his pulse. It was stronger.

The detective was not going to die.

"Deringer. Open your eyes," Merlin said directly into his ear. "Open your eyes!"

There was a flickering in Deringer's eyelids as they opened. "Uhhhhhhh," he groaned from the pain.

"Can you hear me?"

"Yeah," he rasped. He looked down at the makeshift chest tube sticking out of him. Then he winced.

"I want to know about Cutter."

"Kill . . . him."

"Listen to me. Tell me what you know about Cutter."

"He's . . . gonna get away with it."

"What did he do?"

"He . . . was . . . the one with that shrink."

"Valdemar?"

Deringer nodded.

"I saw him go in. I saw him—" he cringed and a horrible sound gurgled out of his throat. "Through the mirror. He pushed him down." He winced again. "It was Cutter."

Merlin looked at Tory before saying, "You sure?"

Deringer reached out his hand and got a weak hold of Merlin's forearm. "Let me tell you one more thing. . . ."

Chapter 27

Tanner Valdemar was making progress. For the past twenty-four hours he had made remarkable improvement, squeezing the nurse's hand whenever he was told to and fighting the ventilator to the point where he was ready to be extubated. He hadn't opened his eyes yet, but that was expected soon. He was a true success story.

The same nurses had been assigned to Valdemar during his ICU stay so that there would be continuity of care. Today it was an eleven-year veteran named Hailey who spent every minute of every break reapplying her makeup. She was wearing a blue scrub shirt and tight yellow scrub pants that showed off the lines of her panties whenever she bent over, which she managed to do frequently when attractive male physicians were in attendance. But she was a terrific nurse, sharp and observant, and it was she who was the first to realize Valdemar was bucking his ventilator.

"Hailey," Mary called from across the ICU. Everyone in the unit looked up, especially the other nurses who were grateful not to have been singled out for a lecture from the charge nurse. Instead of starting her little speech loud enough for everyone to enjoy, Mary hurried across the floor, her thick thighs rubbing together, creating a swishing noise that competed very nicely with the song of the ventilators. Mary was smiling, quite pleased with herself to have such an important and secret mission. "Hailey, I must speak with you."

Hailey looked up from Valdemar's bedside. She was in the process of re-taping one of his IVs and scowled at the thought of having to endure Mary. "What is it?" she said, sounding as annoyed as possible.

"No visitors for Dr. Valdemar until further notice."

"Okay," Hailey said.

"You are the *only* one to be at his bedside unless you hear otherwise from me."

"What if there's a problem with his vent?"

Mary stared right through Hailey. "Unless it's life or death, you're to take care of any problems yourself."

"Under whose order?"

"If you can't handle a simple directive, inform me now."

"Yes, Miss Mary, whatever you say," Hailey said and curtsied as if she were a Catholic school girl responding to one of the nuns.

Marshall Cutter was alone in the staff lounge next to the ICU, thinking about how comfortable his lower back was without the Glock shoved halfway down his pants. With Detective Deringer out of the way, he hadn't bothered searching for it in the grass when he made a brief stop home for a shower and the Grey Poupon jar. He was standing next to the Mr. Coffee machine, helping himself to a Styrofoam cup.

Patting the prominent bulge in the pocket of his blue sport coat, he turned all the way around and scanned the doorway for visitors. He listened for the sound of footsteps. Carefully he withdrew the small, glass jar with its clear contents and dumped it into the cup.

*   *   *

Mary was back at the nursing desk, looking very serious as she talked on the phone in hushed tones, delivering some news about one of the patients. She didn't even look up when Marshall Cutter entered the ICU holding the Styrofoam cup and looking quite handsome in his tailored blue sport coat over a bright yellow open neck shirt. He looked as if he should be on the veranda of a country club sipping a gin and tonic while regaling his friends about his round of golf.

Without hesitation he strolled across the shiny floor, nodding to several of the nurses as he made his way to Tanner Valdemar's bed space.

"Hailey, how are you?" he said confidently to the nurse who was fussing about her patient. Cutter noticed how thin and frail Valdemar looked, his skin nearly the color of the white sheets that covered him. But he was moving both arms, trying to push Hailey away from his endotracheal tube that she was about to suction out, a procedure that inflicted considerable discomfort on patients awake enough to know what was happening.

"Great," Hailey answered with a smile. "And Dr. Valdemar's really doing better. They're thinking about extubating him later today."

Cutter stood at the foot of the bed, balancing the Styrofoam cup on the shiny, chrome railing. First he studied the monitor above the bed, admiring the steadiness of Valdemar's EKG. "He say anything?"

Hailey giggled. "Not with his tube in. But with the way he's improving it's only a matter of time."

"He's really pale."

"He's a little anemic. A transfusion oughta fix that."

"Thank God," Cutter said and lifted his Styrofoam cup as if he were about to take a sip from it. "What happened to him's really gotten to me." He said it spontaneously as if the thought had been nagging him and he needed to get it off his chest. He lowered the cup and rested it on the railing.

Merlin was on the Highland Park Bridge, tailgating a moving van that was slowly negotiating the exit ramp that circled clockwise around a lushly planted garden before going back under the bridge. He was desperate to get to the Medical Center and was becoming frantic with the delay. It had been less than five minutes since he had run out of their Ninth Avenue home and jumped into Tory's Honda.

Already he had called 911 to summon both the police and an ambulance, leaving Tory with the Glock in case Deringer decided to try something stupid. But the Bic pen was clearly the detective's lifeline and he knew it, so he was doing his best not to dislodge it.

Tory's cell phone was on the seat next to him. As he dialed up the ICU for the second time he allowed a gap of twenty yards to form between the Honda and the moving van. "This is Merlin."

It was Mary who answered the phone. "Yes, Doctor," she said crisply, an eager lieutenant poised for additional orders.

"I just wanted to make certain Tanner's doing okay."

"Absolutely."

"Heart rate stable?"

"Yessir," Mary said and at that moment glanced across the ICU and spotted a tall, well-dressed man standing at the foot of the bed chatting with Hailey. The thought of lying to Merlin never actually crossed her mind. Mary was a good soldier who told it like it was, regardless of the implications to her own career. "Uh-oh," was all she had to say to get Merlin to raise his voice.

"What? Is he okay, Mary? Talk to me." His imagination flashed through several frightening scenarios at the same time as the car behind him honked to urge him to pay attention and keep moving.

"He's fine, Doctor. And I know you said not to allow anyone near him, and I realize this is on my shoulders."

Beep! Beep!

"What!!?? What the hell is going on?" Merlin hit the gas pedal.

The moving van came to a stop and was about to back up in order to improve its angle for the turn onto Allegheny River Boulevard.

"I must have been on the phone, but Dr. Cutter is visiting with Dr. Val—"

Crash!

"No!" Merlin screamed as he reacted both to what Mary had just said and the fact that he had rear-ended the moving van.

Once the driver of the van realized what had happened, he came to a complete stop and opened the door of his cab so he could get out and survey the damage.

"Listen to me, Mary!" he said, making no effort to hide his fury. While he was yelling into the phone he jammed the car into reverse and pulled back several feet. "I don't care how you do it, just get him out of there! Call security. Just . . . get . . . him . . . the . . . hell . . . away! Do you hear me?!"

"I'm sorry, Dr. Merlin. I'll take care of it—"

"Mary, stop talking. Hang up the phone and get Cutter out of there." Merlin threw the phone down on the passenger seat and cut the wheel sharply to the right and eased the accelerator down so that the Honda jumped the curb. The garden had a variety of colorful flowers planted in long rows and in seconds Merlin cut a wide path right through them before dropping over the curb on the far side. With a quick turn to the right, he sped off.

"I don't know," Cutter was saying quietly enough so that only Hailey could hear him, "I wake up at night drenched in sweat just thinking about what he's been through." Cutter held out his hand, the one with the Styrofoam cup, and Hailey could see the tremor he almost seemed proud to show off. "See? I'm all shaken up over it."

Mary was hustling across the room, really moving, and the swishing noise her thighs made had moved up nearly an octave. She'd already put a fake smile on her face, the same one she used when the attendings demanded her to do Sisyphean tasks and she didn't want them to know just how stressed out she was. "Oh, Dr. Cutter, I'm so sorry to bother you, but things are going crazy right now."

Hailey looked around. The ICU seemed quiet to the point of being sleepy. She rolled her eyes.

"Could I ask you to wait in the lounge for just a couple of minutes until things settle down? I'll come right out to get you as soon as I can."

"I don't mean to be in the way," Cutter said. He brought the cup to his lips to take a sip but hesitated. "Just wanted to see how he's doing." Cutter turned back to his conversation with Hailey, intending to ignore Mary. "Anyway, it makes you think about your own mortality," he said philosophically.

The phone in the nursing station rang again. This time one of the unit clerks answered it and called across the large room. "Mary, it's for you. Dr. Merlin."

Mary looked back to the nursing station, then at the back of Cutter's head.

The unit clerk called, "Do you want to take it? He says it's urgent."

Cutter must have heard this last bit because he turned to see what was going on just as Mary tore herself away from the bed space and swished her way back across the room.

"This place is friggin' nuts," he said and held out the cup once again to emphasize how shaky he was feeling.

"What's going on?" It was Merlin, calling for the third time, running the Honda flat out up Washington Boulevard, weaving through traffic as if the other cars were standing still.

"I'm doing my best. He's just about to leave."

"Listen to me, Mary. Tanner's life is on your shoulders! You hear me? On *your* shoulders. Get Cutter away from him. I'll be there shortly." Before Mary had finished saying "Yes, Doctor" in her customarily crisp manner, he had cut her off so that he could make one final phone call to the Pittsburgh Poison Control Center.

"Yes, Doctor," Mary replied confidently to the dial tone. She knew Merlin had already disconnected from her, but didn't want the unit clerk to know she had been cut off, so she gamely finished her end of the conversation and immediately turned her sights to Marshall Cutter. Walking briskly, she quickly reached the plastic surgeon and decided on a diplomatic approach. As she sidled up to him, she slipped her sausage-shaped arm through his and said, "I need to have a word with you privately." Then she attempted a gentle pivot so that Cutter would follow her lead, but he resisted.

Mary tugged a bit harder. Cutter stood his ground.

Then suddenly, surprising everyone, Cutter lost his balance. He stumbled badly, pushing Mary out of the way as he struggled to regain his balance. Everyone in the unit was watching, cursing their bossy charge nurse, feeling horribly embarrassed for handsome Marshall Cutter who right at this moment looked like a clumsy old fool who had spilled his drink right on Tanner Valdemar.

"My God! What's wrong with you?" Cutter bellowed as he extended one arm to break his fall.

Hailey dashed from Valdemar's bedside to attend to Cutter.

Mary stood in the middle of the ICU, one hand clamped over her mouth, too frightened and humiliated to move.

"You okay?" Hailey breathed in Cutter's face. She squatted down right next to where he had settled on the floor. The colorless beverage that had splattered the thin white sheet covering Valdemar's frail body had been forgotten.

"She's not going to be when I get through with her," he said menacingly. Both he and Hailey glared up at Mary, who continued to observe the dramatic scene in silent horror. As Cutter began a slow rise from the floor, Hailey remained by his side, watching him closely, looking very concerned.

As quickly as it arrived, the moment of drama passed and the various nurses and respiratory technicians went back to the business of caring for the most critical patients in the Medical Center. Even Hailey's thoughts drifted back to Tanner Valdemar and she turned her head to look at him.

Of course Hailey's wandering eye caught Cutter's attention. "Damn!" he said dramatically. He was clutching his left wrist—the one that he had used to break his fall—as if it hurt, and he began to do a visual exam of it as if he expected there to be some swelling. "I think it's broken."

"Broken?" Hailey repeated in a worried tone as she

turned her clinical acumen back to the plastic surgeon's distal extremity.

Cutter offered his wrist for Hailey to examine more fully. As she gently touched him here and there, Cutter took his good hand and pinched the sliver of flesh between his eyes.

"You want to lie down?" Hailey asked.

"Maybe I better." Cutter purposefully made his voice sound weak.

"Let's go into the lounge," Hailey offered and led him away from Valdemar's bed in the direction of the staff lounge.

Once Cutter and Hailey had moved past her, Mary drifted across the floor toward the safety of her nursing station.

No one in the ICU noticed, but there were two bright yellow complexes scrolling across the EKG readout above Valdemar's bed. They were not the tightly packed up and down complexes that had run continuously since he had been stabilized. These were wide peaks and valleys, painfully out of place. Tanner Valdemar had thrown his first two PVCs.

"C'mon, c'mon," Merlin was saying impatiently as he implored the elevator to fetch him from the ground floor by pressing the button repeatedly. His little fender bender, which ultimately would cause no real damage to the moving van but nearly eleven hundred dollars' worth to the Honda, was nine minutes in the past.

When the elevator doors opened, two women with silvery-blue hair, dressed up as if they should be going to a funeral, were waiting to get off. They weren't in any obvious hurry and hesitated before exiting, looking out into the lobby to be certain this was their floor.

Merlin stood by the doors, holding them open for the two women. "Ladies," he said by way of encouragement.

"Is this the lobby?" one of them asked.

"Yes it is," Merlin answered a bit more curtly than he was used to.

The two women took the hint and made their way out of the elevator but did not smile at Merlin for holding the doors open.

He jumped in. Before the doors had time to close he began punching the button for the eleventh floor.

The monitor above Valdemar's bedside was showing PVCs on a regular basis. They were coming in twos and threes, little electrical cancers hiding out in the normal pattern of the EKG, waiting to take off. No alarms had sounded and no one was close enough to his bedside to take notice.

His sheets were beginning to dry, less from evaporation than the digoxin-laced DMSO finding its way through his pale skin and into his bloodstream.

"You think you should get it X-rayed?"

"No, I think I'm okay," Cutter said. He was sitting on one of the sofas in the staff lounge with Hailey, who was doing her best Florence Nightingale. "It just hurt so much." They had been sitting together in the lounge for more than five minutes. Mary had not shown her face. Cutter was moving his wrist around carefully, going through range of motion exercises to test for pain, bending it up and down and side to side.

"You want some Advil?"

"No, I'm fine. I'll put an Ace wrap on it when I get home." Cutter stood up and prepared to leave. "You better get back before Mary writes you up AWOL."

The two shared a laugh while they took their first steps

toward the door. Both of them heard the sound at the same time, a high-pitched swish-swishing sound, broadcasting the urgency with which their visitor was approaching. Clearly this was not to be an I'm-sorry-for-what-happened kind of visit.

"Hailey, come quick!" Mary said, bursting into the room. "Valdemar's gone into V-tach!"

Without hesitation, Hailey bolted from the room with Mary close behind. V-tach, the verbal shorthand for ventricular tachycardia, was an alarming situation. Valdemar's heart was running wildly, the PVCs having come with greater and greater frequency until they took over and squeezed out any normal complexes.

Cutter was alone. He gave his wrist a couple of quick shakes and smiled. Everything was happening the way it was supposed to.

Part of him wanted to go back into the ICU and observe the denouement. Another part of him wanted to get the hell out of there and take care of Deringer's body. He slowly wandered over to the doorway. He could hear the sound of a monitor beeping its warning that something was wrong.

There was no need to return to Valdemar's bedside. He walked in the direction of the elevators. Just as he was reaching for the button to summon his ride that would take him out of the Pittsburgh University Medical Center for the last time, the musical ding of the elevator sounded and the doors opened.

Marshall Cutter was standing face-to-face with Jack Merlin. At first Merlin had no idea if Cutter was leaving because Mary had successfully thwarted his plan, or if his mission had been accomplished and he was exiting victoriously.

But the piercing sound of the monitor went off again and a voice carried out of the ICU and out to the elevators. It was Mary, loudly repeating precisely what she had evidently just heard a doctor say. "Let's get a cardiologist up here STAT—tell them it's Valdemar."

"Aren't you going to stay to watch?" Merlin asked.

A painful silence followed. Cutter had no doubt whatsoever that Merlin somehow knew why he was in the unit. The two men stared at each other, Merlin clearly waiting for Cutter to respond.

"Excuse me?" Cutter said innocently. He reached out to hold the doors for Merlin to exit the elevator in much the same way the surgeon had done for the silver-haired women moments earlier.

"Don't you want to see him die?" Merlin was speaking more quickly.

"You getting off?" Cutter wanted to know. His tone was indignant.

As Merlin began to walk off the elevator his right hand slipped inside his pants pocket. What happened next transpired so quickly Marshal Cutter had no chance to react until it was over.

Merlin reached out as if he intended to hold the elevator door so that he could have it out with Cutter. But in one quick, furious move, he swept his hand down toward Cutter's wrist. There was no time for Cutter to process the clicking sound. The pain was intense and immediate. Cutter reacted to it before he had any idea what Merlin had done.

"Ahhhhh!" A small chunk of bone no bigger than a pea had been broken off the end of Cutter's radius by the handcuffs Merlin violently snapped on his wrists. The agony it caused was severe.

Cutter yanked his arm away from the door and cradled it much the same way he had done after he had feigned his fall to the floor of the ICU. He would have screamed in misery again if he hadn't noticed the stainless steel bracelet dangling from his wrist. "What the—" he began to say, but before he could finish the thought, Merlin placed his own hand in the other half of Deringer's handcuffs and—quite a bit more gently—attached himself to the plastic surgeon.

The bed space around Tanner Valdemar was a blur of activity. The big, red crash cart had been wheeled into position. Three nurses, not counting Mary, stood in various positions around the bed alternating their attention between the monitor on the shelf and a medical resident who was on duty in the unit and was in charge of the cardiac emergency.

"Ready with that lidocaine?" someone asked.

"BP's dropping," a nurse announced.

"Did anyone reach the cardiologist?" Mary yelled above the din.

Hailey was busy drawing up the syringe of lidocaine, a cardiac medication used to urge an out of control heart back into a semblance of calm. But with the levels of digoxin steadily rising to dangerous levels, the lidocaine would prove only temporary, having little more effect than putting one's finger in the dike.

Reluctantly, Cutter followed Merlin into the ICU. Each time he resisted Merlin gave the handcuffs a swift yank and shot a bolt of pain up Cutter's arm that almost made him pass out.

"Someone get a blood gas!" the medical resident ordered.

"Should I start CPR?" Hailey wanted to know.

"Listen to me!" Merlin roared once he saw the vicious scrawl of the ventricular tachycardia racing across the monitor. Even in the midst of an impending crisis, the tremendous urgency in Merlin's voice secured everyone's attention. "He's got a digoxin overdose. There's no time

to discuss how I know. Draw up twenty vials of Digi-bind, STAT."

Not every poison had an antidote, but Tanner Valde-mar was in luck. Digibind was a clever medication, a one-trick pony created with a single purpose: to treat digoxin toxicity.

For several seconds no one moved. The sight of Merlin and Cutter handcuffed together was enough to cause everyone to hesitate.

"Now! Do it now," Merlin screamed, which brought Hailey back to reality. Within seconds she had opened one of the drawers on the crash cart and was hastily whipping up vial after vial of Digibind and shooting it into Valdomar's IV.

There was little to do now but wait.

Epilogue

"You again. What do you want this time?" Daniel Deringer growled from his hospital bed the moment he spotted Merlin walking into his private room. There were no flowers or get well cards to cheer him up. Just the former cop, naked from the waist up, with a chest tube poking out the left side of his thorax. He held the remote control for the TV in one hand, making no effort to turn off a cartoon he was watching.

"The tube's been in four days. It's ready to come out," Merlin said evenly. He was accompanied by a uniformed cop who routinely left his post in the hallway anytime Deringer had visitors.

"Do what you gotta do, then get the hell out."

Merlin donned surgical gloves and began the slow process of removing the sticky white adhesive tape from Deringer's side. When Deringer had arrived in the emergency room by ambulance, the Bic pen had been plucked out and a standard-issue clear Silastic chest tube had been swapped for it.

Now the air leak in his lungs had healed and it was time to pull the tube.

"You know," Merlin said in a casual tone, "I figured

whoever was doing the work with the ice pick would be someone with medical training."

Deringer stared at Merlin, wincing when a piece of adhesive pulled some hairs on his chest. "Well, you figured wrong."

"Maybe not. Tory did some digging and found out you were a medic in Vietnam."

"Tory Welch. Jesus, that's a name I'll remember. You musta had some fun digging into my soul. Look, I saw some bad shit over there. I'm not gonna apologize for that. Some things you never forget."

By now Merlin had pulled off the last length of tape. All that remained was the chest tube. For the moment, he ignored it. "Thought you'd be interested to know, Tanner Valdemar was able to talk today. He's going to make a full recovery."

"Thanks to me." Deringer rolled his eyes. "Cutter still in jail?"

"Yep. They say he'd disappear into the night if he got the chance."

"Maybe him and I can be roomies." He chuckled to himself, and his eyes glowed with a perverse intensity. "I bet you and Tory Welch have been having a ball making up theories how a good cop goes bad, huh?"

"Something like that."

"I'm listening. I ain't going nowhere."

"Okay. Maybe it started with you looking the other way when a drug deal was going down. Then one thing leads to another and you find yourself up to your eyeballs. This is gonna hurt." Merlin took hold of the chest tube and swiftly pulled it out.

The pain was immediate and intense. As the distal end of the tube scratched against the delicate pleura, a knife-like stitch coursed through Deringer's chest. His entire body went into a brief spasm. Merlin quickly slapped a square of gauze coated with Vaseline onto the wound to keep any air from re-entering the chest.

"Christ, you should've warned me," Deringer gasped. Once he took a few cleansing breaths he immediately got back to business. "So, you've had four days to work on a theory and that's all you've come up with? Shit. I was right about the both of you. You don't know crap about policing." Deringer watched as Merlin finished bandaging his side. "When am I getting outta here?"

"This afternoon." Merlin stood over Deringer for several seconds before walking to the doorway. The uniformed officer refused to look in Deringer's direction as he quickly disappeared into the hallway.

"Goddamn funsie," Deringer pestered, just as Merlin reached the doorway.

Merlin hesitated for a second, running his fingers through his hair as though debating what he should say. Finally he turned around to face Deringer. "There was a second theory we played around with."

"Oh yeah, this oughtta be good." Deringer smiled broadly.

"Seems your sister's married to a fellow named Jackie Tippolito, the New Jersey crime boss. Mr. Tippolito has been indicted twice for arranging a hit on someone in the Witness Protection Program who had the nerve to testify against his organization."

"Indicted. Not convicted. Jesus. I hope you and that friggin' girlfriend of yours drive each other nuts," he hissed across the room.

Merlin smiled. "Tory's not my girlfriend anymore."

"Oh yeah? She wise up and dump you?"

"No. Now she's my fiancée," Merlin declared and walked out of Deringer's room. When he hit the hallway he was already smiling.